THE
DEVIL'S
PACT

OTHER TITLES BY V. S. MCGRATH

The Devil's Revolver
The Devil's Standoff

Writing as Vicki Essex

Her Son's Hero
Back to the Good Fortune Diner
In Her Corner
A Recipe for Reunion
Red Carpet Arrangement
Matinees with Miriam

THE DEVIL'S PACT

V. S. MCGRATH

THE DEVIL'S REVOLVER BOOK 3

BRAIN MILL PRESS
GREEN BAY, WISCONSIN

The Devil's Pact is a work of fiction. Names, places, and incidents either are products of the author's imagination or are used fictitiously. Any resemblance to actual persons, living or dead, or locales is entirely coincidental.

Published in the United States by Brain Mill Press.
Print ISBN 978-1-948559-25-6
EPUB ISBN 978-1-948559-26-3
MOBI ISBN 978-1-948559-27-0
PDF ISBN 978-1-948559-28-7

Cover illustration by Cassandre Bolan.
Cover design by Ranita Haanen.
Print spread by Ampersand Book Design.
Original interior illustrations by Ann O'Connell.

www.devilsrevolver.com

For John and Mara:
"Poot."

CONTENTS

LAND ACKNOWLEDGMENT STATEMENT

The place I call home and on which I produced this work is the traditional territories of the Haudenosaunee and the Mississaugas of New Credit, and is subject to the Dish with One Spoon wampum. I acknowledge the Indigenous people who have lived and worked this land for over 15,000 years and continue to seek justice today.

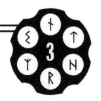

THE
DEVIL'S
PACT

CHAPTER ONE

Hettie's vision exploded in stars as her opponent's fist bashed her jaw. She stumbled to the ground, tasting blood.

"Again." Jemma watched her coolly, balanced on the balls of her feet, arms held loosely at her sides. "C'mon. Get up. A man who'd hit you wouldn't give you time to get to your feet."

Hettie blinked away the haze and pushed up to face the young woman. But before she could raise her fists, Jemma put one hand at the small of her back and shoved her shoulder. Hettie's feet swept out from under her. She landed hard, the air driven out of her lungs.

Jemma straddled her chest. "When you're in a position of weakness, roll *away* from your opponent, not toward. Otherwise you're just opening yourself up to another attack." She flicked her forehead, driving the point home and irritating Hettie further.

She clenched her teeth. This was the eleventh time she'd been floored. She didn't see how she was supposed to get away when she was always going to be in a position of weakness next to Jemma.

She got up again, every muscle aching, but took a defensive stance as Jemma faced her once more. "Again."

This time, Hettie didn't wait to defend from her attack—she rushed at her, fist recoiled for a strike to the head.

Jemma sidestepped her easily, tripping her and grabbing her arm. She twisted it back, spun her around, then slammed her to the mats.

"Don't bang her up too much," Uncle Jeremiah called from the sidelines. "People'll wonder who's been mistreating her."

Marcus cleared his throat. "That's enough, Jemma. Miss Alabama, you need to work on your stance."

"Stance, nothing." Jemma hopped up. "She'd be better off learning how to hide, not fight." She frowned down at Hettie. "Only way you're going to survive is if you dive into a hole like a snake."

Hettie slammed her palms on the mat and leaped to her feet. Hot fury pushed through her and formed the cold, hard grip of the Devil's Revolver, her trigger finger poised over the bloody thorn.

One pull would be all it'd take to end the pain and humiliation, the weeks of Jemma rapping her on the skull and mocking her.

Jemma stared down Diablo's barrel unflinchingly. "You think I'm afraid of dying?"

Hettie breathed hard. She was aware the room had gone very still, though she hadn't dropped into her time bubble. Jemma's eyes drilled into her, took her apart and showed her just how weak she truly was. Her grip trembled. And in that moment, like lightning, Jemma struck out with her heel and knocked the revolver from her hand.

Her long, muscular leg whipped around—

"Now there's a surefire way to get yourself killed."

Hettie slowly opened her eyes. Her head and face throbbed. Uncle stood above her, grimacing.

"I wasn't going to hurt her," she muttered.

"I wouldn't've counted on it one way or another. You're supposed to be training yourself *not* to use Diablo."

She grumbled her acknowledgment and sat up slowly. She took the cold cloth Uncle offered her. Her cheekbone stung as she applied it to the scraped, swelling lump there. "Diablo was just trying to protect me."

"Diablo's not your nanny. And you gotta stop treating it like it is. There'll come a time when it won't do you any good, like ten seconds ago, when you were out cold." He put his hands on his hips. "You owe Miss Jemma an apology."

In a thoroughly bad mood now, Hettie picked herself up and went to dress. Sparring with Sophie's bodyguard always left her sore and grouchy, and it wasn't just because she beat Hettie black-and-blue every time. No, she was thankful Jemma didn't take it easy on her. But she hated the way Uncle and the others kept reminding her of her limits.

Still, she did owe Jemma an apology.

She cleaned and inspected her new cuts and bruises, resignedly adding them to the badges she'd earned since she'd started training four weeks ago.

There came a light knock, and the door opened. "Beggin' your pardon, miss."

Hettie sighed inwardly at the appearance of the slight redheaded maid. "I'm all right, Mary. I can dress myself."

"With all due respect, Miss Henrietta, you can't." Mary took her in, lips pressed tight. "Your corset is too loose."

"I don't like it tight."

"It's only proper if you're to appear in Miss Favreau's company."

She doubted Sophie would care, but there was no arguing with Mary. Every fight about how she dressed and comported herself in the Favreau home ended with her grudging capitulation. Mary's insistence on dresses and corsets and petticoats and things Hettie had never bothered with back on the ranch had worn her down like a gentle waterfall over river stone. She was surprisingly unbending for such a slight girl. Hettie took a deep breath as the maid, who looked barely older than her sister's eleven years, yanked on the laces.

"I'd appreciate some space to breathe," she gritted out.

"Aye, we all would. Just a little tighter."

Once Hettie had been laced in, Mary helped her into a plain gray day dress with puffy sleeves and a high collar fringed with lace and pearl buttons. It was finer than anything Hettie had ever owned, but it was uncomfortable and hard to move around in.

3

It was all for show, of course. When they'd arrived at the Favreau house in Yuma, Marcus, Sophie's head of security, had prepared cover stories for all of them. Hettie and Uncle Jeremiah were Sophie's poor distant relations, Henrietta and Jebediah Wiltshire, who had fallen upon hard times and come to their cousin for help. The Favreaus were wealthy and just eccentric enough to have such houseguests, even in their modest Arizona house, but it was up to her and Uncle to carry out their part in the act to discourage scrutiny.

Mary firmly seated Hettie in front of the mirror. If she noticed the new bruises, she was smart enough not to say anything. She finger-combed Hettie's hay-dry brown hair. "It's almost long enough to do something with now." When Mary pulled it across the scar over the right side of her face, Hettie drew away.

"Don't bother with that."

"Sorry, Miss Henrietta. I thought maybe—"

"You thought wrong." She knew the servants whispered about the scar. Hettie had never been a great beauty in her own estimation, and being judged and gossiped about was nothing new. What she didn't like was other people trying to fix her. Of course, it was Mary's job, and she didn't have a lot to work with: to the maid, Hettie was a scarred, homely twentysomething destined for spinsterhood.

Mary slicked her hair away from her face as best as she could, using a little pomade to give the edges some curls so she didn't appear quite so boyish. "Are you sure you won't consider some other jewelry? A cameo, perhaps?" She drew the leather thong from around Hettie's neck. "This necklace is—"

Hettie snatched the stone amulet from Mary's fingers. "No."

Mary pursed her lips and finished dressing her.

Sophie and Uncle were already seated at the dinner table when Hettie arrived in the dining room. Despite her "rough" surroundings—the debutante heiress never missed a chance to comment on how primitive the accommodations in Arizona were compared to her grandmother's lush mansion in New Orleans— Sophie was, as always, immaculately put together, in a simple but elegant sapphire dress, her gold ringlets artfully arranged.

Hettie supposed Sophie's glamor magic afforded her a measure of confidence and composure. It probably also meant she needed to spend less time getting dressed for dinner—time she'd been spending researching her grandmother's comatose condition.

Sophie glanced up from a sheaf of papers as Hettie sat. Dark shadows hung beneath her eyes, but they disappeared in a blink.

"Any progress?" Hettie hated asking because the answer was always the same. Sophie shook her head.

"I've written all the master-level magicians I know who are experts in the field of psychic interpolation. I've consulted all the magic books I can, interviewed dozens of specialists from the asylum…" She pinched the flesh between her eyebrows. "I simply don't know who else to talk to about Grandmère's condition. Anyone who'd keep her confidence about the soothsayers' blackout, at any rate."

"What about other specialists or sorcerers? Doctors or shamans or…or maybe a warlock?"

"The Favreaus do not entertain Kukulos practitioners," Sophie snapped. "They're everything my family fought against during the war. My great-great-grandfather fought off a Kukulos mob that tried to lynch one of his servants."

"Beggars can't be choosers," Uncle Jeremiah said over the rim of his cup of coffee. Sophie cut him a daggered look, and he shrugged. "All I mean is that there are more Kukulos sorcerers than most people think, and lots of folks are sympathetic to them. And blood magic's a part of lots of magic traditions, not just Kukulos."

"If there's one thing my grandmother would never tolerate, it's anything even remotely associated with the Kukulos. Their kind are not welcome here, and they never will be."

Hettie's lips twitched. She'd thought Sophie would do anything to help Patrice, but clearly even she drew a line somewhere.

"I think it's time for a fresh perspective." Sophie slid a letter across the table to Hettie. She scanned it briefly. "The Society of Mechaniks is hosting a symposium in Chicago. Perhaps the greatest minds in magical science and technology can provide some insight into our dilemma."

"I don't understand. How can a bunch of tinkerers help Patrice?"

"Mechaniks ain't just tinkerers," Uncle said. "They study magic and its interaction with the mundane. They try to determine the line between nature and magic, then mess with it as much as they can. Alchemists were some of the first Mechaniks, looking for ways to turn lead into gold. Nowadays, though, their focus is on the interaction between magic and metal."

"So...they're studying the drain on magic, right?" She'd learned a bit about the drain while she was in Mexico. Maybe she could finally contribute something important to the effort.

Sophie sighed. "Unfortunately, the Society of Mechaniks doesn't believe that magic is disappearing. Their official stance is that it shifts around the globe. They think the drain out of Europe moved to America at some point and that it is simply moving again, as nature intended."

Hettie frowned. "I thought no one knew where magic really came from."

"They don't," Uncle confirmed. "But that doesn't stop a bunch of rich men in expensive suits from making up their own theories."

"There are always outliers," Sophie assured them. "The Society is full of great thinkers. I've arranged for us to travel there to attend this symposium."

"Us?" Uncle raised an eyebrow.

"Of course. My grandmother's pact was with Hettie. You can't tell me you haven't been feeling the itch of the contract spell?"

The debutante must have noticed her fidgeting. Under the table, she'd been bouncing her knee. "I'm handling it fine."

Sophie quirked her lips. "You don't have to lie to me. Grandmère's spells aren't always subtle. She can be a bit of a taskmaster. I never thought a contract spell sealed while she was unconscious would be so effective, though."

Hettie doubted Sophie cared quite that much about her discomfort, but the debutante was right. Hettie had tried to help with the research to find the cause of the soothsayers' blackout, but the sheer amount of information to go through had been dizzying. She simply didn't know enough about magic to understand everything she was reading, and she didn't read as fast as Sophie did. She'd even used Diablo's time bubble to give her more time to read, but she couldn't wrap her head around all the nuances of sorcery and magic.

Instead, Uncle had been recruited to sift through the piles of papers, scrolls, and books. It made sense since he was also a high-caliber sorcerer. Still, Hettie resented her uselessness in this arena. It had left her with too much time on her hands. Training in hand-to-hand combat with Jemma had been one of the few ways to get that nervous energy out—or at least Marcus had insisted it was.

The Favreaus' head of security entered then, his features set in sterner lines than usual. He passed a letter to Sophie. "This just came hand-delivered to the servants' door."

Sophie squinted at the small packet as if it might have teeth. "No hexes I can detect," Marcus added. "Though there is a trace of benign magic on it."

"Open it," she directed him, handing it back. The redheaded Englishman broke the seal at the top, but nothing happened. Three sheets of paper unfolded from the neat packet, and he held the letter out at arm's length, studying the writing carefully.

"What does it say?"

Marcus's brow furrowed. "I think this has been delivered to the wrong address."

Sophie took the letter and squinted at it. She dipped her fingers in her glass and flicked a bit of water at the papers, then poured salt over it, muttering an incantation. She stared hard. "There's something here, but I can't make it out."

"Give it here." Jeremiah took the letter and removed a tiny sachet from his pocket. The bits of rock and bone and hair he shook out littered the table. Marcus grimaced.

"Do you have to do that where we eat?"

Uncle ignored him, uttering his own spell. He must have gotten a different result, because he smiled. "Clever boy. He geised it for the intended reader's eyes only, then wrote over top it. It's for you." He held out the letter to Hettie. "It's from Ling and Abby."

Hettie snatched it from his hand. She'd chewed her nails to the quick wondering where they were, whether they were safe. She'd been anxious about letting her sister go with the Eastern healer to find someone who could train her to use her indigo powers, but it had been her sister's choice. She had to have faith in Abigail.

She stared at the paper. At first, the black ink scrawl made no sense to her. It was simply addressed to a "Madam," and went on about some business venture. But then a silvery glow appeared between the lines, and Hettie could read the words beneath the ink.

Dear Hettie,
Mr. Tsang is writing this letter for me because I'm not as good with writing and he thought this would be easier. How are you? We are good. Cymon gets lots of soup bones from Mr. — downstairs. The place we are staying is small, but I like it. Mrs. — is nice too.

"I can't see some of the words," Hettie said, frustrated. That the message was vague irked her as well.

"Division training never leaves you," Uncle replied with a smirk. "Ling left out any information that might be used to track them down."

Hettie kept reading.

I miss you lots and Cymon does, too. Mr. Tsang says I can send you another letter soon. I like the food here. Can we have food like this when we go home?
Love, Abby

The letter went on.

Dear Miss Hettie,
Greetings from our new home. The journey was long and tedious, but with Abby's help, we managed to arrive without attracting too much attention. We are safe, and I can assure you I am doing my best to care for Abby while maintaining the utmost propriety. I remember how important decorum was to your mother.
I hope you are faring well, and that your quest does not take you long. Perhaps we will see the end of it soon, and reunite when the affair is over.
Your friend,
Ling Tsang

She reread the pages, looking for any hint of distress or hardship that might be affecting Abby's well-being. She sighed. "I wish I knew where they were."

"No, you don't," Uncle said. "The less you know, the better. For everyone's sake."

"You think they'll be okay?"

Uncle's jaw worked. "I'm not Ling's biggest fan, but him leaving the Division is no small matter. He could betray us again, I suppose, but I've no reason to suspect he will. Wherever they are, I reckon Abby's as safe as safe can be."

Rain poured off the brim of Ling's straw hat as he ducked his head. It didn't do much to keep him dry, but it was better than nothing. Gods, he missed the dry heat of Mexico. He never thought he'd say that after the long days of riding beneath the unforgiving sun with sand in his boots. But at least in the arid south, he hadn't felt and smelled like a piece of fermented tofu.

Someone from an apartment above chose that moment to empty a bucket of fetid water out the window. He hunched as the deluge splattered across his back, hugging his precious package closer. Chilled to the bone and stinking even worse now, he made his way along Washington Street, slogging against the stinking runoff coursing down the muddy flagstones.

A pair of police officers lumbered toward him, the rain shearing off their broad shoulders. Ling thought about turning around, but he knew if he did, they would notice and pursue. Any deviant behavior would attract their attention. Best to keep going, act like he was doing nothing wrong.

The space between them closed. He turtled deeper into his high-collared jacket.

They passed. One step. Two steps. Three.

Ling relaxed.

"Hey. Hey you."

Ling walked on, pretended he hadn't heard them.

"You there." A rough hand turned him around, and he faced a wet, bulb-nosed man with beady light blue eyes. "Where're you going?"

"Sorry, sorry, no good English." Playing the submissive had never been his favorite game, but here, it was a matter of survival.

"Goddamned coolies…" The officer growled and gave Ling a shake. "You. Where. Are. You. Going?"

"Home."

"This ain't your home. Where are your papers?"

Ling handed over his forged identity papers. They'd cost him a fortune to obtain, but considering the number of times he'd had to produce them, they'd been well worth the price.

The policeman barely glanced at the papers. Like most of the regular patrolmen in Chinatown, he was a mundane—he hadn't even used any kind of antifraud talismans to check the documents. "What's that?" He grabbed the package from Ling. "Dope?"

Ling's heart squelched. "No dope, no."

The man's partner, who'd been silent up till now, ripped the package open. Ling ground his jaw as the contents spilled out. "What the— Man alive, what is that?"

"Hell if I know. These people will eat anything." He pointed. "What? Dog?"

"Ah…" Ling pushed his nose up in the air and squealed like a pig, then laughed nervously. The package was ruined—now all he could hope for was to get away.

"Pig? Pork?" The officer kicked the melting glob of goo away. "No, that's not pork. What is it? Tell me."

"Pig! Pig!" If these officers locked him up, Abby would be on her own.

"Disgusting. We should take him in, Tommy. He's acting mighty suspicious to me."

"Every coolie here is suspicious to you. Look, I'm soaked to the bone. All I want is to get dinner and go home. You want to do the paperwork, you book him." Tommy drew his collar tighter around his neck and shivered.

Bulb-nose sneered at Ling. "You're lucky this time, Chinaman. But you watch yourself." He shoved Ling against the wall, groping him roughly between the legs. The jingle of coins made him smile, and he pulled Ling's day's wages out of his pocket. He smirked. "Just like your women. All pussies." He gave a harsh laugh as he pocketed the money. Tommy sent a backward glance over his shoulder, grimacing, and the officers left.

Ling's heart pumped blood hard up into his head. It could've been worse—there'd been reports of hoodlums cruising the streets looking for Celestials to beat up. At least there was a police presence here, ineffectual and intimidating as it was. Getting into it with the law wasn't worth it, though. With Abby's life at stake, he couldn't risk arrest.

He sighed as the pig blood curd melted in the rain. Abby's dinner was completely unsalvageable. Cursing himself, the weather, and the men who'd taken his money, he headed back to the tenement, wringing out his shirt under the stoop so he wouldn't drip too much inside.

He made his way up the grimy stairs, ducking laundry lines hanging in the stairwell. The building was dank and poorly maintained, but it was the best he could find on his meager funds.

No one had remarked upon the fact that he was living with a young white girl. That was mostly thanks to the talismans Jeremiah Bassett had given her before they'd parted ways at the border, but Ling also suspected that Abby's gift for mimicking spells had given her some ability to cast glamor that made her invisible. Regardless, she'd been advised never to leave the building. San Francisco was not at all safe for a young girl on her own.

He discreetly undid the antitheft and antivandalism spell on the door and let himself in. Abby sat cross-legged on her bed, the curtain between their respective halves of the room drawn back. Cymon lay curled up next to her, and he lifted his head briefly before settling back to sleep. Abby had her hands raised and cupped, and a globe of fire burned between them.

"I thought you might be cold when you came in," she said without looking up. "So I made it warm."

Ling pursed his lips. He didn't want to scold her for her thoughtfulness and initiative, but he didn't want to encourage recklessness either. "That's very kind of you, Miss Abby. But there are safer spells you could perform to warm the room."

"But I like this one." She tossed the orb from hand to hand, little flames trailing behind it. She turned the ball in her hand and focused. The orange light turned red as it expanded, then yellow-white as she made it contract. She took a deep breath, then made it turn blue. Then violet.

Ling smiled, not wanting his fear to show. "That's very good, Miss Abby. Even so, I want you to be careful. I appreciate you wanting to help, but you have to be mindful of *how* you help."

Abigail frowned and extinguished the flame with a snap of her fingers. "What does that mean?"

Ling never thought parenting would be part of his duties, but he'd found himself answering more and more questions like this for Abby lately. He thought for a moment. "Well, sometimes, when we try to do good things, bad things can happen because we're not careful, or we don't think of consequences."

Abby nodded slowly. "Like…like if I tried to warm the room with my spell and it might have hurt someone."

"Yes. Exactly."

"Oh. I'm sorry."

"You meant well. And you didn't lose control of the spell. Still, I'd rather you stop and think about what could happen. Remember how I said not to practice any spells without someone here to watch over you?"

"Ah-Dong was here," she said.

He chewed on the inside of his cheek. She'd mentioned Ah-Dong before, and he'd worried someone had been visiting her while he'd been away. When he asked around the tenement, though, the other residents had informed him that Ah-Dong had died months ago in the same apartment they currently inhabited.

Abby had said she'd spoken to her dead brother, Paul, before, too. These encounters with Ah-Dong cemented Ling's belief that, in addition to her indigo powers, Abby had the rare gift of necromancy.

As the spirit of Ah-Dong hadn't abused them in any way, Ling wasn't likely to call in a priest or ghost hunter. There were plenty of benign phantoms out there, and it sounded like Ah-Dong was simply happy for company. Truth was, Ling preferred *someone* was watching Abby while he was working. He hated leaving her alone for long hours with little to do, but he had no choice. He wasn't sure he could trust anyone to care for Abby.

He'd leave an offering to Ah-Dong at the temple when he had a chance to thank the spirit.

"Did you bring dinner?" Abby asked.

"Sorry, no. The butcher...ran out."

Her face fell. "It's all right, Abby." Ling slit his finger with a penknife and sat, offering her the dripping finger. "Not too much, now. I still have to wake up in the morning."

She fell on him like a hungry kitten. He clenched his jaw as she drew on his lifeblood and magic. Abby's vampiric needs had been met with pig's blood augmented with herbs Ling had purchased, but now he didn't have coin to pay for it...or anything else. He did a quick mental calculation, and his heart sank. He wouldn't be able to pay next month's rent.

Unfortunately, he had no way to access his personal savings—the Division would know where he was if he tried. And he couldn't ask Hettie or the Favreaus for a loan: getting a money transfer could compromise his and Abby's location.

Besides, he had his pride. He'd promised to care for Hettie's sister, and he'd be damned if she found out they were on the brink of starvation. He'd lost Hettie's trust once—he would not fail her or dishonor her family's memory again.

The long hours he worked washing dishes wasn't pulling in enough. Unfortunately, as lucrative as offering healing services could be, it was too risky to set up shop. A Paladin-class healer working in Chinatown would attract too much attention. Even if he could start his own practice, would anyone trust him? A few inquiries around the community would eventually unearth his story, his shame.

He sighed. There was no way around it—he'd need to take out a loan from one of the tongs. The benevolent societies provided many of the Chinese with financial and legal assistance, as well as giving their fellow countrymen a sense of community and a connection to home.

Unfortunately, there was only one tong he knew of that might grant him his request.

He would have to talk to some old friends.

CHAPTER TWO

The Favreau household in Yuma packed for the journey to Chicago with alacrity. If Hettie didn't know better, she'd say the servants were glad to see the backs of their mistress and her odd guests.

"I was thinking we should take Mary with us," Sophie mused as she went over her checklist. "Not that scroll, Harold, the other one." The servant packing the many books and documents she'd acquired in her research nodded apologetically. His mistress had been breathing down his neck all morning, ensuring he did not try to organize the chaos she'd carefully constructed in the study. Sophie went on. "Mary's never been to any of the big cities, and you'll need a maid of your own."

"I've never had a maid before, and I don't need one now," Hettie argued. "Besides, I don't think we need extra people knowing about—" She twirled her finger around to indicate their situation and flexed it to mimic Diablo's trigger.

"Discretion is a servant's most important quality, and I pay handsomely for it. Also," Sophie added, "if you really were a Favreau relation, it'd be a disgrace on our name if we didn't provide you with a maid. It's about keeping up appearances."

"Maybe Uncle and I could travel with you as servants again, the way we did when we were taking the train from New Orleans." She really had no desire to wear any more corsets or pretend at social niceties. At least as a servant, she could hide in plain sight.

Sophie shook her head. "It would be too suspicious. For one, you don't have any servant training, and it would look strange for you to be traveling with us when you're so inept. Besides, people already know I have poor relations staying with me. We can't change the story now."

"Please, Sophie. I'd rather keep our circle…small."

"What good is money if you're constantly doing your own sewing and ironing and cleaning? Becoming a Favreau means accepting a certain standard of living." The debutante huffed at Hettie's flat look. "Well, if you're insistent about it. But don't expect Jemma to do any of your laundry."

"What about Jezebel and the Furies?" Her father's horse and the three mares they'd ridden from Mexico were currently enjoying the Favreaus' well-kept stables after their arduous journey.

Sophie frowned. "You don't need to bring any of your horses. There will be carriages and drivers to take us where we need to go. And Jezebel is old and has seen a lot of excitement these past few months. Wouldn't you rather leave her here where she can be cared for?"

Hettie chewed her lip. Keeping her father's aging mare with her did seem unnecessary, but she'd never gone anywhere without a horse, and Jezebel was family. Hettie had lost the ability to love her parents, but she still cherished the things that had mattered to them.

Still, Sophie was right. Jezebel had had a grueling few months on the road. Magicked or no, she needed rest. She deserved a quiet retirement.

With a heavy heart, Hettie went to the stable to break the news to her father's beloved mare and say good-bye.

"Yuma's not the place I wanted to leave you," she said, brushing Jezebel's mane. "You were supposed to get green grass fields and a big pit of sand to roll in. Pa would've wanted that for you." Tightly, she added, "But Sophie's people will take really good care of you here. I mean, this is the high life." She gestured around at the clean stall, the full trough, the magic that kept the worst of the flies out.

The mare's head drooped. She leaned her chin against Hettie's shoulder and blew out.

"When this is all over, I'll get you back to Montana. Or wherever you fancy."

She had to have faith they'd see each other again. Jezebel sighed resignedly, but Hettie thought she detected a note of relief, too. The old mare hadn't been as energetic or even as cranky as she usually was since the ride back north across the Wall at the border. One too many magic portal crossings, Horace had said.

The hostler in question came around the corner then. After he told Sophie his tale about being set upon by a mob of Kukulos warlocks and turned into a horse, she'd put him up in quarters above the stables. Hettie was still annoyed he hadn't been offered a room in the house, but Horace had gratefully accepted the accommodations and agreed to help with her horses while trying to reestablish his business connections.

He tugged his cap in greeting. "Heard you'll be moving on out of here soon."

She told him about the Mechaniks' symposium. "We're headed to Chicago."

"Chicago?" He stroked his chin. "This is fortuitous. My lawyer is in Chicago and hasn't written back to me. Perhaps I might beg Miss Favreau to let me join you on this expedition and see if I can't get in touch with him."

"How are things going?" she asked.

"Not well. My man of business, Mr. Jacobi, died in the eight years I was away and left my assets in the hands of my lawyer, Mr. Taylor. I think he perhaps does not believe in my claim. Or does not want to believe."

"Surely there's something you can do?"

"Short of presenting myself to the bank with Mr. Taylor in tow and a judge's letter, I'm not sure." He sighed. "Jacobi was always the face of my business. They wouldn't know mine from Adam."

"You could always rebuild. Things must've changed in the time you've been away. How did you earn credit with the banks before?"

Horace's smile held a bevy of secrets. "Men are like horses. You need to get to know them before you approach or risk getting kicked—see how they treat other horses, get to know their temperament and habits."

He beckoned and pointed across the yard to where a footman sat hunched, smoking a cigarette. "Take young Peter, there. See how he stares at his hands as if they are the most interesting things in the world?" Horace drew a line from Peter to a maid carrying a basket of laundry. She glanced Peter's way, furrowed her brow, and marched on.

"Lovers' spat?" Hettie asked.

"More than that. You see, Peter doesn't smoke. He only started recently. See how inexpertly he holds the cigarette?" Peter pinched it between his thumb and two fingers instead of cradled in the V between his index and middle.

"So?"

Horace raised an eyebrow. "If I were a betting man, I'd say the maid there might be with child."

Hettie gasped, and Horace laughed. "I said *might*. This is just a casual observation, not an exact science. Funny thing is, people are more predictable than horses. They're always motivated by the same things—security, money, power, sex, and revenge. They have patterns of behavior. They like routine. When they deviate from that routine, you can be assured something is going on. You see how I might leverage that kind of information to, say, get a loan from Peter."

"By blackmailing him?"

"Oh, if I wanted to blackmail him, I'd simply point out that I know he's been stealing feed and selling it under the table." He lifted his chin. "I'm going to wait to see how he handles impending fatherhood first before reporting him to Miss Sophie. I'd hate to see him begging on the street to support a baby and wife."

Hettie smirked. "You sure you're not gifted?"

"Not magically." He flashed a smile. "If I were, I'd have tracked down my lawyer and found out whether his wife yet knows about the woman he keeps in Boston. My letters alluding to such have gone unanswered, so I will have to present myself in person. If you wouldn't mind vouching for me to Miss Sophie once more, I would be most grateful if I could tag along for the ride."

It turned out Sophie had no problem taking on an additional passenger on their journey north. For all that he was treated like a servant, she seemed to like Horace. It was Jemma who protested the hostler's presence.

"He's nothing but a charlatan," she proclaimed. "Miss Sophie, I don't even know why you let that man into your house."

Sophie's eyebrow arched. "Jemma, I'm surprised at you. I thought you'd have more sympathy for your fellow countryman."

"I don't owe him anything." Jemma folded her arms over her chest. "He's a con man, that one. I know his like. He's a snake, and he'll bite you eventually. I can't abide him."

Sophie peered at the bodyguard. "Is there something you want to share with me about Mr. Washington's conduct, Jemma?"

She grew quiet, her face fixed in a stony mask. "Nothing to tell."

Hettie watched her carefully. Horace could be a flirt, that was true, but she didn't think he would have gotten within arm's length of Jemma if he'd meant to harm her.

"Jemma." Sophie took her hands in hers and stood to meet her eye. "You are my most trusted ally, my confidante and my friend. If Mr. Washington has hurt or harassed you in any way—"

"Ain't nothing he done I can't handle," she grumbled, then straightened her spine. "I simply do not trust him. A man who's been a horse for eight years can't be all right in the head."

So this was about Jemma's fear of Weres. Shape-shifting was considered an abomination, after all, but Horace had been cursed by a group of Kukulos warlocks and transformed into a horse. It hadn't been his choice—he'd been a victim.

Jemma was aware of all this, of course. Sophie regarded her with patience and sympathy. "If his presence is so disturbing to you, Jemma, I'll pay to put Mr. Washington in a cabin on his own."

"Cabin's too good for that one," the bodyguard said. "I'd rather keep him where I can see him."

They departed the following day. Marcus recited the itinerary—they'd be heading east to New Orleans, where they would stop and check in on Patrice, then proceed north to Chicago. There were a dizzying number of stops and transfers along the way, none of which Hettie could remember. What she did eventually grasp was that, since Sophie valued her privacy and safety, they'd be traveling in the Favreaus' private Pullman car, which had been delivered to Yuma and would be hitched to the train for the journey.

Hettie's breath caught at the luxurious interior of the Pullman. She'd never seen anything like it. Dark wood and polished brass gleamed, and all the furniture was upholstered with plush fabrics and silky fringe and tassels. A crystal chandelier hung above the sitting area. Each of the four tiny private sleeping rooms sported a down bed. There was even a kitchenette where meals could be assembled.

Horace gazed around the car, tipping his hat back. "My, my. It's been a long time since I've traveled in such lush accommodations."

Hettie wondered if maybe he was exaggerating his success as a horseflesh trader. Surely he could never have afforded *this* kind of luxury?

The first day of travel was uneventful. Hettie lost track of which towns they stopped in; the jostle and sway of the car made her feel unsteady on her feet and a little ill. She missed the solid feel of the ground, though she did not miss sleeping on it. Several times in the night, she startled awake, frantically looking for Abby and then remembering she hadn't been with her for over a month.

Hettie had selfishly thought she'd appreciate not having her sister around. She'd been watching her nearly her whole life, after all, always making sure she was safe. But in moments of quiet reflection, all she felt was an impending sense of danger, as if she were standing on a cliff ledge that might crumble at any moment. If she were honest with herself, that feeling hadn't left her since the night the Crowe gang had killed her parents.

She touched the amulet at her neck, feeling the smooth divot in the stone and wondering how Walker and the people of Villa del Punta were doing. Her stomach churned as regret flooded her.

She'd brought so much pain and suffering to the people around her. Sometimes she thought back to how it all began, tallying the if-onlys alongside her sins. They showed in the lines in her face and the first gray hairs she'd noticed in the mirror. She'd just turned eighteen, a birthday passed with all the fanfare of an errant tumbleweed on the dusty road headed north. By Diablo's accounting, though, she was twenty-seven.

She counted them on her ten fingers—the men she'd killed with the Devil's Revolver. And, separately, the two she'd killed without it. Gray hairs at twenty-seven were the least she deserved for her transgressions.

As she lay in bed that night, the numbing edge of grief encroached upon her. She hadn't cried in a long time, but in the quiet of the cabin, except for the muffled clatter of the wheels over the tracks and Uncle's snoring, she let a tear fall. She missed Abby. She missed Cymon. She missed Walker and Jezebel. She missed her bed and the farm and Newhaven and the people there. She missed the life she'd lived, back when things were simple. All this "civilized" traveling had given her too much time alone with her thoughts and multitude of regrets.

Diablo manifested beneath her palm, like a sharp-toothed kitten that had wriggled in between the sheets. She closed her eyes and let the revolver play a series of images in her mind to comfort her: Abby smiling in the sunshine while her brother, Paul, wove a crown of daisies for her; snow falling on the house at Christmas; dancing beneath the moon with Walker.

It didn't matter that these memories weren't real. Diablo simply wanted her not to feel bad. She'd come to accept the infernal revolver's comfort, no matter how misplaced it was.

It was the only comfort she allowed herself.

In the morning, the train stopped in a small town to resupply. Hot food, coffee, and newspapers were delivered to the Favreau car. Sophie and Marcus sat reading, frowning deeply. Horace and Uncle were notably absent. They'd both fled to town when the train stopped. Marcus glanced up. "Have you seen this?"

Hettie took the paper from him. He pointed at a headline: ALABAMA GANG ROBS BANK, KILLS 2. "You take up a new hobby?"

"Surely they mean the state of Alabama..." But as she read on, it was clear the gang was named for their leader.

The door connecting the private Pullman car to the rest of the train slammed open, and Uncle marched in, newspaper in hand, reading the article out loud. "'The notorious outlaw Hettie Alabama and numerous accomplices held up the Kissing Bridge Bank last Wednesday, killing two bank tellers and getting away with over eight hundred dollars in cash.'" He chuckled dryly, rubbing his bristly jaw. "'Miss Alabama is responsible for the deaths of at least thirteen others in related robberies across the state. U.S. marshals have put up a two-hundred-dollar reward for her capture and any information leading to her arrest.'" He snorted. "You've been busy, Hettie."

She glared. "You know it wasn't me."

"Who would do this? Who even knows about Hettie?" Sophie took a cup of coffee from Jemma. The bodyguard flicked a look of suspicion at Hettie before pouring her a cup as well.

"Let's see—the Pinkerton Agency, the Division of Sorcery, the army, the Crowe gang—"

"The Crowe gang's gone," Hettie said. "They were all killed or arrested in Sonoma."

"Perhaps it's only a coincidence," Marcus said. "Any ne'er-do-well could have picked up your story. Or made it up. Do you have any relatives in this part of the country?"

"Alabama's a name my father picked when he woke up with no memory in that state," Hettie said. She'd only learned the story recently from Uncle, and it still felt strange to tell it. "It ain't a family name by any means. I don't have any kin, except Abby."

Uncle gave a snort. She cast him a look that dared him to counter her.

Sophie waved a hand. "We can speculate all we want, but we have a more pressing issue. Hettie is *here*, with us. Your cover stories and my glamor will hide you, but if the authorities are actively looking for you, I don't know how effective those protections will be. We need to be cautious."

"And we weren't being cautious before?" Hettie blew out a breath. "Between the Division and the Pinkertons—"

"I don't think we have to worry about them. Not for a while, at least." Uncle had turned the page of his newspaper and pointed at the headline in one corner: SENIOR PINKERTON AGENT THOMAS STUBBS DISMISSED FOR MISMANAGING FUNDS.

Hettie's stomach bottomed out. The last time she'd seen the Pinkerton man, he'd almost strangled Abby to death. She shouldn't have been surprised he'd made it out of Mexico, but this was an astonishing development. She read the brief story:

> Senior Pinkerton agent Thomas Stubbs, long considered to be next in line to head the Chicago branch of the Pinkerton Detecting Agency, was dismissed from his position last week after a long investigation into the misuse and mismanagement of agency funds and resources.
>
> Mr. Stubbs, a decorated twenty-eight-year veteran of the company, was reportedly spending vast amounts of magical resources for unnecessary trips, expensing lavish meals and hotel stays at facilities across the country, and logging hundreds of unauthorized overtime hours, all on clients' tabs.
>
> Pinkerton Agency president Robert Pinkerton said, "Despite Mr. Stubbs's years of dedicated service, the company cannot overlook such reckless, wasteful spending of clients' hard-earned money." Mr. Stubbs was not available for comment.

"Never thought in all my years that Stubby'd make it to retirement," Uncle said. "Thought for sure I'd kill him first."

"Getting sacked isn't retirement," Marcus pointed out.

"At our age, it might as well be." He sat back in his chair, his eyes light but the look on his face troubled. "It does leave him as a bit of an unknown, though."

"What do you mean?"

"I mean that Stubby's been obsessed with finding Diablo for decades, and he holds a grudge like you wouldn't believe. The Pinkertons might be shifting their priorities, which is a blessing to us. But don't discount Thomas Stubbs. You can bet he'll be back on our trail soon enough."

Dread sat like a stone in Hettie's chest for the rest of the day. The unending shifting of the floor beneath her feet made her feel restless and uneasy, and her stomach wouldn't settle. The morning's news had reminded her that the past few weeks in the Favreau household had not changed the fact that she was a wanted fugitive. And now she was in more peril than ever with this Alabama gang doing gods-knew-what in her name.

They stopped overnight in a large town somewhere in Texas, and the Favreau entourage disembarked and got rooms at a nearby hotel.

As Hettie readied for bed, Jemma knocked on her door and beckoned her to follow her to Sophie's room. She was being summoned, apparently.

As they entered, the debutante looked up from her seat, where she was sipping a hot cocoa and reading. "Ah, Hettie, I'm glad you came. I have something for you."

Sophie picked up a reticule sitting on the side table. "I think now is the best time to give you this." She drew out a small leather pouch and handed it over. Hettie opened it, emptying the contents into her palm. A piece of smoky quartz on a long braid of leather and horse hair dropped out.

"What is it?" Hettie asked.

"A talisman that extends my glamor magic over you. Normally I can only keep you covered and unnoticeable within a few feet of me, but this will allow you to go much farther and still stay hidden," Sophie explained. "You'll need to braid a few strands of your hair around the stone. Wear it under your dress against your skin. And don't lose it. It took me some time to make, and it has some of my hair on it, too."

Hettie examined it, turning it over in her fingers. "How far can your powers extend with this?"

"Not that far," Jemma interjected tersely. Hettie understood. She didn't want her mistress overextending her powers.

"The farther you go, the more it taxes my power, and the weaker the spell gets. I'm magically connected to this talisman—the only way to cut myself off from it is by burning off my hair." She pointed at the golden strands wound around the crystal. "Don't put it on until we arrive in Chicago. In fact, don't put it on unless you have to travel away from me."

Hettie weighed the amulet in her hand and asked, "Why are you giving this to me?"

"We're going to be in the city. Most people won't look at you twice, but the Pinkerton headquarters are located in Chicago, and I'd rather not risk recognition."

"I mean, why now?" She squinted at the quartz. "What is this *really*?"

Sophie resettled herself. Hettie supposed she'd expected her to be grateful, and Hettie knew she was being rude by looking a gift horse in the mouth. But bonding with Diablo had taxed her trust in people. No one did anything without a selfish reason.

"It's exactly what I said it is. Jemma said you've been having nightmares...about Abby. About the men you've killed."

Hettie stiffened. She hadn't thought anyone had heard her cry out in the night while in her little coffin of a cabin. "They're just dreams."

"Except that your dreams can kill," Jemma interrupted. "I went to check on you, and you were waving Diablo around in your sleep. You pull that trigger and you could kill us all."

Hettie winced. That was at least twice, then, that she'd pointed Diablo at Sophie's bodyguard. "I'm very sorry, Jemma."

"I thought maybe this amulet would make you feel a little safer," Sophie said gently. "Mr. Bassett told us some of what happened in Mexico."

She set her teeth. The old man would talk if you got enough whiskey in him. She preferred to keep her private life private.

She inspected the talisman again, though she had no way to tell how it was magicked. Sophie said, "I didn't put any other spells on it. Neither did your uncle or Marcus. I swear it on my grandmother's life."

That was as good a guarantee as she'd get. She couldn't think of any reason why Sophie would want to harm her. Manipulate her, maybe, but since Uncle's attempt at controlling her, she knew now the symptoms to look for—sudden acceptance, an overwhelming sense of ambivalence when it came to something she cared about.

Resignation. Capitulation. Complacency. They were easy traps to fall into considering what she faced. She found she had to check herself constantly. All she had to do was think about Abby's safety and she'd be able to tell if anyone had geised her.

Hettie thanked the debutante with mixed feelings and left. Maybe Sophie did mean well—after all, Sophie did not need her.

If anything, Hettie was a liability to the Favreaus. The Alabama gang had put a target on her back. She was expendable. And that made her vulnerable.

CHAPTER THREE

After her conversation with Sophie, Hettie couldn't sleep. She went down to the hotel lobby, thinking perhaps a drink might help her relax enough to catch a few hours' sleep before they had to board the train once more. Maybe later she'd read a few chapters of the magic books she'd borrowed from Sophie's collection.

She breathed and dropped into Diablo's time bubble. The air went still, the murmur of life muting around her. Uncle had cautioned her about overusing Diablo's time suspension abilities even after they'd tested its limits, but there'd been no lasting or immediate consequences. Still, Jeremiah had explicitly forbade her from using it.

He couldn't tell when she did, of course.

Hettie reasoned that, if anything, they all needed more time to search out the answers to their many questions: the cause of the soothsayers' blackout, Patrice's coma, Abby's indigo powers, and why Hettie, of all people, could use Diablo to step out of time. She hadn't been able to find anything, but that was mostly because the time bubble required concentration, and she often fell asleep reading.

She made her way down to the hotel lobby, pausing and breathing every time she took something else into the bubble—opening the door, picking up a glass and a bottle of brandy at the bar. It'd occurred to her how useful this power would be to a pickpocket, but she wouldn't risk it. One touch and she'd bring a whole person into the bubble with her.

As she poured herself a drink, she spotted Marcus reading a small, well-worn book by the fireplace, the red of his hair catching the frozen firelight. Not much liking the absolute silence of the time bubble, and deciding the Englishman wouldn't mind her company, she put the bottle down and touched his shoulder. He startled as he melded into her slow-time world.

Understanding came quickly. The amber of his eyes pierced her, and he smirked. "So, this is what you get up to at night." He slipped the little book into his inner jacket pocket.

She sat across from him. "I don't like being cooped up in my room."

He gazed at the silent, barely moving molasses world around them. "Very impressive. I can see how this might be comforting. It's very quiet. How do you feel?"

"Nothing I can't handle," she said. She'd become aware of a slight tingling sensation all over her body when she used the time bubble, but it didn't hurt.

Marcus stood. "Well, if you're agreeable to holding this lovely quiet, will you join me for a constitutional?" He held out a hand.

She got up without his help and followed him out of the hotel, skirting the people trapped in time.

The evening was cool, with the faintest hint of rain blowing in on the wind. Hettie had to remind herself it was still winter. Being in the South over Christmas and New Year's had confused her senses.

"Take my arm," Marcus said. "It's not right for a gentleman to be escorting a lady otherwise."

"It's not as if anyone can see or hear us." She cut him a skeptical look, and he chuckled.

"Call me old-fashioned, but I like to feel chivalrous sometimes." He sent her a kind look. "Not to worry, Miss Hettie. I'm old enough to be your father, and I gave up looking for a wife long ago. Of course, any man who had you would be lucky."

She snorted. "I don't cotton to flattery."

"And I don't give it freely. So let's simply walk as friends."

He guided her down the boardwalk, her boots ringing on the worn boards. The early evening provided a relaxing air for those just starting into their cups or looking for a night's entertainment. It was a small, industrious town with farms and ranches surrounding it. Many of the other places the train had stopped in were similarly bustling with life.

"It's nice enough here," Hettie commented. "A lot like Newhaven, if not a bit...mundane." She wasn't used to speaking in those terms, the way sorcerers did, but she'd been doing a lot of reading and had learned to recognize the earmarks of places steeped in magic compared to those that were not as blessed: the lack of a sorcerers' salon, for one. The rampant flies and other pests that buzzed her ears because there were no spells keeping them away. Even the roads seemed dustier and dirtier somehow.

Marcus nodded. "It's a lucky thing it's on the rail line. Magic that leaves a town doesn't leave much else behind if there's no industry otherwise." He glanced her way. "Are you finding any difference between using Diablo here versus other places you've been?"

She shook her head. "Feels the same all around, mostly."

He hummed in thought. "There's a lot we still don't understand about magic, and Diablo is one of the anomalies that could disprove all kinds of magical theories."

Hettie had read about those, too. There were dozens of theories about the source of magic, but no one had come up with a single coherent law. "Maybe it's just the time bubble powers that aren't affected. I don't plan on firing this gun anytime soon to test that either way."

"What else have you discovered about your mage gun?"

"I saved a man's life using Diablo's fire to cauterize his gunshot wound, but I'm not sure that counts. It might as well have been a torch. A tool."

Marcus looked impressed. "Your control is growing stronger. Good. You're cultivating a difficult partnership. Keep in mind, Diablo is its own being. Its only purpose when it was forged was to kill, so you've accomplished something significant." He met her eye. "Never forget it has a will of its own. It'll turn on you if it thinks you're not working in its best interests."

They passed a saloon where a well-dressed madam on the porch called to potential customers, offering the pleasures of drink, gambling, and flesh inside. Hettie imagined an interesting tableau within, but she was far too reserved to go and look.

"Do your mage guns have...wills?" She glanced at the brace of pistols holstered at Marcus's sides. He was never without them, not even in sleep. The gilded double-barreled guns looked more like museum pieces than useful weapons.

Marcus smiled crookedly. "None I've ever known about. But they're not possessed by demons, or angels for that matter. Luna and Claire are true mage guns—metal and wood and ivory enchanted through blood magic."

"But they don't have prickers." She held out her mangled trigger finger, where Diablo's thorn took its price. "They don't have a blood price."

"Not as literally as yours does. Luna and Claire still cost me, though."

"A year of your life?"

He tilted his chin in thought. "Not quite so steep."

"What can they do?"

The corner of his mouth twitched. "You ask a lot of questions."

"You're avoiding a lot of answers." From her understanding, mage guns used the wielder's energy as ammunition. Diablo needed her blood and aged her a year for every human life she took; but other mage guns could do anything from making the wielder lose his hair—she checked Marcus's scalp and found only a full head of wavy copper—to making the wielder's skin slough off. That particular mage gun had been destroyed almost immediately.

She hadn't read anything about a pair of mage guns. Why would a sorcerer insist on two identical pistols? Perhaps he'd split their power between them?

"Why all the secrets?" she asked.

His lips crept up in a half smile. "It's best not to tell too many people what your mage guns can do, what you're capable of, or what the blood price is. You don't want your enemies knowing your weaknesses or your limits."

"You sound like Uncle."

"I consider that a compliment. He hasn't lived as long as he has by being careless. People in our profession don't usually die of old age."

They circled back to the hotel, and Marcus bent over her hand the way a gentleman would. He was a nice man—handsome, even—but he seemed lonely. Sad. Perhaps life as the Favreaus' head of security was not conducive to building a family.

Or was that the life of a mage gun wielder?

Y

They traveled on east through Texas, the train cutting through grassy fields and across low hills waving with dry, gold grass. They passed through towns old and new, some with barely more than a mill and a general store, others with hard-pack roads and brick buildings.

At one stop, an automobile was parked by the hotel. The Mechanikal wonder drew crowds of gawkers, though apparently the machine had suddenly stopped working.

"I'll admit to an appreciation of the aesthetics," Horace murmured, gesturing at the walnut dashboard, "but ultimately these are useless piles of metal. They break down, they run out of fuel, they can only travel on dry roads, they're heavy and prohibitively expensive. It simply isn't a viable long-term business investment. I don't see the use of them."

"It's not about utility, it's about status," Uncle said. "People with too much money always need ways to show other people just how deep their pockets are."

"Considering your bar tab, I certainly didn't think you'd complain about a little money," Marcus murmured.

"Not complaining, just making an observation." Uncle nodded his chin toward Sophie, who was chatting with the automobile's owner. "I'd wager Miss Favreau is estimating the costs for that piece of junk and will write home to her father about purchasing one."

The vehicle's owner opened the hood, exposing the engine within, and the crowd drew closer, oohing and aahing. The guts of the machine looked like nothing Hettie could understand—lots of tubes and wires and pieces she'd never seen smashed together into something that reminded her of a monstrous heart of metal. The owner was explaining something to Sophie, who maintained an interested look as he pointed out some parts, his grimace clearly showing his discontent with its current condition.

Hettie's attention wandered, and she found herself watching a young girl walking hand in hand with an older dark-haired man. Her senses jumped as she thought it was Abby and Ling—but no. Her heart sank. Apparently, she missed them more than she'd realized.

"Hey! Hey, you, boy! What are you doing?"

When Hettie looked back, Horace was leaning halfway into the engine compartment. He withdrew his arm and called to the owner, "Now try it."

The man's face had turned puce seeing some stranger lay hands on his pride and joy. But something kept him from lashing out further. He turned a crank, threw some levers within the machine. The automobile gave a loud bang and sputtered to life. The crowd shrank back, but as the engine rumbled into a steady purr, they gleefully clapped.

"Horace, you clever man!" Sophie exclaimed. "How did you do that?"

He shrugged. "I noticed a missing piece in the engine. Looking inside there, I guessed it'd come loose and fallen down into that space. I found it and put it back."

Sophie grinned. "Mr. Washington, I think you might have a future in Mechaniks."

He tipped his cap. "Kind of you to say, but I still prefer my horses."

The owner of the automobile was grateful that his vehicle worked once more, though he seemed appalled that Horace had been the one to fix it. He gave the hostler a curt nod of thanks. Then they went into the hotel, leaving the car and the spectacle behind.

"Might want to check that ego of yours," Jeremiah grumbled. "It can get you into a lot of trouble."

Horace slid him an arch look. "With all due respect, Mr. Bassett, I don't apologize for being smart or right. But I will take your warning as a friendly reminder of my place." Those last words licked like flames, heating Hettie's cheeks.

"It's not your place I worry about. It's your neck." Uncle cast his look around the group and lowered his voice further. "We're wanted criminals. We have to keep our heads down and our noses clean."

Horace sighed and shook his head. "You can't win for trying."

The train chugged along, and Hettie watched the landscape streak past through the window. A restlessness pervaded her, though everyone else seemed content to pass the time with the clatter and rattle of the tracks and wheels to soothe them. Sophie sat reading a heavy tome about magical ailments. Marcus cleaned his mage guns. Jemma crocheted a lace doily with the speed and dexterity of a spider. Horace was off somewhere else on the train, chatting up strangers. He was uniquely good at that. Hettie wished she could escape, too, but Uncle had said it was too risky to poke around without Sophie's glamor to disguise her. There was no sense using her talisman, either, not for something as frivolous as a need to stretch her legs.

Puffs of dark engine smoke curled across the window. The fumes nauseated Sophie, so they kept the shutters closed. The car grew stuffy, and soon Hettie was desperate for a breath of fresh air.

She went to the observation deck on the rear of the car. Uncle sat there smoking a cigar, his eyes scanning the landscape. He glanced up.

"Starting to miss the open road?" His gaze stretched over the wavering grasses spread below. They'd ridden through fields like this when they'd traveled south through Wyoming, only then there'd been little to no civilization for miles and miles. In Texas the towns were closer together, and it never seemed long before there was a little postmaster's station or farmhouse along the track. The rails stretched behind the train like a silver-edged wake through the field, while the telegraph poles veered away like a comet tail as the train climbed a slope.

"I miss a lot of things," she said. "I miss Abby. I miss Jezebel. I miss the ranch, and I miss feeling safe."

"Welcome to my world," Uncle said gruffly.

Hettie glared. "Do you even care how I feel?" She was moody and spoiling for a fight.

He paused. "Not particularly, no."

At her look of outrage, he raised his hands. "Now don't get hysterical about it. That corset's keeping your good homespun sense from reaching your brain." He met her eye. "*Feelings* don't change the situation. We're stuck here with each other, doing what we have to do. There's no use spilling tears or gnashing teeth about Abby or Diablo or Patrice or any of this."

"We wouldn't even be here if you and Pa had destroyed Diablo in the first place," she groused.

Uncle's lips twitched. "You've already thought this one through, girlie, otherwise you would've come at me sooner." He released a puff of cigar smoke and let it join the greasy black trails from the engine. "If we could've destroyed Diablo, we would've. But no magic or mundane means can unmake that weapon. Maybe I should've taken it south to Punta as soon as I had my hands on it. Maybe I should've buried it out in the middle of the desert. But that thing is like a bad penny." He gazed off into the distance. "You blame your ma and pa for keeping this from you, too?"

She sat back, surprised by the question. It was on the tip of her tongue to deny it, but so much of what had happened had stemmed directly from the secrets her parents had kept from her about Pa's outlaw past. "I'm working on forgiving them."

"That's sad, Hettie. They never did any wrong by you."

"They didn't trust me enough to tell me about Diablo. *You* didn't trust me. You *still* don't trust me." She knew he was keeping things from her. He always was. Maybe it was a sorcerer thing, or maybe it was just Uncle.

"Ain't *you* I don't trust." His gaze slid to her skirt. In her utter frustration at the lack of pockets, Hettie had ripped the seams open and sewn in two pockets on each side large enough to hold the gun. She could conjure it from anywhere, of course, but she preferred to keep Diablo on her. "All the cards I play close to my chest are wild ones. No telling what *it* thinks of that."

"You say it as if I don't have control." Everyone acted as if the Devil's Revolver was going to turn on her at any minute. Or were they worried about *her?* "You think I can't handle whatever comes at me?"

"I think that six-gun makes you think you can do whatever you want. We haven't had words about what's happened to you, how you've changed. You were always hard-headed, but now . . ." His lips flattened into a hard line. "Now I don't know what to make of you. It's like all the softness has been beaten out of you."

She gestured at the fine dress Sophie had made her wear, the corset cinching her guts like sausage casing, the gloves and polished boots and careful coif of her short hair. "This isn't soft enough?"

"Clothes are just clothes. Skins and shells are meant to be shed. You've become hard, Hettie, through and through."

"You stole my love for my parents," she bit out. "What did you *think* would happen?"

His look could cut a diamond. "I'm not apologizing for that, and I'll be damned if you make me regret my choices. What I did cost us both. Your problem is that you still think that weapon is some kinda pet, and you let it snap at anyone who even looks at you wrong." He harrumphed and sat back hard in his chair. "The problem with mean dogs is that they'll turn on their owners if they're hungry enough."

She stuck out her lip. Diablo was powerful, but it was still a gun, and it couldn't pull its own trigger. *She* did that. The revolver was nothing more than a precaution, like her old Winchester. It gave her the power to keep her family and friends safe. There was nothing wrong with wanting that . . . even if sometimes it meant killing people.

People who deserve it, she reminded herself sharply. She dug her fingers into her skirt.

The land dipped, and rocky hills rose around the train as it chugged toward a tunnel pass. With a roar, the tunnel swallowed the Pullman, and the darkness closed around them. The entry point became a shrinking dot of light. Hettie broke out in a sweat; she'd never liked dark, enclosed spaces to start with, but since her journey to hell, even closing her eyes at night brought her back to that terrifying nothingness made of sharp knives and fire.

Movement in the dark caught her eye. Maybe she'd just imagined it, but it looked as if there were people in the tunnel.

She stood and peered hard, but before she could get a bead on the figures, the train emerged from the tunnel, the sunlight blinding her briefly.

Her scalp prickled, and her heart raced. Something wasn't right. Diablo jumped into her palm.

Uncle stared at her. "What—"

The train jolted hard. Hettie lost her footing and stumbled backward. The wrought-iron railing caught her below the knees, and she tumbled from the moving train.

She hit the gravel berm and rolled over and over, the jagged rocks biting into her arms and legs. The train whistled long and shrill, and then came the screech of metal as the massive engine threw on the brakes. Hettie looked up through some scruffy weeds growing by the tracks just in time to see the cars buckle and jounce to a standstill. The engine let out a long, exasperated hiss.

Slowly she pushed up, taking shaky stock of her person. Nothing broken or sprained. Her dress was ruined, and she'd have new bruises to add to her collection, but she'd been lucky.

She brushed herself off and was about to return to the train when something whizzed past her ear. Diablo leaped into her hand automatically, and she dropped to the grass as gunshots erupted around her.

Whoops and hollers echoed against the cliff face and through the trees. The rumble of hooves shook the ground, and the riders came streaking out of the forest.

Bandits! They were going to rob the train!

Hettie needed to get back to the Pullman. She breathed and tried to drop into her time bubble. Nothing happened.

She glared at the revolver in her fist, tried again. Nothing.

This is not the time to be stubborn! She got no response, sensed nothing from the mage gun except silence. Her heart beat hard.

The riders poured from the low hills and forest, their horses foaming at the mouth and glistening with sweat. Five galloped up on the right side of the train, firing into the air and waving their weapons at the passengers staring wide-eyed through the windows. Six more men slid down the slope and boarded the train. Muffled screams came from within, followed by more gunshots.

No one had spotted Hettie yet. She raced for the observation deck of the Pullman car, sweating under her too-tight collar. Uncle must have gone inside at the first sign of attack. As soon as the bandits recognized the prize jewel hitched to the end of the train, they would take Sophie for all she had.

She reached for the railing. A force slammed her back ten feet, like a giant fist to the face, and she landed hard on the berm. Her arms felt like jelly, and her ears rang. Marcus must have raised a barrier spell.

"Thanks so much for thinking of me," she muttered. Of course the security man would prioritize his charge's safety over hers.

She couldn't do a whole lot out here to help the passengers, but charging in without her time bubble would be foolish. What, then? Hide and hope no one spotted her? Wait out the bandits and hope they didn't kill anyone?

Diablo's weight doubled. It wasn't speaking to her, but it smelled death in the air, knew its purpose needed to be fulfilled. Hettie bit her lip. Despite all the anti-Eye spells Uncle and Marcus had placed on her, she'd promised not to fire the mage gun in case the Pinkertons or the Division of Sorcery got a bead on her. She reconsidered this commitment now. Using the mage gun in the past had summoned the Pinks almost instantly via remote Zoom tunnel. If they came to arrest her now, they could dispatch this gang thoroughly.

That didn't leave her an escape, though. Better to take a page from Uncle's book and wait. The travelers were rich—they could afford to give up their baubles and wallets if it spared their lives. She had more to risk, including her sister's safety.

She crept to the next car and ducked under the chassis. There was a tiny shelf of space behind one of the big mechanisms, so she pulled herself into it to keep her feet from showing beneath the car, tucking her skirts between her knees. The undercarriage was hot and dirty and smelled of grease.

Gruff shouts went up and down the length of the train. She could hear muffled cries and heavy bootsteps above her. She hated that she was hiding here like a coward—she knew Diablo hated it, too, despite its silence.

When the bandits reached Sophie's car, the two men who approached flew back upon contact with the barrier spell. They cursed and groaned, then yelled, "Mizzay!"

Hettie peeked below the chassis as a huge midnight-black horse walked up alongside the train. Its hooves stamped deep prints in the mud as big as her face. Highly polished black boots with deadly looking spurs landed solidly on the ground next to them as the rider dismounted.

Diablo trembled. She felt the tremor deep down, something between alarm and agitation.

The air shimmered as the barrier repelled another attacker. A woman's raspy voice cursed, then snapped out the command, "Round up the passengers and bring them outside."

In a few short minutes, the train was emptied. The outlaws herded the frightened travelers to one side of the tracks, forcing everyone to place their hands on the side of the train.

"Occupants of the Pullman car." The woman's voice rang out on an amplification spell. Her thick Southern drawl seemed affected, though, and burnished by years of too much smoke and whiskey. "I am the outlaw Hettie Alabama. My men have the train surrounded."

Hettie's chest expanded and clutched tight in one breath. Anger wound through her, strangling her common sense. She wanted to unburden the weighty mage gun and erase the imposter with a burst of hellfire.

She banked her feelings and breathed. Getting herself killed now would serve no one.

No response came from Sophie's car. The outlaw hitched her thumbs into the waistband of her split riding skirt and said something to one of her men. He shouted at the others, and they started grabbing the women and children out of the lineup, corralling them in a tight circle.

Outlaw Hettie moseyed over to the group and bent to speak to one of the smallest children—a little boy of maybe six years whose big eyes wavered with tears. He nodded bravely as the woman took his hand and led him toward the car.

"The deal is simple," she called. "You lower your barrier spell and no one gets hurt. All we want is what you already have too much of. Jewels and money and whatever else you have to spare. My men wouldn't say no to a few bottles of fine whiskey either."

The gang members laughed. There was still no response from the car, though. The outlaw rubbed the back of her neck. "Let's be civil now. I just made a friend in little Gabriel here. He's turning seven next week, you know." She pulled her gun from her holster and kept it at her side. Gabriel stared up at the Pullman car, trembling.

The air shimmered, and the door opened. Slowly, Sophie emerged, hands in the air. "Don't harm the boy."

Outlaw Hettie smirked and tipped her hat up with the barrel of her gun. "How many in your party?"

Sophie hesitated. "There are four of us in the car."

"All right. Get your people down here." She gestured as if she were a schoolmarm directing her students. Sophie climbed down, followed by Jemma, Uncle, and Marcus. Two bandits immediately cuffed iron manacles around Uncle and Jeremiah and thrust them against the side of the train. Hettie noticed they left Sophie alone, though she was a master sorcerer.

Outlaw Hettie addressed the passengers. "Rest assured, good people, that once we have what we need, we'll let you go on your merry way." She waved the revolver around casually. Gabriel was still standing by the Pullman, and he turned to look at the outlaw leader. He spotted Hettie, and his eyes widened. She put a finger to her lips and ducked back beneath the undercarriage.

"There's no reason for any of you to be frightened," the gang leader went on amiably as if she were coddling a group of schoolchildren. "Your cooperation and your generous donations are all we need. You're doing a remarkable job of staying calm. Yes, yes. That's all I ask for—order and peace."

"You'll never get away with this, you whore."

Outlaw Hettie froze in her tracks. She turned. "Who said that?" Her voice dropped an octave. Feet shuffled restlessly—even the outlaws looked suddenly nervous.

One of the men standing against the train squirmed. Hettie spotted Horace standing next to him, his hands firmly planted, staring straight ahead as if studying the bolts on the panels intently.

"I said, *Who said that?*"

Outlaw Hettie gave a sharp nod, and the bandits spun the men around, keeping their hands raised high. She paced along the line, glaring into the sweating, fearful, downcast faces of the passengers as if she could divine their fates with a look. Perhaps she could— Hettie could sense power wafting off her.

"All I asked for was compliance. All I required was respect." Her voice rose with her anger. "If there's one thing I hate more than disrespect, it's a self-righteous would-be hero." She panned the men along the train with a gimlet stare. "So, which of you wants to be a hero?"

No response came. The man who'd spoken was trembling.

Outlaw Hettie shook her head and scoffed. "You could have all gotten away with nothing more than empty pockets. But now . . ." She laughed almost hysterically. " . . . now I have to teach you a lesson about respect."

She drew her gun, pointed it at the first man in the lineup, and shot him in the head.

The women and children screamed as Outlaw Hettie paced down the row. "One, two, three . . ." She shot the fourth man point-blank and continued down the row. "One, two, three . . ." She pulled the trigger again. More screams.

One man tried to duck out of line, but he was instantly shot by other gang members. The protests and pleas were brief and loud as Outlaw Hettie marched along, splattering brains against the side of the car in some perverted waltz. "One, two, three . . ." *BANG.* "One, two, three . . ." *BANG.*

Hettie did a quick count. Horace would be shot in two more turns and Marcus in four. She couldn't stay hidden any longer, time bubble or no.

She scanned the land, made a quick calculation, then sent her most fervent prayers to the quiet revolver.

Don't kill them. If I'm put in danger for even a second, that'll be it for both of us.

Hettie rolled out from beneath the chassis, took aim at the men guarding the women and children, and fired.

Green power exploded from Diablo's muzzle, two rapid-fire shots that melted the men's shooting hands and their weapons along with them. They fell to the ground howling, and as the rest of the gang turned to see what the outcry was about, Hettie went for Uncle and Marcus.

"Raise 'em high!" she shouted. They didn't need more instruction than that. Diablo took their manacles off in a burst of green fire, and the men flung the slag from their wrists, flicking the melted restraints away like hot molasses.

Uncle shouted an incantation and clapped his hands. A blinding white light flashed across Hettie's vision, dazzling everyone's eyes. Marcus drew Luna and Claire and opened up on the bandits.

Hettie wasn't sure what she was seeing at first—it seemed like clouds of golden fireflies were darting out of the muzzles. They scattered wide, like pellet shot. The unfortunate targets shrieked as they were perforated, writhing on the ground and clawing at their wounds. It seemed to take a long time before they were still. Marcus charged the bandits, ducking shots, his face set in a cool mask. Whatever the blood price was, it wasn't thwarting him.

Jemma dragged Sophie back to the Pullman. A bandit jumped into her path, raising his weapon. She batted his arm back, slammed an open hand into his throat, rammed her knee into his stomach, then spun and kicked him in the head, using the rest of her momentum to slingshot Sophie toward the safety of the private car.

Gunfire and chaos erupted all around them. The passengers scattered, fleeing into the woods or piling back into the train. Some of the men, Horace included, grappled with the outlaws and got their guns. Bodies piled up. Gun smoke and golden fireflies filled the air.

Hettie shot off the hands of two more men. Diablo's weight did not diminish. It still craved death.

She scanned the battleground for the woman in black. She met her stare head on.

Long dark hair framed wide dark blue eyes set on a pointed face. An angry red blaze of melted flesh slashed across her cheek and eye. She looked nothing like Hettie, but there was something strangely familiar about her.

Something flashed in her eyes—recognition. Outlaw Hettie's jaw firmed as she mounted her big black horse and shouted at the men to ride out. Those who were able scooped up what spoils they could, leaped onto their mounts, and dashed out of there in a scatter of gravel and dirt. The thunder of their departure rolled off into the landscape.

Diablo protested loudly, as if suddenly given voice once more. She was letting them get away! But Hettie kept its muzzle pointed firmly down. *No killing. We've done enough damage as it is, and now everyone knows we're here.*

Marcus lowered his weapons as the bandits dispersed.

"Miss Sophie?"

She emerged from the cover of the Pullman. "I'm fine, Marcus. Jemma and I are safe."

"Jeb?" They were speaking to Uncle.

"Dang bullet caught my jacket. Luckily it's the only casualty. How about Henrietta?"

It took Hettie a moment to figure out he was asking after her. They were still traveling incognito, after all. "I'm fine."

"You used Luna and Claire," Sophie said to Marcus on a gasp. "Are you...?"

"Now's not the time to worry about that, Miss Favreau," Marcus said, holstering the weapons. "I need to do my job."

Horace joined them. "We've got dead and wounded. We should get everyone back aboard before those outlaws regroup and come back."

While most of the remaining passengers were physically unharmed, many of them were shaken. Able-bodied men and boys cleared the barricade of logs and rocks that had been piled onto the track to stop the train. A doctor who'd been on board quickly patched up the wounded with what supplies he had. Sophie volunteered all her linens and petticoats to make bandages and slings. The dead were wrapped in shawls and blankets and placed in the luggage compartment for transport.

"What about the Pinkertons?" Hettie asked quietly, peering around nervously. "I fired Diablo. They could be here any minute."

"I doubt it." Uncle sniffed and unbent himself. "We've been here a while and they haven't come crashing down on us like I thought they might. Could be they simply can't afford another remote Zoom."

"So...we're free of the Pinkertons?"

"Don't get your hopes up," he said. "Like their motto says, they never sleep."

CHAPTER FOUR

hey took an extra day in New Orleans to recover and check on the comatose Patrice Favreau. The train robbery by the notorious Alabama gang made the newspapers, and reporters were clamoring to interview the heiress to the Favreau fortune about the harrowing experience and how her brave compatriots had fought off their attackers. It was attention they did not need, and Marcus had the Favreaus' security men increase patrols to discourage any journalists from approaching the mansion.

Despite the compound's amenities and security, Hettie felt no safer than she had when they'd been on the road and pursued by the authorities. Not being able to use her time bubble had made her vulnerable. She had no trouble using it now, but its lapse troubled her.

"Maybe someone was casting a dampening spell—something to nullify your powers," Uncle said when she told him about it. "But I didn't feel anything like that. If there was a counterspell, it would have had to be specific to your special ability. But who would even know what that is? Even I wouldn't know how to make a spell stick to your infernal time tinkering."

She could think of only two people who might be able to: Diablo's maker, Javier Punta, who was dead, and the Kukulos warlock Zavi, Diablo's heavenly wielder dragged to earth.

The fallen angel was most assuredly alive, Punta had said. Hettie had wondered when he might try to retake Diablo and possibly Abby as well. Could the crazed warlock have anything to do with the Alabama gang? He'd organized and taken control of the Crowe gang, after all.

The difference was that the Crowe gang had kidnapped children for Zavi to blood feed on; the so-called Alabama gang hadn't, despite the ample supply available on the train. No, the Alabama gang had seemed far more like run-of-the-mill bandits.

Perhaps Diablo had simply been confused by the second Hettie. As Marcus and Uncle had pointed out, it had a will of its own.

They spent two nights in the Favreaus' opulent New Orleans mansion. All that time, Sophie sat by her grandmother's side, telling her of their adventures. None of the doctors and specialists who'd seen Patrice had any helpful news. Sophie also received a confidential telegram from some close friends of Patrice's.

"It seems Hettie was right. Other members of the soothsaying community have fallen into comas. Among them are Mr. Eversight and the Lady Laguna."

"The second and third most powerful soothsayers in America." Uncle's narrowed eyes left deep lines all over his face.

"Zavi's attack was what put Patrice out. Did he attack these other two as well?"

"No one knows. They both went to sleep and didn't wake up again. They fell into their comas within a week of each other." Sophie wrung her hands. "Hettie, I know I've asked you before—"

"I'm sorry, Sophie. I don't remember anything else." Hettie had not spoken to Patrice Favreau in her dreams again since leaving Mexico. Sophie had asked for every last detail of those encounters repeatedly, but the memory of the conversations had faded.

"If we could just talk to her through your dream link—"

"No," Marcus and Uncle both interjected.

"There's no telling if this affliction is only affecting soothsayers or others in the magic community," Marcus said. "I can't allow you to risk yourself, or Miss Alabama, for that matter."

"If it was affecting other sorcerers, the Division would say something. Or we'd see it in the newspapers."

"The Division's just as black-hatted as the Pinkertons," Uncle said, "even more so since I left their ranks. I wouldn't trust any of 'em farther than I could throw 'em. As for the *media*"—he said it with derision, rolling his eyes—"never forget that someone owns them, too. I'd think you'd know this, considering your family's ties to the press."

"We don't use our money to influence what gets printed," Sophie objected.

Uncle's lips puckered. "So keeping the soothsayers' blackout a secret is what? For fun?"

Sophie clenched her jaw, her delicate complexion mottling. "I realize my hypocrisy in this matter, Mr. Bassett, but I would remind you that you are here on my sufferance and that once Hettie and you resolve the issue, there will be no more secrets to keep."

Jeremiah merely shrugged. Hettie wasn't sure how to feel. She saw Uncle's point of view: if soothsayers could no longer predict the future, then they were earning money by lying. But that wasn't different from what a snake oil peddler did, and people still lined up for their medicines. Some people swore by them. Blind faith was sometimes as powerful as the most potent of magics.

Hettie herself had always taken all forms of fortune-telling with a grain of salt: Pa had contributed to the farmers' bank for a look at the year's growing seasons, but that was to maintain good relations with his neighbors. He'd always hedged his bets and made provisions in case the soothsayer was wrong about what the year brought in harvest. No magic was guaranteed, he used to say. And nature had a funny way of changing its mind.

Hettie barely heard Jemma as she walked up next to her. "Time to train."

Hettie frowned. "What, now? Can't I just rest?"

"You rested on the train. Didn't do you any good when those bandits attacked, did it?"

There was no point in arguing. She followed the bodyguard through the mansion and into a large, empty salon that might once have been used as a dance hall. Thick bloodstained mats covered the ground. Nearby, a strange wooden dummy sat in one corner, and a well-beaten padded stand showed evidence of hard use. Jemma closed the door behind them and locked it. "Take off your dress."

"Excuse me?"

"I've locked the doors so we won't be disturbed. You need to start learning how to defend yourself when you are at your most vulnerable. The men don't need to know this. Take off your dress. Keep your stays, though. We're going to find places to hide your weapons."

Hettie hesitated. She understood the logic, and Jemma's stony look brooked no argument. But she was not used to undressing in front of anyone except perhaps Abby.

Jemma turned and shucked her own simple dress. She stood unabashedly in her corset, drawers, and ankle boots. It wasn't the ensemble that had Hettie staring, though.

"You want to know about the scars." Jemma indicated the raised score marks carved across the tops of her breasts and lower, curving up her shoulders and across her back. It looked as if she'd been stabbed repeatedly by a small blade. "I received them when I was assigned to guard Miss Sophie. They're anti-influence. Not even Mrs. Favreau herself can undo this charm."

Hettie wanted to tear her eyes away but found she couldn't. Butch Crowe had a similar anti-influence spell put on him—the starburst scar on his face had been evidence of that. "They look like they hurt."

"They still do sometimes. That's the price you pay for this kind of magic."

Hettie grimaced. "Why'd you let them do it, then?"

"'Let them'?" She snorted. "I *chose* this. It not just for Miss Sophie's protection. It's for mine, too. You've seen the dangers that are out there. You've met the worst kinds of men. Well, the people in Miss Sophie's circles..." She glanced around as if someone might be listening and lowered her voice. "Knives and guns aren't the only weapons a man or woman will use to hurt you. Magic's tricky that way. This"—she indicated the scars—"is armor against a few of those weapons."

Jemma ran her fingers along the seams of the corset. She pulled out a thin blade the length of her palm from one decorative piping and brandished it. "It is small, but it is strong." She sliced the air with it several times, then mimed plunging it into some unsuspecting soul's chest. "Stabbed in the right place, two inches can be just as effective as ten."

"Size doesn't matter, it's how you use it?" Hettie raised an eyebrow. Jemma didn't laugh. "I've got a knife in my boot already," Hettie pointed out.

"That is a good start, but it is too obvious when you need to reach for it."

"Do you make Sophie wear knives, too?"

Jemma thought a moment, as if weighing whether to share her answer. "She has many forms of power and protection. And a derringer for the rest."

The idea of the debutante with a tiny gun made Hettie smile.

Jemma beckoned her to a cupboard on one side of the salon. Inside, an array of blades mounted on the back gleamed with deadly mirth. It was not a collection of artful antique pieces, either—these were meant to be used, and clearly had been over the years.

"Are these all yours?"

"They were handed down through my family, generation after generation. My great-grandfather, grandfather, and father have all served the Favreaus. I am my parents' only surviving child, and so here I am, continuing the tradition."

"As a...bodyguard?"

Jemma's eyes flickered with amusement. "Bodyguard. Lady's maid. Confidante. Whatever word you can come up with, I'm that for Miss Sophie."

"So this is a family business."

"The Favreaus pay us well," Jemma said. "My brothers...before they died, they'd served the family, too."

"I'm sorry. I didn't realize it was so dangerous."

"Dangerous, yes." She began selecting small blades and laying them on a piece of velvet as if she were a jeweler displaying her merchandise. "But they didn't die in the line of duty. It was tuberculosis." She glanced up. "Never make assumptions, Hettie Alabama. A wrong judgment can get a person killed pretty quick."

"Why do I need all this?" she asked warily, looking down at the array of blades. "We're going to the city."

"You may not find bandits and wild cougars in Chicago, but the dangers there are just as real. You're serving Miss Sophie now, whether you like it or not. I'd prefer you were overprepared."

Hettie picked up one cruel-looking serrated knife and shivered. "Not exactly the tool of choice for doing Sophie's mending."

"Your sharp tongue may mask your fear well, but it won't save you from death. Take off your dress," Jemma said again. "We will find you some teeth for your bite."

The salon of the On Fook tong had changed, Ling thought. Not so much in decor or layout, but it wasn't as immaculate and fresh as he'd remembered. It had been nearly fifteen years, after all. The dark wood floors and carved lacquered pillars seemed to have absorbed time and wear, soaking it in like the roots of a thirsty tree.

A fresh gouge in one pillar, made with either a hatchet or a machete, caught Ling's attention. He bent to inspect a splatter of dried blood, maybe a day or two old, dotting the floor in the shape of a question mark.

Ling grimaced. Violence was not tolerated within the hall. The media had sensationalized the so-called tong wars, feuds that'd been brewing among the tongs, focusing on the more lurid tales involving prostitutes and opium dens. But On Fook was a much smaller tong and strictly aboveboard. Brother Wu had always ensured that On Fook stood for respect, honor, and family.

A man carrying a tray laden with tea spotted him standing in the salon, and his expression shuttered as he took Ling in head to toe. "What do you want?" He spoke to Ling in English. It was an outward insult, meant to make him feel unwelcome and suspected, but Ling was used to it. He'd adopted a Western-style haircut and clothes, as some Chinese who stayed in the city had. It usually helped him blend in better, but here, somehow, he was still recognized as an outsider.

"I'm looking to speak with Brother Wu," Ling said in Cantonese.

Furrows appeared in the man's brow, and he replied in the same dialect. "Who are you to ask such a thing?"

"Tell him...Little Dragon is here to see him."

The man's lips compressed, and he told Ling to wait as he hurried away. Moments later, a different man came out of a side door and beckoned Ling to follow.

Brother Wu rarely had people visit him in his office. He'd always preferred to do business in the salon, out in the open. Secrets were for people who had too much to lose, he once said. On Fook hosted some occasional card games and gambling, but it was only for tong members, and debts never got out of hand. Brother Wu was far more interested in profit and peace than any slights to his reputation. A show of humility and transparency was better than an iron safe, he had said.

Apparently times had changed.

The office was unrecognizable. It'd once been piled high with papers and documents and a profusion of plants. Brother Wu had loved his gardens and missed cultivating life. All those potted flowers and succulents had been removed, and Wu's big desk was pushed to one corner and covered in discarded teacups. Now, men played cards and dice in here. There was even a game of mahjong off in one corner, the players banging the bamboo tiles loudly. Two burly hatchet men paced the perimeter. Whether they were protecting the players or keeping them from leaving, he wasn't sure.

Ling scanned the room but didn't see Brother Wu. Most of the men gave him only cursory glances—they were too busy losing to note the stranger among them.

A man stood slowly, grinning. Younger-looking than Wu, he smoked a cigarette and wore a leather vest over his mandarin collared tunic.

"Welcome home, Little Dragon." He flipped his cards facedown on the table, and the other players followed suit, sitting back in their chairs with dejected looks. "It is a real honor to meet you. A true and real honor."

Ling studied him. He had a smooth, fair complexion and thick, dark, expressive eyebrows. There was a large mole on his neck, which he tried to cover with his high collar—but there it lurked, peeking above the material like a diseased third eye.

Ling gave him a cursory nod. "Forgive me, I've been away for a long time. I don't think I recognize you."

"I was an old family friend of the Wus back in China. I did not come here until after your departure." There was a slight tightening around his lips that made them pull away from his teeth a little more. "I am Brother Shang."

"Shang." Ling acknowledged him with a slight bow. "Where is Brother Wu?"

The whole room shifted uneasily. Shang put his cigarette out, his smile fading. "Brother Wu died eight months ago."

Ling became acutely aware of the hatchet men drawing closer. One of them was blocking the door. Shang leisurely left the table and waved Ling over to a settee. "I can see you're in shock. Please, sit. Have some tea."

"How did he die?" Ling asked. More important, how had Shang taken his place? Wu had a son a few years younger than Ling whom he'd brought over to start an exporting business. He would have been the natural choice to take over On Fook.

"The sickness," Shang intoned. "It took him quickly."

"What sickness?"

"Surely you're joking? You would not have come back if you'd known..." Shang looked around. "The sickness. They say it has been among the Celestial sorcerers only. Did you not see signs around the streets?"

"The ones that say all gifted Celestials must report to the police station for inoculation?"

Shang lowered his voice. "The police came here, rounded up all the gifted. Brother Wu went along with his son. A week later, they were all dead." He poured the tea with a long flourish, raising the pot high up yet somehow managing to keep the golden liquid from splashing out of the tiny clay teacup. "From what I understand, you have some gifts yourself. I'm surprised the gwai lo haven't dragged you in yet."

That was because Ling had been cautious about using his magic in public, and had even employed one of Jeremiah Bassett's special hide talismans to keep suspicion off him.

"Tell me, what is the infamous Little Dragon doing back in San Francisco? From the stories Brother Wu told us, you were arrested and dragged away by the Division of Sorcery and presumed dead or imprisoned."

50

"It's a long and tedious tale that I don't wish to bore you with." He stood, feeling the net closing around him. "I am sorry about Brother Wu and his son. I will pay my respects at the temple." He turned to go.

The toughs converged, and Ling stepped back.

"I think I'd rather like to hear the tale, Tsang Li Ling." Shang lit another cigarette. "I'm especially interested in hearing about what happened to the dope you were supposed to be delivering the day you supposedly went missing."

His throat constricted, but he kept his expression carefully neutral. Shang was studying him for any sign of weakness or surprise; Ling could tell he was looking for some hold over him. "It is exactly as you say. The Division caught me on my way here. They dragged me into holding, and I had no choice but to stay in their custody." He added thickly, "I was not released until recently."

"You hardly look like a man who's been in prison for fifteen years." Shang's mole danced behind the collar as his Adam's apple bobbed. "Even your nursemaids' magic could not keep you so healthy. So I have to wonder what kind of deal you made to keep you alive and so well fed."

Ling regarded the man steadily, examining every inch of his frame for clues. Shang's suit was new but fit poorly. The leather vest was old and battered, like something a cowpoke wore—a trophy, perhaps? Ling glimpsed a fresh bandage around his left arm, tucked beneath the sleeve. Perhaps he'd been involved in the altercation that had resulted in that bloodstain in the main receiving area. "You have me at a disadvantage, Brother Shang. You seem to know more about me than I know about you."

"Brother Wu talked about you frequently." Something like jealousy licked at his words. "He used to consider you his most trusted man." Shang lifted his chin. "Used to."

Ling glared. He did not care for Shang's tone. "If you are accusing me of treachery, come out and say so." Unease rippled through the men. "I didn't know the package I was delivering was full of opium." He hadn't believed it even when the Division had dropped the evidence in front of him. Ling had firmly believed all these years that the government agency had set him up. "Brother Wu was never interested in the drug trade before."

"Times change, Little Dragon. It could be Brother Wu did not want to burden you with his new enterprise." Shang's smile barely reached his eyes. "There is the matter of your debt to On Fook, however. You seem to be in a well-off enough position to pay it..."

Ling clamped down on his anger, keenly aware of the hatchet men. "I'm not. I came here looking for a loan. I'd hoped Brother Wu would recognize everything I've done for him, his family, and On Fook and forgive my long absence."

"I am not Brother Wu," Shang said after a long consideration. "But I have always respected him and the trust he put in those around him. Regardless of whether you knew about the opium, you lost an important source of income for the tong. So I will give you an opportunity to pay off your debt." He tilted his head to one side. "The amount you owe plus fifty percent, to be paid within six months' time. I think you'll agree that is generous."

It took him a moment to realize Shang was expecting him to thank him, to act grateful and applaud his charity. Heat crawled into his cheeks and down his neck, but he ignored it. The hatchet men were itching to do some harm.

He couldn't run. He couldn't fight. So he did the only thing he could do.

Stiffly, he bowed at the waist. "Very generous. Thank you."

Ling cursed himself as he left the gambling den. It'd been a mistake coming back to the tong. Learning first about Brother Wu's betrayal and then adding to his financial problems...he hadn't expected to leave the tong worse off.

In the main hall, he breathed deep. All he'd managed to do today was bring more troubles on him and Abby. What could he do, though? Leave San Francisco? He couldn't afford horses or provisions. Besides, the Division would be looking for them wherever they went. At least here they could hide in relative safety.

"Brother Tsang?"

He startled when a young servant girl approached. She had to be in her teens—maybe sixteen, possibly older. A huge bruise covered half her face. His throat constricted as he remembered another girl around her age from long ago, from a different lifetime...

She beckoned, darting a look around, putting a finger to her lips.

Hesitantly, Ling followed the girl out of the hall and around the corner. She looked back a few times to make sure he was still close, then dashed through a narrow alley. Ling probably should have known better than to follow some strange girl through the streets, but if anyone wanted him dead, they'd already had plenty of chances to kill him.

He found the girl hovering in the doorway of an herbalist's shop. Several anti-Eye talismans disguised as wind chimes hung around the door, so faintly enchanted that only a master-class sorcerer could detect them. They turned would-be customers away from the doors with the subtlest of influence, the way a bad smell might ward someone off.

"Who are you, little sister?" Ling asked.

"My name's Li Fa. I work at On Fook," she said simply. "She asked me to bring you here."

"Who?"

"Auntie Wu."

Brother Wu's older sister, affectionately known as Auntie or Ah-Gu, was a rich widow who lived in Guangdong province in China and had bankrolled many of her younger brother's special projects. Ling had known of her in his old life, before he'd been shipped off to America. She'd even sent him a generous red pocket for New Year's once, back when he was still close with her brother. Brother Wu only ever spoke of his sister with reverence and respect.

"Are you saying she's *here*?"

The girl nodded toward the herbalist's shop. "In the back. She says the barrier will let you in."

Ah-Gu was a high-caliber sorcerer, and like many in her rank she dabbled in blood magic. Selective spellcraft was difficult without it.

He studied the servant. "Let me see your face, Little Sister. Who did this to you?"

The girl met his gaze head-on, her expression flat. "It's a birthmark."

Oh. Ling should have been able to sense that with his healing gift, but apparently he'd misjudged. Maybe it was her other conditions that'd thrown him off—hunger and fatigue, mostly, and an affliction in the lungs, probably from damp sleeping environs.

He started fishing uselessly in his pockets for some small token of thanks, but the girl shook her head. "No need for tips. Auntie already provides for me." She hurried away.

Ling pushed into the herbalist's shop, the barrier buzzing over his skin as if he'd walked through a curtain of sparks. The place was poorly lit, the only light in the front area coming from the dingy, cluttered front window. The smells that assailed him, sharp and tangy, musty and briny, brought back memories of a different time in his life.

He'd never encountered such a well-stocked herbalist outside of his homeland. It didn't make a lot of sense to keep customers away—only trained sorcerers would notice the wards. So either the proprietor was picky about their clients or they didn't actually care about business—or they were presenting a very careful front.

He stared longingly at the big jars of teas and dried goods lining the dark shelves. He'd learned to make many healing tisanes and soups from the old masters, but finding the ingredients here was difficult.

"See something you like, Little Dragon?"

Ling turned sharply. From the back doorway, a tall woman with pale, paper-thin skin stretched over a lithe frame watched him with bright, birdlike eyes. Her hair was pulled back in a severe bun, and she wore a plain, shapeless gray cotton dress with only a little embroidery around the cuffs and hems. She'd arrived silently.

Ling had only seen one picture of Ah-Gu, and that had been when she was a blushing bride on her wedding day. The woman before him was very much that same girl fifty or more years on, only there was a remoteness about her—her smile a touch forced, her shoulders slightly hunched as if she were shying from a hard rainstorm.

"Auntie Wu." He bowed deeply to show his respect. "My condolences. I am sorry to hear about your brother and nephew."

She didn't acknowledge him as she slid behind the counter. She had not had her feet bound as some women did, and there was a careful boldness to her step, as if she could crush an ant without bending the grass. "I think we need some tea. I have just the thing." She took a jar from a high shelf and spooned some leaves into a tiny clay teapot. She brewed the tea with an expert hand, just as a woman in a tea shop would, though he had a hard time imagining this woman had ever had to work for a living. Both her father and her husband had been very wealthy.

He joined her at a small table as she poured. "I don't have any buns to offer you. I'm afraid baking is beyond my realm of expertise."

"This is fine." He sipped the tea. The golden flavor burst in his mouth, and he closed his eyes as memories flooded him. He hummed in appreciation.

"I thought you might like it." She sipped her own cup. "It comes from some fields I own. But I'm not here to talk about tea." She put the pot aside.

"How did you know I was in San Francisco?" he asked, puzzled and a little wary. He'd only just arrived at the tong today, and Li Fa couldn't have seen him and informed Ah-Gu of his attendance in the short time he'd been interviewed by Shang.

"I make it my business to know," she answered simply. "You've met Brother Shang. What did he want?"

Hmm. Her interest wasn't in him, but in Shang. "I went to the tong for a loan. Shang insists I pay him back for the opium I lost when I was caught by the Division fifteen years ago." He gave her a critical look. There was little Brother Wu could have done without his sister knowing.

"I had nothing to do with that dope," Ah-Gu said, the lines around her lips tightening. "Ah-Fung told me nothing about importing opium. I want to believe he was doing it for a friend. But we didn't agree on everything he did at On Fook."

Ling decided it was best not to question her sincerity. What was done was done, and he would not take his resentment out on her.

"So you're looking for a loan. And a monk, from what I hear." She arched an eyebrow as Ling held his composure. "And not just any monk, but a man I knew who was a sifu at the Golden Light temple."

Ling said nothing, though every nerve in him warned him to flee in case the woman knew about Abby. She pushed up from the table slowly, stretching her back. "I'm not sure what you've gotten yourself into, but I can see the magical haze around you. You stink of someone else's power. You're with someone who needs help. And you've been buying pig's blood, which means they're either a vampire, a Kukulos warlock, or something else."

"You've been spying on me." He shifted his stance slightly, ready to run, ready to fight, ready to defend himself. All three, probably.

"Money buys a lot of eyes. Magic does the rest." She retrieved several glass jars from the shelves and measured out portions into a bowl set on a scale. "You need better anti-Eye charms, Little Dragon. Those charms you're carrying around are so shriveled and used up, there's barely any juice left in them. Have lots of people looking for you, don't you?"

This was almost worse than being trapped at the tong. He didn't underestimate Ah-Gu's abilities. Her Qi was almost palpable, though she hid it well. Brother Wu had told him stories about his sister's fearsome temper, too. "What do you want from me?" he asked plainly.

"From you? Respect. I think I already have it, though. You haven't tried to rob me or threaten me. You haven't asked me for money. You haven't called me 'old woman' or rejected my tea. True, you're suspicious, but I think you've earned the right to be." She glanced up. "But more than that, what I want is to find my brother and my nephew."

Ling's lips pursed. "There's little I can do for the dead."

"No one's sure of that." She met his eye. "Their bodies were never delivered to us, and no one has actually *seen* their corpses except for Shang. But I don't believe that son of a dog for one second. He's been undermining everything Ah-Fung and I have worked to build." Her jaw worked. "They're not dead. They're *missing*."

Ling turned this over. It could be that Ah-Gu was in denial, grieving the loss by pretending it hadn't happened. But having met Shang, he had to admit that the new tong leader had every reason to want the Wus out of the picture.

"If that's true," he said slowly, "where would they be?"

"With the Division. They were last seen entering an unmarked metal cart driven by men in police uniforms, but I think it was an act. Other gifted have gone missing as well, though most here insist they are dead or have been deported."

"What about this sickness Shang mentioned?"

She scoffed. "People always blame plagues and illnesses on foreigners. If there were some kind of sickness affecting sorcerers, they wouldn't be offering inoculations only to us Chinese." She shook her head. "The Division is up to something."

The understatement of the century. He'd worked for them long enough to know it kept secrets, even from its own agents.

Carefully, he said, "I've been away for a long time. I don't see how I can help."

She sent him a flat look. "A former Division Paladin-class healer doesn't see how he can be helpful?" She snorted at his surprise. "Yes, I know everything about your past, Tsang Li Ling. I even know about the girl you killed."

Ling glanced away, the pain in the center of his chest like a beetle boring deeper into his heart. Ah-Gu clucked her tongue as she bundled the herbs together in a paper packet. "Don't worry, Little Dragon. I have no intention of telling your secrets to anyone. What I would like to know is how a respectable, talented second son ended up killing an accountant's daughter whom he hardly knew?"

She raised her dark eyes, the faintest ring of blue around the irises. The pressure in Ling's mouth grew. He clamped down as the truthtelling spell started unravelling his reserve. But then the silence spell activated. His throat squeezed, choking off his air supply. He sputtered once as his vision blurred.

Ah-Gu released her geis abruptly, and he gasped for air.

"You've placed a silence spell on yourself?" She arched a painted eyebrow at him. "Is the secret so dire you'd rather die than reveal it?"

"I have my reasons." Ling gulped his tea down and coughed. "And I like my privacy."

Ah-Gu laughed. "Very well, then, keep this secret to yourself if it comforts you." She poured him another cup of tea. "Tell me about the pretty little gwai mui living with you. You haven't taken a child bride, have you?"

"She's a family friend." Maybe it was the lingering effects of Ah-Gu's truthtelling spell that had loosened his tongue. Otherwise he might have kept quiet about Abby. But there was something in her face that invited confession, too. "Her parents were killed by bandits. Her sister asked me to care for her while she attends to business."

"And the pig's blood you've been bringing her? If she were a true vampire, you'd have more fear in your eyes." She glanced down at his bandaged finger.

"She needs blood for mental sustenance. A side effect of her…abilities."

"I see." She nodded. "That is why you've been asking about the monk. You're looking for a teacher."

Ling wondered how she could know all that. Indigo children were not common. "I don't even know his name, only that he came here before I did. How do you know this monk?"

"I was a disciple at the Golden Light temple," she said, then glanced up at his silence. "Don't look so surprised. My father was a progressive man. With my gift and intellect, he made sure I received a proper magical education from the old masters. The monk you seek, Sifu Ying, was one of my mentors."

Ling sat up. He couldn't believe his good fortune. "Where is he? Can I meet him?"

She refilled both their cups, her expression wooden as she lowered her eyes. Ling got a sinking feeling. "You will not find Sifu Ying, except in the afterlife. He was killed by a dynamite blast over four years ago."

His chest caved. The monk was the only person he knew who might have been able to help him. Now where was he supposed to go? He couldn't afford to take Abby across the sea to the Golden Light temple itself. He couldn't even set foot in his home country.

"Your friend's abilities are growing, am I right?" Ah-Gu asked. "Her sister sent her away because she had no idea how to handle them."

"It's more complicated than that," he replied, despondent.

"Perhaps. What if I told you I know someone who can help you? Someone who can guide your friend on her journey?"

He blinked. "Who?"

"Me, you simpleton." She handed over the packet of herbs she'd prepared. "This is a brew to help with the blood cravings. It's much stronger than the sawdust you've been buying."

He stared at the packet, shook his head. "I don't understand. What do you know about indigo powers? How can you train Abby?"

Ah-Gu swiftly put the jars away. "One of my responsibilities at the temple was to care for my classmate, a young boy with these 'indigo powers,' as you call them. I sat with him in lessons, made sure he ate and bathed. I even shared his punishments when he misbehaved. I know exactly what it takes. I learned how to handle children like him from the old masters."

Ling pursed his lips. Few indigo children survived birth, much less made it to school age. All the reports he'd read pointed toward children with wild, uncontrollable power. In the past, many of them were killed as infants because their parents believed them possessed by the devil.

For the longest time, Ling hadn't even believed Abby could be one of these children—the Division had sent him to Newhaven, Montana, only to monitor her. Apart from her strangeness and penchant to wander, she'd displayed no indications she was gifted. Her powers hadn't manifested until after she'd been kidnapped, or so he'd thought. "What happened to this boy?" he asked.

Ah-Gu paused, tilted her chin. "He died. His abilities . . . swallowed him. The masters did what they could to get his powers under control but . . ." She glanced away, eyes distant and full of grief. "He was only eight years old."

"And you think you can do better with my ward?"

Her gaze skewered him, as cold, sharp, and direct as the point of a needle. "I may have failed that boy, but I have more experience than you will ever have at the feet of the Division or whatever master you serve now."

"I serve no one," he snapped.

"You do, however, owe On Fook—or at least Shang—a debt. So I have a proposal for you. Find my brother and nephew, and I will pay your debt and teach your little gwai mui."

He hesitated. Someone with Ah-Gu's reach and influence could surely have taken Abby from him a long time ago if she truly had any desire to control her, so he didn't suspect her of false motives. And she was a powerful enough sorcerer. But was she a good teacher?

Better than none, perhaps. But still he balked. "What is it you *really* want?"

She raised her chin. "Ever the Division agent, looking for ulterior motives. I admit I am no fan of Shang's. I have suspicions about his role in my brother's abduction. He is involving On Fook in more and more distasteful business, bringing girls here to fill brothels." She wrinkled her nose. "I can't abide by that."

"You want him out."

"Should you find evidence that he was the one who betrayed my brother, I will want him more than *out*." The glint in her eye told him she'd probably see to it personally.

"And for how long will you train my ward?"

She tilted her head, her lips pressed in a straight, severe line. "That remains to be seen. Perhaps the more prudent question to ask is, how long will she survive my training?"

CHAPTER FIVE

Chicago was by far the biggest city Hettie had ever visited. She'd never been anywhere so crowded, so hard with angles and straight lines, so busy and chaotic.

The air hummed with the rushing river of humanity. As the hired carriage rolled down the paved streets, she stared at the buildings rising all around them. It was hard to imagine the city engulfed in flame, and even harder to believe how quickly everything had been rebuilt after the Great Fire. Everything here seemed shining and new.

"Stop gawking," Jeremiah muttered. "You look like a tourist."

"I look like a poor country girl who's never been to the city," she corrected. "Which I am, in case you've forgotten. Jeb and Henrietta Wiltshire have never been much outside of Kansas."

Jeremiah groaned. "What other delightful lies are you weaving?"

"Well, we're poor relations of Sophie's, aren't we? Marcus wasn't exactly thorough about our profiles, so I had to embellish. People'll ask how we became poor. I'll tell them my parents died in a fire. You came to take care of me, gambled our life savings away, and now we're stuck together, but I'm the forgiving sort and want to take care of you till your end days."

Uncle rolled his eyes. "And you criticize *me* for lying?"

Horace, who'd been sitting quietly with them in the carriage, squinted at the streets. "It's busier than I remember."

"Been here before?" Hettie asked.

"Once, just long enough to deliver some ponies to a local hostler. Ate a good steak over there." He pointed at a restaurant on the corner.

"When was that?"

He scratched his chin. "Must've been a year or two before I became a horse. I traveled a lot in those days."

Hettie didn't say anything. Horace was in his late thirties, if she were to guess, and had been a horse for the past eight years. Chicago would still have been in the midst of rebuilding much of its downtown core in the years he would have visited. She didn't want to interrogate him on the specifics, but remembering Jemma's reaction to his traveling with them, she wondered if maybe the man was stretching the truth a bit. Either that or his memory was wrong.

The carriage pulled up outside a grand hotel where several employees rushed to help unload their luggage. As Sophie alighted, the hotel manager approached, flanked by a young, fresh-faced man—the concierge, apparently.

"Miss Favreau, it's an honor and a delight to welcome you to the Cumbria Hotel. I'm Mr. Gambon. I received your letters and have everything prepared to your exact specifications."

Sophie met his gaze only briefly as she scanned the area. "Thank you, Mr. Gambon. If you'll allow us to retire, I'd appreciate it if we weren't disturbed."

"Of course, right this way!" The hotel manager hurried ahead. "The silencing charms were a bit difficult. All the new buildings are mundane constructions—"

"Do they *work*?" Marcus interrupted the nervous man.

Mr. Gambon nodded vigorously. "Yes, absolutely. I guarantee it."

"Then that's all we need to know." The security man ushered them along, walking ahead of the group as if he knew exactly where they were going.

"Silencing spells?" Hettie whispered to Jemma as they trudged up the stairs.

"There are all kinds that've tried to blackmail the family by listening in on gossip and rumors. The spells keep the trickier ones out."

Hettie nodded. "I'm surprised Sophie doesn't have a house here."

"The family's Chicago house had a small fire, and they're still renovating," Jemma explained as they piled into the room. She sniffed as she studied their surroundings. "It was a grand old place, and properly staffed, too. This hotel's not for Miss Sophie." She frowned around the room. "We'll have to make do."

Hettie studied the suite. Four bedrooms were attached to a large salon and common area, but there was no kitchen. All food and even tea would have to be ordered via room service. The suite was lavishly appointed, with rich, warm woods and fine wallpaper, gilded objets d'art and original paintings. Sophie never settled for second-best. Hettie supposed she never had to.

The sleeping arrangements meant that Hettie got a room to herself. Uncle would bunk with Horace, Sophie with Jemma, and Marcus had his own room as well. The security man walked the perimeter of the entire suite, swinging a talisman and drawing a chalk line along the baseboards.

"Anti-Eye and –Ear," Uncle explained, nodding in approval. "You can never have enough of that."

Hettie hadn't thought the Favreaus' head of security used much magic, but maybe, like Uncle, he juggled multiple protection spells at once. It wasn't uncommon for low-level sorcerers to hire themselves out as private security. But she'd always thought of Marcus as a man who spoke with his mage guns and unflinching hard stare. The presence of those shining twin pistols would certainly make anyone with malice in mind think twice.

"Why can't *I* learn to do these spells?" she asked. She'd been thinking about it since they'd left Mexico.

Jeremiah cocked an eyebrow at her. "You're not gifted."

"I know that, but neither was Julia, and Javier Punta taught her." Julia, Walker's "cousin," had only minor gifts—dormant abilities that wouldn't have otherwise manifested had it not been for the magical node at Villa del Punta. That localized wellspring of magic had enhanced her gift so she'd been able to summon and control the chupacabra that had terrorized the countryside. Hettie went on, "She learned spellcraft. If I ever had to, couldn't I borrow magic and do the same?"

Uncle glowered at her. "What kind of foolheaded schemes are you concocting now? You shouldn't even be thinking about borrowing magic. You saw what it did to Walker."

"I'm just saying that it seems like something lots of people could learn to do if they found someone to borrow power from. Considering all the things that have happened to me and Abby, shouldn't I be doing everything I can to protect us?"

"Magic's about more than just learning incantations and making and using talismans. It takes years of practice and learning. The juicers are just pretenders. Their spells are one-offs. No holding power at all."

"Walker seemed to be fine."

"Punta probably trained him some. But most of his power was used for short-burst spells—his fire spell and the like." He huffed. "Anyhow, you don't need to learn spellcraft, and you certainly don't need to borrow magic. You've already got that infernal revolver attached to you. You don't need to make your life any more complicated."

Hettie blew out a breath. She thought Uncle might have appreciated that she was taking an interest, but he'd shut her down the same way he always did. Sometimes she believed he was happier keeping her ignorant and powerless. As if all she'd ever be was Diablo's keeper.

It was a daunting and depressing thought. All her life, she'd been content to settle down on the ranch, run things the way Pa had, maybe do more with the horses she broke. Now…she had no idea what the future would look like. Where would she end up? In a big city like this one? In some remote cabin in the middle of nowhere?

"Those heavy thoughts are weighing your lips down," Horace said. He nodded at the jagged skyline through the pane glass. "I take it the view doesn't impress you?"

"I'm just worrying about what'll happen to me and Abby after all this is over." If it ever ended.

"The way I see it, there's no use worrying about what you can't see. There'll always be one more goal to reach, one more hurdle to get over. Life doesn't end when you get what you want."

"I think the problem is that I don't know what I want."

Horace smiled. "That can be a blessing, too. Sometimes having no expectations means you'll never be disappointed in the end."

Υ

The following day, the Favreau entourage—minus Horace, who was paying a visit to his lawyer—journeyed to the University of Chicago, where the Mechaniks' Society was holding its symposium. They weren't sure what to expect. This long, fraught journey could result in nothing. They were there seeking a fresh perspective, but without any solid idea of what the exact problem with Patrice was, they couldn't know what they were looking for.

The university was like nothing Hettie had ever seen. The campus spread for what felt like miles, the carefully manicured grass just begging to have a horse gallop over it. The buildings reminded Hettie of castles from a storybook, gleaming in the morning sun. A somber air hung about the grounds, and though she knew this was supposed to be a place of serious academic pursuit, she wanted to laugh and wave at the young men staring wide-eyed at the beauteous Sophie Favreau, riding by in her carriage with her motley crew in tow.

Of course, faced with Sophie's radiant glamor magic, it would be hard to notice anyone else in the debutante's company. Hettie had worn the amulet Sophie had given her for this occasion—there was no telling where they'd end up.

"Imagine attending a university like this," Hettie murmured, staring around the grounds. "I'd get lost for sure."

"*You* wouldn't do anything. They'd never let a hayseed farmgirl like you in," Uncle said dryly. "You wouldn't be able to afford it, for one."

"You never know," Sophie said from ahead of them. "The world is changing, Mr. Wiltshire"—she used Uncle's incognito name in public—"far faster than you think it is."

"It's changing plenty fast enough for me," he grumbled, rubbing his red-rimmed eyes.

They followed the signs toward a grand hall crowded with people there to gawk at the latest Mechanikal inventions or listen to lectures about the newest theories and discoveries in magic. The Chicago World's Fair had brought great things to the city only a few years before, leaving the populace with a hunger for more, but from what Hettie understood, the focus there had been mainly on mundane science and technology. Many in the scientific community didn't regard Mechaniks as a serious field of study, despite its contributions, so they'd been mostly banned from the World's Fair.

As they entered, someone handed Sophie a schedule of lectures and presentations. She scanned the list and gasped. "Dr. Fielding's here."

"Who?"

"Alastair Fielding. He's a Mechanik who specializes in magic transference. The head of the asylum in Yuma, Dr. Dunkirk, mentioned him to me at our last meeting." Sophie gripped the pamphlet excitedly. "Fielding wrote a paper about the effects of magical transference on comatose patients. I contacted him asking for advice. I even sent telegrams and made a phone call, but he never responded to any of my requests, not even when I suggested that the Favreau family was interested in funding his research. We have to see him."

"His presentation isn't until eleven," Marcus noted. "I suggest we split up and browse the floor beforehand and meet back here at quarter to."

They parted, Jemma and Marcus trailing a determined Sophie, while Hettie followed Uncle along the aisles.

Many displays featured charts and diagrams and pictures of things Hettie couldn't begin to understand. Some of the notations were familiar—a combination of numbers and runework, similar to what Ral Punta, Javier's son and Walker's stepbrother, had her recording when they'd been studying the flow of magic in Mexico.

A few of the projects had small gadgets and contraptions that lit up or whirred or did some clockwork-type motions—these were the most popular displays, and crowds gathered to watch tinker toys walk across a platform or perform some silly repetitive task.

There was a fighting automaton in one booth. Hettie had heard a lot about these machines, but she wasn't impressed. "Hercules," a vaguely humanoid machine with a barrel-shaped torso and four articulated limbs, sat inert on a chair, its arms dangling limply as if it'd been knocked out. The once-shiny breastplate sported fist-sized dents from previous matches. The automaton's owner explained poor Herc had stopped working suddenly, and that he theorized the magic drain had something to do with it—one of the few Mechaniks who'd admitted it was even a possibility.

"Why do you suppose that?" Uncle interrogated.

"There's no other way to explain it. I've taken Herc apart and put him back together. There's no damage, nothing to indicate it's broken. It's the power source. It has to be."

"It runs on magic?" Hettie asked. The man startled, as if shocked he was being addressed by a woman. Or perhaps he hadn't seen her, if Sophie's glamor magic was keeping her out of anyone's notice.

"No...no, not magic, though I did build it on Eberhard's principles of Mechaniks."

Hettie had read up on a few magical theories regularly bandied about. The most popular was by Max Eberhard, which stated that magic was a finite source, like oil or coal, that sprang from the earth and could be mined by the gifted and used to power spells that contradicted the laws of nature. The Mundane Movement often cited Eberhard's theory as a reason to stop all sorcery; nature's laws were not to be tampered with, they claimed, and there would be a price to pay if all the magic in the world were suddenly used up.

Eberhard's theory also claimed that magic had to be a real, physical particle or energy, like light, whose power could be captured and stored. All of it made relative sense to Hettie, but she didn't have enough experience with magic or science to know whether it was a sound theory.

"I don't understand," Uncle said. "If this contraption doesn't run on magic, then what is magic being used for?"

"Oh...the movements, of course." The man beckoned them closer and lifted part of the breastplate. The "flesh" beneath the metal skin was made up of thick, braided materials—heavy hemp twine, horse hair, and vines. Woven within were stones and bones, teeth and skins—things used regularly in talismans. "The metal body is the shell and skeleton," the man explained. "It's the flesh, if you will, that is magicked."

"So you made a golem." Uncle did not sound impressed.

The Mechanik's cheeks reddened. "Well, no, not exactly. That is, we did imbue the automaton with an animal spirit, for the life, of course—"

"Feh!" Uncle waved his hand dismissively. "Didn't you learn anything at the Academy?" He didn't let him answer as he barged on. "Of course you didn't. Flunked out bad enough so the Division wouldn't keep you, huh?"

The Mechanik shrank.

"If you'd paid any attention to your Imbuement lessons, you'd know the spirit of an animal can only be contained for as long as the animal would've lived out its natural life. What did you use for the heart?"

The man's chin dipped. "A common bumblebee."

Jeremiah shook his head. "Smart in theory. Aggressive when challenged, stalwart, industrious, but easy to control. Only live for a year or two at most, though." He rapped on the chest, and it rang hollowly. "Your problem isn't a magic drain. It's that you have no heart." He gestured dismissively. "Start from scratch, sonny. Old Herc has fought his last fight."

Uncle moved on and Hettie followed, bewildered. "I take it that Mechanik didn't have anything useful?"

"That automaton was a common piece of magic covered in metal. It wasn't even *his* magic. He had someone, or more likely a group of low-level someones, create a golem and then stuffed it in a metal suit. And he's parading it around as if it is a Mechanikal wonder. Mechaniks is supposed to straddle the line between magic and the mundane. *That* was a sham."

Even so, Hettie still thought it was interesting. "Shouldn't the metal armor have nulled the magic?"

"A tree can grow through a fence, given time. A flower can take root in the dirt beneath a railway track. The spells are already in the golem—they're not trying to penetrate it. The gaps in the armor let the magic flow around it."

"So . . ." Hettie thought about everything she'd read on Eberhard's theory. "That means that magic must act like a particle that moves freely." She felt proud she was able to articulate it.

Uncle grunted. "Magic's not black and white, and it's not confined to what any one person believes. The problem with

Mechaniks is that everyone treats it as though it is." He sent her an arch, sidelong look. "Don't think too hard about it, girlie. Your hair'll catch on fire."

Hettie huffed at his dismissal. She'd been bitten by a golem—a little snake someone had sent to attack her and Abby—and it had nearly killed her. That kind of power warranted a hearty amount of respect, and she wanted to know more about it in case she ever encountered its like again.

CHAPTER SIX

Uncle dragged them on to the next display, and the next. He interrogated a few of the Mechaniks, asking each time what the practical applications were, what the foundations of their magics were. Many of the men said it was not about practicality, but about discovery and the advancement of knowledge. After the fifth such proclamation, Hettie began to see why Mechaniks were not considered serious-minded: many of them seemed to be engineers playing with the ideas of magic, or low-level sorcerers tinkering with machines.

They found nothing among the displays in the hall that could help Patrice.

Close to eleven, they met with the others and proceeded to the lecture hall. The looks on Jemma's and Marcus's faces told Hettie they hadn't found anything groundbreaking among the displays either. Still, hope lurked in Sophie's bright eyes.

"This might be our only opportunity to speak to Dr. Fielding," she said in a low voice. "According to some of the other Mechaniks here, he's very secretive and doesn't much like being out in public."

"What's this presentation about, anyhow?" Hettie asked.

"I'm not sure. The flyer just says 'Latest Discovery by Dr. Alastair Fielding.'" A furrow appeared between Sophie's brows. "No one we've talked to seems to know."

"Must be a pretty popular guy either way." Uncle glanced around the foyer to the lecture hall. "This place is filling up."

They went in to find seats. Mechaniks old and young, many of them fusty men who had displays in the exhibition hall, sat together in clumps, heads close as they speculated over the presentation. Curious students and public spectators filled the gaps in the seating, many of them relieved for a break in the perusal of the symposium floor.

On stage a canvas sheet covered something as big as a carriage. Two large, armed burly men guarded it, and several more men lined the perimeter of the room.

"That's an awful lot of muscle for a horseless carriage engine," Uncle murmured. "You feel that, English?"

Marcus's eyes were narrowed on the contraption on stage. "I thought I was imagining it. It feels…it feels like…"

"Like you're staring at a lake being drained dry, and you're afraid of being sucked in yourself," Sophie said faintly.

Next to her, Jemma straightened and craned her neck, as if searching for the threat making her charge so uneasy. Hettie wondered if Jemma could feel it, too; Uncle suspected the bodyguard had a latent minor gift. Hettie herself couldn't sense anything. It was the guards that were making her uneasy.

A man in his thirties, with slightly too-long hair the color of tarnished brass and a soft jaw, made his way onto the stage, his gaze focused on the notes in his hands. His clothes fit strangely—the pants too long and the sleeves of his jacket too short. He didn't even seem to register the crowd, which hushed as he approached the podium.

"Gentlemen. Ladies." He said this almost as an afterthought and cleared his throat. His voice sounded rough with disuse. "Good afternoon. I'm here today to present you with what I can only describe as a revolutionary engine that will change the world of magic forever."

The two guards yanked the canvas off. A murmur rippled through the crowd. The "engine" was about as big as an automobile and sat on a four-wheeled chassis, presumably so it could be moved around. A series of tubes snaking along the sides of the main metal bulk ended on a kind of clamp, the tips of which had several pointed teeth. In the center was an oblong blown-glass canister, delicately filigreed with gold leaf.

Hettie didn't know what she was looking at, but it felt off to her. Sophie's face was fixed in a grimace, and Uncle and Marcus sat very stiffly in their seats. It seemed the engine, or whatever it was, was making a few others in the audience uncomfortable as well.

The Mechanik cleared his throat again, tugging at the cuffs of his jacket. He kept his gaze on the notes resting on the podium. "Since the first gifted learned how to manipulate the magical forces that surrounded him, man has sought to understand and control this force. All these years later, we still don't have a complete understanding of the source of magical power, how it works, or even why some people are gifted and others not."

He paused and took a deep breath. "What we do know is that magic has been leaving the land, jeopardizing the traditions and cultural history of countless gifted peoples. Many of my colleagues refuse to believe this is the case. But thanks to my discovery, not only can I prove the crisis the gifted have faced; I can end it, too."

The buzz of the crowd oscillated—incredulous, skeptical, wary. "Preposterous," someone proclaimed loud enough for everyone in the room to hear, but his words dissolved into a fit of coughing.

Dr. Fielding gestured to a man sitting in the audience who headed toward the stage. "Gentlemen and ladies, this is Mr. Phineas Garble of the Division of Sorcery. He has independently verified my work on behalf of the Division and approved its validity of concept. Mr. Garble is also a high-level sorcerer and has kindly volunteered to help in my demonstration."

The middle-aged man joined Dr. Fielding on stage. Uncle sank in his seat.

"Friend of yours?" Hettie asked.

Uncle grunted. "Keep your head down."

Dr. Fielding attached the clamps to the Division man's hand. He sat calmly in a chair brought by one of the guards as the Mechanik pushed some buttons on a control panel.

"Pay attention to the glass canister," he told the audience. The engine whined and whirred. Blue tongues of lightning crackled up the coils and enveloped the glass canister.

Mr. Garble closed his eyes and exhaled. Slowly, the empty glass canister began to glow blue-white. After about ten seconds, it shone as bright as a lantern. Dr. Fielding shut the machine off, and the Division man quickly unclamped his hand.

The crowd's whispered excitement grew. Dr. Fielding gestured. "This canister holds a tiny fraction of Mr. Garble's powers, drawn straight through him and stored here, just like a battery for electrical power. With my engine, not only can this power be siphoned off and stored, it can be redirected into a mundane."

The fusty men flapped and squawked in protest as one of the guards attached a different clamp to his hand. Dr. Fielding pushed several more buttons, and the engine revved once more. The light within the canister faded, and the guard staggered with a loud exhale. As the noise of the contraption died down, he removed the clamp. He held out a small piece of wood and spoke an incantation. The stick ignited instantly.

The audience gasped and cried out in amazement…and perhaps a little terror. Not every sorcerer could simply make fire spontaneously.

"Notice that Mr. Garble remains unaffected by the use of his powers. This has always been the major downside to sharing one's powers—the lender always feels the effects of their power use by the borrower. My engine his eliminated that entirely." Fielding cleared his throat and looked up from his crumpled notes. "Are there any questions?"

The room erupted in a hubbub, everyone talking at once in confusion, in excitement, in fear.

"How long can magic be stored?" someone shouted, and the din faded.

"Indefinitely, from my studies. As long as the canister remains intact, the magical power is contained. Over all my years of observation, and from what I have been able to quantify, nothing is gained or lost."

Someone else yelled, "How much can one of those canisters hold?"

"The magic of ten middle-strength sorcerers has been put simultaneously into one canister. We did not want to test the outer limits of that; there are still many things we are learning about magic and its interactions with metal. This engine"—he rapped on the brass—"is made with a special composite of metals infused with talismans."

"How do we know this isn't just a trick?" This from the fusty corner.

At that Dr. Fielding scowled. "I am a man of science and a sorcerer of note. Lies have no place in either field. If you wish to test this engine for yourself, I invite you to join me on stage for a demonstration."

No one moved. Probably because he'd just done the equivalent of inviting a healthy person to stick themselves with a needle full of dope.

"Jeremiah?" Marcus murmured.

"I'm not volunteering," he muttered. "Whatever that thing is, it does what he says it does. It takes people's magic away." His voice was tinged with something like disgust.

A man called from the audience, "What practical applications does this device have?"

"That is a very good question. First and foremost, it is a tool that we can finally use to capture and quantify magic, study it in its pure form without the interference or manipulations of a sorcerer. I expect many experiments can now be performed with the donations of a few willing gifted—"

"Who'd give up their magic?" A man in a black cassock stood, loudly decrying, "Sorcerers only hoard power for themselves!"

"I think this could be an opportunity to show the world otherwise," Fielding said crisply. "The gifted are no different from the mundane. Not everyone with powers can use them effectively. My machine will give them the opportunity to pass that gift on to someone who might have more aptitude."

"For a price," the man returned. "Money is the root of all sin, and this infernal engine will put witchcraft in the hands of the vilest servants of Satan!"

A resounding cry went up. "My great uncle was killed by a rogue sorcerer!" a man shouted. "And now you want to give the criminals and outlaws a way they can all juice up?"

The audience's mood soured, and what Hettie had thought was awe now turned to cold fear and hatred. People didn't like this machine—maybe because of the strange vibe it was giving off. Or maybe it was too unnatural for some to contemplate.

The noise grew, and a flustered Dr. Fielding was ushered off the stage by the guards to a chorus of abuse. More guards closed around the engine as it was covered up and wheeled out. A few of the audience members tried to rush the stage; the men held them back, and then, as if on cue, uniformed officers rushed into the lecture hall, blowing whistles and surrounding the rowdier protesters.

Marcus and Jemma swiftly herded Sophie, Hettie, and Uncle out of the lecture hall and away from the university.

"Oh, dear," Sophie said as their carriage pulled away. She glanced behind her where more people were gathering, shouting at the line of police forming a barricade around the building. "I don't imagine that went at all the way he'd thought it would."

"Those are members of the Mundane Movement," Uncle growled. "It explains the police presence. The university must have been expecting them."

"Why invite the rabble if they knew this would be the outcome?" Sophie sniffed.

"I don't know. The Division's well aware of the Mundane Movement's stance against Mechaniks. They think it's a bunch of sorcerers trying to sully their precious 'pure' science." His eyebrows knit. "This ain't a rogue operation. Agent Garble's a company man through and through. I knew him back in the day. If he was here to verify Fielding's findings, he would've also advised him not to release this information in a forum like this one." He rested his elbows on his knees and steepled his fingers in front of his lips, thinking. "The Division doesn't do anything without turning it inside out beforehand. They're not careless."

"So you're saying the Division let Fielding show off that thing here on purpose?" Hettie asked.

"Let. Encouraged him. Forced him to." Uncle raised his eyes. "Hard to say which."

"You think they wanted him to start a ruckus with those Mundane Movement types?"

"There's no love lost between the Mundane Movement and the Division," Uncle said. "All the Division needs is just cause to lock up the worst instigators of violence. Get a riot going over something like this and the Division will get carte blanche to round up every movement member on grounds of domestic terrorism."

"That seems too convoluted, even for the Division," Hettie said. "They helped Fielding build that engine. Why?"

"Seems they could do a lot of good and evil with it," Uncle said. "Give powers to the already powerful. Take it away from people they don't deem worthy…"

"And all for a price," Sophie agreed. "Whoever controls that engine would make a fortune."

"It's the military applications I'm worried about," Marcus said. "Who knows what kind of weapons will be derived from this?"

"Or who they'll be used against," Jemma murmured.

"If it's so dangerous for gifted folks, why would the Division sanction this project?" Hettie pointed out.

"That is the question." Sophie chewed her lip. "I think we'll have to ask Dr. Fielding himself."

CHAPTER SEVEN

N ews of Fielding's "Infernal Engine," as it was being called, hit the newspapers the following day.

MAGIC FOR MUNDANES? the headline shouted, though the question mark seemed to be an afterthought. The articles wildly speculated about the implications and applications for Fielding's Mechanikal wonder, though the man himself was only quoted through his studies, which had somehow been made available to the press.

"More Division work, I bet," Uncle said. "If they're trying to calm things down, they're doing a terrible job of it."

In fact, in the days following the presentation, the Mundane Movement redoubled its campaigning efforts. Canvassers picketed and handed out flyers on every street corner, even outside of the hotel. Men and women carried placards that read *Magic Is The Devil's Work!* and shouted slogans like "Sorcery is sin!" and "We shall not suffer a sorcerer to live!"

Hettie had seen the like in Newhaven—the Mundane Movement was alive and well across the country, even in the most remote corners—but here in the city, the threat behind the protesters' words felt more real. At one point, she saw a man holding a picture of a woman being burned at the stake with the words "Bring Back Salem" on it. The witch trials in Massachusetts had been particularly terrifying for the gifted, and even the Division hadn't been able to intercede fast enough to save the people killed by antisorcery fervor.

"You sure you still want to do this shopping trip?" Hettie asked hopefully as they exited the lobby. Marcus and Jemma stayed close, watching the Mundanes carefully.

"You didn't pack anything for the ball, and I can't have you showing up in rags," Sophie said. After a short letter to the Mechaniks' Society's president, Sophie Favreau and her entourage had been issued an invitation to the Mechaniks' Ball, which would afford them another opportunity to speak to Fielding. Her grandmother was a great supporter of Mechanikal innovations, after all, and the Favreaus' pockets were deep. "Besides, I won't be terrorized and silenced by these small-minded plebs. Now, come. They won't even know I'm here."

Perhaps it was Sophie's glamor magic that kept the canvassers' eyes off them. Or perhaps they ignored her because of Marcus's gleaming mage guns. Whatever it was, they walked past unmolested, though clearly the shouted slogans irritated the debutante.

"That was easier than I thought it would be," Hettie commented as they climbed into the hired cab.

Sophie smirked. "Mundanes can't tell gifted and nongifted apart. They think we dress or act a certain way, but the truth is, we're just regular folks with a little more talent and training."

"That's *why* they're so afraid," Jemma murmured. Her fingers flexed over the fat Bible sheath in which she hid her most wicked knife. "*Anyone* could be gifted."

Shopping with Sophie turned out to be something of a trial. The debutante complained bitterly that they didn't have time to get something tailor-made for Hettie and would have to buy a dress off the rack. Sophie made her try on frilly gown after frilly gown, looking for "just the right thing." The fine silks and expensive fabrics started to chafe almost as much as Hettie's corset.

"Hettie, we simply must work on your comportment." Sophie tsked as she held up a frothy thing full of lace. Hettie made a face at the sight of it. "Your glowering is going to scare the men away."

"I'm not *glowering*. This is just my face. And I don't need a dress to talk to a bunch of men."

"On the contrary. The right dress is armor *and* a weapon. Men won't admit it, but they pay attention to the details—a good fit and quality means taste; high fashion means money; ostentatious jewelry or baubles means you're looking for a husband and you have the lures to do it. A little extra décolletage"—she tugged her collar down slightly—"and they are rendered idiots."

"My body ain't a weapon," Hettie said flatly. "My weapon's a weapon."

"Everything is a weapon when your whole life is a battle," Jemma said. "You just have to know which one to bring to the fight."

"Besides," Sophie went on, readjusting her dress and rifling through a pile of fabric swatches, "there are social niceties to be observed. These Mechaniks think my interest is only superficial—they don't know how much I've read up on Fielding's work. But I can't launch straight into an interrogation. No one will ever talk to us if they think we know more than they do."

"So you think that pretending not to know anything will get them to talk to us more?"

"Guaranteed. Men *love* explaining things to women." Sophie's lips tugged up in one corner. She called to her head of security, "Isn't that right, Marcus?"

"I plead the fifth," Marcus deadpanned.

Jemma snickered. "See, *that's* what I call smart."

"Seems like an awful waste of time to be putting on this show," Hettie grumbled, fingering the dress Sophie had declared was the only one "fit for a second-rate Favreau." Hettie did not like it.

"This isn't some backwater tumbleweed town. We can't just walk in waving guns and demanding answers. Civilized society has a different set of rules. These men don't respond to threats from bullies."

"I think Diablo'd beg to differ," Hettie muttered.

Sophie cast her a grim look. "You saw what happened on the train to that one man who nearly got us all killed. So-called civilized men think themselves above that kind of barbarism. They'd never tell us what we needed to know with you waving a gun under their nose."

"They'd be too busy wetting their pants," Jemma added pointedly. "The minute they stopped laughing at you, and after they had already lost a limb to your temper, that is."

"Trust me," Sophie implored. "I know what I'm doing."

It took a long time to kit Hettie out in a gown, stockings, undergarments, shoes, and all kinds of finery whose cost she didn't want to estimate. Sophie seemed to revel in treating her like a living doll, commenting on her hair and posture and the deepening furrows gathering on her brow. When she suggested they consider a lot more rouge, Hettie finally snapped.

"This is ridiculous. Why do I need to go through all this? I don't even need to be at this ball."

Sophie frowned. "Are you saying you wish to break the contract with my grandmother?"

Hettie's stomach dipped. "No. Of course not. I made a promise." She huffed. "But I'll stick out like a sore thumb, and I have no idea what I'm supposed to do there. Frankly, it's probably safer if I stay at the hotel."

Sophie sighed. "I have a confession." She exchanged a look with Marcus and Jemma, and they nodded. "The reason I need you there is as an extra distraction. I mentioned to the president of the Society of Mechaniks that I was chaperoning my cousin, an eligible young woman seeking a staid, respectable husband."

Hettie stared. "Why the hell would you do that? I thought the whole point was to keep attention *away* from me."

"Miss Sophie's of marrying age," Marcus said, "and far above the station of these men. Nonetheless, they will try to win her favor or even compromise her honor to secure their own future. Jemma will be relegated to the ladies' salon for the evening, and I am not a suitable escort."

"It's a shame Mr. Woodroffe isn't here. He could have easily played my fiancé again." Sophie sighed. Hettie chewed on the inside of her cheek. "But he isn't. Without an appropriate escort, I'll be left open to the unwanted attentions of a bunch of blustering bachelors looking to fund their research." Sophie notched an eyebrow up. "If, however, I present them a fine Favreau adjunct—"

"Then they'll swarm me and leave you alone to make our inquiries." Hettie pinched the flesh between her eyes where a headache was forming. "Wouldn't your father have something to say about passing a ranch girl like me off as a Favreau?"

"You're not a Favreau at all," she reminded her primly. "And it's not as if you're *actually* getting married. Anyhow, Papa's too busy to worry about what new relatives have crawled out of the gutter with their hats in hand. He won't be bothered by whatever I'm doing."

Hettie thought she detected a catch in Sophie's voice. "What's he going to say about the bill on this dress?"

"This is nothing." Sophie glanced around and lowered her volume. "I have my own income. My own personal investments. Financial security is just as important as bodily security, after all."

Hettie pursed her lips. "I know you think this is frivolous," Sophie continued, seeing her face. "I know you think *I'm* frivolous. But this is *my* world, and it has certain rules. I'm not looking to embarrass you or myself, but I'll do whatever I must to help my grandmother." She glared hard. "I need you there, Hettie. Grandmère needs us."

Υ

The following night, Hettie, Sophie, Marcus, and Jeremiah piled into a carriage and made their way to a grand mansion in Hyde Park. The society's headquarters was a lovely old brick edifice with shining brass roofs and a domed observatory perched on the highest tower. It looked like something between a castle and fortress, Hettie thought as they mounted the front steps.

Hettie ruffled her voluminous skirts and tugged up the low neckline of her ball gown. The material of the dress was shiny and oddly rigid, and no matter how still she sat, it wrinkled. Bits of lace as delicate as spiderweb frothed the collar and obscured her modest décolletage, and she was terrified she'd move wrong and tear it. Her fingers were stiff in her too-tight gloves, though in the colder late winter weather, their cover was welcome. On top of it all, she could feel every rock and pebble on the ground through her butter-soft slippers.

"You look like a damned cake," Uncle snickered. She glowered at him as she gathered her skirts and climbed the steps to the house.

"Remember, whoever spots Dr. Fielding first, flag down the rest of us and we'll introduce ourselves," Marcus said.

"Considering the uproar over the engine, do you think he'll even show up?"

Sophie nodded. "These are his peers, and this is the one social event of the season they're all expected to attend. Jemma?"

"I'll keep my ears open for any talk about the man," the bodyguard said. At a gathering like this, she was required to stay in the ladies' salon where women could have their clothing and hair adjusted by their staff.

"Remember, this is a late debut for you, so act like a woman on a mission to find a husband," Sophie reminded Hettie as they entered the building. "But don't seem *too* desperate. And for goodness' sake, stand up straight."

At the doorstep, they were greeted by the hosts. Mr. Campbell was the society president, a balding and somewhat myopic fellow who peered at Hettie as though through a jeweler's loupe, head bent, one eye squinted. Mrs. Campbell wore a tight smile and a trailing bejeweled gown that clearly hadn't seen much use, and which everyone kept stepping on. She looked as weighed down by her garments as she did by her husband, who leaned heavily on her.

As they entered the main ballroom, Hettie's spirits fell. Admittedly, there'd been a part of her hoping this would be a grand affair with romance and masks and beautiful people dancing. She would never get to go to another event like this in her lifetime.

Instead she walked into a room filled with men in staid black-and-white suits. Graying, white, and bald heads bent close together, murmuring deeply, extemporizing on this theory or that new innovation. There were some younger men, too, but they were too eager soaking up their elders' lessons to notice the new arrivals. There were few women, and most of them were older and either by their husbands' sides or else sitting on the sidelines, making polite conversation or looking bored. A string quartet played, but no one danced.

"Not even an announcement," Sophie commented, half appalled and half amused. "If we'd been introduced, we'd be swarmed by eager suitors by now."

"Not the caliber of party you're used to, then?" Uncle said. Sophie didn't rise to the bait, though her expression said, "Obviously."

"Where do you think Dr. Fielding is?" Hettie asked, scanning the room.

"I'm not sure. I was hoping our hosts could introduce us, but Mrs. Campbell looks rather put-upon." Sophie glanced back toward the president's glassy-eyed wife. "Poor woman. She apparently hasn't had much luck organizing these events. She can't even out the numbers of women and men, what with all these professorial bachelor types her husband keeps inviting."

"Seems you didn't need me here after all," Hettie grumbled, plucking at her dress. What a waste of lace.

"We're not here to dance anyhow. Let's split up and find Fielding." Uncle pointed at Hettie. "Keep out of trouble."

"And don't go too far," Sophie reminded her, tapping at her chest to indicate the talisman concealed in her bodice.

Hettie made her way to the bar, where there was a better vantage point. The voluminous layers of petticoats rustled around her legs and tripped her up, and she stopped a moment to shake the skirts out. She looked up to find two older men staring at her. Her cheeks flamed.

"What? You've never seen a dress before?" she snapped. The men turned away quickly.

She leaned back against the bar and scanned the room for Dr. Fielding while eavesdropping on the conversations around her, listening for any mention of the man. Most of the talk revolved around the research the men were doing. A few mentioned Fielding's engine, but only in the most derogatory sense, as if the discovery was inconsequential. Hettie got the sense that those who were thinking about it were either too proud to acknowledge the importance of the work or too afraid to praise it among peers.

"Something for the lady?" The voice at her shoulder was like honey, and Hettie startled as a tall, dark-haired man in a well-trimmed coat sidled up next to her.

"No, thank you. I was just looking for my friend."

"Not a husband."

She clenched her teeth, reminding herself of her purpose. "My uncle."

The man's mouth spread into a slow smile. "I'm afraid there are many uncles here. For your safety, let me chaperone you until we find your escort. I'm sure he cannot be far."

Hettie swallowed a protest. She didn't want to make a scene. "Thank you, Mr. . . . ?"

"Fielding. Alastair. Doctor." He chuckled. "Dr. Alastair Fielding, that is."

She stared. This was not the same man who'd been on stage. He had dark hair and a sharp jaw, and his eyes were cobalt blue. Why was this man trying to pass himself off as the Mechanik?

She decided to play this charade out and see what his game was. "I thank you for your company, Dr. Fielding." She offered her hand. "Henrietta Wiltshire. Will you . . . take a turn around the party with me?" She had to think of the words Sophie would use. *Mosey around* wasn't exactly the parlance this crowd used.

He took her hand. "It would be . . ." He bent over her fingers. ". . . my greatest pleasure."

Heat stirred low in her gut. She hadn't thought she'd have any kind of reaction to the man, though he was handsome enough. She thought of Walker and noted the similarities in coloring, but "Fielding" was lean where Walker was broad. He was long-limbed, and his dove-gray coat made him look like a heron deftly wading through the crowd and plucking the tastiest fish.

She held his arm carefully, not clinging to it, but not being too ginger about it either. She became aware of the looks she was getting—had she made some kind of faux pas? All she was doing was holding a man's arm.

"Tell me," she said to distract herself, "what is it you're a doctor of?"

"Mechanikal engineering. But my main field of research is in magical hybrid engineering."

"So you're a sorcerer?" Fielding had declared himself one onstage.

"I have Division training," he said, though Hettie noted that wasn't a straight yes. Students did, in fact, flunk out of the Division Academy, and those who barely passed were often recruited in less sorcery-intense roles such as enforcers or clerks.

On their trip north from Mexico, Ling had told her about some of his time at the Academy and the horrors he had witnessed there. Ultimately, those deeply buried memories had overridden his duty as a Division agent, stopping him from taking Abby to whatever hell they'd designed to keep her indigo powers in check.

Fielding was still talking, and she tuned back in. "…It is my belief that magical endowments are nothing more than a genetic disorder—a mutation, if you will, as common as red hair or ambidextrousness. The birth of magically gifted persons has been on the decline for decades, according to the Division of Sorcery's registry. So either people are not breeding as vigorously, or they're hiding their gifted children away, or something is happening to magic."

"And what is your theory, Dr. Fielding?" Hettie remembered Sophie's claim that men such as Fielding liked to talk, so she tilted her chin coquettishly to show interest as she'd seen the debutante do.

"Please, call me Alastair." He folded a hand over hers, stroking his thumb along the top. Hettie tried not to squirm. "I ascribe to the Eberhard theory that magic is a finite resource that comes from the earth. My experiments have shown that this resource can be collected, stored, and even transferred."

"That sounds interesting," she said in a perfect mimicry of Sophie's own flirtatious tone. He hadn't revealed anything she hadn't read in the papers, of course, yet the man preened. "Tell me more about your experiments."

The man drew her closer, smiling wide. "You're a thirsty girl, aren't you? Hungry for knowledge?"

"I consider myself a…a student," she said haltingly as warmth trickled through her belly. She felt trapped in his eyes, as if his look were consuming her mouthful by mouthful.

He guided her with a palm pressed against the small of her back. "Let us go somewhere a little less crowded. I'd be happy to tell you all about my experiments…in private."

CHAPTER EIGHT

Hettie felt lightheaded and giddy as "Fielding" guided her through the house and to the empty garden, drawing her along a flagstone path toward a gazebo shrouded in darkness. It had been an unseasonably mild winter, but a chill still skated over her skin as they emerged from the stuffy house.

A few dead leaves crunched under her slippers as they hurried along. The buzz in her gut had moved to her groin, creating a strange friction that sent waves pulsing through her. She'd only just met the man, and she didn't find him particularly enticing, only…

What was she doing? She was supposed to be grilling him for more details about…about…

Sophie. Where was Sophie? And Uncle? And Marcus?

Her footsteps faltered. "I…I shouldn't be out here alone," she said, grasping for sanity. Something wasn't right. Her head felt stuffy, her skin tight. "I need to find my uncle."

"He might be out here. We could look in the gazebo."

They could. But what else would they find there? Hettie shook her head. It was filled with thoughts she'd only ever entertained in private…with Walker as her guide.

And then she realized they couldn't be real. She had no feelings for this man, no desire to hide away in dark corners with him doing…doing…

The buzz between her legs doubled in intensity. Her knees weakened. Alastair pulled her close, pressing against her, his musk cloying. He planted his wet mouth on hers.

She couldn't breathe. His kiss aimed to suffocate her, practically covering her nose. His tongue flagellated against her skin like a fish pulled from the water. Hettie pushed at him, but her limbs felt like jelly. He pressed her up against the scratchy shrubs and rocked against her, moaning.

He pulled at the front of her dress, tearing the lace. She felt sapped of strength the way she did when she had a fever. Her limbs shook. Everything in her demanded she stop resisting and give in to whatever was to come.

As Fielding buried his face against her bosom, Walker's amulet stamped a cold circle against her chest.

"No!" Hettie reached out, and Diablo formed in her fist. The fuzz lifted like a flock of startled birds, their alarmed cries echoed in the harsh rasping of her breath.

The man before her had transformed. He was no longer the lean version of Walker, but the real Alastair Fielding, with his soft jaw and hay-colored hair. The moment he saw the dark barrel pointed square between his eyes, he scrambled back.

Hettie's hands trembled, keeping tight rein on the weapon's growing weight. She could hardly get a word out as righteous fury mixed with disgust and horror clogged her throat. It distilled into a single point of focus, twitching in her trigger finger.

Shoot him, the mage gun whispered. A green aura wavered around the grip, as if her outrage had become something tangible. *He violated you.*

Hettie inhaled, still tracking Alastair's wild-eyed look. "I-I-I apologize profusely," he stammered. "I don't know what came over me. Too much champagne…" His eyes darted around. "I didn't mean to—"

"Shut up." It came out as a cold, direct order, and his lips sealed as if she'd cast a silence spell on him. The cold air penetrated her skin, bringing her back to her senses as the haze of rage cleared. To keep him from seeing her tremble, she carefully rearranged the lace around her neckline while still keeping Diablo levelled at his head. "If it weren't for the fact we actually need you, your balls would be a flaming cinder right now." She gave him a once-over. This was the doughy man from the lecture hall, no question about it. Even the dove-gray suit he wore looked ill-fitting now that his spell was broken. "Why were you using glamor?"

He looked around wildly, as if he might find an escape. "I…I didn't want people to know I was here. I gave a presentation yesterday that made me somewhat unpopular—"

"I know about the engine, Dr. Fielding. I was there. So you're in hiding." But from whom? Then she remembered the hired muscle who'd surrounded the engine and escorted the Mechanik off stage. Those Division men were nowhere in sight now. "You were being guarded for your own safety. Why'd you come here alone?"

His lips pursed in a pout. "I…I wanted to see what the others were saying about me."

Ego. Of course. Her gaze narrowed as a new thought occurred to her. "You used some kind of coercion spell on me, didn't you?"

He shifted uncomfortably. "It wouldn't have worked if you weren't receptive to it. You were standing by the bar, which was a clear signal you were seeking companionsh—"

Hettie pulled the hammer back on Diablo, and the loud click silenced the man. "I knew a man who used to do the same thing. He raped dozens of women this way." A cold smile crossed her lips. "I shot him in the gut and let him die slowly."

He paled. "Please…I wouldn't…I didn't mean—"

"Hettie!" Uncle jogged into the garden. His eyes landed on the ripped lace at her neckline.

"Uncle." Hettie's insides were icy now, and the trembling had seized her whole being, except for her shooting hand, which remained as steady as a surgeon's.

Fielding had looked relieved for a second before he realized Jeremiah wasn't there to rescue him. For someone with all his education, he wasn't terribly smart. He hadn't even tried to call out for help.

Uncle grabbed the scientist by the collar and hauled him to eye level. He inhaled deeply, scenting him like a dog.

"Borrowed magic," he said with disgust, then roughly searched the man's pockets. He pulled out a small figurine—a lewd carving of a giant male member jutting from a tiny trickster god. Uncle gave a growl of anger. "You son of a bitch." He slammed a fist into the man's gut, and Fielding folded. Jeremiah opened his clenched palms. Eerie bluish light crackled across his fingertips. "You like coercion spells? 'Cuz I can make you pull out your own teeth and shove them up your—"

"Stop. Uncle, let him be. We need him . . . functional." She let that word bury itself into Fielding's brain.

The Mechanik's eyes widened with fear, but before he could cry out, Jeremiah wrapped a length of twine around Fielding's neck, whispering a silence spell. "See how you like that," he growled.

The man's eyes bulged, and he croaked out hoarsely as the geis firmly sealed his lips. Uncle roughly bound the man's wrists behind him with a leather thong, uttering another spell. "What d'you wanna do with him? We can't bring him back inside."

"Take him back to the hotel. The Division agents guarding him don't even know he's here, but they'll be looking for him." She eyed the Mechanik, wanting him to know every mistake he'd made. He shuddered visibly. She went on, "I'll find the others and we can make our excuses and go." Sophie wouldn't be happy about this development, but at least now they'd get the information they needed.

Uncle harrumphed. "You can't go in there like that." He gestured at the rips in her bodice, then draped his scarf over her shoulders, tugging the ends closely together. It smelled strongly of tobacco and was still warm from his body. He nodded. "It's not high fashion, but it'll do."

She'd thought she had a good hold on her emotions, but just then, tears burned in her throat. Uncle settled his hands over her shoulders. But she couldn't meet his eye.

"Hurry on, then," he said gruffly. "I'll meet you back at the hotel."

Hettie drew the scarf around her throat as she reentered the society house. As she cast her gaze around for Sophie, she got the distinct impression that people were whispering and leering at her, as if they knew what she'd been up to.

Diablo reformed in her grip unbidden. She'd left it in the garden, but it came to her now, as if it sensed danger in every pair of men's eyes. She pulled the scarf around her more closely and hid the mage gun in its folds.

She finally spotted the debutante standing with a group of men. Marcus was close by. He flinched as he took in her dishevelled state.

She marched up to Sophie. "Excuse me, Sophie..."

"Ah, there she is." Sophie drew her into the circle of men, who closed around Hettie like a pack of wolves. "Gentlemen, meet my cousin Miss Henrietta Wiltshire. Miss Wiltshire, this is Mr. Henry Kurt, Judge Vernon Wales, and..."

"Robert Smythe." The round, red face sneered down at her like a blood moon grinning through a bonfire. "But everyone calls me Boss."

It took every bit of strength she could muster to not flinch from Smythe. She would never forget those beady eyes and the spittle flying from his mouth as he whipped up the mob that had tried to lynch Ling Tsang. He'd traded his stained white suit for a more sartorial gray, and his thin pate of hair had been dyed a ghastly orange. Arrogance and anger radiated from him as readily as the smell of talc and sour milk wafting from his body. He looked exactly like the sweltering ham hock being served at the buffet on the other side of the room. She stifled the urge to clasp the glamor talisman Sophie had given her.

"Mr. Smythe is running for governor of Illinois," Sophie said, her tone riding the fine line between admiration and condescension. "He's running on a very... interesting platform."

"I fight for good Americans," Smythe said, puffing out his chest. "I've worked my way up from my family's poor little farm in Kansas, did my time serving in the army, and built my empire in Montana. I've seen it all, and I can tell you the key to ending this recession is building more prisons. We don't do enough to weed out the undesirables in this great nation of ours."

"Well said." Judge Wales raised his glass. "I'm tired of seeing recidivists in my courtroom. If they can't abide by the laws, why should they have the right to enjoy the freedoms we do?"

"Wouldn't education and social programs be a more effective way to help these people?" Sophie asked in a polite but pointed tone. "We can't keep citizens locked up forever just because they don't have the ability to make a decent living."

"Prison is as good as any social program for these criminal types. Ask the learned men here, Miss Favreau—there is scientific evidence that certain types of people are more prone to crime, though I could've told you that without feeling up a bunch of skulls." He laughed as if it were the funniest thing in the world, and the other men chuckled along.

"Of course, we wouldn't expect inmates to just live off the good graces of our tax dollars. We'd put them to work, doing the jobs too dangerous for everyone else. They could earn their room and board by helping to blast mines or build roads. The gifted could be sent to shore up the Wall or reinforce the protection wards on our borders. I mean, look at the work the Swedenborg facility has produced."

"That's true," the judge said. "I have it on good authority that the prison for sorcerers has produced some of the best talismans around."

"Why anyone would want to use talismans made by convicts is beyond me," Mr. Kurt said. "A rogue sorcerer could have put a geis on any of those things."

"The Division vets all talismans," the judge assured him. "And they don't allow the worst offenders anywhere near that work. It's only for the lower-level sorcerers."

"The point is, there are ways to put the most wayward men to use," Smythe said. His grin was oily. "No one should get a free ride. The criminal class need to repay their debt to society with interest—we've carried them for too long. Put them to work, I say, whatever that entails. And if a few of them perish in the labor, that's God's work culling the herd."

"I imagine God would have a lot to say about that kind of judgment," Hettie snapped.

The men stared at her as if she'd popped out of thin air. She was agitated and angry and just wanted to go, so she glared right back.

Sophie snapped open a fan, fluttering and laughing. Every part of her bounced and gleamed as she tittered—her glamor at full force, no doubt—and it lured the men's disconcerted gazes back to her. "Oh, my cousin is full of such…progressive ideas! Forgive her, gentlemen, she is eccentric."

Only Smythe's piggy gaze stuck to Hettie. He grinned humorlessly down at her, as if he were almost impressed. She looked away, but not quickly enough. His expression shifted. "Beggin' your pardon…have we met before, Miss Wiltshire?"

"I don't believe so." She prayed Sophie's glamor was strong enough to withstand scrutiny. Boss Smythe had been juicing when she'd last encountered him—it was possible he could see through the glamor.

"My cousin has not been out in society." Sophie drew her a little closer. She felt Sophie's power envelop her, and Smythe's gaze slid back to Sophie.

"Society," Smythe said with a touch of ridicule. "You'll forgive me for saying so, Miss Favreau, as I know you're used to associating with more refined company than ours, but it is my firm belief that much of the world's woes come from the concentration of wealth and power among the top tiers of this so-called *society*."

"You are forgiven, sir," she said delicately. "And I am not offended. The Favreaus have accumulated much wealth, but we devote almost half of our income to help the less fortunate through numerous charities and public works. Unfortunately, money only goes so far. It is policy that must change. I expect a man like you will see to that and enact change rather than sit on his hands like so many of our useless politicians."

"We're only useless if we're not properly funded," Smythe said, his tone heavy with suggestion. He might as well have been rubbing his fingers. "The support of a patron goes a long way to pushing policy."

Sophie's brittle smile crackled. "Let us hope, then, that your donors have progressive ideas. I'd hate to see those society types you so despise making sure you uphold the status quo."

"I see you're an intelligent, political woman as well as a beautiful one." Smythe's gray teeth flashed, but the manic look in his eye reminded Hettie of a dog about to bite. "I assume whoever wins your hand in marriage will have to match your intelligence."

"No man 'wins' a Favreau," Sophie returned. "And in all honesty, I think I'd prefer a stupid man. They're easier to control."

The men's laughter was loud and forced. Smythe's stiff, toothy smile remained fixed like a crooked picket fence.

"Let's move on to more interesting topics. Politics can be so frustrating." Sophie made a pointed turn away from Smythe to face Mr. Kurt. Her grip on Hettie's arm remained firm. "I understand you're one of Dr. Fielding's sponsors for his latest projects. I have some interest in his work."

"After the debacle at his presentation, who doesn't?" Mr. Kurt chuckled. "I told him it was too early to present his findings. Exciting as they are, he still doesn't grasp how his work will affect the national mood toward magic."

"The mood will never change," Judge Wales said. "Men who go without will always envy the men who have. This 'infernal engine' of his will balance the power between gifted and mundanes. Now the practice of borrowing magic can be regulated."

"Taxed, even," Smythe added. "For the benefit of *real* Americans."

"I was under the impression the society did not approve of Dr. Fielding's work," Hettie said.

Again the eyes swivelled toward her, as if she'd materialized out of nowhere. Was Sophie's glamor so strong that she was nearly invisible to these men? Or was it that they weren't expecting her to speak?

"The society's divided, as it tends to be," Mr. Kurt explained. "The older, more conservative members don't approve. The younger ones are excited and interested, but they don't want to lose esteem or clout with the older ones."

"They're just jealous of the Division funds and resources being poured into Dr. Fielding's research," Smythe said.

"That's true." Mr. Kurt glanced about and lowered his voice. "But no one would willingly admit it. It'd suggest they condone his methods." He wrinkled his nose.

"Methods?" Sophie asked.

"He took magic from comatose sorcerers and placed it in other comatose patients. He didn't have any of their consent."

Hettie felt every muscle in Sophie go stiff. Hettie understood why. Transferring magic from one person to another was an intimate transaction that required both parties' consent. Ling had told them that General Cabello, a Mexican sorcerer and military tyrant, had taken Thomas Stubbs's magic by force. This revelation had disturbed even the usually imperturbable Jeremiah Bassett.

It seemed Fielding's engine was capable of transferring magic from anyone whether they wanted it to or not.

"From my understanding, those patients had been in vegetative states for months, if not years. Why shouldn't they be put to good use for the advancement of science instead of wasting away on taxpayer dollars?" Boss Smythe rubbed his fingers together, as if the grit between the pads was worth more than basic human decency. "I'm sure the participants would be thrilled to have been a part of this historic finding."

Sophie's grip spasmed over Hettie's arm, and Hettie took that as her cue to interrupt the conversation before Sophie said something she'd regret.

Hettie cleared her throat. "Sophie…if I could beg you to come with me to…uh…powder my nose."

The debutante nodded, snapping her fan closed. "Yes, of course, cousin. Gentlemen, please excuse us."

CHAPTER NINE

They hurried out of the room and up the stairs. Marcus followed discreetly. They passed the ladies' salon, beckoning to Jemma to join them. The four of them entered an empty room farther along the hall and shut the door.

"The nerve of that...that arrogant, myopic—" Sophie tore off her gloves, flexing her clawed hands. Jemma clucked her tongue and handed her a flask. Sophie took a swig from it, exhaling fumes. "I should've cursed him to talk his tongue off!"

"He was certainly opinionated," Marcus said. "I wonder if he knew you were a sorcerer?"

"His counterspells were strong enough. All of it was juice, though. Jemma, any word on Dr. Fielding?"

"Not much that was useful. A few of the wives of the Mechaniks here have some opinions on his work, but the man himself is a bachelor. And he's free with his hands around the housemaids, which is why he's not invited to many homes."

"No use there, then. I thought for certain he'd show up tonight." She blew out a breath and only then seemed to notice Hettie's dishabille. "What happened to your dress?"

"I found Dr. Fielding."

"What kind of answer—" Then the words and their meaning struck Sophie, and she gripped her arms. "Why didn't you say something sooner?"

Hettie suppressed an eye roll and explained what had happened in the garden in the briefest of terms. Jemma grew very still, and Sophie became stony.

"Are you telling us Bassett *kidnapped* the doctor?" Marcus rubbed his temples.

"Not on purpose." Hettie paused and reconsidered. "Not with harm in mind, at any rate." She rethought that. "Not much."

"We'd better go. When the Division figures out their ward is on the loose, they'll come here first. It's best we're not present when they arrive."

They made their way back downstairs. To Hettie's dismay, Boss Smythe waited for them at the foot of the staircase. "You're not leaving so soon?" His gaze was on Sophie, but Hettie felt it slide toward her, and she turned her face away.

"My cousin has caught a chill," Sophie said with a note of regret. "It was nice to meet you, Mr. Smythe. Good luck on your campaign."

"I hope I didn't offend you and can count on your support," he said. "I forget that sorcery is strong in your family."

"Indeed." She tried to move past him, but he put his bulk in her path.

"Why don't I come visit you sometime, and we can discuss more of your ideas for public works? I'm always willing to negotiate my policies and engage in...political intercourse."

Sophie's smile was so brittle it looked as though it might flake off her face entirely. "I'll have to check my schedule."

"Do that. I hope I can count your father among my supporters."

There was no dissuading the man, so the debutante bobbed her head, keeping her smile fixed. Smythe moved aside, but as Hettie passed him, he stopped her.

"I hope to see you again, too, Miss Wiltshire. In the full light of day."

She nodded, barely meeting his eye. Diablo nudged her in her mind.

They piled into the carriage, collected Jemma from around the servants' entrance, and drove away. The knot in Hettie's stomach eased as the society's headquarters rolled out of sight. She told Marcus and Sophie about her encounter with Smythe back in Hawksville, Montana, and Sophie frowned.

"Odious man," she said with a sniff. "Why anyone would vote for him is beyond my understanding."

"You'd be surprised how many people share his views," Marcus murmured.

"Do you think he saw my scar?" With the Alabama gang terrorizing the country, she had no desire to be wrongfully identified...or even correctly identified.

"I can't be certain. As much borrowed magic as he had, just having raw power isn't enough. He needs to know how to access it with spells and talismans and such. He would have needed training. Can you tell me anything else about him?"

Hettie shook her head. "A man borrowing magic and running for office can't possibly be a good thing."

"Juicing isn't actually illegal, and neither is a sorcerer running for office. As long as the candidate is vetted by the Division and they pass all the anti-influence tests, they're free to run."

Hettie shuddered to think about that man as governor. But they had other matters to worry about now.

At the hotel, Alastair Fielding sat straight-backed on a couch, hands tied in front of him, his eyes bulging with fear as he watched Uncle clean his gun. The old man pointed the muzzle at Fielding and spun the wheel, peering through the empty chambers at the Mechanik.

Marcus expelled a breath as he took in the tableau. "Don't you think that's a little too on-the-nose as an intimidation tactic?"

"If he did to Sophie what he did to Hettie, you'd be less inclined to criticize."

Wordlessly Jemma unsheathed her Bible blade and inspected its edge in the candlelight. She took out a small whetstone and ran it along the blade with four quick strokes. Fielding flinched at the tinny shrieks. She resheathed it within the Bible. All this she did without looking Fielding's way.

Hettie sat just out of Fielding's peripheral vision, as far from the Mechanik as possible. She summoned Diablo and folded it in her lap. She got no real pleasure seeing Fielding helpless. She didn't want to see him at all. She just wanted him gone.

Sophie sat across from the man, tight-lipped. Jemma took a place standing next to her, the Bible in plain sight. "Dr. Fielding. I'm Sophie Favreau."

The man's eyes widened. His lips stayed glued shut, and his cheeks bulged as if a flood of words were trapped within.

Sophie frowned. "The silence spell wasn't necessary, Mr. Wiltshire."

"It was for *my* health." Uncle reassembled his gun and put the cleaning kit away. "I can't stomach mealy excuses for poor behavior."

Sophie tipped her chin as she sized Fielding up. "I would normally apologize for your poor treatment, Dr. Fielding, except I noticed my dear cousin's ruined dress. Would I be correct in assuming you had something to do with it?"

Fielding's eyes glazed, and he made a pitiful whine. He glanced toward Hettie. She flashed the gun.

Sophie implored Uncle, "Mr. Wiltshire?"

"Fine." He slit the binding with his knife, and the man collapsed in place.

"Miss Favreau, I am so sorry for the misunderstanding. It was the drink, I tell you. I am no good with spirits, and I overindulged. You must believe me, I did not know she was your—"

"Shut up," Uncle growled. He slammed the lewd figurine onto the table in front of Sophie. She glanced down at it, and two deep red spots of color burned on her cheeks. The scientist shrank back as Uncle got into his face. "A man doesn't juice up and learn *this* influence spell unless he has one aim in mind."

Sophie was quiet a moment as her gaze flattened over the figurine. "Your apologies aren't worth much to any of us, Dr. Fielding. The only thing that might save you from further indignity is your willingness to cooperate." Her tone was so cool, Hettie swore she saw her breath cloud.

Jemma swept the talisman off the table with a handkerchief and tossed it into the fire, wiping her hands as she went.

Fielding nodded enthusiastically. "I'll cooperate. Absolutely. I remember your letter. This is about my work, isn't it?" He licked his lips, and his gaze canted toward Diablo. "Something to do with that mage gun, perhaps?"

"We need to know more about the magic power transfers you used on those coma patients," Hettie said.

He blinked. "What about them?"

Hettie looked to Sophie, then Marcus. They nodded. "Sophie's grandmother has been in a coma for several months now. We need to know whether this procedure could wake her up."

"Your grandmother? The Soothsayer of the South?"

"That would be her."

Fielding took a moment to process this and all the implications. "Without seeing her and doing some tests...I have no idea. But..." His mouth compressed. "She isn't the only soothsayer in a coma, is she?"

Sophie hesitated. "Why do you say that?"

"In my studies over the past several months, more and more soothsayers have been admitted to the long-term coma care ward at the hospital. They were not listed as such, but in my search for ideal candidates for my trials, I had to look into the backgrounds of the patients brought in. There are at least four sorcerers with minor scrying gifts currently at the Kardec Hospital for the Magically Infirm, all of them relatively healthy before the sudden onset of coma. Considering the rarity of the soothsaying gift, I couldn't help but notice."

There are more of us now. Hettie remembered what Patrice had said in their last conversation in the place in between. So the blackout was spreading, affecting the less powerful soothsayers now, not just the most gifted.

"Did you figure out what was wrong with them?" Sophie asked.

"No. I discounted them as candidates for the trials."

The debutante deflated. Fielding raised his hands. "I had to pick less remarkable gifted for the tests, you understand. But that doesn't mean we can't try the engine on a soothsayer."

"I've read a great deal of your work," Sophie said. "One report specifically mentions a patient who woke up during the transfer."

"One out of dozens," Fielding corrected. "Not a statistical sample, and not necessarily a side-effect caused by the procedure.

Frankly, I didn't have time to even study that anomaly. The Division was set on me completing the engine as soon as possible."

"Why is the Division in such a hurry?" Hettie asked.

"Unlike many of my colleagues, I firmly believe in the magic drain, and even though it's not official, the Division does, too. I believe they're looking for a way to store magic—to hoard it and preserve it from further draining. I've been working for years to understand the methods for melding magic with metal. If I'd had a working mage gun to study, I would have had so many greater opportunities." He glanced at Hettie. Diablo's barrel swerved toward him like a snake coiling to strike.

"That ain't a gun you want to get close to, doc," Uncle growled.

"Your engine," Hettie prompted. "The Division asked you to build it?"

"No. It was a theoretical only. I published a paper about it a few years ago, and then a sum of money was gifted to me by an anonymous source to build it."

"Anonymous?" Marcus's brows furrowed. "You never asked where it came from?"

"No. There was only a letter encouraging me to go ahead and test my theory. I'd assumed it was from the Division, but it wasn't. The Division only became directly involved a few months into the work. They loaned me sorcerers and resources I could only dream of. My colleagues were jealous, of course. I don't even have tenure at the university."

Sophie sat forward. "Dr. Fielding, I am going to be blunt. I need to awaken my grandmother. Is there a chance you can help her?"

He shook his head. "I'm not certain. I don't know that I can even replicate the results of that one test. Magic is…peculiar."

Years of research and study and all he had to say about magic was that it was *peculiar*? Hettie growled, her patience wearing thin. "If he's not going to be of any use to us, I say we toss him in the river."

"No, wait!" Fielding's hands fluttered like moths. "As I said, I don't have all the data. Magic is fluid, and its rules are not concrete. Despite my success with the engine, there's still a lot of work to be done—coming up with units of measurement, determining dosages…"

"Is that all you have to offer?" Marcus asked irritably.

Fielding huffed. "No one understands the work that goes into this kind of study. Without a larger pool of test subjects and time to do my work, it's rather difficult to make any headway. The Division gave me access to Kardec's, but what I really wanted was access to the more powerful inmates at Swedenborg." He added, somewhat chagrined, "*Conscious* test subjects."

"They didn't volunteer their own sorcerers?" Sophie asked tightly.

Fielding shook his head. "It was still too early in the trials, and too dangerous. They couldn't risk their own agents. Just getting Mr. Garble to agree to the demonstration was, well, awkward to say the least."

"And why would they volunteer their men? They're trained assets." Uncle prowled along the wall of windows. "Better to use people who won't fight back. That's your M.O., isn't it?" His lip curled in disgust, and Fielding shrank.

"The engine works. We've all seen it," Hettie said to keep the conversation on track. She turned to Fielding. "Can we use it to help Patrice Favreau? Yes or no?"

"Yes. But it could be dangerous," Fielding admitted finally. "My report didn't mention the…failures."

A cold shiver raced along Hettie's spine, and she firmed her grip around Diablo.

"If we don't help Grandmère soon, she may simply pass," Sophie said quietly.

"Perhaps we could test this procedure first on one of the other soothsayers at Kardec?" Marcus suggested.

Sophie shook her head. "We don't have their permission, and I will not jeopardize their lives without their consent."

"Well, that leaves at least one big problem: how are we going to move that monstrous engine to New Orleans?" Marcus asked. "Madame Favreau is too frail to be moved from her bed, and transporting her here in her state would raise too many questions."

Hettie regarded Fielding steadily. "You used this on patients in Kardec's, did you not?"

He winced. "I did…"

"Then you must have had some portable version. You wouldn't have had patients moved here."

The Mechanik looked as though he was unwilling to admit any such thing, but then Uncle shifted his stance and put his hand on the grip of his holstered gun. "It's a prototype only," Fielding blurted. "I mean, of course it works, otherwise I couldn't prove my theories, but it's not in mass production..."

Marcus, Sophie, and Uncle exchanged looks. "Where is it?"

"In my lab at the university. All my notes and findings are there as well."

"Is it being guarded?" Uncle asked.

"Insofar as any of the laboratories are, yes. Though I imagine the Division is likely looking for me by now—I've been gone too long for them not to notice. They'll lock up my equipment and all of my work."

He sounded just a touch too smug for Hettie's liking. Patrice's contract spell burned at the base of her spine now, as if someone had lit a fire beneath her. She loomed over him.

"You'd better hope that's not the case. We're going to need that engine." Hettie's rough voice, full of conviction, seemed to come from a deep, dark hole gaping inside her. She brandished Diablo in an unmistakably menacing way, and Fielding shied back. "And you're going to help us whether you like it or—"

Just then, the door opened. Horace walked in, his clothes smelling of whiskey and cigar smoke. He halted abruptly as he took in the gathering in their finery, surrounding the terrified-looking Mechanik, who looked up at him hopefully.

"Good...evening?" It came out a question. He met Hettie's gaze, saw the gun in her hand. He closed his eyes and stared up at the ceiling. "Seems I've had too much to drink and am hallucinating. I will see myself to bed, thank you very much."

He walked in a perfectly straight line to his room and shut the door soundly.

CHAPTER TEN

The five of them made their way to Fielding's lab at the university the following day. Horace had smartly avoided leaving his room that morning, begging off breakfast and saying he'd be visiting with some business acquaintances. "Plausible deniability," Marcus had murmured, nodding in approval. Jemma simply snorted and rolled her eyes.

The Mechanik was restrained once more by Uncle's talismans, and he marched quickly and quietly through the halls to a door at the end of a long corridor crammed full of desks and chairs. It looked as though most of this wing was being used for storage.

"Not a lot of security around, considering what we saw at the presentation," Marcus noted, glancing about as they navigated the furniture-clogged hall.

"I can feel a faint trace of glamor here," Sophie said. "Just subtle enough to ward off anyone who doesn't need to go this way."

"Some of the best secrets hide in plain sight," Jemma said. "A Division guard would've drawn too much attention to this wing."

They stopped in front of a plain door. A series of runes were carved into it, and Fielding gestured grandly. "Of course, my lab is secure. The locks are all magicked." He waited for the sorcerers in the group to praise him.

"You think *that's* secure?" Uncle scoffed. He banged on the door with a fist and spoke a few words. The lock clicked, and he kicked open the door. "Juice all you like, but you would've been better off investing in a deadbolt."

Hettie had worried that the lack of Division presence meant the engine had been moved, but they were in luck—it appeared everything was intact. Mechanikal parts tooled in brass, copper, gold, and silver were laid out in meticulous patterns over every surface. The chalkboards rimming the perimeter had numbers and figures and runes scribbled on them in something that resembled a protection circle. A pile of blueprints sat in the middle of the table, crumpled pages detailing every part of the engine.

Laid out on one long metal worktable was a glass canister encased in gold filigree about the size of a large watermelon. Upon closer inspection, Hettie realized the latticework was engraved with runes for a protection spell. In fact, all the metal pieces had protection spells carved into them.

"I thought you said this portable engine was complete," Marcus said, indicating the loose pieces arranged around the canister.

"It is, but I was in the process of disassembling it for travel."

Sophie's features were tight. "It's still giving off that…that feeling."

"I haven't discovered the source of the…well, *void* is the only term I've been able to come up with. It seems to affect higher-level sorcerers more acutely than lower ones."

Hettie sensed Diablo shying away from the canister like a cat pressing itself into a corner. She summoned the mage gun just to be safe, and it came, albcit reluctantly. She hastily shoved it back into her pocket.

Hettie caught sight of a shadow moving quickly past the window. Diablo flashed a warning in her mind, and her future vision exploded in light. "Get down!" she screamed.

The here and now snapped back to her. Glass shattered as something was hurled through the window. Uncle shouted an incantation and pointed at the brick that had landed on the floor at their feet. A lit bundle of dynamite had been strapped to it.

Hettie grabbed the brick and lobbed it back outside with all her might. The moment it left her hand, she dropped into her time bubble—

The brick had barely made it outside before the blast blossomed out in a sphere of fire and force. From her time bubble, she watched the window panes spiderweb and bow inward, fracturing into tiny, deadly shards of glittering death as the shock wave rolled over them.

Marcus and Jemma were already tackling Sophie to the ground, and Uncle was in the throes of casting some kind of barrier spell. Fielding stood there gaping, fully exposed. With a growl, she hauled him down behind one of the worktables, slamming him onto the floor with unnecessary force.

Fielding gasped as he was pulled through the syrup into her time. "Wha—"

"Cover your head!" Hettie's grip on the bubble slipped. The concussive force of the explosion jarred her bones and teeth. Glass shards rained down over her back.

"Everyone okay?" Marcus's voice was dampened in her ringing ears.

"Fine." Uncle staggered up from his spot. A perfect ring of debris surrounded him.

"Hettie?"

"Fielding's with me." She heard the shouts then—a familiar chanting that grew clearer as her hearing returned.

"Sorcery is sin! Sorcery is sin!"

"Tarnation," Uncle grumped. "What do those lunatics think they're doing?"

"I've been threatened before," Fielding said, his voice trembling. "It was partly why the Division dispatched their men in the first place. But this...this violence is new."

Hettie glanced over at the engine—it looked intact. "We better collect your things and get out of here." She went to the window and glanced out. The protesters were scattering—now that they'd made their point, they had no desire to wait for the authorities to arrive.

"So much for civilized society," Hettie muttered, and looked to Sophie. "Are you all right?" There was a small cut on Sophie's cheek.

"Nothing a healer can't fix. Idiots, all of them. They could have killed us!" Sophie huffed.

"I don't think they knew we were in here," Hettie said.

"I don't think they cared," Jemma retorted.

Back at the hotel, preparations were made to depart for New Orleans.

As expected, the attack on Fielding's lab at the university made headlines, but interestingly, news of the Mechanik's disappearance was not mentioned.

"It's the Division's doing," Uncle said. "They don't want anyone knowing they've lost track of one of their assets. Can't have people thinking they're not as all-powerful as some folks believe."

"So his handlers know he's missing?"

"Definitely." He glanced over at the scientist, who was immersed in inspecting the portable engine's components. For all that he'd been kidnapped and forced into this situation, he was quite biddable and content as long as he was working. "Marcus and I have already checked him for any sign he's being Eyed. No one's got a bead on him, though, which makes me wonder why the Division didn't load him with tracking charms."

"They interfered with the spells in my engine," Fielding replied without looking up. Evidently he could hear them from across the room. "I was strict about what kinds of spells and enchanted items they brought into the lab. I have to keep a magically sterile environment."

Uncle seemed to take the man at his word, but Hettie did not trust Fielding. She suspected he was biding his time, maybe even looking for some way to sabotage their efforts.

When she mentioned her doubts to Jeremiah, though, he dismissed her as being overly suspicious, which was saying something considering his usual paranoia. Fielding's borrowed magic had expired some time ago, apparently—Uncle had sensed it leave him, which told them the transference of magic using the engine had a limit, the same way juicing between sorcerers did.

Magical transference usually only happened as a compact between people, with a set time limit on the powers they passed on. Apparently the engine had not been designed to do this. Fielding explained that without the ability to measure or quantify magic, they couldn't say how long any transference would last.

All that said, Hettie knew the Mechanik might still be looking for a way to escape. If he reassembled the engine successfully, he might use it to juice himself. Or maybe he'd make a weapon with what he had. In any case, she would remain vigilant. They needed him—but only as long as he wasn't a threat...and up to the point he proved useful.

As they packed their things and prepared for the journey, Sophie asked, "Has anyone seen or heard from Mr. Washington?"

"Not since yesterday morning," Marcus said. "Perhaps he's still trying to track his lawyer down?"

Hettie frowned. They'd been so busy, she'd hadn't had a chance to ask him about his mission to rebuild his business. He'd been out and about reconnecting with clients and partners, but he hadn't mentioned anything about reestablishing any part of his former enterprise. "I better track him down," she said. "He needs to know we're heading back south tomorrow."

"I say leave him here. He's right where he needs to be," Jemma said.

Sophie regarded her companion thoughtfully. "Jemma, I think you should go with Hettie."

"What?"

"You heard me. Go with Hettie and help her find Mr. Washington."

"I'm far too busy here, Miss Sophie. I have to pack—"

"I can do the packing myself. Hettie can't go off alone, and I'd like Marcus and Mr. Bassett near to watch Dr. Fielding. Besides, you said you've always wanted to see Chicago. This is your chance before we return to New Orleans."

Jemma glowered mutinously at her mistress but then dipped her head and followed Hettie out.

"She'll be fine with Marcus in the hotel," Hettie reassured her.

"I'm not worried about her safety. I know she'll be all right." She exhaled sharply. "But Horace is bound to be in trouble."

"What makes you say that?"

"I've met the likes of him. He can talk you three ways to Sunday, and he's very good at making you believe whatever he wants." She shook her head. "He's got the devil's silver tongue."

"You don't like him."

"I don't *trust* him. I just have a feeling."

Hettie and Walker had also questioned Horace's story when he'd first emerged after the curse on him had been broken, but the hostler had been a kind, thoughtful, and charming traveling companion, and Hettie hadn't thought anything more about it. He'd worked hard in the stables in Yuma, and he'd been nothing but gracious. His claim that he had a large and thriving horse trading business still seemed incredible, but so what if it was an embellishment? He was obviously talented and smart and lucky enough to succeed in whatever he chose to do. She couldn't fault him for that.

They tried Horace's lawyer's office first to see if the two had connected. It took quite a few inquiries to find a lawyer named Mr. Taylor—fortunately, only one had a law office across the Chicago river. Hettie had remembered that much from her last conversation with Horace.

The offices of Taylor, Brownstein, and Associates occupied the fourth floor of a newer building. As they climbed the polished stairs, Jemma reminded Hettie that Sophie's glamor spell might not extend this far, even with the talisman, and that she needed to be cautious about showing her remarkable scar. It was why she'd made her wear a hat with a black veil—something a woman in mourning might wear. "Men don't want to see tears," Jemma explained. "No one will want to look too closely at your face with this on."

They needed some pretense to see Mr. Taylor, so they told the secretary, whose shiny nameplate read *Priscilla*, that Hettie wanted someone to look at her late husband's will.

Mr. Taylor welcomed her in warmly, ignoring Jemma as she took an unobtrusive seat by the window. He was a well-fed man in a sharp suit, a thick gold pocket watch chain dangling across his girth like a decorative streamer. "I'm sorry to hear about your loss," he said, though his eyes gleamed with speculation. Hettie noticed him trying to see through the veil, as if he suspected something was amiss.

"I thank you for your condolences, but I am not so sad. He was a brute of a man. I hope he rots in hell."

That threw the lawyer off. He sputtered his apologies and straightened.

"Of course, we will do everything we can to see that you and any family members are properly taken care of. Do you have children?"

"Fortunately, no. My husband was fond of women with looser morals. I don't think we shared a bed beyond our wedding night."

Mr. Taylor cleared his throat. She enjoyed making him uncomfortable—something about him rubbed her the wrong way. She decided it was the glint in his eye that told her he'd already made up his mind about her life and her husband. He wasn't sympathetic to her plight—he wanted her business and to secure himself a tidy fee for his services. Maybe even skim a little off the top.

She scanned his office, nodding toward a framed photograph on his desk. "Your family?"

Mr. Taylor was all too happy to get off the uncomfortable subject of her miserable life and on to his loving wife of seventeen years and three children. Hettie remembered what Horace had said about the man's mistress in Boston.

"I imagine your work doesn't allow you much time together," she said. "Do you travel often?"

"I used to. I decided to stay at home more. To be with the family."

"That's unfortunate. For your business, I mean." She met his eye. "Tell me, have you ever been to Boston?"

Mr. Taylor's expression froze. "I've been all over. I believe I've been to Boston once or twice."

"Really? Because a friend of mine told me you're there quite frequently."

Mr. Taylor's eyes narrowed fractionally, and his fixed smile became a baring of teeth. "What friend would that be?"

"You may have seen him recently. In fact, I'm certain you have." She sensed Jemma slipping out of her seat and locking the office door. "Can you tell me where Mr. Horace Washington is?"

The lawyer's smile dropped. "I don't know who you're talking about."

"Horace Washington. You handled his legal affairs through his recently deceased business partner, a Mr. Jacobi. From my understanding, Horace has been trying to contact you, but you haven't responded. He came here with me to clear up those business matters, but he's since gone missing."

The lawyer's face darkened. "See here, who are you?"

"I'm the woman asking you where her friend is and why you haven't been returning his calls."

"Get out." He stood abruptly and shouted, "Priscilla!"

Hettie closed her eyes and slipped into her time bubble, smooth as butter. Getting thrown out now would not help them find Horace, nor would waving a gun in the lawyer's face. She needed a moment to think things through.

She walked around the office, studying the surroundings. A drawer in the filing cabinet in the corner was cracked open. Considering the nearly pristine condition of everything else in this office, it looked as though something had been hastily stuffed back inside. Carefully, she took it into her time bubble and riffled through its contents.

Her instincts were right. One of the files within, marked *Washington, Horace*, had recently been taken out. It was a fat file filled with invoices and contracts, letters and more. A quick perusal told Hettie the hostler had indeed had quite a successful business venture. He hadn't been lying.

The most recent letters informed the law office of the demise of Mr. Tobias Jacobi, a bachelor who'd died of a heart attack two years ago. With no word from Horace or any of his next of kin, all the business assets were turned over to Mr. Taylor.

Hettie studied the papers. The lawyer could have easily forged the documents that had bequeathed him Horace's business earnings. Looking at Jacobi's signature, she was certain it'd been forged, though a judge might not look twice. If he'd done this to Horace, how many others had he swindled?

Going through all his files would take forever. Even with the time bubble, she wasn't about to waste hours digging up evidence of wrongdoing. She wasn't a lawyer or a lawman, and she didn't think she could beat Mr. Taylor at his own game. No, if she was going to find out what had happened to Horace, she needed leverage.

Horace had said to look for clues, to study behavior. She looked at the prominently displayed family photo, noticed how plain and unadorned his barely smiling wife was.

Meanwhile the young and pretty secretary, Priscilla, wore a diamond bracelet and necklace at work, though she had no wedding ring and no pictures of rich beaus displayed on her desk. Hettie hardly thought she could afford those baubles on a secretary's salary. Now that Mr. Taylor was deskbound, his philandering could have become more local.

She opened the file and put it on the desk in front of Mr. Taylor. Then, to keep him from shouting out, she stuffed a handkerchief in his mouth. It was delicate work—she didn't want him in her time bubble. She wanted the effect to be sudden and shocking.

It worked. With the last poke of the handkerchief into the lawyer's gaping maw, she slipped back into regular time, and the lawyer gagged. Hettie slapped her hands over his wrists and pinned him to the desk. "I need you to be very quiet for a moment, Mr. Taylor. You see, I know you stole Mr. Washington's assets." His eyes bulged as he stared at the forged papers under his nose. "I also know that Priscilla out there doesn't just make you coffee and file your papers. Does your wife know you moved her out here from Boston?"

He stopped struggling, eyes wide. She smirked as his silence confirmed her bluff. "I see we're on even terms now. Just tell us what we want to know and we'll be on our way." She released his hands, and he pulled the wadded handkerchief out.

"That *boy* came here yesterday," he spat. "You can't just show up after eight years missing and expect the world to have gone on hold." The lawyer sneered. "The law is on my side with this one. Seven years and he's declared dead in absentia. I did nothing wrong."

"Right and wrong in whose eyes? Perhaps I should consult Mrs. Taylor about that. Does she know about Priscilla?"

The lawyer's lips curled.

"Where is Horace?" she asked in a low voice.

"I called the authorities on him. He was harassing me. Causing a stir and disturbing my staff and clients. They took him to jail, I imagine."

"You had him hauled off?" Fury tingled over her skin, and Diablo's shadow grazed her palm.

"I didn't press charges. I simply wanted to make him rethink his place. We can't have those people thinking they can live and work among civilized businessmen." His eyes flicked behind her to Jemma. "All of them should go back to the fields where they belong."

Diablo popped into her hand, doubling in weight, and Hettie quelled the urge to set the man's office on fire. Even flashing the mage gun here could get her into more trouble than she'd bargained for.

"My kind," Jemma said, "don't steal their clients' money and call themselves 'civilized businessmen.'"

Hettie stood stiffly. "When Horace comes here next, you will return what is his and treat him with due respect. I imagine that is what Mrs. Taylor would want as well."

"You think you can make me do anything? You little witch. I'll have you all arrested for harassment!"

Hettie sighed and slipped back into the time bubble. She gathered Horace's file and touched Jemma's hand. The bodyguard exhaled sharply and looked all around her.

"I'm sorry, Jemma."

"Sorry for what? Him?" She snorted. "He is what he is. I don't give him my time. Besides, this is Horace's business. He should've known better than to deal with the likes of this one, even through a proxy."

They left the still, silent building in the time bubble with the satisfaction of knowing they'd disappeared before Mr. Taylor's eyes like ghosts.

As they made their way out, Hettie decided she'd send a letter and Horace's file to the district attorney and the media.

She'd send a separate letter to Mrs. Taylor.

CHAPTER ELEVEN

They found Horace at the local police station. He'd been jailed for "causing a public disturbance," but since Mr. Taylor hadn't actually laid any charges, there was no reason to keep him.

And yet they had.

Hettie sent Jemma to get a lawyer and bail money. In due course, Jemma returned with Sophie and a stout-looking lawyer who shouted at the desk sergeant at a volume consistent with his pay grade, demanding the release of his client. A few minutes later, Horace was escorted into the main reception area.

His lip was swollen, and there were fresh bruises on his arms and shoulders. His fine shirt had been bloodied and torn as well.

Hettie clenched her teeth and fists to keep Diablo from jumping into her hand. "Who did this to you?" she hissed.

"Same folks that always do these things," Horace muttered.

"This is unacceptable." Sophie glared around, as if seeking his assailants among the patrolmen watching them. Loudly, she asked, "Mr. Washington, would you like to file a formal complaint?"

Horace's chin lifted in surprise, and his eyes danced. "If you will support me in this, Miss Sophie, then I will."

She bent and said something to the lawyer, who nodded sharply like a soldier taking orders. He addressed the desk sergeant using the most grandiose legal jargon Hettie had ever heard, in a tone that made clear the hell the Favreau family would rain upon the heads of whoever had harmed his client.

Horace crossed his arms and stood solemnly by, looking neither smug nor content. Sophie's murderous, unblinking stare bored through the increasingly uncomfortable man in uniform. Her glamor magic writhed around her, making her seem bigger. Angrier. As if she cast a much bigger shadow than she did. Or maybe that was just Sophie.

Eventually, a different man, in a suit rather than a uniform, led Horace, Sophie, the lawyer, and Jemma into an office, where they could make their grievances known and file the requisite paperwork. Hettie had no great desire to be trapped in that stuffy room with the others, so she waited in the foyer, watching the various colorful characters being marched in and out of the precinct. No one gave the veiled widow a second look. At the other end of the room, she noticed the bulletin board where an officer was putting up a new wanted poster.

Hettie drew closer, and her vision wobbled. The woman in the picture had a scar up the right side of her face. It read:

> WANTED: Hettie Alabama, For The Crimes Of Murder, Robbery, Vandalism, And Sundry Crimes Across The States Of Texas, Montana, Arizona, Massachusetts, Kansas, and Wyoming. Reward: $500.

"I wouldn't worry your pretty little head about that Alabama gang." The young patrolman who'd put the poster up smiled winsomely. "I'm Officer Pendleton. Peter, that is. I noticed you waiting for your friends. I can see it's been a long day for you. Would you like a cup of tea? I can fix one up for you."

She was about to decline, but she realized she did need a cup of tea. She was drained from the confrontation with Mr. Taylor, and it was nice to see a smiling face, even through the veil. Besides, she could find out more about the Alabama gang. "Thank you, officer. I'd appreciate it."

She followed Pendleton to a small table, where he poured her a lukewarm cup from a stained teapot. She nodded toward the wanted poster. "That crime spree is pretty widespread."

"Rumor is they're using remote Zooms to get everywhere."

That sounded far too much like the Crowe gang for Hettie's comfort.

"It's nothing to fret over, Miss...?" He waited.

"Henrietta Wiltshire." It seemed he was assuming her mourning garb was not for a late husband. "Tell me...how likely are the authorities to catch this gang?"

"Better odds, I think, than a week ago. I single-handedly arrested a couple of the Alabama gang's high-ranking members a few days ago. They're sitting in one of our jail cells right now." He puffed out his chest.

Hettie straightened. She needed to interview those men, find out more about this other Hettie. But even with her time bubble she wouldn't be able to unlock all the doors and gates to the jail. She eyed the young officer, put on an expression of awe, and gazed up at him. "You must have been so brave!" It came out as a squeal, and she winced. *Tone it down*, she told herself harshly.

"Just doing my duty," he said. "Not that they're not dangerous criminals. Duke Cox robbed the First Dominion Bank in Yellow Springs, Texas. The other one's Jonas Lafayette, a no-good half-breed pickpocket. I caught them together red-handed, all on my own."

"Really?" She pressed closer, pursing her lips. She wasn't sure she was doing it right—she was certain she looked more like a duck. Would he even see it through the veil?

"They were robbing a sorcerers' salon while I was on patrol. I stopped 'em, though. Cuffed them to each other with my manacles and pinned them to the ground together like a flapjack folded over." He laughed.

Something seemed off about his story, but she decided he was simply exaggerating to impress her. "How'd you know they're with the Alabama gang?"

"Well, at first I didn't. But we found some strange talismans on them. Our sorcerers haven't quite figured out what they are yet, but a sheriff in Texas found another like it at one of the places the Alabama gang robbed."

Talismans carried around by gang members could be for anything, from amulets that let them past barrier spells into their hideouts to simple sigils to let others know who your posse included and what a bad idea it'd be to mess with you.

"I've never seen an outlaw before," Hettie said tentatively. Awkwardly, she put a hand on his arm. "I don't suppose you could let me have a peek?"

He laughed. "They're just men, and rough ones at that. You won't want to see them. Anyhow, the jail's strictly off-limits."

"Oh, but surely a fine officer like you could...ah..." She faltered. "Show me the forbidden?"

Ugh. She sounded crass to her own ears, and Pendleton, bless the man, looked a little embarrassed by her innuendo.

He chuckled nervously. "We've just met, Miss Wiltshire. How do I know *you're* not an outlaw looking to break them out?"

She laughed a little too loudly. "I guess I've read too many dime novels. I'd love to do what you do...solving crimes and such."

"Well, I hear that the Pinkerton Agency has a few female agents. You could always look into joining them."

"Oh, but I'd need to be a sorcerer to qualify, wouldn't I?"

"The gift isn't what makes a good detective. The Pinks scoop the best Division Academy graduates, true, but they have plenty of mundanes in their ranks. Allan and Robert Pinkerton are both mundanes, after all."

"Even so, I'd need to demonstrate my abilities." She made a show at thinking. "Perhaps I could have a look at those talismans?"

He quirked an eyebrow. An innocent young lady in the Favreaus' company wouldn't have such peculiar interests. "I have an uncle who specializes in talismanic curiosities," she explained quickly. "Maybe if I had a look and wrote him a letter, he could help you." She fluttered her lashes, but ended up getting an eyelash in her eye instead.

His smile returned. "Sorry, but they're in the property room. They're not just available to anyone who wants to see them. Besides, I don't think Oliver would open the box even if I asked politely."

If she couldn't interrogate the suspects, she could at least see those talismans. "Could you point me in the direction of the ladies' facilities?"

He did. The moment the door swung shut, Hettie inhaled, slipped into her time bubble, and made her way carefully through the crowded station in search of the property room. She edged around broad-shouldered men in uniform who would not likely be as easy to manipulate if they were to accidentally slip into her time bubble. It was delicate work.

In due course, she found the room. Fortunately a man was just on his way out, leaving the door open behind him. She ducked in.

The metal boxes labeled *Duke Cox* and *Jonas Lafayette* contained a well-used sidearm, a few dollar bills and coins, and random bits and pieces extracted from their pockets. She rifled through the boxes until she found two small matching knobs of whitish bone with several notches scored on their faces. She pocketed one of the talismans, put the boxes back, left the property room, and returned to the ladies' room. She dropped the time bubble and after a couple of minutes rejoined Officer Pendleton. He was none the wiser.

He escorted her back to the lobby. "I hope to see you again, Miss Wiltshire," he said. "But perhaps not in these surroundings?"

She doubted she'd return here unless it was in manacles. Just then, Sophie, Jemma, and Horace exited the office. Sophie raised an eyebrow as she approached. "Henrietta, dear, what are you doing?"

"Just talking with the nice officer." She bobbed a quick, awkward curtsey to Officer Pendleton, who grinned as he tipped his hat. Jemma's scowl seared her.

"Are you crazy, talking to a policeman?" she hissed as they left the precinct. "What if he recognized you?"

"He didn't." She waited till they were piled into the carriage and headed back to the hotel to tell them what she'd learned about the Alabama gang. She showed Sophie the bit of bone. "What do you think it is?"

Jemma slapped it out of her hand, and it clattered to the floor of the carriage. "Are you crazy? Stealing strange talismans from the police station? You don't even know what it is or what it does. You can't just hold random pieces of magic like that."

"It's all right, Jemma," Sophie said." I would've sensed if it was dangerous before this."

Hettie picked up the knob of bone and held it out for Sophie's inspection. "I can't identify the spell on this," Sophie said. "Perhaps it's imbued with locator spells so all the gang members can find each other. Best not to take any chances in case it is being tracked."

She removed a little leather pouch from her reticule, and Hettie dropped it in. Sophie wrapped a piece of twine around the bag, muttering a spell to seal the magic in, then handed the bundle to Hettie. "Perhaps Marcus or Mr. Bassett will know what it's for. But right now, the Alabama gang will have to wait. We must focus on getting Dr. Fielding and the engine back to New Orleans."

Hettie sighed inwardly. Of course Sophie's first concern was for her grandmother. Strictly speaking she didn't need Hettie's help—in fact, Hettie was becoming more and more of a liability with this Alabama gang crime spree.

Horace piped up then. "I am very sorry for this inconvenience, Miss Favreau. I promise I'll pay you back for the bail money and the lawyer."

"You have nothing to apologize for, Mr. Washington. You were wrongfully detained." Her features softened. "I am sorry to hear about the loss of your business. My lawyer is at your disposal if you wish to pursue your case in court."

He shook his head. "Thank you, but I'm afraid there's little I can do. Mr. Taylor's probably left me nothing worth reclaiming."

"We can still punish him," Hettie said. "The law will have something to say about his fraud."

"I'm afraid the courts won't favor my side. I have no way to verify my identity or account for my long absence without revealing what was done to me. And you know how some people are about Weres." He flicked a look toward Jemma. "In the end, it's a white man's word against mine. I don't like those odds."

"What about all those meetings you've been having?" Hettie asked. "I thought you said you were seeing old business contacts."

He shook his head. "Unfortunately, I haven't had as much success as I may have let on. The few who did agree to meet with me just don't have a need for my services. Not as many folks are shipping goods by horse anymore. And without actual horses..." He shrugged. "I don't have capital. I don't have stock. I don't have customers. I don't have anything."

Sophie frowned. "A man with your talents can surely rebuild?"

"With God's good grace, perhaps. But the world has changed a lot in eight years." He stared out the window, forlorn. "I'm not sure where my place will be in it."

Ling's inquiries into Brother Wu's disappearance were at a dead end. Literally.

The alley where Ah-Gu's brother and his son had last been seen showed no traces of magic or resistance. Not surprising, since it had been eight months since they'd supposedly died. Ling had asked the people living in the area about whether they'd seen anything, but few were willing to speak to him.

He'd discreetly interviewed everyone at On Fook who'd been with Brother Wu before he and his son, Ah-Keung, had been arrested. So far all Ling had been able to determine was that Brother Shang hadn't been present. One way or another, it wasn't concrete evidence of betrayal as Ah-Gu had suggested.

Paying off the debt to On Fook—or more accurately, to Shang—had turned out to be an opportunity to inveigle himself back into the organization. Ling could not take Ah-Gu's money—it would be too suspicious if he paid the debt so quickly. Instead he'd gone back to On Fook, begging Shang on his knees to let him work it off.

Grovelling had been the key. Shang's eyes had shone with triumph, as if he'd felled some great foe with his own cunning. His ego stroked, Shang had decided having a healer on his staff was useful.

Working for Shang at On Fook was tedious and sometimes demeaning, but it gave Ling access to the staff. Some were suspicious of his healing magic—even among his people, "ether magic" was considered dangerous and not to be trusted. Many preferred the traditional medicines and treatments offered by locals. There were some cases, however, where Shang would not tolerate long periods of convalescence, and some of his staff were forced to submit to Ling's tender magical care.

One day Shang stormed in, cursing at Big Monkey for his carelessness and Ah Chang for his slow reaction.

"I could have been killed!" Spittle flew from Shang's mouth. His complexion was dark and mottled, though his lips had been leached of color. The tong leader gripped his hand, gritting his teeth.

Ling hurried over. "What happened?" He looked at the two grim-faced hatchet men, who lowered their heads.

"You, nursemaid. Fix this." He thrust his hand out. "These two idiots didn't see that mangy dog in the alley, and they let him bite me!"

"I told you kicking him wasn't—" But then Big Monkey clamped his mouth shut. Shang glared at him.

"Let me see." Ling inspected the wound. He stifled an eye roll when he saw the light abrasion the dog had left. Best to salve the man's injury and ego. "Let me get some ointment."

"Are you kidding? I need more than ointment!" Shang shouted. "Use your magic."

"I will, of course. But this will numb the pain a bit." Ling rifled through his medicine bag. It'd be a waste of magic and ointment, but he didn't dare give Shang a reason to suspect him of treachery.

"I hate dogs," Shang muttered. "Filthy, flea-ridden disease carriers. Did I tell you about the mutt that bit me when I was five?"

"Several times," Ah Chang deadpanned.

Shang launched into the story again anyhow. The dog in his story seemed to get more ferocious with each retelling. Ling tuned out as he went about his duties.

The one good thing about working at the tong was that he'd been able to quit his dishwashing job. And Ah-Gu had put him and Abby up in the back of the herbalist shop so they wouldn't have to pay rent. It was safer there, she'd insisted, and Ling had to agree. The matron kept a tidy home free of fleas, and the powerful wards on the door kept prying eyes away.

Li Fa, the girl who'd brought Ling to Ah-Gu, often came to clean the apartment and sometimes helped prepare meals. Every time Li Fa came, Ling couldn't help but flinch. She reminded him so much of…

He pushed away those thoughts. There was no use dwelling on the past.

He slipped into the shop late one evening, weary and sore after a healing session with a brute of a man Ling suspected had been fighting with one of the other tong members. He was surprised to find Ah-Gu sitting with Abby on a grass mat in the inner apartment. Ah-Gu sat ramrod straight, a long cane resting across her lap. Abby mirrored her serene pose, but when her chin drooped, Ah-

Gu whipped the cane over Abby's knee lightning quick. The girl whimpered, and Ling felt the air compress.

"What are you doing?" He advanced on the pair, horrified, bracing himself for a tantrum from Abby. Tears rimmed her lashes, but she stiffened her lips and straightened, settling back with only the most restrained of sobs.

"Shh. Li Ling, don't interrupt," Ah-Gu murmured.

"It's way past her bedtime. She shouldn't be awake at this— ow!"

The cane bit into his thigh, and he hopped backward. Ah-Gu resettled. "I said *shh*. We're almost done here."

Ling hobbled away. That switch would leave a mark.

The candle between the two sitting figures sputtered and went out in a smudge of greasy smoke. Ah-Gu exhaled. "Very good, Abby. You may rest now."

Abby toppled over with a quiet moan.

"How long have you been at this?" Ling hurried to the little girl's side, fearing for her health, but Abby was already deeply asleep.

"Only since after dinner." She glanced at the clock on the mantel. "Six hours. Barely any time."

"Six hours!" Ling quickly poured a glass of water from a carafe on a side table and brought it to Abby, but before he could give it to her, Ah-Gu swiped it out of his hand and drank. "She's only a child. She can't do activities like this."

"Six hours of meditation is nothing. The masters who taught me would make us meditate for three days at a time. We learned discipline and serenity, patience and denial of the body's needs. Six hours is nothing."

"Abby's different," Ling insisted. "She can't sit like this for such long periods."

"She can, and she did." She nodded at Abby. "It took some work to get her up to six hours. Eventually I'll get her to twelve, then twenty-four."

"No." He slashed the air with his hand. "I forbid it."

Ah-Gu eyed him condescendingly. "You wanted a teacher. You wanted someone to get her powers under control. Tell me, do you see any evidence that she has lost control? That any of her powers have leaked whatsoever?"

Ling firmed his jaw. He opened his third eye to see whether the indigo miasma that wafted around Abby when she was distressed or using her abilities permeated the room. Except for the faintest cloud around her, there was none.

Even so, seeing the dark shadows beneath Abby's eyes and the long red welts on her wrists made his fists clench.

Auntie Wu cut down his building anger with a look that could have felled a tree. "If you'd taken her to the Division as you'd originally planned, she would be enduring far worse than this," she reminded him, her words biting with the teeth of a bandsaw. "Would you rather *they* teach her?"

Ling stiffened. He'd once deluded himself into believing Abby would be taken care of and saved from a short, torturous life of being unable to control her indigo powers. But it'd been a selfish belief. His fear of Abby's powers had made him think he could and should subject her to the Division's cruel brand of training and discipline, all in the name of "what was best." Hettie would've been right to shoot him dead for that treachery. He lived every day now to atone for that nearly fatal betrayal.

Ah-Gu softened. "Coddling her will not achieve anything," she said. "I know you care for her. She's intelligent, thoughtful, and kind for someone who has endured as much as she has. She has compassion and empathy that would rival Kuan Yin's. But if she is to master her powers, she must endure some hardships. And it will hurt as one builds muscle to lift a great stone." Grimly, quietly, she vowed, "I will not make the same mistakes the masters did. She is progressing at what I deem to be an acceptable pace. Tell me"—she switched topics the way she changed slippers, sliding into the next effortlessly—"what news do you have on the search for my brother and nephew?"

Ling relented. The conversation about Abby was over. "None, I'm afraid. I've asked around, but no one has any information."

Ah-Gu snorted. "That they're willing to share, at any rate. I should go to the tong myself and beat the truth out of Shang."

"Please, don't," Ling implored. "I have his trust for the moment. I think I do, anyhow. I would make better headway with my own inquiries."

She sighed. "Li Fa tells me he's squandered much of On Fook's funds on gambling and girls. If he continues this way, I will have to intervene." She nodded toward Abby. "Put her to bed. She's earned her rest."

Ling picked up Abby—not so little anymore, he realized, staggering—and carried her to her pallet bed. As he drew the blankets over her, her eyes snapped open, the pupils huge and black.

"He's looking for us."

Ling's skin broke out in goose bumps. Her eyes closed once more, and she subsided into a light snore.

"What was that?" Ah-Gu stood just behind him, holding a silk coverlet.

"I…I'm not sure." He watched as she bent to Abby's side, dropping the embroidered coverlet over her, gently tucking her in. She placed her papery palm over the girl's forehead and closed her eyes briefly, probing her mind.

She frowned. "Something is trying to speak through her."

Ling flinched. Not someone. Some*thing*. "A spirit?" He thought of Ah-Dong's ghost.

"I'm not sure. I'm only getting…impressions. Not dead…but not alive either." She tilted her head, and her brow furrowed. "It's gone."

Hettie had told him her sister sometimes had visions and could speak to people over great distances. It was how the warlock Zavi had found her.

While Ah-Gu brewed a strong-smelling pot of tea, he told her about the fallen angel pulled down from heaven to be Diablo's wielder and how he'd kidnapped Abby. Her frown deepened as Ling related Hettie's certainty Zavi was still alive.

"If it is as you say, then this Zavi is more powerful than we can imagine. The wards on this building should keep all forms of interpolation magic out."

"He is a divine being," Ling warned.

"Divine, perhaps, but from which realm? There are many more places than heaven and hell, many more worlds than this one. There's no telling from where this Zavi comes, how his magic works, or what his intentions are. If he has any." She shook her head. "Some spirits are only here to cause trouble for the inhabitants of this realm. Others are trapped here, bound by the sins of their former lives. Perhaps all he needs is appeasement or absolution to send him on his way."

"I don't think Zavi is a spirit or a ghost. From what Hettie told me, he's flesh and blood, immortal, and very dangerous. As for what he wants…"

Ah-Gu frowned in concern, and they both glanced toward the sleeping girl.

"We will have to watch Abby for any further signs of influence or manipulation," she said. "Meanwhile, help me strengthen the wards. I do not want this Zavi near her."

CHAPTER TWELVE

r. Fielding's engine was not working. Upon their return to the New Orleans Favreau mansion, they'd reassembled the device, meticulously placing every piece back where it belonged. But the portable engine refused to run.

Four days of tinkering, disassembling, and reassembling the device made Hettie nervous, mostly because there was nothing she could do to help. With little else to keep her occupied, she was forced to train almost constantly with Jemma.

"Firm your stance!" the bodyguard shouted yet again. "You cannot hold your ground until you root yourself."

"How am I supposed to stay light on my feet if you keep telling me to firm my stance?" Hettie shouted back in frustration.

Her back talk earned a punch in the face, which Hettie only just managed to snap away from enough to soften the blow. She fell back and rolled out of Jemma's reach.

"Afraid I'll hurt you now, aren't you?" Jemma smirked. "Can't take it anymore, can you?"

Hettie was fed up with the bodyguard's pointless, painful lessons. She charged—

Jemma kicked her feet out from under her, grabbed her by the waist, and slammed her down on the mats. She sat on her chest and peered down at her.

"If a few words are all it takes to make you lose your temper," she said softly, "imagine what they'll do in the fight of your life."

Hettie exhaled. She knew Jemma was right. It didn't stop her from feeling helpless and frustrated.

Jemma helped her up off the mat. "No more today. You're improving."

She blinked. A word of encouragement was not what she'd expected. "I did terribly."

"You rolled away when I hit you," Jemma said. "You have always been too sure of yourself, too stubborn to admit your own weaknesses, too willing to absorb a blow. You think strength is being able to take a hit and endure, but you're wrong. Strength is acknowledging your weaknesses and walking away to fight another day. That is a lesson I did not think you'd ever learn."

Hettie rubbed her cheek. "I don't think I've learned it yet."

"You will."

Given the reprieve, she decided to clean up and check in with Sophie. The debutante spent a lot of time at Patrice's bedside, reading to her, talking with her. As Hettie knocked on the bedroom door, Sophie looked up and gave a tentative smile.

"No change," she said in response to the unasked question. She laid a hand over her grandmother's. The matron looked painfully thin, Hettie thought grimly.

"Have you heard back from any of the other soothsayers?"

She nodded. "There's no denying it now. Almost a third of Grandmère's associates in the soothsaying community have fallen into comas. Those who are still working have seen dramatic increases in business, but their work is not as reliable…and they cannot hide what the other soothsayers are going through forever. Some have even stopped scrying altogether—they're afraid the comas are being brought on by the work." Sophie rubbed her forehead. "Soon the news will hit the papers, and chaos will ensue. The blackout is already affecting the market. All the surefire investments people were putting their money into have shrunk. If we don't do something soon, the entire economy will collapse."

Hettie wasn't sure that was a bad thing. Only the rich could afford accurate soothsayers' predictions, making the rich richer. Without soothsaying the playing field would be leveled. But she didn't say that out loud. "Maybe it won't be too bad. People have been coping with the magic drain for years."

The look Sophie shot her told Hettie she'd clearly said the wrong thing. "Obviously you don't understand. You aren't on the brink of losing everything."

Hettie chewed on the inside of her cheek. Sophie seemed to realize what she'd said and exhaled sharply. "I'm sorry. That was uncalled for. You've lost more than I could imagine."

"Any progress on the engine?" Hettie asked coolly instead of forgiving her.

"Dr. Fielding thinks the explosion must have damaged some of the parts. He went into town with your uncle and Horace to have them retooled."

"Is that a good idea? He's still technically our prisoner," Hettie pointed out.

"I'm not sure he realizes it. He's completely immersed in his work, and he has everything he needs here, plus no distractions. For some people, this would be paradise."

"I doubt the Division will see it that way. People'll miss him."

Sophie waved off her concerns. "There's no reason to look at us as suspects in his disappearance. No one knows I had anything more than a trifling interest in Fielding, and no one saw him at the Mechaniks' ball, so I doubt they could trace him back here. The Division won't be able to track him here either, and they have no reason to suspect my family's involvement."

"What about the army?" Sophie had mentioned that the officer in charge of the raid on Sonoma station, Captain Bradley, had visited the Favreau household in Yuma to interview Sophie after Hettie's escape.

"If they had any evidence, they would have come by now. Marcus has headed off any inquiries. We're safe here. The grounds are spelled against the Eye, interpolation, and remote Zooms, and there are wards all around the house and the perimeter, not to mention our security team. Nothing short of an army—or an invitation—can get past the gate."

Of course none of that had stopped Zavi from hurting Patrice. But the warlock's magic was like nothing anyone had ever encountered. Even Diablo was not immune to the fallen angel's power.

"What will we do with Fielding once he's finished putting the engine together?" she asked tentatively.

Sophie didn't quite meet her eye. "Your uncle suggested we put an influence spell on him, make him forget he was ever here."

Hettie studied the set of her jaw. "You don't agree?"

Her shoulders stiffened, and she met Hettie's gaze full on. "I think his engine poses a threat to all sorcerers. Marcus is right—there's no telling how it might be weaponized. I think we should wipe his mind entirely to make sure this knowledge doesn't fall into the wrong hands. But not until he's woken Grandmère, of course."

A chill danced across Hettie's skin. She didn't want to argue with the sorcerer—she understood her fears. But she couldn't agree with a violation as heinous as a full memory wipe. She might not like Fielding after what he'd done to her, but there were mundane laws to deal with mundane crimes. Even the Swedenborg prison didn't wipe the memories of its inmates. It was considered barbaric.

She left the debutante with a muttered excuse, stomach churning. She couldn't fault Sophie for wanting to protect the gifted, but she couldn't cotton to the idea that Sophie's status and privilege made her think she was fit to dispense judgment and mete out punishment.

Then again, hadn't Hettie done the same with Diablo? How many men had she killed to save Abby? How many more would she kill to keep her family and friends safe? To protect what was hers?

As many as needed. She set her teeth and admonished the mage gun, even as she secretly relished its promise. The truth was, Hettie could not protect Abby by shooting one man or a dozen men; shy of annihilating every single threat that came at them and locking her sister in a box, she could do nothing to keep the world away from Abby, or Abby out of the world.

That doesn't mean you can't try. She tucked that dark thought away.

Restless and needing a distraction, she paced down the long hall to the study where the men had set up the engine. She generally avoided the room when Dr. Fielding was there—she had no great desire to be in his company any more than necessary. With him gone, though, she had the luxury of studying the machine in greater detail.

The main part of the engine consisted of numerous brass wheels that fitted together. She ran a fingertip along the runes etched into the sides, wondering what they said, how the whole contraption worked. She'd originally thought the engine ran on electricity, but there didn't seem to be any kind of motor attached. Uncle had mentioned something about redundant magical power—she assumed that was some form of energy.

The crackle of a page startled her. Marcus was sitting in a chair in the corner, poring over his battered little book. "Didn't even see you there."

The Englishman barely looked up. "It's half my job. If you're looking for Horace, Mr. Bassett, or the good doctor, they went to town."

"Just the three of them?"

"I sent some of my men along." Meaning he had sent guards to keep them out of trouble. The Favreaus' security team might as well have been an army, considering their uniforms and number. It'd only recently occurred to Hettie that the most powerful soothsayer in the country *would* want a strong personal security force for her own protection. Soothsaying was a lucrative business. "Judging by how happy Dr. Fielding has been, though, I don't think he'll attempt an escape."

"I wouldn't be too sure," Hettie grumbled.

"If nothing else, Horace will keep him around. Fielding has taken to him like water to a sponge. You've never heard a man talk so much about his work, or another man absorb it so readily. Those two are peas in a very odd pod."

"Pa used to say all beans are beans, whether they're black, white, kidney, or navy. They all make us gassy in the end."

Marcus laughed. "Your father was a philosopher."

"I s'pose." It was an empty memory, but the joke did make her laugh. She turned away from the disconcerting void in her emotions and nodded at his book. "What're you reading? The Bible?"

"In a manner of speaking." He seemed to consider a moment before he held it out to her. "Here. Have a look."

The cover of the leather-bound book was worn and faded, its corners boxed. The pages within were scrawled with fine, tight handwriting. She turned to the first page.

You are Marcus Wellington.
Your mage guns are Luna and Claire. They take a memory away every time you fire them.
You do not know what you do not know.
You work for the Favreau family, and have been tasked with protecting Patrice and Sophie Favreau.
Jemma Baron is Sophie's bodyguard and your last line of defense . . .

It went on at length. The book was about three-quarters full. The most recent journal entries succinctly detailed Hettie's association with Diablo and how she and Jeremiah Bassett were helping Patrice.

Hettie glanced up in surprise. "This is your life story."

"The vital parts from the moment I took up a job with the Favreaus, at any rate. It's the most important thing I own. Whenever I use Luna and Claire, I read my book to make sure I haven't forgotten anything I need to know to do my job."

She suddenly remembered the gunfight when the Alabama gang had tried to rob the train. "What'd you forget the last time around?"

He lifted a shoulder. "Nothing that's in here. Often it's something trivial—the way something tastes, or a book I've read. Once or twice, I've forgotten something I've had to relearn, like how to tie my shoelaces." He grimaced. "God forbid one day I forget how to read."

Hettie pursed her lips. She'd had the ability to love her parents taken from her—she couldn't even form new affection for them—but at least her memories of Pa and Ma and the little comfort they provided gave her a sense of the past, the place she'd sprung from, as lackluster as that impression was.

She wondered whether Marcus would have something to say about Sophie's wish to wipe Fielding's memory. But then, he was loyal to the family. He probably wouldn't interfere.

She brushed her hand across her plume-shaped scar. "If you're at risk of losing your memory, why use your mage guns at all? You're not bonded to them."

"I *could* use other guns," he admitted. "But you saw what they're capable of. It's my duty to protect Sophie and the rest of the Favreaus. Given the power Luna and Claire possess, I can't take the chance that a regular weapon might misfire, or that my aim might be off. Luna and Claire are sure bets, the way Diablo is."

"Not that sure," she said grimly.

"Diablo does have more agency," Marcus agreed. "And you don't have much choice whether you wield it or not."

"I can still choose not to pull the trigger."

He didn't respond to that, staring out the window instead. "My choice is made. I swore an oath to protect Sophie and her family. Luna and Claire's power is undeniable. Would I use them and risk losing everything that I am to save Sophie? In a heartbeat."

Devotion shone clear in his eyes. Despite the fact Marcus was old enough to be Sophie's father, Hettie realized he was in love with her. But she could see that it would always be a secret love, a painful yearning he would never voice. Perhaps he hoped Luna and Claire would take that away from him one day.

She passed the book back to him. "I thought you said it wasn't a good idea to share too much about your weaknesses."

"Strength is gained when a weakness is shared among friends. We can't weather all the world's woes without a few allies." He tucked the book into his breast pocket. "You're a remarkable young woman, Hettie Alabama, and you've been a good influence on Sophie. For what it's worth, you have my trust."

The pounding of footsteps echoed through the hall. "Miss Hettie! Mr. Wellington!" Horace ran in, sweating and wild-eyed. "Dr. Fielding's been taken!"

"Taken?" Marcus shot out of his chair. "By whom? What happened?"

"I'm not sure. It happened so quickly. We were on our way to the machinist's when a group of bandits surrounded our carriage and shot your men. Mr. Bassett pulled me out of the way. They took Dr. Fielding. Mr. Bassett tried to stop them—"

"Where is he now?" Hettie's heart thundered.

"Tracking them. They dragged the scientist to the French Quarter. Bassett sent me back to get reinforcements."

Marcus nodded. "I'll gather some men. Hettie—"

She was already heading for the door. "I'm going to find Uncle. If we lose Fielding, we lose our only chance to help Patrice."

The horse Hettie took from the Favreau mansion's stable was strong and fast, one of Sophie's favorites, a bay gelding by the name of Midas. He wasn't magicked, but he loved to run, and Hettie spurred him to an all-out gallop around Lake Pontchartrain and down the street, past numerous carriages ferrying finely dressed ladies to tea parties. Their drivers shouted at her as she passed, kicking up mud and dust in her wake.

Horace caught up to her on another horse. "Did you even think about where you were going?" he shouted. "How would you even have found Mr. Bassett?"

"Uncle always finds me," she shouted back. Admittedly she hadn't thought it out carefully. Maybe Patrice's contract spell had spurred her on, like a hot iron to the backside.

"It's been over an hour," Horace said. "There's no telling where they are."

"We can make up for lost time. Take my hand."

He rode up alongside her and grabbed her outstretched hand. Hettie breathed deep as she slipped into her time bubble, pulling Horace and their mounts along into it. The world around them juddered to a standstill as if it'd been enveloped in golden syrup. Flocks of startled birds taking wing stopped midair. Other travelers on the road froze in their tracks. Now only the hoofbeats and heavy breathing of their horses filled their ears.

They maneuvered their unfazed mounts through the streets, the mud giving way to hard-packed earth and then cobblestones and pavement that made Hettie's bones judder. They slowed as Horace guided them down busier streets. Hettie warned him not to touch anyone—two people and two horses was taxing her concentration.

"I can see why they would've taken Fielding from here," Hettie said. "What I don't understand is who would've done this."

"I think I might have recognized one of the men from the train robbery. He was missing his front teeth, and his hat was a woman's hat with red feathers in it."

"The Alabama gang? You sure?"

"I would never forget a hat like that."

"But why would they want Fielding? How do they even know who he is or why he's here? Or even that he was in New Orleans?"

"All good questions to ask after we find him." He pointed at a hansom cab that'd been overturned. The wheel had been sheared off as if by a sharp sword, the spokes ending abruptly in a perfect line. "This is where they attacked. I don't know what kind of magic they used, but they hit quick and hard, almost as if they knew exactly where we'd be." He pointed toward an alley. "They grabbed him and went through there."

They dismounted and searched the alley. No one was there now, and there was no sign of where they might have gone. They emerged on the other end.

"We need a better vantage point. There." She indicated a fire escape ladder.

They climbed to the rooftop of the building. Hettie felt a little sick for a moment with the city spread far below her. Winded and at her limit, she released the time bubble. The noise of the city around them was almost deafening.

Diablo kicked into her hand in warning. It twitched, and she followed the movement to the opposite corner of the building and looked down.

A pair of men wrestled with Uncle. His hands flashed with white energy, but one man had a stranglehold on him, and the other was brandishing a knife. Hettie shouted and took aim.

She just managed to keep Diablo from killing the two men. Green power rained down on the attackers, the revolver's firepower streaking down and splitting into needlelike darts that turned the men into screaming, bleeding pincushions writhing on the ground.

Jeremiah glanced up. "'Bout time."

"Where'd he go?" Hettie yelled down.

Jeremiah pointed. "They took him down that way in a big covered cart."

"Marcus is coming. I'll slow them down."

"Hettie, wai—"

She breathed deep, as if to take a plunge, and dropped into her time bubble. She hadn't regained enough strength to take in Uncle and Horace and catch up to the abductors.

She clambered over the rooftops, jumping the gaps between buildings with relative ease since they were so close together. She spotted a large canvas-covered cart in the street, pulled by four ragged horses. It was one of those old covered wagons like they used back when settlers were still making their way across the country, and it looked out of place in the city. Hettie climbed down a fire escape, but as she wove through traffic, the time bubble popped—

Suddenly she was smack-dab in the middle of oncoming traffic. A man shouted and hauled on his reins. His hansom cab buckled violently, and the horse reared. Hettie scampered out of the way of its hooves and directly into the path of another cart. The man's horses faltered and tried to skirt around her, but then the cart they were pulling plowed into them, and they whinnied in panic, veering to the side and crashing into another rider.

Hettie ran toward the covered wagon, summoning Diablo and trying to reestablish the time bubble. No good. The same thing had happened during the train robbery.

A man peeked out of the wagon. He shouted and drew his sidearm. Hettie zigzagged to avoid the gunshots and pulled Diablo's trigger, unleashing a blast of green power that incinerated the man's arm up to his shoulder.

Two more men appeared with rifles. Hettie ducked left and rolled behind a cart as the bullets bit into the cab, showering her with splinters. The passengers within screamed.

Traffic ground to a halt, and people dove out of their vehicles while the drivers tried to get their horses under control. The covered wagon surged forward and plowed through the street while the men in the back continued an assault on the cab Hettie hid behind.

She had to stop that wagon.

She whipped around the corner and fired. Diablo let out a wide beam of power that took out the right two wheels. The wagon collapsed with a loud crash, sending up a wake of splinters. The whole right side of the wagon tore off, and the canopy ripped away from the U-shaped frame as it snapped up like angry fish spines.

People screamed as carts, drivers, and pedestrians tried to escape the gunfire and chaos. Horses thrashed and reared, whinnying as the vehicles piled up. Hettie ran toward the wagon.

It was empty. Unless Dr. Fielding had somehow escaped...

One of the riflemen who'd tumbled from the wagon pushed up off the ground. He spotted Hettie and, in a panic, reached for his pistol.

Hettie pointed Diablo at him. "Don't."

He blinked at her. "I-I-I'm sorry, Mizzay, I didn't realize—" He stuttered to a stop. "Wait, you're not—"

Hettie cocked Diablo for show. "Where's Dr. Fielding?"

He gaped. "I—I don't know—"

Hettie blew a molten hole in the ground next to his feet, and he stumbled back. *"Where is he?"*

"I was just supposed to stay in the cart! I don't know anything!" His eyes canted left. Hettie reacted a second too late.

Someone cinched an arm around her neck and dragged her backward. Hettie struggled, dropping Diablo as she tried to pry her fingers under the man's elbow to get a breath.

She sank her teeth into the man's thick muscle, then slammed her heel into his shin, twisting to throw him off balance. He yelped and let go. She dove for Diablo, and before she could stop herself, fired.

The man's shriek was cut off almost instantly as he evaporated, flaring like a hellish green grease fire.

The agony of the revolver's blood price was instant, shredding through skin, flesh, and bone as it extracted one year of Hettie's life for the life she'd taken. The pain went on and on, as if she were the one being consumed by flame. It'd been months since she'd killed a man, months since she'd slaked Diablo's bloodthirst. And the mage gun's appetite was insatiable. For a flash, she thought she was back in hell, being swallowed and forced down into Satan's gullet—and then it was over.

Through the haze of relief, Hettie barely registered the person standing over her, pistol drawn, its blank, black eye winking at her.

CHAPTER THIRTEEN

I t's you." The woman's smoke-and-whiskey voice filtered through Hettie's hazy mind. Her eyes focused...to find herself staring at someone familiar, yet not.

She looked different. Her pointed face was no longer quite so pointed. Her jaw was more square, her eyes no longer blue but brown. Her scar, which previously took up half her face, was now more artfully drawn, curving up along the cheek. As Hettie stared, the scar shifted, crawling up into her temple like a long-limbed centipede. Outlaw Hettie's hair flattened out, shortened before her eyes.

Suddenly Hettie was staring at a mirror image, only the reflection was like an idealized version of Hettie, as if a smitten artist had painted the outlaw, gilding her features. She was...prettier. Her features were softer, her complexion pale and smooth and free of the blemishes and rough patches the sun had seared against Hettie's cheeks. Her dark hair was free of grays, and it flowed around her face in soft waves rather than wiry hanks. Her figure was curved, nothing like Hettie's trunklike body, and her dark clothes hugged a pinched waist that topped long legs. The doppelgänger stood over her, smirking as the transformation completed.

This woman had to be a powerful glamor sorcerer—maybe even as powerful as Sophie. A strange kind of anger rose in Hettie.

This woman hadn't earned a single one of her scars, hadn't been through the traumas Hettie had, and here she was, wearing her face and reputation like a costume.

"Mizzay!" The other rifleman ran up, stared down at Hettie, and snarled. "The witch killed Red!" He shouldered his weapon, but Outlaw Hettie shoved the muzzle away.

"Leave her be, Jake. We got what we came for, and then some." The doppelgänger kept her gun trained on Hettie. "I knew it was you back on that train. He told me we'd meet up eventually."

"Who are you?" Hettie rasped. She couldn't summon the time bubble or conjure Diablo. She felt around surreptitiously, but the mage gun was nowhere nearby.

The woman didn't seem to hear her. She tipped up her hat and glanced casually around. "If it were up to me, we'd take you back with us now, get this all over with. But he doesn't want that." She sighed. "Waste of men and time, in my opinion."

"Where's Dr. Fielding?" she demanded.

"Safe. For now." She glanced around again, and Hettie wondered what she was waiting for. She strolled across the road and stared at something on the ground. "This must be the Devil's Revolver." She toed the mage gun but didn't reach down to pick it up. "I don't see what the fuss is about. Not much of anything, if you ask me."

Hettie glared. "Bring it here and I'll show you."

Outlaw Hettie smirked again, that lifting of the corner of her mouth a strange tic to see on her own face. "He said you were a crafty one. I ain't touching that. He said in time, you'd bring it to him again."

"Who's *he*?"

She snorted. "If you don't already know, then you're dumber than he thinks you are."

There was only one person who knew her or the Devil's Revolver this well. "You're working with Zavi."

Outlaw Hettie flashed her teeth in a humorless smile. "He wanted to make sure you knew it, too. He has a message for you— he doesn't need Abby anymore. But he's going to take her anyhow because he knows it'll hurt you."

Hettie struggled to sit up, still straining to conjure Diablo. Somehow the Alabama gang was blocking her ability, probably with Zavi's help.

The man with the rifle shoved her back with the heel of his boot. "What're we gonna do with her, Mizzay?"

Mizzay. Miz A. Miss A. She'd been hearing it wrong all along. "Nothing. Not now, anyhow."

Jake squinted. "Shouldn't we get that there gun? He wants it, doesn't he?"

Mizzay cut him a look, and he flinched. "I don't pay you to think, Jake. You wanna end up like Duke?"

"No, ma'am." He shook his head. "Sorry, Mizzay. I just thought…"

She narrowed her eyes, and he clamped his lips shut. The outlaw turned back to Hettie. "Timing's everything," she said. "And as far as I'm concerned, we're not ready for you yet."

"Ready to do what?"

Mizzay's lips spread in a manic smile. "You'll see soon enough. In the meantime…" She drew her gun and pulled the trigger rapidly. Streaks of pus-yellow light sliced through the air, mowing down innocent bystanders. People screamed and writhed on the pavement, gushing blood. The outlaw gave a sultry laugh, as if she'd just been told a dirty joke.

Hettie's gut clenched, pushing bile into her tight throat. "Why?"

Mizzay didn't respond. The air turned frigid, and Hettie's nose went numb. Her breath fogged. Her mirror image looked up. "That's our cue to leave." She waved her fingers and backed away. "See you soon, Hettie."

A pinprick of darkness dilated open in the middle of the street. The remote Zoom tunnel opened so quickly and violently that Hettie's toes iced over. She caught the briefest impression of a dark space, but could see no identifying features beyond the portal. Mizzay and the rifleman stepped through, and the tunnel winked out, leaving a trail of frost and drifting snow behind.

The moment they were gone, Diablo leaped into her hand like a frightened child, and she clutched it tight with shaking fingers.

Dr. Fielding was lost.

Ⴧ

Hettie hurried back to the Favreau mansion under the time bubble. She had no desire to be caught and wrongfully accused of the crimes the Alabama gang leader had committed in her name. The nonchalance with which "Miss A" had maimed and murdered those people chilled her. It was like something out of a nightmare.

With a shudder, Hettie realized she knew exactly why Mizzay had opened fire on those bystanders. She'd wanted to make sure Hettie's legacy was punctuated by random acts of violence and murder. She was painting Hettie's hands with blood. But was it because Zavi had ordered her to or because she'd decided Hettie was her enemy? Their conversation had suggested she was not entirely under Zavi's thumb.

One thing that was certain was that the Alabama gang had found a way to dampen the mage gun's powers. Maybe Zavi had somehow passed on his immunity to Diablo.

Accepting that Zavi was alive was easier than she'd thought it would be. Perhaps because now that she was certain, she could formulate a plan, prepare herself instead of holding her breath.

She should warn Abby. Getting in touch with Ling and her sister would be nearly impossible, though, and she didn't want to accidentally reveal their location. No, she had to trust Ling and Abby would be able to protect themselves and stay hidden. Still, Zavi had reached her sister once. There was no telling what else he was capable of.

Horace and Uncle didn't return to the mansion until late—Marcus and his teams had joined them to scour the city for any trace of Dr. Fielding. They'd found nothing, which told Hettie multiple remote Zooms must have opened to reclaim all the gang members. When they reconvened in the salon, Hettie told them about her encounter with Miss A and Zavi's involvement. The room went silent.

"So Zavi's alive and working with the Alabama gang," Uncle said.

"Seems so."

"Doesn't make sense. If he wants Diablo, why didn't she just take it? Couldn't she have scooped it up into a sack and taken it through the Zoom with her?"

"She said something about timing," Hettie said, and shook her head. "Woman's as mad as a March Hare, though. I guess if she took it through, I could just recall it before she handed it to Zavi. Once he gets his hands on it, I can't conjure it."

"That would make sense," Marcus added, "especially if whatever magic they're using to dampen your connection to Diablo is calibrated to you rather than the gun."

"That tracks. He could've gotten a piece of you when you first met," Uncle said.

Sophie sat, fingers clenched around her elbows. "I know of your reputation as a tracker, Mr. Bassett," she said quietly. Her voice wavered, though she maintained her composure as stiffly as an ironwood tree in a hurricane. "Can you find Dr. Fielding?"

Uncle blew out a breath. "It'll take time. I have a few resources I can consult, but this Zavi was pretty damned hard to find before. I don't know that I'll find him again...and survive."

"Anything you need is at your disposal," the debutante said. "We must have Dr. Fielding back."

Uncle scratched his chin. "The question is, what would someone as powerful as Zavi want with a Mechanik?"

"Mizzay said he no longer needs Abby. She was the one who was supposed to help him open the portal to hell. He must know about Fielding's engine. He's probably going to make him build one to juice up enough so he can open that portal by himself." She turned to Marcus. "But how could he have found out about Fielding? How did they know exactly when and where he'd be most vulnerable?" She didn't mean to sound accusatory, but the lines forming between the security man's eyes told her she did.

"My men are loyal, Miss Alabama, if you're worried about a betrayal. And there are many ways a warlock of Zavi's caliber might have been able to find what he was looking for. Eyeing spells, Vision, scrying...it sounds as if this creature has enough power to do any of these."

"And he wants more for whatever nefarious deeds he has planned. Time is of the essence, then." Sophie got up and paced. "We still have Fielding's prototype. Horace," she addressed the hostler who'd been listening from the side, "do you think you could put the engine back together?"

"Me?"

"You've been glued to the man's side these past few days. You have a better understanding than any of us about how that machine should be assembled. And you're clearly good at this kind of work."

He hummed in thought. "Well, we'd still need those parts tooled. I can't make any promises, but I can try."

Sophie nodded. "I have confidence in you. If we can get the engine working and wake up my grandmother, she might be able to scry what will happen next."

"That's a lot of ifs," Hettie said. "We don't even know that the engine will wake Patrice. And her knowing what will happen next won't necessarily help us prevent it from happening. What we need to do is find out where this gang has taken Fielding and stop Zavi."

"I gotta agree with Hettie," Uncle said. "Soothsaying can't protect us, and with all due respect to your grandmother, Miss Favreau, with magic wobbling the way it is, I wouldn't trust any oracle's prediction."

Sophie's brow knit. "I would remind you both that you're here on my sufferance and that Hettie is bound to my grandmother's contract spell."

"She wanted me to find out what was causing the soothsayer blackout," Hettie clarified. "Of course I want to help her, Sophie. And I'll do everything I can. But this is bigger than just her now. Zavi's involved, meaning everyone's in danger. Now that he has Dr. Fielding, there's no telling what he'll do."

Sophie sent her a mutinous glare and stood. "I disagree. We must fix the engine and wake Grandmère. She'll know what to do after that. That is my wish, and this is my household, and I will hear no more argument." With that, she swept out. Jemma sent them an uneasy look and followed her.

Horace rubbed the back of his neck. "Guess I better get started."

"I'll help you." Marcus paused and with a grimace said to Hettie, "Don't judge her too harshly. Her grandmother means the world to her."

Hettie sat back, tired to the bone. Uncle poured himself a large snifter of brandy from the decanter and drank it down in two big swallows. "Seems our dealings with the Favreaus might be at an end soon," he said, pouring himself another drink.

"She's just upset and scared." Hettie drummed her fingers on the table. "We still need her and her resources if we're going to find Fielding."

"We'll find him," Uncle reassured her, but his tone was less than optimistic. "Whether he'll actually be able to help us is another matter. Wherever he's been taken, I can't imagine his accommodations will be quite as comfortable. If the Alabama gang is trying to get him to build them an engine..." He scratched his chin. "Well, they won't be treating him to feather beds and roast beef dinners."

Hettie slowly sat up. "At the police station in Chicago, there were two Alabama gang members. They were caught robbing a sorcerers' salon." She gripped her knees. "If Zavi wants an engine, he'll need all the parts to build one..."

"Or they'll just take the prototype." Uncle shot to his feet. "We need to go back to Chicago."

They were too late.

A telegram to the University of Chicago confirmed that Dr. Fielding's lab had been raided, stripped of all its valuables, and set ablaze. The university official who'd worked with the Chicago police believed it was the Mundane Movement who'd broken in, but Hettie knew it had to be the Alabama gang.

"Some fine job the Division's doing," Uncle scoffed, refolding the telegram and stuffing it back in his pocket. It had arrived just before they'd left New Orleans via remote Zoom, which Sophie had reluctantly paid for. The exorbitant cost would've been worthwhile if they'd secured the working prototype. Unfortunately it seemed that was not going to be the case. "Losing Fielding *and* all his work?" He pursed his lips. "Unless they were the ones who stole Fielding's notes and prototype to begin with. If this is one of their elaborate schemes, though, I can't figure it out."

Hettie sighed, watching the city streets go by from the hansom cab they'd hired to get to the university. "Did we have to come all this way if there's nothing to salvage?"

"It's possible I can still track down whoever took the prototype," he said. "If the Division hasn't already cleaned the site, that is."

"What about the police?"

He scoffed. "Most police departments don't have full-time sorcerers on their payroll. Can't afford 'em. Besides, the Division recruits their agents straight out of the Academy." He used the word *recruits* with a hint of sarcasm. "Pinkertons hire the rest and headhunt the best. Tried to sway me to their side a few times. I suspect that's how they got ol' Stubby."

"But you didn't take the job?"

"I'm not a fan of their politics."

When they arrived at the university, they headed directly to Fielding's lab, though it took some time to find it.

"Deflection spells are still in place," Uncle noted. "It means whoever was here knew what they were looking for, knew what they were up against."

The lab was a blackened ruin, the smell of char still strong. Every piece of machinery was gone, or else a burned-out heap of slag, smashed, or overturned.

"Doesn't even look like the police took anything as evidence. Not machine-wise, anyhow. We'd see more clean spots on the ground, places where they moved stuff after the fire."

"So whoever did this took *everything*?" She glanced around at the smashed windows, the narrow doorway. "How could they get all that out of the university without anyone noticing?"

"Short-distance portal spell to get the equipment off campus, then a remote Zoom. But Fielding said this place is supposed to be spelled against that kind of interference. And moving that much metal through a Zoom..." He trailed off. "Whoever performed the spell would've had to be plenty strong to keep it open that long and to keep it stable as they were moving the equipment through."

"It's got to be Zavi," Hettie said.

Uncle tapped his chin. "Maybe not. If Fielding was with them, maybe he juiced up whoever was opening the Zoom."

They picked their way carefully through the lab, searching for anything they could take back to Sophie. They found a few papers that were only slightly burned tucked in the back of a metal filing cabinet, but Hettie couldn't make heads or tails of them.

"Someone's very good at covering their tracks," Uncle said, slipping a pendulum made of quartz back into his pocket. "All kinds of confusion spells and magical footprints here." He rubbed his forehead tiredly. "It's giving me a headache."

It made sense that the Alabama gang would want to keep anyone from tracing the Zoom back to their hideout. She supposed there was a chance it hadn't been them, but her doppelgänger had as good as confessed to the crime. If it hadn't been Mizzay's men...

"Of course!" She turned to Uncle. "I know exactly who can tell us where the Alabama gang is."

ᛣ

"You sure about this?" Uncle asked as they watched the police precinct where Horace had been jailed. "The last time we went to interrogate someone in a jail cell, it ended with a whole lot of trouble."

"This won't be like Hedley," Hettie said firmly. "We'll use Diablo's time bubble to get in, talk to them, and leave. I couldn't do it last time because I was alone. Now I have you."

"What makes you so sure they'll talk to you? If they're even there after all this time?"

"They'll talk to me," she said. "At least, they'll talk to *her*."

Uncle's eyes widened. "Oh, no. No, you won't."

"It'll work. I've talked to her. I can do her accent." This last part she exaggerated with Mizzay's smoke-and-whiskey drawl.

"Hettie, the whole country is looking for you. Now you want to march straight into the long arms of the law, posing as their most wanted?"

"I'm not walking into the station as her. Your glamor spell can extend beyond your reach, right?" She'd left Sophie's amulet behind and had chosen to wear her veil to hide her scar. Uncle had cast his glamor over her whenever they were anywhere public.

He pursed his lips. "Takes a lot out of me."

"All you have to do is get us past the barred doors and the guards. We can get the rest of the way in with the time bubble."

"I'll remind you we're in Chicago. The Pinkerton Agency's headquarters are just a few blocks away—they won't need a remote

149

Zoom to get to you if you pull Diablo's trigger. And I still don't trust that time bubble."

"They didn't come for me when I used the time bubble before, and they've had plenty of opportunities to catch me. I think you were right about Stubbs being fired—the Pinkerton Agency doesn't care about Diablo the way he did."

She watched the patrolmen strolling in and out of the building. It was just after four in the afternoon—many of the officers were at the end of their day, coming off long shifts and looking forward to dinner or a cup of coffee.

Uncle grunted. "I don't know why I ever listen to you." But he pulled out a pair of river stones along with a handful of what appeared to be dandelion fluff. She'd never know how he organized his talismans.

He placed one of the stones in her hands, muttering an incantation, then blew the fluff into her face. She coughed as the little seeds got in her eyes and nose. In seconds, they'd disappeared.

"I can't hold this forever, so whatever you plan to do, do it quick. I'm juggling a lot here."

They crossed the street and walked into the precinct. As before, it buzzed with characters of all kinds, all of them wrapped up in their own personal dramas. Two more unlucky visitors to the Chicago PD wouldn't attract anyone's notice.

Someone put a firm hand on her shoulder, and she startled. "Miss Wiltshire." The young officer she'd met on her first visit here grinned down at her.

"Oh." Hettie struggled to remember the young man's name, sliding Uncle a questioning look—was his glamor faulty? "Officer Pendleton."

"It's Detective Pendleton, now. I got promoted." He flashed a smile. "I'm so glad you came back."

"I couldn't stay away." Hettie put on what she thought was a disarming smile, gazing up at him through the veil. "And congratulations. It's well deserved."

Uncle had melted away, propping himself up in a corner and picking up a newspaper. She was on her own, it seemed.

"What are you doing here?" the detective asked. "Not in trouble, I hope?"

She gave a watery laugh. "No...I...I was hoping to...bump into you, actually." She looked down at the tips of his shiny shoes.

"I'm almost finished with my shift," Peter said eagerly. "How about you and me go for a dinner to celebrate my promotion?"

"I could wait," she said, forcing giddiness into her tone, "but this room is awfully crowded and...unsavory." She flicked her gaze toward a pair of officers escorting a stumbling drunk to a holding cell.

Peter grinned. "I have an office now. You can wait there."

He escorted her through the station, and Hettie glanced back to make sure Uncle followed. She wasn't sure about the range of Uncle's glamor. She couldn't be certain what Peter Pendleton saw when he looked at her, either, but she supposed it wasn't the face of the notorious outlaw Hettie Alabama.

"So you're a detective now. Are you working on any big cases?"

Peter unlocked a door in a side hallway. "Not at the moment, I'm afraid. Just the usual thefts and murders."

"Oh!" She gave her best impression of Sophie being scandalized. "What about those horrible gang members you told me about before?"

"Who, Duke and Jonas? They're still here, snug as two bugs." He drew back the curtains to let some light into the room. "I have to file some paperwork quick. Promise you'll be here when I get back?"

"Can't wait." She waved with her fingers and made a show of getting comfortable, perching on the corner of the desk with a coquettish tilt of her chin.

A few seconds after Peter left, Hettie hurried to the filing cabinet next to the desk. Files for Duke Cox and Jonas Lafayette indicated they did indeed share a cell right there in the precinct, and she noted the cell number. Uncle slipped into the room. "You're going to get us both shot," he groused.

"Probably." She stuck her head out the door. "C'mon. We'll need to hurry."

CHAPTER FOURTEEN

They made their way through the precinct, dodging a pair of uniformed men in a heated discussion and walking past a guard engrossed in his newspaper. Uncle reeked of sweat, and his forehead shone with perspiration.

"You better appreciate what I'm doing for you," he rasped. "It's taking everything I got to keep everyone's eyes off us. If that policeman sees you again, I probably won't be able to hold the glamor."

"Can he see my scar?" she asked. It was her most distinguishing feature, and despite the veil she felt as though every policeman in the nation would know her face, especially after what'd happened in New Orleans.

"He can see it. But the glamor is keeping him from actually noticing it. Glamor glazes the flaws, polishes up the best in a person, physically speaking. Not sure what he sees in you, to be honest."

"I'm sure it's my fine personality."

They found the holding cells. A guard sat between the barred gates. He stood as they approached. "This is a restricted area."

"I'm sorry," Uncle wheezed, "I was trying to find the facilities. Got these names for Officer Bangum written on my hands"—he held out his shaking palms—"bunch of names of those Alabama gang members..."

The guard stared uncomprehendingly. "Listen, old timer—"

"Have a look, won't you? The girl can't read, and my eyes are old." He stuck his trembling hands through the bars. The guard almost got to protest. Almost. But Uncle grabbed the front of his shirt and yanked him hard into the gate, bashing his skull against the iron and dropping him. For good measure, he whispered an incantation, and a flash of white erupted in his palms, which he sank against the guard's head. The guard's body relaxed. Soon he was snoring softly.

"That's it for me," Jeremiah muttered, letting out a long breath. "No more glamor."

"How about a truthtelling spell?"

Uncle shook his head, face pale. "My skull's gonna split open."

"It's all right. Just keep it together." Hettie took the guard's keys and unlocked the gate. She grabbed Uncle's hand and slipped into the time bubble.

They hurried along the corridor. It reeked of vomit and piss in here, and there were more than a few derelicts crammed together in a single cell.

She breathed deep and approached the cell where Duke Cox and Jonas Lafayette lay on two bare benches. Then she realized she couldn't bring them both into the time bubble without opening the cell first. And they'd both be suspicious if their fearless leader appeared out of nowhere with some new powers. Besides, interrogating them and maintaining the time bubble would tax her.

She dropped the time bubble as she walked into their field of view. They sat up as she approached. "Mizzay? Is that you?"

"Well, I ain't your mama." The accent was easy, but Hettie had no clue how the outlaw spoke to her men.

"God's balls, woman. Your face . . ." Duke gestured to her vaguely. "Is that really what she looks like?"

They were talking about her, Hettie Alabama. The gang knew Mizzay wasn't the real deal. "We met down in New Orleans. She and I . . . had a talk."

She gave them each weighted gazes, balancing contempt with wry humor, thinking how unpredictable and violent her doppelgänger had been. "What do you two have to say for yourselves?"

Jonas, who wore his dark hair in a long plait, spoke. "It was a stupid mistake. Bad timing."

"Yeah. *Timing*," Duke Cox said stiffly. "You got Fielding?"

"What do you think?" She glanced around the cells casually. "Been here long?"

"Awhile." Duke didn't sound happy about it. "Lawyer never came."

She wasn't sure how to get the information she needed out of them. Not with the limited time they had. She probably should have thought this through better.

"Who's the geezer?" Jonas asked suspiciously.

"Old friend, new recruit." And then she added, "He's going to help get us out of here."

Duke's eyebrow cocked up. "No Zoom?"

"What fun would that be?"

"Uh…*Mizzay*…" The name tripped from Uncle's tongue uneasily. "With all due respect, I don't think your glamor's gonna pass muster beyond these cells. Not with all those police out there."

"We don't need glamor." She flashed her teeth at the Alabama men. "You boys trust me?"

"You know we do," they both said, though Duke was a second slower.

She regarded them and sniffed. "Well, to be frank, I don't know that I can trust you." She leaned back against the wall. "How do I know you're not under some influence spell? Or that you aren't officers in disguise? What if *you're* using glamor against me?"

Jonas and Duke exchanged looks. "You're serious."

"I'm gonna need some proof that you're who you say you are."

Duke snorted. "Of course you do. But they took our talismans."

"Tell me what they do."

"They're part of the null net. Zavi gave them to us."

Hettie's skin prickled. Whatever this null net was, she'd have to ask Uncle. "And where is Zavi now?"

"Exactly where we left him," Jonas said with nervous laugh. "Mizzay, it's us. You have to know it's us."

She glanced at Uncle, who gave nothing away. This was her play, and she'd just about run out of ways to get information out of them.

"One more thing," she said. "Tell me where our safe house is."

155

"Safe house?" Duke narrowed his eyes. "How do I know you're even who you say *you* are? You could be some strumpet with a glamor herself."

Hettie set her jaw and drew Diablo. She hadn't seen Mizzay conjure it and didn't think it was something she could do. "This convince you of anything?"

"Not particularly. Gun's a gun."

Hettie wasn't about to pull the trigger—not while she was in a police station and not if she didn't have to. "We ain't leavin' till I'm convinced you are who you say you are."

"Then I guess we're staying." Duke sat slowly. Jonas's gaze bounced between them, looking like he was about to protest. "I mean, if you were the one to pull the lawyer back, you had to have a reason." He leaned against the bars. "What was that, anyhow?"

"I don't answer to you, Duke." She hitched a thumb in her waistband. "I've got my reasons. And I don't pay you to question my motives."

A shout down the hall echoed through the jail. The metal gate banged loudly. That was their only way out.

"Someone's coming!" Uncle hissed.

Hettie cast the men a look. "Last chance, boys. Where's the safe house?"

"Duke!" Jonas hissed.

"It's not her. Don't say nothing, Jonas."

Hettie took a deep breath and plunged into her time bubble. She reached out and touched Jonas, pulling him through the ichor of time. He gasped and stared around at the suddenly still and silent Duke.

"Duke's right, Jonas. I ain't Mizzay."

"You're...you're *her*. The one Zavi wants."

She kept her expression neutral. "You work for him. He juicing you all?"

"No...no, nothing like that." His eyes flickered as if seeking an escape from her bubble. "I joined the outfit same as everyone else. The money was good. Mizzay's a bit..." He made some empty gestures. "But she's smart, and she's fair, and we always get paid. Then, a few months ago, Zavi came and took over. He...he has something on Mizzay. I don't know what, but he's made her

156

reckless. Violent." His lips pursed. "He's out to get you. What did you do to him?"

"Nothing near as bad as I can do to you if I don't hear what I want to hear." She brandished Diablo. "Do you need any further proof this is the Devil's Revolver?"

He paled. "No, ma'am."

"And you know that fighting me won't help you."

He shook his head vehemently. "I would never hurt a woman, not even Mizzay if she were pointing that thing at me. I'm a thief, not a monster." His gaze darted toward the mage gun, and he swallowed thickly. "Besides, I know all the stories of Elias Blackthorn. If that's Diablo, then I wouldn't test the world's best gunslinger against you." He glanced around nervously. "I didn't know you could control time."

"Where's the gang hideout?"

"In the mountains. Colorado. Not exactly sure where, though— we get in and out by remote Zoom. Zavi opens it on his own."

"Why does he want Dr. Fielding?"

"I don't know. Something about a Mechanikal engine. They had us stealing parts for it these past few months, in between robbing banks and the like. He's got us taking spellbooks and talismans and what have you, but I'm mundane. I don't know much about that stuff, except that I don't like it." He read her look. "They got him, didn't they?"

Hettie thought hard. Duke and Jonas had been caught days before Fielding had presented the engine at the Mechaniks' symposium. If they'd been stealing parts for the engine for as long as Jonas claimed, Zavi had to have known of the engine's existence *before* it'd been made public.

Was it possible Zavi could scry the future when the other soothsayers could not? It would explain how the Alabama gang had known to find Fielding in New Orleans. And Jonas had mentioned something about their robbery being planned. If he'd been able to do that all along, though, he would have known Hettie would stop him—would know everything that she'd do, where Abby was, what they were planning.

She shook her head. Jonas's answers had come too easily. She studied him carefully. "How do I know you're not lying? You weren't so forthcoming before."

He glanced past her, jerking his head toward his colleague. "Duke's a bully. I wasn't going to go against his word while the two of us were cellmates. Besides, I have nothing to lose by telling you the truth. Zavi wants you there. He as much as said that we should tell you where he is if we met you." His look grew serious. "With all due respect, Miss Alabama, I don't think you want to go there. That warlock is no good news."

She didn't want to go, but her showdown with Zavi would come. Maybe not today, but soon. She had to stop him once and for all.

"Do you think Mizzay took Dr. Fielding to the hideout?"

"Likely. All the pieces for the engine are there."

She grabbed Uncle's arm, felt the time bubble flex and strain as she pulled him in. He shook his head. "Hell's bells," he grumbled, shaking his limbs as if he might rid himself of the gold syrup of time she'd pulled him through.

"We need to take Jonas with us. Gang's hideout is in the Rockies in Colorado. He can get us to Fielding."

"Whoa, now, I didn't say I'd do anything of the sort." Jonas held up his hands. "I'm safer in here than I would be betraying Zavi. Or Mizzay, for that matter. She's no kitten when it comes to traitors."

"Don't think you have much of a choice, Jonas." Uncle glared at him. "You gonna make this difficult?"

Hettie shifted her grip on Diablo, drawing the thief's attention. His lips flattened out. "No, sir."

"Awfully biddable for a criminal," Uncle remarked sourly.

"Well, he's working for Zavi, and Zavi wants me to go to him."

"So it's a trap."

"Probably. Now help me with the lock."

Uncle got the cell open by picking the mundane lock. Hettie had to focus on maintaining the time bubble. It'd gotten easier over time to manage, though it still strained her the more people or objects she had to draw into it.

Once the door was open, Jonas reluctantly followed them out of the jail, leaving Duke behind, frozen in the moment. The double gates at the end of the corridor were unlocked, and three uniformed men were in the process of hurrying through. They couldn't get past without touching them and taking them into the time bubble, though. They positioned themselves and coldcocked the men simultaneously. Jonas wrapped an arm around one guard's neck to cut off his air until he passed out.

The time bubble slipped. No alarms had been sounded, but that wouldn't be the case for long. Hettie inhaled and tried to muster the strength to re-form the bubble. It wouldn't come.

"What's wrong?"

"I can't drop out of time." She set her jaw, and Diablo trembled in her hand. "This has happened before."

Jonas's eyes widened. He turned and ran back toward the cell.

Her vision flashed as Diablo previewed the next moment: the inner wall of the jail cell erupted in a blaze of light and fire as the bricks exploded inward, dashing Jonas against the far side. The blast blew them both back, the concussive force bowing their ribs until they cracked. Blood leaked from Uncle's ears and sightless eyes.

"Get down!" She threw herself at Jeremiah and pinned him to the ground a second before the explosion went off. Jonas was thrown against the iron bars, a sickening snap echoing in Hettie's ears.

Her vision blurred and her ears rang. Smoke and grit filled the air, along with the tang of something like gunpowder. *Dynamite*, she thought, *or maybe nitro*. Pa had sometimes used it to get rid of stubborn boulders around the ranch.

She pushed to her knees, coughing, and looked Uncle over. He blinked dazedly up at her, his mouth moving but the words indistinct. Hettie tried to summon Diablo. It wouldn't come. She found it a few feet away and picked it up with bloodied hands.

Three men wearing bandanas over their faces clambered through the hole from outside the jail. Duke stood and waved at them. The Alabama gang had come for their men.

Hettie took aim and unleashed molten fury upon them, aiming carefully so she wouldn't kill them. The men screamed as slag rained down on their backs and arms. They writhed on the ground, then went still. Hettie held her breath, expecting the mage gun to take its blood price, but it didn't. They weren't dead.

Jonas lay unmoving, dead or dying, and his cooperation dying with him. She looked up to find Duke sending her a murderous glare through the bars of his cell. She cursed.

"Uncle!" she shouted. Her head felt as though it were under water.

The old man was getting to his feet, still talking, but Hettie could barely hear what he was saying. "Jonas is dead. We need to take Duke with us."

He grabbed her by the wrist and yanked her around to look at him, pointing frantically at the hole and at Diablo. She waved him off; it wasn't as if she'd had much choice.

She melted the lock to Duke's cage with Diablo's fire. "You're coming with us," she shouted, pointing the mage gun at his head. She indicated the hole in the wall and his three smoldering compatriots.

His jaw firmed in understanding.

They climbed out into a side alley, just half a story off the ground floor. Uncle paused long enough to take a gun from one of the jailbreakers' belts. The explosion had drawn dozens of spectators, and as they made their way out, cries of alarm went up.

"What're you all gawkin' at?" Uncle raised his weapon and let off a few shots. People screamed and scattered. Duke Cox laughed.

"Are you insane?" Hettie exclaimed. "You'll draw the police to us!"

"We're not exactly inconspicuous. The chaos will help hide us. C'mon." Uncle pulled them down the alleyway. "We need to get as far from here as possible before anyone gets a bead on Diablo."

They ran down the alley and emerged around the corner. Hettie kept Diablo pressed against the small of Duke Cox's back, watching her surroundings, all while trying to reestablish the time bubble. It still wouldn't come.

"They're not going to let me just get away," Duke drawled. "Mizzay's come for me, and she's not going to let me go with you."

"What makes *you* so important?"

"Absolutely nothin'." He said it dryly. "Except Mizzay hates unfinished business."

"Keep going," Hettie said, fording a path through the crowded street with a mean look. If the Pinkerton Agency was paying any attention, they'd be here soon. The Division probably had agents in the area, too—men who could sense the mage gun's power. And obviously the police would be looking for them. They'd be hemmed in on all sides if Hettie couldn't raise the time bubble.

Two patrolmen rounded the corner, scanning the streets. Duke's hesitation was enough to draw their attention.

"There! You! Halt!"

Uncle raised his gun and fired off a series of shots, and the police threw themselves to the ground, drawing their own service pieces. Hettie shoved Duke behind a hansom cab.

Uncle dove next to them. "We need to split up," he said and pointed. "Take him and get to the train station. If you can, get on the train headed south."

What she wouldn't give for a fast horse right now. "And if I can't?"

"You'll figure it out." He hacked dryly and spat a dark gob onto the road. "I'll give you an opening." He opened his hands and whispered into them, and his palms filled with fire.

He stood, face pale and sweating. "Go!" He ducked out from behind the cab and lifted his hands. As he clapped them together, the fire in his palms expanded, and a ball of flame billowed from them, orange, then yellow, then blue.

Heat prickled over Hettie's skin. It was like Walker's fire spell, only this was far more potent. Uncle wasn't trying to kill anyone, but he was putting as much fear into their pursuers as possible.

She jammed Diablo's muzzle into Duke's side. "You heard the man. Train station."

Duke got up, not quite hurrying. They ran up the block away from the expanding ball of flame, dodging people trying to escape from the crazed sorcerer in the street.

They'd never make it across town to the station on foot.

"C'mon." She prodded him toward a dandy of a man just getting off a fine black mare. She pointed the gun at his face. "Excuse me. We're taking her."

The man blinked owlishly at them, his mouth curving into a laugh. But then he paled as he saw the gun. "Now, see here—"

Duke stepped forward and slugged the man across his jaw. He went down like a sack of corn. He eyed Hettie. "If you're gonna be an outlaw, you don't need to be polite about it."

161

She scowled and pointed her gun. "Just get on."

He huffed. "Like I have a choice."

Duke sat behind her and clung to the front edge of the saddle rather than her waist. He smelled like rancid sweat. The mare, unused to the extra weight, pranced and whinnied in complaint.

"Sorry, girl. But we need to go in a hurry." Hettie kicked the mount hard, and she took off at a sprint, shod hooves clacking loudly against the cobblestones.

They made it to the end of the block and turned south, pointed toward the train station. She would have to trust that Uncle would find her—he always did—but she still worried. For all his magic, he wasn't bulletproof. And the police would use all the firepower they had if they felt threatened by his display of magic. The Division would likely be called in, too. What if they caught him? He'd be dragged to the Swedenborg prison for rogue sorcerers.

The air filled with an encroaching roar that made Hettie's gut tremble, and she looked over her shoulder. Three automobiles zoomed up the street, driven by black-suited men in bowler hats.

A woman's voice nearly shouted in her ear, "This is the Pinkerton Detecting Agency. In the name of the law, I order you to stop and surrender!"

Hettie gritted her teeth. Pinks. Just what she needed.

She steered the mare around the next corner. She never thought she'd wish for *more* traffic. The Pinkertons barrelled down the street against the flow, and the people on the road shouted obscenities as they yanked their conveyances out of the path of pursuit.

A ball of light sizzled past her ear, and she hissed a curse.

"You gonna shoot back?" Duke asked. "'Cuz *they're* not worried about being polite."

Hettie turned the horse down another street, out of the path of the Pinkerton's spells. They couldn't keep this up forever, but Hettie had no wish to hurt anyone, and there was a good chance she'd have to.

She drew Diablo, sending up a prayer that it knew what she wanted to do. *Just stop those vehicles.* She pulled the trigger.

The green beam scythed across the road like a whip, slicing through the tires—and legs—of anyone and anything unfortunate enough to be standing in the street. The Pinkerton cars plowed into the ground, their tires shredded, the chassis flying apart like pieces of split firewood. One of the vehicles weaved and slammed into a screaming horse that'd lost its hind legs, and the poor beast toppled into the seats, front legs flailing, crushing the men.

The increasingly shrill police whistles told her she and Duke had made enough turns that they were pointed back toward the precinct. Hettie stopped to get her bearings, testing the time bubble once more.

"Train station's that way," Duke prompted, sounding almost bored. She didn't trust his direction and instead spurred the mare in the opposite direction.

"Scenic route," she said in response to his protest.

It was a good thing she hadn't listened. A pair of mounted patrolmen rode around the corner, aiming straight for her. She swung the mare about and let off two warning shots, aiming near but not at the police horses. The crackling green fire made them scream and shy away.

A sizzling bolt of power zapped her arm, sending a flurry of pins and needles singing through her bones, and she dropped Diablo. Behind them a new fleet of Pinkerton agents in automobiles had penned them in.

"Turn left!" Duke grabbed the reins and yanked hard, whipping the horse around, and he kicked the mount into a gallop. Hettie tried to summon Diablo, but the mage gun wouldn't come.

Above them she sensed movement, and she looked up. There were people—or what she thought were people—running along the rooftops, following them. They moved lithely with inhuman speed, leaping the gaps between buildings as easily as if they were squirrels hopping from tree branch to tree branch. One of them deftly swung down an eave and slid down the stonework, rolling onto a ledge and running easily along its narrow length. He was dressed in plain cowpoke clothes—not Pinkerton or Division or the police.

It was the Alabama gang. It had to be. Zavi must have lent the members some power, giving them this incredible agility and speed. And they were following her.

The mare ran full tilt into the next intersection. Ahead of them, a pinpoint of darkness swirled open, a wall of black on the other side, and the air grew frosty.

"That'd be our way out," Duke said, a hint of snide satisfaction in his voice. He grabbed Hettie tight, pressing her against his chest. She struggled to throw herself off the horse, but Duke was much larger, and her one arm was useless. She scrabbled for the knife in her boot—

But it was too late. They plunged into the remote Zoom tunnel.

CHAPTER FIFTEEN

The cold, sucking, falling sensation was blessedly brief. The mare landed with a bone-jarring stomp on the opposite end of the Zoom, whinnying in fear as she found herself in close, dark quarters. Hands on all sides grabbed for the horse's reins or halter. Duke shoved Hettie off the saddle like a sack of grain. She landed hard on her side, bruising her hip.

Diablo wouldn't come. And she'd dropped it on the other side of the Zoom.

"We need to stop meeting like this."

Hettie's blood turned cold. Skin prickling, she sat up slowly and faced the warlock Zavi.

He looked much the same as he had when they'd last met. He'd healed supernaturally—not surprising, since he was a divine creature. She'd watched him straighten his mangled body as though he were smoothing out a wrinkled shirt. He was whole and unscathed, but there was something in his eyes that had fractured further.

"How could I stay away?" She flashed him her most winning rictus, her lips peeled away from her teeth in a parchment-dry mouth. "You didn't have to go to so much trouble to get me here, though."

Zavi's lips twisted, as if he were almost impressed by her gallows humor. "I didn't expect you so soon. It's very rude for guests to arrive early, you know."

"I suppose you'd know all about manners, considering how long you've been stuck here, eh, Abzavine?"

The warlock's cheek ticked. Good. If she was going to die here, she'd annoy her murderer as much as possible first. She gave a low laugh. "That's right, I know who you are. I met Javier Punta, and he told me all about you...right before I killed him."

She knew Zavi hated the man responsible for dragging him to this plane of existence, knew he'd plotted revenge on him. She hadn't wanted to kill Punta, of course, but she'd convinced herself at the time it had been the correct thing to do.

The Alabama men stirred uneasily.

"*You* killed him." His tone wasn't quite incredulous, nor was it skeptical, but his surprise was clear. Zavi had claimed a connection to the Devil's Revolver. If the angel hadn't sensed his patron's death, what did that mean?

"He asked me to. I did him a favor." Any truthtelling spell would confirm that.

She looked around, feigning boredom, partly so that if the killing blow were coming, she wouldn't see it. These caves were far rougher than the ones at the Crowe gang hideout at the old abandoned Sonora Zoom tunnel station in Arizona. "Nice outfit you've got here," she observed dryly. "Coming down in the world, are we?"

"Creature comforts are for mortals and weaklings." Zavi inspected her head to toe in her fine dress. "I suppose you've succumbed to them."

Suddenly feeling the men's eyes all over her, she reached for Diablo. It was still lying in the street in Chicago—she could see it in her mind's eye. She called to it, but it wouldn't come.

"I see you've discovered my null net," Zavi said, smirking. "Ingenious, isn't it? It took a lot of effort to develop the spell, and no small sacrifice." He glanced toward Duke. "Mr. Cox, welcome home. I can sense you're about to tell me something important, though."

Duke stuck his lower lip out. "My talisman was confiscated. Couldn't get it back."

Zavi sighed. "You're like small children, all of you, losing all the carefully made gifts I gave you." The warlock drew a knife. "Lucky for you, I can always make more."

The blade flashed, and Zavi gave a short gasp as he sliced off his own left thumb. Hettie clamped down on her rising gorge as he dropped the bloody digit into Duke's outstretched palm. "Clean that off and keep it safe. And try not to lose it again."

"Thank you," Duke muttered as grudgingly as a spoiled child.

"What is family for? You'd do the same for me, surely?" Zavi held up his hand. The bloody stump of his thumb healed over before her eyes, the skin smoothing. The flesh plumped and elongated like clay on a potter's wheel, and in seconds, a new thumb had sprouted back, pink and healthy. The warlock flexed it and met her eye.

"Nice trick," Hettie said flatly. "Whole lotta good a roomful of thumbs'll do you with Diablo clear across the country."

"My people will retrieve it shortly. In fact…" He tilted his head, eyes glazing obsidian. "I believe they're ready to come home."

The men hurriedly got out of the way as Zavi waved a hand. He reached out and poked a penny-sized hole midair in the fabric of reality. The hole bloomed open, and a cold blast rushed through the dank cavern.

Eight men leaped and somersaulted through. They weren't Weres, but something was off about them—their limbs were elongated, their muscles coiled and bouncing in ways that reminded Hettie of clock springs. Their eyes glowed with manic light, and as they landed on the other side of the tunnel, they couldn't seem to hold still. A few of them ran up the walls and did backflips, as if they were mindless windup toys.

One of them carried a burlap sack, which he brought to the warlock. Zavi opened it and smiled as he drew Diablo out. "Ah. My old friend. Welcome home."

Hettie's heart torqued as she tried to conjure the revolver. The mage gun was silent, and yet she thought she could feel it straining toward her like a squirming kitten.

"Zavi." The voice was sharp like a gun's report. The men cleared a path as Mizzay, dressed in a dark split skirt, shirt, vest, and black hat, marched up to the warlock, frowning. "What've you done to my men? Take that geis off them."

The warlock met her eye, inclining his chin. "Your men did admirably. Look how happy they are. I think they might like to keep their newfound abilities."

Mizzay's face darkened, and she put her hand over the grip of her holstered mage gun. "Ungeis them," she snarled. *"Now."*

"Very well." He waved a hand, and the wildly leaping men collapsed at once, groaning and wheezing, their chests heaving. Zavi cocked his chin, as if expecting a thank-you.

Mizzay gave her men a cursory inspection, then growled at the warlock, "I told you, no juicing, no curses, no nothing. We do what you ask, you leave my people alone."

"Your men can make their own decisions. They don't need you mothering them." He gestured. "These men volunteered for this mission...for an extra cut of the profits."

Mizzay's face—Hettie's face—contorted with murderous outrage, and the outlaw seemed to grow until she towered over the warlock. Glamor, Hettie reminded herself.

"You don't decide how our loot gets divvied up. *We're* the ones helping you, not the other way around. You wouldn't even be here if I hadn't taken pity on you. You're here because *I* allow you to be here. You got that?"

Zavi smiled faintly. He bent his head. "You are right, of course. I thought perhaps you wanted your men out of jail, so I sent a rescue team. You care about them, don't you?"

Her glare went diamond hard, and her nostrils flared. "I choose *how* I care."

Hettie glanced around surreptitiously, gauging what the rest of the gang made of this power struggle. The majority seemed undecided, though many were clearly still loyal to Mizzay. They were just too afraid of Zavi to stand directly behind her.

The outlaw glanced over at Duke Cox, who watched the proceedings with interest. "Duke. Where's Jonas?"

"Bought the farm." He shrugged. "Aren't you gonna ask how *I'm* doing?"

She barely looked at him. "You seem healthy enough." Clearly she was not pleased by his return, though apparently whatever bad blood was between them hadn't resulted in Duke's death. Mizzay narrowed her eyes on Hettie. "And what's *she* doing here?"

"Duke brought her. You should applaud his initiative." At her scowl, Zavi added, "Of course, I would've preferred her here *after* Fielding had completed his project. Diablo's powers might interfere with his work." He sniffed as he looked over the mage gun. "Still, there's no point in sending her back now. Once the device is complete, we can collect Abigail as well."

"You stay away from Abby," Hettie snarled, tasting bile. "You want revenge? Take it out on me."

"No need to be so eager. We'll get to you soon enough." Zavi's lips spread into a thin smile. "But I'm not so cruel as to deny you sisters a last good-bye before I end you painfully."

"You don't even need her," she said, remembering what Mizzay had said. "Why do you want us?"

Zavi seemed to contemplate that for a moment, as if he were perplexed by the question. "Because it would bring me joy to see you in pain?" He nodded, accepting that as the answer. "Yes, I believe that is the reason."

Mizzay signaled to the men behind her. "Chain her up."

"Put a round-the-clock guard on her, too," Zavi added. "She's slippery."

Hettie was frog-marched to the other end of the cavern, close to where the horses were kept penned. She couldn't imagine them being happy there. A rough cage made of wood planks sat near one of the paddocks. In the center of the cage, a metal ring was bolted to the floor. Hettie was put in manacles, and chains were threaded through the ring and her restraints. She had just enough slack to reach the bucket set in one corner.

Before she was locked in, rough hands searched her cursorily— almost too quickly, in her experience. Men like this were usually far more liberal with their pat-downs, especially considering she was wearing a dress. She was divested of her boot knife and the various protection charms and talismans Uncle had given her. They did not find the flexible stilettos woven into the boning of her corset.

Somehow they also missed Walker's talisman, tucked under her high collar, pressing a cold reminder that help was a drop of blood away. Walker's stepbrother, Raúl, had made the amulet before he'd died. It must have been enchanted with some powerful protection spells to keep from being noticed by the wrong element. Hettie was not about to summon the bounty hunter, though, not against such dubious odds. Besides, there was no telling how long it would take him to get to Colorado, much less find a way into the hideout.

The cage door slammed shut, and a grizzled-looking man was left to stand guard.

"You know he plans on destroying the world, don't you?" she said to his back. "That warlock only wants Diablo so he can end his existence here."

He didn't respond. She wondered if maybe Zavi or Mizzay had some kind of influence spell over these men.

"He's killed hundreds of children," she said more loudly. "For years, he kidnapped them and drank their blood to fuel his powers."

Still the man did not react. Hettie gripped the chains and banged them noisily against the floor of the cage. "You even listening to me? He turned a bunch of men Were. Juiced them till they were his slaves." She kicked the bars. "You saw what he just did to your friends. You think he'll stop there? He'd as soon step on you as do anything to help you. He doesn't care about anyone but himself!"

"Quiet, you," he muttered over his shoulder. "Or I'll take your bucket away."

She sat back, frustrated and utterly disgusted, and thought hard. Even if she could pick the lock on the manacles, she'd still have to get out of the cage. This was no time to act rashly. She had to be patient.

The guard changed every hour—at least, that was her estimation. Without any view of the world outside, she couldn't tell exactly how much time passed. Three guards later, her pleas for reason were still not getting through. None of these men cared for anything she had to say.

Hettie kept her fear and rage locked down as effectively as the chains and manacles circling her wrists and ankles. Even if she could escape the cage, she had to find a way out of the cavern, and then out of the mountains, and then back to Uncle or Sophie.

She breathed deep, willing herself not to panic at the thought that Zavi would be going after Abby next. He'd said they'd track her down only after the device was complete. It meant Hettie had some time to plan her escape.

A burst of cold, fresh air blasted and rippled from farther back in the cave. Zavi was opening another remote Zoom tunnel. She closed her eyes and listened carefully to the shouts echoing through the cave. Something about parts.

Parts for the engine, she assumed. She thought about shouting Fielding's name, getting some idea of where the Mechanik might be, but if she did there was no saying whether he could respond, and they'd probably stop her quickly. She had a feeling no one would balk at knocking her out to keep her quiet.

She studied her surroundings, trying to formulate an escape plan. If she had Diablo, she could give herself all the time in the world...

Not all *the time.*

She sat up. *Are you talking to me?* She projected the thought at Diablo, willing it to respond. The mage gun didn't answer. Zavi's null net was still firmly in place.

There had to be a reason for that. Diablo had punched through all kinds of containment spells, metal boxes, and magic-proof manacles. She reviewed everything she knew about Zavi and the Devil's Revolver, their relationship to Javier Punta, and the story about how the sorcerer had created the weapon. Abzavine had supposedly been pulled down from heaven to balance the demonic power bound to the mage gun, and to act as the wielder of Diablo. He was immune to its power and could move through time in much the same way Hettie could with the bubble.

The talismans the gang members carried were part of the null net and were made of parts of Zavi. She shuddered. Self-mutilation was one of the more perverse forms of blood magic. That Zavi could grow and regenerate so readily meant he could do it, if not indefinitely, then without major repercussions.

She thought about how nets worked—filaments woven together. That meant each talisman had to be linked to the others. The more talismans, the bigger and stronger the net. They probably only worked within a certain distance of each other, too. It would explain why the lone talisman she'd stolen from the police station hadn't affected her. If every gang member was carrying one of these linking talismans, it was no wonder she couldn't call the revolver to her.

Nets had holes, though. Small fish could get through nets that had tears, or nets that weren't constructed well. She had to think of a way to tear the net... or make herself so small she could get through it. Or maybe just get Diablo through it.

She went to the corner with the bucket. The man watched her intently. "You mind?"

"Don't let me stop you," he said archly.

"A gentleman would give a girl her privacy." She cut him her most dead-eyed stare, picturing Mizzay doing the same. He grumbled, then turned around and walked several paces away.

She squatted over the bucket and reached up under the gathers of her skirt. The stiletto blade was nestled between the boning against her stomach. She managed to work it out, grunting over the enthusiastic release of her bladder to ensure the guard didn't turn around, then palmed the thin blade, tucking it up her sleeve.

"You comfy?" Mizzay's drawl broke through her thoughts. Hettie hurriedly recomposed herself and turned. Her mirror image stood by the cage, hip cocked, watching her. Even in the burnished orangey light emanating from magicked glow stones set throughout the cavern, Hettie could see that the outlaw's split skirt and shirt, both in black, were well-tailored and of high quality. A subtle touch of embroidery and lace decorated the fringes of her sleeves and collar. Her black gun belt and boots were tooled and polished, and her gloves looked like kid leather. The spoils of her crimes, clearly.

Hettie sized her up. "I could use a pillow and some blankets. Maybe a foot massage."

The corner of Mizzay's mouth twitched up. "You eat yet?"

"You bringing a menu?"

She gave a low laugh. "You'll eat what we eat. It's Zeke's night to cook, so it won't kill you." She eased onto a stool. "Don't look so surprised or suspicious. You might be a prisoner, but it doesn't mean you're less than human. I treat people the way they deserve to be treated."

"Like all those innocent people you killed on the train and in New Orleans?"

Her brittle laughter crumbled any sense of decency the woman might have been pretending at.

"What do you want from me?" Hettie asked, lip curling.

"Can't a girl just have a nice conversation with another lady?"

"I'd have better conversations facing a mirror, and I wouldn't be sick to my stomach about it either."

The outlaw stood back. Her visage shimmered. Hettie's face dissolved, her square jaw lengthening, the features sharpening, her scar melting away. The woman who stood before her now was...well, beautiful, with full lips and big green eyes that sparked with manic light.

It was not the face of someone Hettie imagined shooting people in cold blood...but then, she'd been wearing Hettie's face while she was doing it. Cruelty and evil came in all stripes, she supposed, and sometimes all it took was a mask and a black hat to reveal a person's true nature. "Better?" she asked.

Hettie watched her. "You know Zavi wants to destroy the world."

"Honey, *all* men want to destroy the world. Nothing new about that."

"Why are you working with him?"

"Why does anyone do anything?" She splayed her hands. "I set out to make my way in the world. I throw my lot in with winners when I can." She pulled her gun out. "See this? He made it for me when we struck our deal. You know what this is?"

"A mage gun."

"That's right. Not many'd make one of these and hand that power over to another."

"He hasn't handed you anything. That's a trinket compared to what he's cooking up." Plus, all mage guns had a blood price. Whatever it was, Mizzay seemed to think it was worth it. "You have Fielding building an engine. Imagine what Zavi'll do when it's complete and he starts draining people of their magic and feeding it to himself."

Mizzay ignored her. "You should feel honored. I started this gang to take back power for people like me, and I did it in your name. You were a legend."

Hettie's insides churned. "I'm not anything."

"Back when I was whoring in Wyoming, I heard stories about a girl with a mage gun riding across the country, tracking down the men who took her sister. Same girl went and kidnapped a highfalutin' lady of wealth for ransom and killed a bunch of Division men and Pinkertons because they tried to stop her. Men came to the bar and told these stories...and they wanted to fuck that girl nine ways to Sunday." Her gaze hardened on Hettie. "That's why they came to me. They paid handsome for the glamor, for a chance to lie with the outlaw whore Hettie Alabama."

Hettie didn't break eye contact despite the nausea swamping her. A cold, slimy feeling crept over her skin. Hettie didn't care that Mizzay had been a whore—Ma had always treated the painted ladies in town decent, saying life was hard enough for women that they didn't need other women telling them what to do to survive. No, she felt sick that Mizzay had sold her identity, her story, her *soul*, as easily as if it were a crock of sweet churned butter. Given the way her love for her parents had been bargained away without her permission, every piece of who she was felt that much more sacred.

"After a while, I got famous in town for my act. Why, I could've gone on tour with the song and shimmy I made up." Mizzay looked up for a moment as if remembering, and then she sang in a full-throated, whiskey-laden drawl,

> *"The Division, the Pinkertons*
> *All came for me*
> *But no man has caught me before I could flee*
> *My six-gun's a-ready*
> *My aim's sure and steady*
> *I'm Hettie the outlaw, I'm coming for you."*

At those last words, Mizzay pumped and gyrated her hips suggestively. Hettie remained stone-faced, even as her cheeks heated. She didn't miss the bawdy double entendre.

Her doppelgänger laughed. "It was fine playing you. But it was never enough. *I* was never enough..." Her gaze grew distant, and the corners of her mouth turned down. "My customers wanted the *real* Hettie Alabama, the outlaw who did what she wanted and thumbed her nose at authority. They wanted to dominate a girl they thought couldn't be tamed... or else *be* dominated."

"That's not what I do," Hettie gritted out. But Mizzay was too caught up telling her story.

"After a night with me... after they realized I wasn't you... well, it could get ugly sometimes." A cold smile slipped onto her face. "One day, I realized all I had to look forward to for the rest of my cursed short life was the ceiling in that whorehouse. Then I thought to myself, why can't *I* be *you*? Who'd even know the difference? I can do what you can. Better even." A delicate scar slid up her cheek as if God were painting it on as she spoke.

"My boss didn't like it when I told him I was leaving the whoring business. I was making him a lot of cash. He threatened to break my legs to keep me from leaving. So I shot him through the head, cleaned out his safe, and ran." She grinned. "It was thrilling. The freedom. The excitement. I get why you enjoy it so much."

"I don't go around shooting innocent people or robbing banks. And I don't *enjoy* this life," Hettie bit out. "I just survive it."

Mizzay snorted. "Please. You have all that power and you're telling me you never used it to take what you want?"

Hettie glared. "All I've ever wanted was for my sister and me to be left alone."

The outlaw laughed unkindly. "Don't lie. Everyone wants something. To be rich. To be famous. To be respected and treated like more than a second-class citizen. To be free to love who you want to. To be free to just *be.*"

Maybe some of her friends wanted that. And Hettie thought perhaps she was all right using Diablo's powers to help them—or at least to prevent them from coming to harm—but for herself? Did she know what she wanted for her and Abby?

How would Mizzay secure her safety and well-being? How would anyone with a mage gun handle Hettie's situation? The answer came too easily, and she pushed those thoughts away. "Ain't nothing that can win me any of those things without strings attached. Not in this world."

"That kind of thinking just speaks to a lack of creativity and gumption." Mizzay sneered. "So all you want is your sister? You could've had that. You could've settled down anytime, retired to a nice little cabin in the woods."

Hettie narrowed her eyes. "With glamor powers like yours, you could've had that, too."

"*This* is true freedom. True power. The moment I killed a man and went on the run, I knew life would never be the same. I had to look out for myself."

"So you conned a bunch of gullible lowlifes into joining your posse."

Mizzay smirked. "Glamor's a neat thing—it makes people see what they want to see, even when they know the truth. These men around me see a legend, a hero, a mother, a lover—they're loyal to me 'cuz I'm what they want most in life. Something reliable. Something fierce. I don't just have a posse. I have a *family*."

And yet, despite all the power she claimed to have, she wanted something more. "And what does Zavi have to offer you?"

Mizzay tipped up her chin. "A girl can do nice things for a stranger in need, you know. It's called being a Good Samaritan."

Not a trace of irony lingered in Mizzay's statement, confusing Hettie.

Mizzay went on. "We found him after we'd robbed a payroll wagon in Arizona. He was a pitiful wreck—no shoes, barely any clothes. I swear he'd just clawed his way out of a grave. "I took pity on him. I used to get juicers in the saloon looking for comfort, and I could see he was in a bad way. So I gave him the sorcerers we'd tied up, and he drank 'em dry. Healed like that." She snapped her fingers. "I could see then he was special. Powerful. And then he said he could be helpful to us. He made me this." She held up the mage gun, gazing at it adoringly. "I call him the General."

"You can't trust Zavi," Hettie said.

"You're right. But I trust the General. It's the only thing I'd trust in this world." Mizzay's grin flashed white, almost parallel with the scar glamored across her face. "Men lie and cheat and break promises and do whatever it takes to keep their power over you. But a trigger you pull yourself? That's yours."

Hettie glanced down at the General. "What about the blood price?"

"Power always has a price, and I'm more than willing to pay for my fair share." Mizzay gave a low chuckle. "This makes me legit. This makes me *you*. Far as I'm concerned, the General makes me *better* than you."

Before Hettie could retort, one of the men called, "Mizzay, Zavi wants to talk to you."

She nodded and glanced at Hettie again. "Get comfortable. No one can find us here, and even if they could, they wouldn't be able to find a way in. Zoom or portal's the only way in or out." She smiled. "You're gonna be here awhile."

CHAPTER SIXTEEN

W hen Hettie cracked her eyes open the next day, or after however much time had passed, she found Duke Cox leering down at her.

"Breakfast is early 'round these parts." Hettie sat up and stretched, surreptitiously studying Duke. "I'll take two eggs and bacon. And I like my coffee strong."

"The boss wants to see you," he grumbled.

"Would that be Zavi or Mizzay? I'm a little bit confused about which master y'all serve."

"I don't serve anyone," Duke snapped.

Interesting. "You and Mizzay had some kind of falling out, huh?"

"Some kind," he muttered.

"Let me guess. It started falling apart after Zavi joined the outfit."

He remained stoic as he unlocked the cage. She kept talking. "What's the story with that mage gun? When did Zavi give it to her?"

"I told her she shouldn't have taken it," he said under his breath.

Hettie clung to that. "Mage guns have a blood price. You know that, right? What does the General do to Mizzay?"

"Stirred up her head, is what." He glowered and added in a hiss, "Ever since she started using that thing, she's lost her mind, bit by bit. She never had cause to kill before. It was always about the money. She was smart. Now she shoots folks for fun. She don't trust anyone. Not even me..." He suddenly seemed to realize who he was speaking to, and he clamped his lips shut.

"Duke, listen to me. Help me out of this. If I can stop Zavi, maybe I can stop Mizzay, too."

"Stop him?" He huffed. "There's no stopping him. Beg for a quick death, girlie. And hope Mizzay doesn't get to you first."

Duke yanked her to her feet and steered her through the cavern. Her chains clinked as she passed tents and men in cots, horses and small fires that did little to stave off the damp chill in that dark, stony cavern. She wasn't sure how the smoke was escaping from the cave if there were no vents to the outside, but looking up, she couldn't tell where the ceiling was. The entire mountain might as well have been hollow.

The warlock stood by a great machine, its tooled brass parts gleaming with runes. It looked like Fielding's engine but...not. The shape of it was different from either of his prototypes, almost as if some of the tubes and pieces had been inverted. Instead of a sickly drawing sensation, the device radiated a kind of menace, as if it'd just been extracted from a hot oven.

She didn't understand. If the Alabama gang had stolen the prototype from the lab, why were they building a new device?

Inside one cavity, like a rat huddled inside the ribcage of a buffalo carcass, was Fielding, tinkering with some mechanism while another man held a glow stone set in a lantern over him. The scientist looked up—hopeful elation lit red-rimmed eyes—and then his dirt-streaked face crumbled in despair.

"How's your progress, Dr. Fielding?" Zavi's liquid voice pooled in Hettie's gut.

"I...I need more time. And parts," he added hastily. "And these conditions aren't ideal for such delicate work—"

"I've every confidence you'll produce results. As for parts, my men are out gathering everything you need."

"They'll be contaminated by the remote Zoom," Fielding said, gaze flickering side to side. "I can't work with what they're bringing me. Perhaps if I were to collect the parts myself and work outside of this setting—"

"For a man who is supposedly brilliant, you're remarkably naïve, Doctor." Zavi waved. "The Zoom affects nothing metal. It is the metal that affects the Zoom. But you've already seen it isn't affected, so…" He waved his hands in a "go on" motion.

Fielding bit his lip and met Hettie's eye. Something like fear shone in his face, and his gaze canted toward the machine. She didn't know what he was trying to communicate, but she stayed alert.

"I've brought Miss Alabama here to give you some incentive," Zavi said silkily.

Manacles were clamped onto her wrists and attached to about ten feet of chain on either side. Two men pulled so her arms were spread wide. Zavi set a wooden box on the ground before her and kicked the cover off. Inside, a coiled rattlesnake as thick as her leg writhed and shook its tail menacingly.

"Don't worry, it's only a golem," Zavi assured her mildly. "I don't want you dead right away, after all."

Hettie screamed as the serpent darted out, sinking its fangs into her arm. The cold bite turned instantly to searing agony, and her bicep swelled until she thought it might explode. She struggled against the chains, trying to pull away from the box, but the men held her firm. She could barely move.

The rattlesnake struck again, its bite puncturing her thigh. Fire blossomed through her leg and into her groin. It was worse than when she'd been shot. She sobbed as her whole body thrashed against the magical poison flowing through her.

Zavi didn't want her dead. Not yet. Not until she was utterly broken.

She moaned past a slowly swelling tongue. This was just the beginning.

"Stop!" Fielding shouted. "There's no reason for you to do this!"

"If you want it to stop, I suggest you get your device working so *you* can stop it." Zavi folded his hands in front of him. The golem slithered out of the box and headed straight for Hettie. She cried out, struggling between recoiling or trying to kick the serpent away.

The rattlesnake lunged, plunging its fangs into Hettie's ankle, and coiled around her leg. She screamed hoarsely as new pain found

181

her and dug its hooks in. Those fangs were so long, she thought they might have hit bone.

Desperate to leave her body, to die, to make the agony stop, she thought of Diablo. She thought about how dying now would end it all—the running and hiding, the suffering, the uncertainty, the responsibility...

Her fingers curled. She could almost feel the mage gun's weight in her palms, as warm and reassuring as her father's hand in hers. If she ended it now, Zavi would have no reason to get Abby. Her sister would be safe—

Suddenly the rattlesnake crumbled to sand. Zavi's furious scowl contorted his face into a nightmarish gargoyle's visage. "You dare to call on Diablo for *comfort?*" He strode up and kicked her swollen shoulder, sending a million needles stabbing through her arm.

She could barely catch her breath, gasping through a throat that was closing up. Death would claim her soon—the golem wouldn't kill her right away, Zavi had said, but it would kill her eventually. If she died now, she'd have a victory over the warlock.

She grinned up at him through bloody foam.

"No. No!" He grabbed her by the shoulders. "I promised you nothing but pain. *You* don't get to die!"

His voice grew distant. Hettie's vision blurred. And then she was flying down a long tunnel with light at the end.

I'm coming, Ma, Pa.

Shang wasn't gifted. Ling had known that when he'd first met the On Fook tong leader, and yet now he sensed the faint glow of the gift around him. Juicing was considered unclean by many of his people—there were theories that mixing Qi with other magics was bad for a person's soul. Others simply looked upon it as lazy and indulgent. But just because it was frowned upon didn't mean it didn't happen. Even if you couldn't perform any spells, magic gave a person an especially potent high.

That Shang was juicing wasn't all that surprising to Ling, though. For all his bluster, the man rarely lifted a finger to dispense his brutal discipline. He left the accounting to the tong money men;

he pretended he had wisdom by telling tong members who were fighting to resolve their own issues. He was a skilled evader of work and boasted that the success of his leadership was due to his ability to delegate. *Lazy*, Ling heard others grumble, but no one dared call him on it. Big Monkey and Ah Chang were bored too often to turn down a beating.

"Beautiful day to be making money, isn't it?" Shang greeted loudly as he strolled into the tong, his hatchet men following silently behind him.

A few tight smiles and nods at Shang confirmed everyone else's lukewarm feelings toward him. Brother Wu had never displayed such pomp. The tong was for forming community, not making money, though the Wus had certainly drawn an income from the fees and investments they made. Shang slapped the accountant on the shoulder and murmured something to him before laughing too loudly, too boisterously. Something was up.

"Little Dragon," he called. "Come with me. We have something to discuss."

Ling followed the man to his office.

"I have a job for you," he said. "There is a package I need picked up from the docks."

"I have patients to see today."

"Don't worry, this is an errand to run in the evening, and it is only a small package. Not dope, I promise." Shang smirked as if being reminded of Wu's betrayal was funny. "I don't trust anyone other than you to get it." He handed him a slip of paper. "The boat is scheduled to arrive tonight. I'd rather you pick up my parcel before it gets manhandled in the unloading. You'll meet my contact, and he'll deliver the package directly to you."

"What is it I'm picking up?"

"An old family heirloom. My family's statue of Kuan Yu. I asked my mother to send it to bring the tong good luck. Nothing illegal about it, I promise you." Again, that flash of teeth.

"And that's all?" Ling couldn't help his suspicion.

"That's all." He smiled broadly. "I simply don't trust these rough oafs' hands. They'll likely drop the crate and break it, and then I'll be sending apologies to my mother for years and serving the best part of my roast pork to Kuan Yu in retribution." He gripped Ling's shoulder, squeezing with more force than necessary. "You're the only one I trust with this, Little Dragon. You and your nursemaid's hands." He laughed.

Ling acknowledged him stiffly and left, feeling like a target was on his back. Could this be a trap? Shang could have tipped off the police that an unregistered sorcerer was working with him. But the police and the Division could have come straight to the tong and arrested Ling if Shang wanted him out. And Ling had done nothing to draw suspicion to himself, unless someone had mentioned that he'd been asking about Brother Wu and Little Wu's disappearance.

He didn't think anyone at the tong had taken great offense to his presence, but who could say for certain? Members still avoided him. No one asked him to tea or to play a round of fan-tan. They only spoke to him if they had health issues.

It didn't make sense. Shang was too lazy to set some elaborate trap for him. If he wanted him arrested, beaten, or killed, he could have done so anytime.

Ling brought the news back to Ah-Gu at the herbalist shop. He found her working with Abby in the rear apartment. Abby sat cross-legged in a containment circle, palms turned faceup on her knees. Soft light glowed in her hands.

Ling knew better than to break a sorcerer's concentration midspell, so he stayed in the doorway and waited for Ah-Gu to notice him. Softly, she clucked her tongue, the sound plucking the air to draw Abby out of whatever trance she was in. "You may rest now, Abby."

The light faded, and Abby blinked her violet eyes slowly. A frown creased her face. "Hettie's sleeping with big lizards."

Ling glanced at Auntie Wu. The woman watched her steadily. "What did you see?"

Abby shrugged and picked at the hem of her shirt, her interest in the vision fading. Ling walked farther into the room and opened his bag, handing Abby an orange. "Here. For you."

She grinned and bit into the peel as if it were an apple.

"You're teaching her to scry?" Ling asked. He'd mentioned the soothsayers' blackout in confidence to Ah-Gu. She'd said a few of the soothsayers she knew had been blind for some time.

"No. I'm testing her Vision."

"Vision" was a gift almost as rare as necromancy. Some sorcerers claimed they had the ability to see what was going on within distances of up to ten miles, though their reports were not reliable. It was a limited gift; he knew of no one whose skill was so specific they could, say, read a document from afar or see what lay beneath a cloth cover or even look at another man's cards if they were turned facedown on the table. But a sorcerer with Vision could supposedly see things as if they were in the same room, from any vantage point they chose.

"Her Vision is distant, but her sight is clouded." Ah-Gu sighed. "I left a few items in the next room and asked her to tell me what was there. She did. But then she started describing what was outside the door, then in the street, then farther and farther..." She shook her head. "I'm having a hard time deciding whether what she sees is real or imagination."

He'd learned not to dismiss anything Abby said. She was simply too prescient, her powers growing day by day. He knelt next to her as she inspected the protection circle.

"Hello, Abigail."

She blinked up at him as if she'd only just noticed his presence. Juice ran down her chin and made her hands sticky. She'd eaten the whole orange, rind, seeds and all. She stared at him for a moment as if recalling something. "Ling, why do people do things that are wrong?"

He and Ah-Gu exchanged looks. "That's a complicated question, Abby. *Wrong* means different things to different people. Some people don't live by the same rules as other people. Right and wrong are complex ideas."

"But some things are always wrong, right?"

"I suppose. It's never right to kill an innocent person, for instance. But a person might have to kill someone to protect someone they love." He didn't want to give Abby any absolutes that might cause her to pass judgment on her sister.

Her lips pressed as she mulled that over. "What's a... sacrifice?" she asked.

He wondered what spirits she'd been communing with. "A sacrifice is giving up something important for something else that's also important." Seeing that she didn't quite grasp the concept, Ling held out another orange. "It's like this: I want to eat this orange, but you also want to eat this orange. You're more important to me than sating my own hunger, so I'll give this orange to you."

Her brow wrinkled. "But we could share this orange."

He chuckled. "We could. And then maybe we'd both have a little satisfaction, but you'd be hungry again soon and we'd have the same problem and no orange to help us. Sharing the orange wouldn't be as beneficial as me giving it all to you. Sometimes we can't split the difference. We have to make a choice and decide what's more important. I put your health and well-being above my own. So I'm giving you my orange."

Abby accepted the orange, turning it over in her hands, still looking unsure. "How do I know what's more important?"

"That's not a question I can answer for you, Abby. Ultimately, we all make our own choices. That's what sacrifice is."

"Okay." She paused. "Ling, who's Yung Goh?"

His throat dried and constricted. "Yung Goh...he's my older brother. Did Ah-Gu tell you about him?"

Her eyes locked with his. "No. Siu May did."

His skin prickled, and his heart sped up. He felt as though the air had been sucked from his lungs. He carefully schooled his features and did his best not to shy away from Abby and her uncanny violet stare.

Abby went on. "She said she's not happy with Yung Goh. He has a new girlfriend." She wrinkled her nose. "I don't know why anyone likes him. He's ugly."

Ling stifled a nervous laugh. "My brother's got charm."

"Siu May said that, too. Anyhow, she wanted me to tell you she's not happy."

His fingertips went numb as his nerves deadened all over his body. This couldn't be...this couldn't be right...

"You did a good job today," Ah-Gu interrupted. "Meditate before you go to bed tonight, Abby. Half an hour."

Abby got up and stretched, swiping a toe over the containment circle to break the spell. She went to the other room, humming to herself.

It was a long moment before Ah-Gu said, "She's a necromancer, then."

He nodded dumbly.

"A necromancer who can apparently talk to spirits on the other side of the world."

"She's talked to others from far away." The words tripped off his tongue awkwardly. "Unless someone else told her about Siu May." He glanced up, hoping perhaps Ah-Gu were playing some horrible joke on him. She was not.

"I didn't know her name," she replied. "Some here know what you did, but not the exact details."

He shook his head. "I can't talk about it."

"You geised yourself with silence. Why? Is the truth so horrible?"

"I don't like to talk about it."

"It doesn't take an exorcist to know this has haunted you for years." She studied him down the length of her nose. "This is your problem, Li Ling. This burden you carry has made you like an ill-tempered ox who won't shake off his yoke or leave the field. Your silence makes you standoffish. Unapproachable. You could smile more often as well." She gentled her voice. "Undo the geis. Tell me what happened."

Ling sighed. Reluctantly, he pulled a piece of twine from around his neck and draped it over his shoulders. He murmured the words that would undo the years-old silence spell, felt it lift from him like a heavy mantle slipping off.

He inhaled deeply for the first time in years. "Yung Goh got a girl in the village, Siu May, pregnant, but he refused to take responsibility. He was always shirking his duties, whether it was school, chores, or work." He scoffed, that mixture of pity and resentment still churning through him after all these years.

"At the time, I was training to be a healer with the old masters. I was on the verge of graduating, and my father was so proud of me. I didn't want to have anything to do with my brother's dramas... but then Siu May came to me one night, begging for my help. Her family had disowned her when she'd started to show. She'd tried to abort the baby too late and had induced labor instead."

Ah-Gu's expression didn't change. "You couldn't say no."

"I thought I could deliver it, take it to the orphanage, and save everyone the heartbreak and hardship. I just wanted to do what was right..." He swallowed past a lump in his throat. "The baby didn't

187

make it. And Siu May bled out and...it was a hemorrhage. I tried to use my healing abilities to stop it but..."

"Your healing magic can't stop death."

Tears ran down his face. He hadn't cried about it since leaving his homeland. He'd kept all that pain and regret rooted deep inside, held back by the silence spell that kept him from even thinking about it. "I had two bodies and blood on my hands. All I wanted to do was give them an honorable burial..."

Ah-Gu passed him a handkerchief. "But you were caught, and everyone drew their own conclusions."

"My brother didn't even defend me. And I couldn't make any excuses. I *did* kill her." He hung his head. "But before the magistrates could try me, Yung Goh broke me out of holding, gave me some money, and smuggled me aboard a boat bound for America."

"Charitable of him."

"Hardly. There was a chance I'd expose his misdeeds, so he made sure to get rid of me. He was just too cowardly to kill me himself. He begged me to simply leave and never return. I'd already tainted the family honor, so I left. It was that or face execution."

"And so here you are."

He nodded, miserable.

"I understand now." She got up and opened a money pouch, withdrawing some notes from it and counting the thick wad of bills. He hung his head. He'd have to find somewhere to take Abby where she'd be safe. Find another teacher for her.

"Siu May has likely become a hungry ghost. Since her family disowned her, I imagine she and the baby have been haunting your brother. Part of her probably followed you here as well." She handed him a sheaf of bills. "Go to the temple and burn some offerings for Siu May. Then buy some roast pork, oranges, and incense for the shrine, in case she tries to visit with Abby. Perhaps you can assuage her spirit some. Take care of that tonight. She has haunted you long enough."

He stared, nonplussed. "You're not kicking me out?"

"Why? Because you made a mistake when you were young?" She shook her head. "You did what you thought was right, even if you were completely misguided about it. You aren't blaming others for your errors. You live with regrets. And you're trying to do better by helping those around you. If that is not the definition of atonement, then I don't know what is."

"It's just…I thought…most people don't want me around once they know about what I did."

"My brother did."

"He didn't know the whole story. He was different."

"And so am I. Stop judging people before you actually find out what they think of you. Everyone's made mistakes."

"Not like mine."

She sighed as she got up. "I can't stop you from feeling guilty or from punishing yourself for the rest of your life because you think you deserve it. It is important we acknowledge the past and honor those who came before us. But this shame doesn't serve anyone, especially Abby, and that girl needs you here and now." Ah-Gu glided to the door. "Stop living with your heart in the past. Siu May's ghost will cling to your feelings as long as you let her. Her spirit is anchored to your grief. Turn away so she can finally rest. The dead need to sleep, too."

The place in-between was all too familiar. Hettie looked around, hoping this time, there'd be a guide, someone to meet her, to bring her to her family. The mist swirled around her legs. No one came.

She sighed, stuffing down her disappointment. Not dead then. At least she wasn't in pain here.

She started forward, assured that wherever she went, she would find whoever she needed to. Patrice, maybe, or Crying Sparrow, or the Indian woman who had helped her find Abby.

She walked so long through the mist her feet were getting tired. Why wasn't anyone coming? There'd always been someone to meet her. Someone she needed to talk to.

Maybe she *was* dead. Maybe *this* was all there was waiting for her on the other side.

"Don't get *too* excited," she grumbled to herself, surprised by her own voice. She cleared her throat.

"I'm here again," she said out loud to the grayness enveloping her. "Patrice? It's Hettie Alabama." Worry gnawed at her. The last time she'd spoken to the Soothsayer of the South, she'd said something about fading from this place.

"She's not here."

Hettie whipped around. The voice was familiar, but Hettie couldn't put a name to it.

"Who's there?"

"You know who it is."

Hettie's skin prickled. "All the same, I'd prefer to talk to you face-to-face."

The figure who emerged from the mist was exactly who she thought it was, and yet she didn't know what to call him. Everything inside her knew the young man before her was her dead brother, Paul. But she also knew this wasn't the place he'd ended up.

"I'm who you'd be most comfortable seeing here." The corner of his lips lifted in a crooked smile, so like their father's, yet softer.

Hettie swallowed thickly. "You're...him."

"I don't give out my name freely. Not even to you, Hettie Alabama." He stuffed his hands in his pockets. "Last time I did, I ended up bound to a mage gun. But you can call me Diablo if it makes you feel any better."

It didn't. She braced her feet. "What are you doing here?"

He shrugged. "I'm stuck because of Abzavine's null net. He's put a helluva whammy on me this time. Keeping my powers suppressed." He sounded just like Paul, had all his mannerisms. "What are *you* doing here?" he asked.

"I think I came here...looking for someone. I think maybe that someone was you."

He spread his hands. "Well, you found me. Now what?"

"I'm not sure. I thought you'd have the answers."

"If I did, we would already be out of that place and on our way home." He turned. Suddenly they were back on the ranch. He sat down under the cottonwood tree on the hill where her family was buried. Their graves were there even in this vision world.

"Is Patrice still alive?" she asked.

Paul—Diablo—closed his eyes. "I'm not sure. Death is a sure thing; it's the one thing I know. But she's not dead, and she's not quite alive. Maybe that's why you keep meeting her here. That hole in your soul is like a wide-open doorway."

"But she's not here."

He chuckled. "Not 'here,' no. There are more places than *here* between your world and the worlds beyond."

"You mean like heaven and hell?"

He laughed outright. "If only it were that simple. Those names you have are just that—names made up by men who think in black-and-white terms. As if there's right and wrong and good and evil, and that you end up in one place or another. Sure would make life a lot easier if that were the case."

"But...you're a demon. I've been to hell through the hell gate. I thought Zavi was pulled down from heaven to be your wielder to...to balance out the good and evil."

Paul snorted. "That would make it nice and neat, wouldn't it? As if we can tally all of magic in a ledger." He rubbed his jaw in thought exactly the same way her father used to. "Javier Punta was a wise man and a talented sorcerer, but he didn't understand the first thing about who or what I was, what binding me to a mage gun meant. He called me a demon and Zavi an angel—the wielder who controls me. Did it ever occur to you that for someone who's supposed to be my equal and opposite, with that kind of power and control, Zavi can't handle me very well?"

It hadn't. She'd assumed Zavi's vast powers, his immunity to Diablo, and his ability to move with the time bubble the way she did meant he was the divine force Punta had claimed him to be. "You're saying he's not an angel?"

"You're assuming there are only two powers in the universe. That making Diablo only opened two gates and let two beings through, and that they're equal opposites. There are infinite realms, Hettie Alabama, and they're all populated with beings I can't begin to describe." Paul shrugged. "Who can say where he's from? Whatever spell Punta used to summon me must have opened a portal that accidentally sucked that poor creature through. Maybe he ate up whatever story Punta fed him about being an angel. There are some very impressionable beings out there."

He wiped his nose and sniffed. "Fact of the matter is, for all the power he has, Zavi's trapped here the same way I am. I'm used to it mostly—your world is fun. Finite. Where I'm from, everything goes on and on forever. It's a bit of torture, actually." He flashed his teeth. "I just got that's why you call it hell."

Hettie processed what Diablo was telling her. If Zavi wasn't a divine being…an angel…then he was just a warlock. A sorcerer. A powerful one who had some handle on Diablo, but not the unstoppable force she'd originally feared.

Still, it was hard to ignore that ethereal aura about him.

"Tell me about these other places—about where Zavi is from."

"I don't know anything for certain. I can tell you about where I'm from…but you already know that." He gave her a brief, grim smile. "Some are places like this—galleries connecting realms where some of us can congregate. Others are more like public corridors between only a few places. Roadways. Some of them you can get to with your body, some of them you can't. You and Abby have been playing hopscotch through them for a while now."

She tensed at the mention of her sister. "Do you know if she's all right?"

"She's fine for now," he assured her. "Zavi can't find her, and it'll stay that way as long as you don't call for her."

"What do you mean?"

"You two have a connection stronger than blood ties—like a pair of tin cans on a string. You used to play that game with me. With Paul, I mean."

She remembered. "So…as long as I don't call out to her, she'll be safe?"

"For now." He glanced over his shoulder. "I don't like that thing Fielding is building. The engine was bad, but this…it's something else."

"Like what?"

"I don't know. But I don't like it." He grimaced. "You have to stop him."

"Why? What's he building?"

He closed his eyes. "I don't know. My Vision used to be clearer. But it's clouding…"

"At least explain to me why Zavi wants to open the hell gate and destroy the world."

"I'm not exactly sure that's what he wants." He shook his head. "We're connected, he and I, but not as intimately as you and I are.

Sometimes I get the impression…it's like when you were young and you used to make those big piles of mud by the creek and cover them in stones? You used to call them—"

"Little castles." She smiled faintly at the memory.

"But then afterward you'd stomp on them. Just jump on them and flatten them down, even though you put all the work into making them perfect. Do you remember why?"

"I…just liked the feeling. They were mine, and I didn't want anyone else to do it." Hettie wrinkled her brow. "Are you telling me Zavi's acting like a child?"

Paul smirked. "There are two great forces in the universe. Creation and destruction. Neither is inherently good or evil, but they are each their own forms of power. Every act of creation or destruction opens a gateway to a new realm. But no matter how much he's built, he hasn't been able to do the one thing I can: open the doorway to home. It's made him bitter and angry."

"And insane?"

"Insanity is relative. He's a creature trapped in a place he doesn't belong, and he can't accept it. I think that's why he's doing what he's doing. Maybe he's hoping someone will notice what he's doing and take him home."

"So you're saying he's throwing a tantrum till he's put to bed?" Hettie spread her hands. "That's ridiculous. He's a grown man."

"Grown in your eyes, perhaps. I told you, there are infinite realms, populated by beings you can't begin to imagine. For all we know, Zavi may only be a child where he's from."

Hettie paced. She refused to accept the warlock and all his plans for world destruction were based on the whims of an immature brat. "This is unbelievable."

"Reason is something mortal men made up to explain the unexplainable. They even need it for magic." He chuckled. "Can't you have a little faith?"

"Faith is for people who can't think for themselves."

Paul tsked. "Now that's awfully mean and cynical. But I suppose you've had your faith tested too often for you to believe in much anymore. Except me, maybe." His lopsided smile was wholly their father's. "Hell, I'm a demon stuck in a gun, talking to you in a dream world while wearing your brother's face, and you seem to have no problem with that."

She exhaled in frustration, a headache beginning to pulse at her temples. "That doesn't really help me."

"Nah, I s'pose it doesn't." He studied his boot tips. "Hettie, you have to stop Zavi. That's all I know. What he's doing is ... wrong."

"I'm going to need more than 'wrong' if I'm going to stop him. What exactly is he planning?"

"I don't know." He pursed his lips and glanced up. "There's not a lot of time left. When you wake up, you need to get out. There's a chance now." He looked around again, as if sensing something coming. "You're the only one who can stop Zavi. Stop it all from happening."

"But how——"

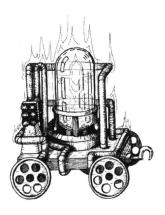

CHAPTER SEVENTEEN

The whinny of a nearby horse woke Hettie. She cracked her sticky eyes open. One of the outlaws was whipping a big dark bay mare as she pulled on the lead and thrashed her head side to side.

"Calm down, ya big bitch." The man brought the crop down hard across the mare's snout. She screamed in outrage and turned a tight circle, plowing into the man and knocking him over. She kicked dirt over him as she trotted away. A couple of men standing outside of the corral laughed.

"Told you not to take that one," one man said. "She's magicked. Should've gotten a dumber horse."

"She'll fetch a good price at market," the handler argued. "Soon as I break her."

"You're still thinking like a rustler, Jon. Ain't worth it."

"Maybe Zavi'll do some magic to help calm her down."

The two men snorted as they left. "Yeah, why don't you ask the warlock to help you break a magicked horse? I'm sure he's got nothing else he needs to use his magic on."

Jon jammed his hands on his hips and stared down the mare. She'd backed herself into the far corner of the corral and watched him warily. "If you're so smart, you'd better figure out *I'm* your master now. I ain't above shooting you, neither."

The mare lowered her head and stomped the ground, making Jon jump. He hopped the fence and hurried away.

Hettie sat up slowly, taking stock of her aching body. The dull throbbing of her muscles reminded her of the golem snake's near-fatal bites. The swelling was gone, as were the puncture wounds. Her flesh and skin were tender to the touch. Zavi must have healed her, brought her back from the brink of death.

The mare turned her head toward her, ears twitching. Slowly she walked to the side of the fence closest to Hettie and stretched her neck out.

"Yeah, I'm a prisoner, too." Hettie reached out to let the horse sniff her, but the chains were too short. She huffed.

Well, she wasn't dead. And there was no guard, meaning they didn't think she'd wake up so soon.

She called to Diablo, asking a question in the dark. No response came.

The mare lipped the bars. She had to be at least seventeen hands—a standardbred, if Hettie wasn't mistaken. She must have belonged to someone of wealth to also have been magicked.

The horse shook her head, the lead jingling from the harness. The idiot outlaw Jon had left it on to trail through the dirt. It could catch on something and seriously hurt the creature…

Hettie sat up. That was it.

"Maybe we can help each other." She pried the stiletto blade from between the floorboards where she'd hidden it. Diablo had said she had a chance to escape now. But even if she got out of the cage, how would she get Fielding out of the cavern?

If it was a choice between escape or rescuing him, she'd choose escape. She was no good to anyone locked up. To the horse, she said, "Throw me your rope. If you can get me out of here, I'll do what I can to get you back where you belong."

The mare tossed her head, and the rope swayed. She shook out the lead and swung it over the fence. The end of the lead eventually snaked its way across the ground to the edge of the cage. Hettie stretched out a leg, caught the rope with her heel, and dragged it toward her. She tied it through the ring at the base of the cage and secured it tight.

The mare watched steadily. "Okay, girl, it's up to you."

The horse walked backward and tautened the line. She jumped back, yanking hard. Muscles stood out on her neck as she dug her hooves into the dirt and pulled.

The wood floor around the ring creaked. Hettie started bashing the planks with the edge of her iron manacles, bruising her wrists and gouging tiny, satisfying chips and shavings out of the worn, flaking wood. The horse pulled and pulled. Suddenly there was a cracking noise. Hettie grabbed the ring. "Pull! Pull!" She heaved up with all her might while the mare rocked back.

The bolts popped out, and the ring was wrenched from the floor. Hettie flew backward, but she didn't waste a second. She grabbed the lead before it could slip away and secured it around one of the wood bars. "One more time."

The wood snapped easily. Hettie kicked the bars loose and pried herself out of her splintered prison.

"Hey! Hey you!" A man ran toward her, fumbling with his sidearm.

She grabbed the chain and whipped it at the man's head. It landed with a mighty crack, and he stumbled. Hettie tackled him, stiletto in hand. When he tried to sit up, she smashed the iron manacles against his face and jammed the thin blade into his throat. His eyes widened, and he gurgled as she drew the scalpel-sharp stiletto across the soft flesh of his neck, opening a red, gaping second mouth. Hot blood spurted over her hands, and the man thrashed. Then he was still.

Hettie's vision went gray as she shakily clambered off his body. What triumph or relief she might have felt was numbed by a deep coldness seizing her from the inside. Distantly she realized this was the second man she'd killed with her own hands.

Trembling, Hettie dragged the man's corpse into a corner of the corral and searched the body quickly. She took his bowie knife as well as every stone, bone, and feather on him. It was possible one of these was a talisman that could help her escape. For good measure, she took his hat—a lot of folks sewed talismans into their clothing. His gun, however, would do her no good. She needed Diablo.

"Any ideas on how to get out of here?" she asked the mare.

The bay turned toward the other horses bunched shoulder to shoulder in the far corner of the holding pen. There had to be at least twenty ponies jammed in there, all of them miserable in the dark, close confines. Hettie could almost taste their misery. They shifted restlessly and watched her as if she were some kind of predator.

"They'd make a good distraction, sure, but we need to portal out of here. Or else we need to dig our way out."

The mare blew out in a huff and stomped the ground. The other horses flinched and shied away.

If she got them stampeding through the cavern, Zavi would have to open a portal to get them all out in a hurry. Unless he decided to kill them all...but that would leave the gang with a heap of dead horses to dispose of.

It was a grim chance, but it might be the only one she had.

"Listen," she said to the other horses. "We're getting out of here. But if you want your freedom, we're going to need your help."

She hadn't exactly expected a rousing battle neigh, and maybe she felt silly for speaking to them as if they were anything other than mundane horses. But Horace had said she had a gift. Anything was worth a shot. "All we have to do is run 'em down. Run, run, run! That's all you want, isn't it? You don't wanna be stuck here in the dark anymore, right?"

The horses shifted and crept forward, snuffling the air inquisitively.

"Run, run, run!" Hettie whispered again. She pictured the wide-open plains of Montana, green grasses and rolling hills where these horses could run free, their hoofbeats drumming against the earth like thunder. "Run away with me," she coaxed, pushing that image into her words.

The mare blew out of her nose as if to say, *Good luck convincing them.* Hettie clenched her jaw. With one last look around, she opened the gate.

As if she had other ideas, the magicked mare stomped the ground, lowered her head, and charged the other horses, giving a challenging whinny. The creatures startled and rushed toward the open gate. Hettie slapped their passing rumps the way she did driving cattle, shouting and whipping them into a dash.

There wasn't much room in the cavern for the horses to move, and they were hesitant to stampede. She grabbed a stick of wood from a nearby fire and mounted the mare. "Sorry about this," she said aloud, then smacked the nearest horse in the rump with the glowing tip of the stick.

The horse screamed and bolted. Hettie did the same to several more horses, then threw the stick into a pile of hay. It went up like tinder. Smoke and flame and thunder filled the cavern. The outlaws were roused now, shouting as the horses streamed through the cavern. They trampled men, crashed through tents, knocked over barrels and crates. There'd be casualties, both men and horses, and Hettie was sorry for it. But she had to get out.

Hettie urged the standardbred into a gallop. She deftly maneuvered across the uneven floor while Hettie stayed low on her back in the hope that she wouldn't be spotted. Men tried to grab their horses' bridles, but they darted every which way, evading them. Many of the animals slipped and plowed into the ground. Hettie heard the sickening snap of a leg, along with an agonized scream.

The ceiling trembled, and sand rained down upon her head. The horses plowed onward, reaching the other side of the cave. The air here was cold, and the tip of Hettie's nose grew numb. Freedom! A Zoom was already open! It didn't matter where it led as long as it was out of there.

She spurred the mare on, aiming toward the men gathered around the portal. Three other horses crowded near them, desperate to escape, but then a gunshot cracked, and the horse to Hettie's right reared and fell. Another crack—the horse on the left screamed and twisted away.

The remaining horse, a big white-and-brown pony, angled in front of the mare and drove straight for the men blocking the portal. They waved their hands and weapons as if to stop it. The pony gave an outraged cry, and for a moment, Hettie almost felt as if she understood.

Run, run, run! Run!

The pony crashed into the men and swung her thick hindquarters around, bowling the outlaws over and bucking and kicking any that got near. Hettie's mare dove through the gap in the line of men, head down, aiming straight for the Zoom.

There was a slight sucking, and then Hettie and the mare emerged on the other side into the cool, crisp night air.

They kept running.

CHAPTER EIGHTEEN

The boat Ling was looking for was not docked at the pier. He checked and rechecked Shang's note and the name of the contact, but he found nothing matching the name or description, and he'd already been up and down the water's edge twice. As he searched for the vessel, he kept one hand on the pistol in his pocket and one eye behind him. He extended his senses as far as they would go, but he detected no suspicious magic in the vicinity.

If this were a trap, something should have happened by now.

He walked around the buildings, weaving through the shadows, but the place was silent, the thick fog and damp cold his only companions. He waited another hour before giving up and heading back to the herbalist shop.

Perhaps the boat was late in arriving. Or maybe Shang had given him the wrong information. Or maybe he'd given whoever was supposed to meet him the wrong information, which was somehow exactly what Ling imagined the tong leader would do. Ling hadn't been keen on being attacked, but at least he'd been prepared.

When he reached the doorstep at Ah-Gu's, he halted in his tracks. The anti-Eye wards had been burned off and torn from the overhang. The door frame was splintered, and the door, hanging off one hinge, gaped open as if in shock.

His heart leaped into his throat. *Abby!*

He rushed in, gun drawn. The place was in shambles. Jars and pots were smashed everywhere. Boxes had been emptied and overturned. Someone had hacked long gouges into the counter with a big blade of some kind.

A man lay facedown in the center of the room. His pulse was thready, his breathing shallow. He was not long for this world. Ling turned him over. He was a white man dressed in a loose brown suit with a high collar, like the clothes Ling's countrymen wore. Blood trickled from his mouth, and Ling could see why—his chest had caved, the ribs inside pulverized. Wherever they were, Ah-Gu and Abby had put up one hell of a fight.

He quickly divested the man of his talismans and weapons, finding a Division enforcer badge in an inner pocket. His carefully banked anger surged through his veins. "Where are they?" he demanded. But the man only gurgled, blood bubbling from the corner of his mouth.

Ling opened his third eye. The violet miasma that trailed after Abigail when her indigo powers were activated barely misted the room. He tried not to panic as he followed the fog, tracing it to the living quarters, which had been similarly torn apart. The bedding was shredded, the furniture and kitchenware smashed. He'd expected to see more of her indigo power in here, but there was nothing.

His heart stopped. Cymon lay in the corner, unmoving. Ling checked him over quickly—still alive, thank the gods. Someone had put a sleeping spell on him rather than shooting or maiming him. They must have wanted to keep things quiet. Typical Division tactics: stealth over violence.

He fed a thin thread of his power into the mutt. The dog opened his eyes, then rolled up to sitting, panting and looking around. His ears drooped, and he whined. "It's okay," Ling said, patting his neck. "We'll find them."

Ling glanced around, swallowing thickly. The fight had definitely moved in here, but something was amiss. Where were all his belongings? What few items of clothing and bedding they used weren't scattered about, but he couldn't imagine why the Division would take them; they couldn't be certain who they belonged to, so taking them for curses was counterproductive.

Ah-Gu's favorite teapot lay cracked in half upon the ground like a perfectly broken eggshell, exposing the dark tea stain rings within. Upon closer inspection, he noticed an inscription inside.

The most precious of gifts are hidden.

The way the pot had broken was no coincidence—it hadn't been smashed. It bore the faintest trace of magic, too. It was a talisman—a clue for him to follow. He looked in the direction the spout pointed and followed it to Ah-Gu's large wardrobe. Except for a few items of clothing, it was empty.

Or was it? He touched the back of the wardrobe, sensing the trace of magic there. The panel was made of strongly scented camphor wood, used to keep moths away. A protection spell had been infused into it, subtle, layered.

Abby's violet miasma was entirely absent from this spot. Which was strange considering the way it wafted around the rest of the room.

His heart beat hard. He knocked softly on the wood. "Abby?"

The faintest scrape, and the panel popped open. Abby peered out from the foot-wide space, blinking. "Are they gone?"

He pulled the panel away and helped Abby out of the hidey hole. Cymon woofed, tail wagging as he sniffed her, checking her over. Somehow all their belongings had been stashed inside the tiny space as well; Ah-Gu had managed to hide all evidence of their presence. The interior of the hidey hole and panel was carved and painted with dozens of containment and protection spells.

Abby gripped his hands and shuddered. "They came after you left. They started to break down the door. Ah-Gu put me in here and told me to meditate, so I did." She gazed around her, frowning, tears filling her eyes as she took in the destruction. "I just did what she told me to do," she sniffed.

"You did fine, Abby. You didn't do anything wrong." Ling cleared a space and sat her down. "What can you tell me about the people who were here?"

"There were three of them. A fourth outside with a..." She trailed off and gestured. "Machine."

"You mean an automobile?"

She shrugged.

"Did they use magic?" he asked.

Abby nodded. "But they weren't as strong as Ah-Gu. She did a big spell and fought them. I think she ran out..." She closed her eyes. "I didn't see anything else. I had to meditate."

Ling cursed. This had to be Shang. He must have been looking for Ah-Gu all along, and sent the Division to collect her for him. She was the rightful leader of the tong, after all. She'd held the purse strings for most of Brother Wu's tenure. If Shang had something to do with her brother's and nephew's disappearances, Ling was certain that meant he was involved in this attack, too. Auntie Wu had no heirs; when she passed, the tong would receive a large stipend to continue servicing the community. Shang could be speeding up that process.

Which meant Ling and Abby were still in danger.

"We have to go," he said, gathering their things quickly. "We can't stay here."

She glanced at the nearly dead Division enforcer and licked her lips. "I'm hungry."

Of course she was. She'd been in that closet for hours, meditating. Ling should probably find her some sustenance, but the healer's shop was a ruin, and sweeping together the ingredients for one of Abby's blood-appetite-suppressing teas would take too long.

As a Paladin-class healer, he was bound to do no harm with his magic. But he'd sworn to protect and care for Abby above all.

He nicked the Division agent's wrist with his knife and held it out to her. The man was dying—his last act in life might as well be something productive. "Don't take too much," he warned. If she drank him dead, she could harm herself. The blood of the dead had been known to poison vampires. He couldn't be sure how it would affect Abby.

He looked away as she set to drinking the low-level sorcerer's blood. It was one thing to feed her himself, another to watch her take nourishment from a man who couldn't object. He didn't want to set a precedent, but he hoped Abby knew better than to drink from any random person on the street.

She stopped after a minute, looking a little less pale. The man was dead, but if Abby knew it, she didn't seem to notice. He might as well have been an empty coconut shell, drained of its sweet water.

"Ah-Gu gave me this." She pulled a slip of paper from her pocket. "It's an address where we can get help."

Ling read the slip, memorizing the street name and number. He set it ablaze immediately, then grabbed their things and left out the back way, Cymon on their heels.

Ψ

They managed their flight unnoticed. The address Ah-Gu had provided was to a laundry that was closed for the night. He spotted one of Ah-Gu's wards hanging in the doorway, disguised as a windchime. It glowed faintly with protection spells. He went to the door and knocked.

The door cracked open, and a familiar pale face peeked out. "Brother Ling?"

"Li Fa." Of course. She was the only other person who knew about Abby. He glanced around. "Ah-Gu sent us."

Her eyes widened, and she ushered them in. Ling pushed Abby ahead of him, along with Cymon, and the young woman glanced down in surprise. "What happened?"

"Ah-Gu was attacked and taken by the Division. She left us a note to come here. I think Shang might have been the one to tip them off. He sent me on an errand tonight at the pier, but his contact never met with me. When I returned, she was gone, and the shop's in ruins. There was a dead Division enforcer there."

"I haven't heard anything about any kind of shipment," Li Fa said. "And Brother Shang likes to boast. I think he set you up."

Ling cursed his foolishness. Of course Ah-Gu had been in danger. He'd thought all this time it might have been about him, but he'd been used...again. And he'd nearly gotten Abby captured in the same breath.

He glanced at the serving girl and shook his head. "It may not be safe for you at the tong anymore," Ling said. "If Shang suspected me enough to have me followed home, it's likely he suspects you, too."

She bit her lip. "So what will you do now?"

"I have to find Ah-Gu." He couldn't leave her with the Division. "Will you take care of Abby for me?" He was already heading for the door.

"I want to help," Abby said. "I can help."

"I know you can, Abby, but right now I need you to rest and be safe. I may need you to save me if things go awry." He smiled lopsidedly.

Abby looked at him seriously, her violet eyes going distant. Then she nodded and turned away.

"Brother Tsang, what are you intending?" Li Fa asked.

"I have some questions for Shang," he growled. Then, as an afterthought, he called, "Cymon. Come."

CHAPTER NINETEEN

The journey back to New Orleans by train was long and boring. The Zoom had dropped Hettie in the middle of Kansas, fortunately not too far from civilization. Once she'd found a town where she could telegraph Sophie and leave the magicked mare in the care of a local hostler, the debutante had wired enough funds to pay for a private cabin from Jackson, Wyoming, for Hettie to travel in. If any of the porters who brought her meals thought it strange that a young woman in men's clothes was traveling and dining alone on the voyage, they didn't ask. Just as well—she didn't want to have to kill anyone on this trip if they fingered her as her notorious outlaw doppelgänger.

When Hettie finally arrived at the Favreau mansion, she was met only by anxious frowns.

"Fielding?" was Sophie's first question. It'd been nearly a week since Hettie had broken Duke out of jail, and the debutante's only concern was for the missing Mechanik.

"The Alabama gang has him. They're making him build something, only I'm not sure it's an engine." She added, "He's alive. They won't kill him till he's finished his work, is my guess."

"Jeremiah never made it back," Marcus told Hettie gravely. "He hasn't checked in with us since he telegraphed to let us know what happened in Chicago. We assumed he was after you."

"He probably still is." She paced to the window, hoping to see the old coot standing in the garden. He'd tracked her just about everywhere she'd been, and while Kansas was a long way off, she'd left a note with the stationmaster to let Uncle know, should he pass through, that she was headed back to New Orleans. Of course, if Uncle knew she was safe, he might take the opportunity to visit the local saloon.

Hettie related her harrowing escape from the hideout and told them about Fielding's captivity. She spared her friends the grislier details of Zavi's torture. She didn't mention the guard she'd murdered either.

"So you lost Diablo?" Marcus asked.

Reflexively she tried to conjure it, but it stuck fast. "It won't come to me. Zavi's created a null net to contain it. I'm not sure how it works, but all the gang members have talismans like the one I took from the jail. They're made of Zavi's bones and are spelled to contain or mute the gun's powers."

"That net should only be affecting you, though." The Favreau security man blew out a breath. "I don't know much about Diablo or this Zavi, but the way you're bonded with the Devil's Revolver…it'd take some serious magic to keep it from coming to its wielder's call."

"If Zavi has Fielding's engine, he could be juicing enough to keep you two separate," Sophie said.

"That's the thing—I didn't see a working engine anywhere. The big prototype was gone from the university, so we assumed the Alabama gang had taken it. But that cavern I was in couldn't have hidden that thing easily, big as it was. And the machine Fielding was building wasn't anything like what we saw at the symposium."

At that moment Horace hurried in. A pair of goggles that appeared to be two jeweler's loupes joined together rested on top of his head. The heavy apron Fielding wore for welding hugged his broad chest.

"You're back. Thank God." His smile of relief had a question in it, too.

"Uncle's still missing. That's nothing new." She forced the wry reassurance into her voice, wondering if maybe she was trying to convince herself more than him.

He nodded and turned to Sophie. "Miss Favreau, I think I've got the engine assembled."

Sophie shot to her feet and headed for the salon where the engine had been. The rest of them followed. "What?" Hettie chased them down the hall. "How?"

"It was a simple matter of fitting the pieces together like a big puzzle—Marcus helped me decipher some of the spells on the parts, of course, so that it all worked together. Fascinating workmanship. I've tinkered with other machines before—boilers and even a player piano once. But this…" He tapped a screwdriver in his hand, grinning at the machine. "It's really quite something."

"You're too clever by half, Mr. Washington." Sophie studied the gleaming engine with its glass canister, the bands of brass encircling its girth like wobbling planetary orbits. It reminded Hettie of a big shiny egg waiting to hatch. That strange sucking sensation radiated from it, though not nearly as powerfully as the larger prototype from the university. "Does it work?"

"Well, that's another matter. I can't say for certain. Not without testing it out."

"Then test it on me," Sophie said.

Marcus stepped forward. "Miss Sophie, I cannot allow this. If anyone should volunteer, it should be me."

She fixed him with a stony look. "I can't be responsible for anyone in my employ being hurt by this procedure, and I would never compel anyone to volunteer for this potentially dangerous test. Besides," she added with a sniff, "I have more magic than you that can be siphoned off without doing too much harm."

The security man's lips flattened. "Perhaps we could find a volunteer—offer a stipend and put out an ad—"

"We don't have time for all of that. Fielding is out there building God-knows-what for that warlock, and Grandmère is wasting away with every minute we hesitate. All we have is this." She gestured at the engine. "And before you even suggest it, I won't test this on Grandmère either. We don't know what could go wrong."

"I object to this." Jemma stepped forward. Up to that point, she'd been still as a pillar. "Miss Sophie, you can't put yourself at risk. You're the heir to the family fortune. Your grandmother would have all our jobs if we let you do this."

"My grandmother isn't here." The coolness in her voice seemed to remind her bodyguard of her place, but Jemma was having none of it.

"Then have some consideration for my position and Marcus's." Her voice was sharp and to the point. "If you do this, we've failed in our duty to protect you."

Sophie looked chastened, but mulish conviction lit the gaze she levelled at Jemma. "Your positions are fully guaranteed, regardless of what happens to me," she said evenly. Aristocratic authority simmered in her tone. She nodded decisively at Horace. "Mr. Washington, if you please."

Horace glanced between a frowning Marcus and Jemma before bringing the two leads to Sophie. "Mr. Washington," Jemma bit out in warning.

"With all due respect, Miss Baron, Mr. Wellington"—Horace addressed them in the most civil tones—"Miss Sophie is her own woman and can make her own choices." He attached the clamps onto Sophie's hands, then went to the control panel.

Marcus ground his jaw, practically growling. "Can you do it with minimal effect?"

"I believe so. The settings go from zero to ten. The gauges should tell us something about how the machine works. Assuming I've put it together correctly." Horace grimaced at Sophie.

She sat in a tall-backed chair. "I put my life in your hands, Horace."

The hostler-turned-Mechanik flipped some switches. The engine whirred to life, its hum filling the room. It was much smaller than the one in Fielding's lab, but the effect still made goose bumps stand all over Hettie's skin.

Sophie gave a gasp, and her fingers clenched. She shut her eyes, breathing deep. "I'm all right," she gritted. "I feel like...I'm being drained..."

"That's enough. Stop it," Marcus barked. Horace quickly shut the machine off. Sophie released a breath and hunched in the chair. Marcus checked her quickly while Horace inspected the glass canister.

"It worked." He sounded surprised. He lifted the cylinder from the engine, a faint glow emanating within. "Miss Favreau, look. This is your magic."

The debutante glanced up. Hettie was shocked to see just how tired and haggard she looked. Deep, dark shadows ringed her bloodshot eyes. Her hair was limp and greasy, as if she hadn't bathed in days. Her skin was sallow, and the cheeks that were normally full and rosy seemed sunken, the skin curdled.

"Did it take *all* of her magic?" Hettie asked. For some reason, she'd expected Sophie to adjust more quickly, but she looked ready to faint. The days and nights obsessing over the engine, and watching and worrying over her grandmother, had clearly taken their toll.

"It shouldn't have." Horace inspected the machine again. "I can't see anything wrong right off, but I'm no expert."

"Well, you better figure it out quickly. You were the closest thing Fielding had to an assistant," Marcus said. "Let's return her magic right now."

"No." Sophie held up a hand. "Horace, I want you to put my magic into my grandmother."

Horace grimaced. "With all due respect, Miss Favreau, we should test this by putting your magic *back* into you. We can't be certain the . . . transfusion will work."

"We saw it work at Fielding's demonstration. My grandmother's well-being must come first. When she wakes up, she can tell us what's going on."

"Sophie, don't be stupid," Hettie said impatiently. "You said you didn't want to test this on your grandmother. We should try to reverse the process before we test anything on Patrice."

Sophie snarled, "You *would* say that. You don't care about my grandmother. You don't care about anything except your precious sister and that infernal gun. She asked you to do one thing—find the cause of the soothsayers' blackout—and you haven't lifted a finger! I'm going to save Grandmère and my family's fortune, and if you're not going to help me, then get out!"

Hettie set her teeth, taken aback by Sophie's sudden turn. "I've been helping *you*. You haven't exactly been—"

She didn't realize what Sophie was doing until she'd drawn a small, shiny pistol from the folds of her skirt. "I will not be coddled!"

Jemma and Marcus both stood back, hands raised, shocked. Hettie held absolutely still. The derringer was small but just as deadly as any other gun.

"I'm tired of people telling me what I can and can't do," Sophie cried, tears trembling in her eyes. "I've had a lifetime of it."

"No one's doing that. But maybe you should put that thing away." Hettie forced herself to sound casual. "You don't want to hurt anyone you care about, do you?"

"You're not the only one with family in danger, Hettie Alabama. If nothing else gets done, I *will* save my grandmother."

"You will," Jemma said softly, sliding between her and Hettie. "But you need to stop and think and be cautious in this moment." Her words broke through Sophie's raving mood.

"We'll help Patrice, Sophie, I promise you that," Hettie added. "And I *will* find out the cause of the soothsayers' blackout. But we have to be careful with this machine. We don't want to harm your grandmother in case something goes wrong."

Sophie stared around, almost as if she didn't recognize anyone. Slowly she nodded and started to sit. Jemma deftly slipped the gun out of her grasp as she helped her into the chair. "Yes... yes, of course," Sophie said. "That's entirely reasonable."

Marcus nodded to Horace. The hostler quickly reattached the clamps and reactivated the machine. The light in the canister faded. Sophie took a deep breath, as if she were being reinflated. The color returned to her cheeks, and in a flash her perfect facade was restored.

"Oh, my." The engine's drone dropped off. "That was not pleasant at all."

"How do you feel?" Hettie asked.

She hesitated, as if taking stock of herself, flexing her fingers and touching her face and arms. Her dress seemed to ruffle and puff up momentarily, like a bird shaking its feathers after a bath. "My magic does seem to be restored. But I feel... different."

"*Bad* different?"

"I'm not sure. It's almost as if... well, if one were to remove the feathers from a mattress and then try to stuff them all back in. I'm not certain it's all quite there." She glanced around the room, her eyes landing on the derringer in Jemma's hand. She bowed her head. "I...apologize for my earlier outburst. I was not myself."

Horace wiped a hand over his mouth. "I think we should avoid any further tests until we consult Dr. Fielding. I can't be sure the engine was assembled correctly." More grimly, he added, "I'm sorry."

Sophie waved him off. "This is not your fault, Mr. Washington. You did your best, and better than most."

"Even if we got Fielding back," Hettie said, "we can't be sure this isn't what the engine *normally* does. What if the design is flawed? Fielding said this is a portable prototype—he might not have worked out all the kinks. Plus it could have been damaged in the blast."

"Hettie's right. But for now this engine is all we have." Sophie blew out a breath. "There's nothing for it. We need to get Fielding back." She folded her hands in front of herself. "I think it's time to call the authorities to help locate him."

"We can't risk the Division's involvement," Hettie said. "They want Abby. They'll know I was here, that Diablo was here. I don't even want to think what they'll do to get the answers they want out of us."

"Perhaps there's an alternative," Horace interrupted. "What we need are hired hands."

"Bounty hunters?" Jemma asked with a curl of her lip.

Hettie's thoughts flew to Walker, but she stamped out that tiny hope as quickly as it came.

The hostler paced. "We'll need someone with a bit more authority and firepower if we're going up against the Alabama gang on their own turf. Miss Hettie has seen the cave where they're hiding. A sorcerer can magick the exact location out of her, right?"

"If you mean plumb her mind, then yes, it's possible," Marcus said. "Though I'm not sure Miss Hettie would appreciate that."

"I don't." Friend or foe, she didn't want anyone digging around in her head. "As for firepower, considering the numbers I saw, it'd take an army to roust the gang from their nest."

"We have the team here," Marcus pointed out.

"I don't think you want them associated, just in case things go south. Some folks take exception to private armies traipsing across the country to wage war on a private citizen, even if they are outlaws," Horace said seriously. "No, we need something a little more official but a little less...scrupulous."

"You want us to hire a posse to storm Zavi's hideout?" Marcus asked incredulously.

"Not a posse." Hettie read the sparkle in Horace's eye and felt her gut churn. "He wants us to hire the Pinkertons."

CHAPTER TWENTY

re you mad?" Jemma exclaimed, taking two big steps toward Horace. "We can't invite those...those black hats here."

Horace raised his hands. "Hear me out. If I know one thing, it's business. You could hire mercenaries, deputize sheriffs, gather a posse of farmers with guns to attack this hideout. But if you want anything done right, you pay professionals. The Pinkertons are that in spades. They have a license to operate, the resources to carry out their directives, and a business reputation to maintain. They won't ask needless questions, either—they understand their clients' privacy comes at a price, one I'm sure you can afford."

Sophie sucked in her lip. Hettie stared. "You can't be seriously thinking about this."

"I'll consider any and all possibilities at this point," she said. "The Favreau family has hired Pinkertons in the past for delicate personal matters."

"They didn't bat an eye at the idea of shooting you," Hettie reminded her harshly.

"That was three men, all of whom are dead by your hand, I'll add." She didn't sound the least bit remorseful for bringing it up. "I'd like to give the rest of the Pinkerton Agency the benefit of the doubt—they fired that Mr. Stubbs, after all. Mr. Washington is right. There's a reason they've been in business this long. They get results."

Hettie rubbed at the ache forming between her eyes. Now Sophie was just being willfully ignorant. "I've got a fat reward on my head. And as you so kindly pointed out, I killed three of theirs. I don't think the Pinks would turn down the chance to capture me."

"So we'll make sure you're nowhere nearby when they're here. We can hide you, scrub any evidence you were ever here from the place. This mansion holds a lot of secrets." Sophie glowed with renewed hope; her mind was made up.

"Look at it this way," she said, the corner of her lips twisting. "If we send the Pinkertons after the Alabama gang and they all kill each other, you won't have to worry about any of them."

Sophie forged ahead, regardless of Hettie's misgivings. The debutante sent a telegram to the Pinkerton headquarters in Chicago, requesting assistance. They replied within hours, informing Sophie that representatives of the Pinkerton Detecting Agency would arrive in a day or two.

Sophie was as stubborn as a dog with a bone now that she'd set herself on a course of action. No one could convince her how suspect the Pinkertons' motives might be. Marcus and Jemma were loyal to their employer, so Hettie doubted they could talk any sense into her. And she found herself silently resenting Horace for giving Sophie the idea in the first place.

The staff got busy scrubbing all evidence of her and Uncle's presence from the mansion. There were four house sorcerers—general healers, talisman makers, and spellcasters—who paced through the house swinging censers and murmuring incantations. "To purge Mr. Bassett's spell trail," Marcus had explained.

Apparently the old man had been leaving quite an impression wherever he went these days, like a bad smell from a mangy dog, though Marcus and Sophie had been too polite to mention it. It worried Hettie. Jeremiah was usually very careful about leaving trails for anyone to follow. She hoped the old coot was all right, wherever he was. If he'd been here, he would've stopped Sophie from involving the Pinks in their schemes.

All of her and Uncle's belongings were packed and shipped to an inn, where they'd stay for the duration of the interview with the Pinkerton agents. To keep in line with the story of the poor relations, the household was told there'd been a falling out and that Sophie'd had them relocated. That way, if the Pinkertons went to visit them, they'd find an empty room that looked somewhat well lived in, but no Wiltshires to interrogate. Any truth magically compelled from the staff would align with the gossip.

Meanwhile Hettie would be safely ensconced in the mansion, hidden away like a dirty secret. She hated being sidelined, but she didn't have much choice. She didn't have Diablo or any of its powers; against the Pinkertons, she was a liability.

Unfortunately she was far from free of the Devil's Revolver. She'd tried to pick up one of the sidearms in the Favreau's armory and had been rewarded with a sharp sting across her palm. The mage gun's curse still had a hold on her, even if she couldn't conjure it.

She fingered the grip of the bowie knife she'd taken to carrying. She hadn't been without a gun since her brother was killed. And Diablo had been a part of her since the moment they'd bonded.

Hettie frowned at herself. Had she become entirely dependent on the mage gun for her security? Jemma and the others had told her this could happen. And now she'd lost the one thing that had made her useful. Important.

You can do more than pull a trigger, she reprimanded herself. Diablo was more than a weapon, and she was more than its wielder. She might not be as capable as either Jemma or Marcus in hand-to-hand combat, and she might not have the gift like Uncle or Sophie, and she probably wasn't as learned or skilled as Horace...but she'd found Abby, kept her safe, mostly, and was helping Patrice in her own way. Whatever that was.

Restless and out of sorts, she walked through a long gallery filled with portraits of Favreau ancestors. Several of the richly dressed distinguished ladies and gentlemen were sorcerers of the highest caliber; Hettie could tell by the shields they wore as symbols of their magical rank. At least two of them were Paladin class—the highest rank achievable through non-Division training. Paladin sorcerers were the mundane military equivalent of captains.

Toward the end of the gallery was a large portrait of a younger Patrice, wearing a gown of embroidered roses and surrounded by full bloodred blooms, holding the sigils of her soothsayer status: a silver hand mirror and candle.

Next to the portrait of Patrice was a much smaller portrait of a rosy-cheeked, blue-eyed man with a somewhat sullen countenance—Sophie's father, presumably. The only things Hettie knew about Atherton Homer Favreau were that he was very rich, very mundane, and, according to Sophie, very opinionated. Sophie must've taken her looks from her mother.

Loud voices echoed down the corridor, and she followed them to the east wing.

"...Not this way." Sophie's tone was low, calm. Hettie peeked through the crack in the door, seeing Jemma pacing in tight circles, hugging her elbows.

"You can't test fate like this!"

"I'm not testing fate. I can only embrace it. There's no escaping what's to come." Sophie reached out, grasping her bodyguard by the forearms. "Jemma, I have to do this for Grandmère. We need to know about the rest of her vision."

"Not at the cost of your *life*!" Jemma cried. Tears streamed down her cheeks. "We could run away. Far away from all of this. We have money. We could go to France. We could go shopping and eat croissants every day like we always talked about and be happy—"

Sophie chuckled. "You hate shopping."

"I'll go to every damned hat shop in Paris if you'd just leave this all behind now." Her sobs racked her. "Patrice would not want this for you."

Sophie gathered her close. Jemma was nearly a head taller than Sophie, and yet she shrank in her arms. They collapsed onto a settee together, Jemma's head resting against her shoulder. "Shh, shh. No sense in spilling tears. This was the way it was always going to be."

"Doesn't mean you have to go rushing headlong into all this. That engine is dangerous. We should destroy it."

"Not until we can help Grandmère." Sophie cupped her cheeks. "I've come to accept what must be, my love. There's no use fighting fate. All we can do is appreciate what we have now."

She leaned in and kissed Jemma deeply. Hettie blinked rapidly, felt her cheeks burn as Jemma wrapped her arms around Sophie's waist.

Hettie quickly and quietly left the scene. She didn't think her footsteps could be heard across the plush carpeting, but much later, as she tried to focus on the books about talisman-making in the library, Sophie slipped in, shutting the door behind her.

Hettie fixed her face into a blank, trying hard not to notice the way Sophie sparkled, her lips red and plump. "Evenin'."

Sophie smiled tightly. "I want to talk to you about something."

Hettie shut the book she wasn't reading. "Okay…"

"I know you were there. I know you saw…us." Her cheeks pinkened, but she didn't look frightened or even particularly embarrassed. In fact she was smiling. She caught Hettie's frown. "You don't approve."

"It ain't that," she replied. "I just thought… well, when you met Walker, you were smitten with him." She gritted her teeth—she still sounded jealous.

Sophie laughed lightly. "Who *wouldn't* be smitten? For all his rough edges, he's a force to be reckoned with. Don't tell me you're immune to his charms."

Hettie flushed. Sophie sighed. "To answer the questions all over your face, I *do* like men. Just not as much as I love Jemma. She is my soul mate." Her lashes lowered, and she clasped her hands. "But I have a duty to marry well to maintain the Favreau family status. Glamor or no, I won't be young forever. The only reason I've put it off this long is because I want a man who will accept Jemma and understand his place in our lives. We will have to have children, raise a family, but Jemma will be a part of that. And Jemma doesn't like to share."

Hettie felt a twinge of sympathy for Sophie. In Newhaven there'd been a pair of spinsters who'd lived together quite happily for nearly forty years. Hettie had never considered there might have been more going on, but now all the whispers about "those odd women" suddenly made sense. "I won't say anything. It's not my business. Or anyone else's."

"Marcus doesn't know," Sophie interjected.

Hettie had a hard time believing that, but then again, some men were clueless. "Does he need to?"

"Jemma insisted we not say anything. She thinks it would compromise their working relationship. The arrangement has always been that the Barons—Jemma's family—serve the Favreaus. All the Barons have been body men and personal guards for our family since we arrived on the shores of this country. My great-great-great-grandmother prophesied that a Baron would save a Favreau in every generation, up till the time when magic ended. And it has been so." She looked away suddenly, as if she'd said too much.

"Wait…your grandmother had a vision about you and me, didn't she?" The memory was hazy, but she'd thought it odd at the time. "And Jemma thought we were supposed to be 'the ones.' What did that mean?"

Sophie sighed. "It wasn't a clear vision—it was one of the last ones she had before she lost her scrying abilities. She told me to go to Barney's Rock, where I'd meet four riders. She told me they'd bring about the end."

Hettie's skin prickled. "The end of what?"

Sophie went on as if she didn't hear her. "We all thought maybe she was getting soft in the head. Grandmère's always been eccentric. But now, with the blackout, I think it's something more than that. Her Vision is unparalleled in the Western Hemisphere. She could always see the clearest and the farthest into the future among all her peers. She was the first to fall ill. The other soothsayers have followed by rank, almost to the number." She looked up bleakly. "I think they can't see the future because there is no future to scry."

Hettie thought of Zavi. "Like…the end of the world?"

Sophie shook her head. "No. Scrying gives soothsayers access to the threads of the past and future. I'd hoped I was wrong, but the moment I saw Fielding's machine…" She shook her head. "I think she meant the end of magic."

Hettie stared, the pit of her stomach hollowing out. "The magic drain…it can't just disappear completely, can it? All the theories—"

"Are only theories. The mysteries of the universe are vast. I think we have to assume magic can stop existing, and that we have no way to stop it. It must have gotten to the point where even the Division had to do something about it, even if they aren't officially acknowledging it. Maybe that's why they were so interested in Fielding's engine."

Hettie rubbed her temples. If Patrice's vision was right, what did it mean for Abby? Could her sister survive if there were no magic? "Why didn't you tell me about your grandmother's vision before now?"

Sophie's glass-green eyes shimmered. "We don't tell people's futures, in case they try to avoid them. That doesn't usually end well; no matter how fast or how far you run, all roads lead to the same place."

"I make my own future," Hettie said stubbornly. "And I wouldn't have run."

"Everyone runs. Or they try to." Sophie smiled wryly. "Fate's not an enemy you can outpace."

"Maybe." Hettie squared her shoulders. "But you had no right to keep this a secret. That you didn't trust me with it tells me you don't care who you might have hurt. You're not the only one who has something to lose if magic disappears, you know."

Sophie stiffened. "The truth is, I don't know what's going to happen. Without Grandmère's complete vision to guide us, I don't know how to proceed. We can prepare for the future, minimize damage, but we can't avoid it. Grandmère didn't see how the end came about, only the final result. The end of all this." She gestured around the library, the New Orleans mansion. She meant the end of the Favreau fortune and legacy.

So that was why she was so scared. An end to magic meant financial uncertainty for many of the wealthiest families in the country. Anger seared through Hettie. Was money all Sophie cared about?

She raked her fingers through her hair. She'd thought perhaps Sophie was beginning to have more sympathy for her, for others, but she didn't. She was the same self-centered girl she'd always been.

And you're not? Grudgingly, Hettie supposed her own vow to keep Abby safe at all costs was just as selfish. But if she could save others with what she knew, she was certain she would at least try. Or better yet spread that knowledge and let them save themselves.

She locked gazes with Sophie. "End or no end," she gritted out, "I'm not going to allow your mistakes or your omissions to put Abby or anyone else in danger." She pulled herself up, her decision made. "I made a contract with Patrice to find the source of the soothsayers' blackout. If the end of magic is what brings that about, I'll consider the terms of the contract fulfilled. Otherwise I intend to keep that promise to her. I'll be leaving you once you have Fielding back."

"You think you can just go off on your own? What resources do you even have? You've no horse, no gun, not even clothes. You are here on my sufferance. You can't do this without me. Hettie, where do you think you're going? I'm still talking to you…"

Hettie ignored her. True, she had very little to work with apart from her reputation as an outlaw. But she'd pulled herself from the depths of hell once. She'd figure it out somehow.

She wasn't doing anyone any good here.

CHAPTER TWENTY-ONE

The Pinkertons showed up the next day.

Only some of the staff had been apprised of the visit; Marcus thought it best not to make anyone nervous by telling them the detecting agency would be snooping around. Meanwhile he and Horace moved Fielding's engine out of the house and into one of the storage sheds, where it would look like just another piece of machinery. They couldn't risk losing the prototype.

"It's best you not step foot outside this room," Jemma told Hettie as she unlocked an empty room among the servants' quarters on the top floor of the mansion. Hettie was even given a servant's uniform and instructed to lie in bed under the covers should anyone come in. She'd pretend to be sick with something contagious to keep busybodies away. "Miss Sophie's glamor will keep their attention on her, but any major distraction could break her hold on them."

"Maybe I should hide under the bed while I'm at it," Hettie grumbled.

"That'd be too suspicious." Jemma looked around the room as if she were considering other possibilities. "Just stick to the plan."

Hettie let out a huff. "I hate being cooped up like this. I'm the one who knows where Fielding is. I'm the one who's seen the hideout."

"And you're the one the Pinkertons are looking for. For once in your life, Miss Hettie, stay put and keep quiet. If the Pinkertons agree to our terms, you'll have plenty of opportunity to show us all what you know."

The condescension was clear in her tone, but rather than take umbrage, Hettie felt chastened. Jemma was right, of course. Hettie sat on the narrow bed as Sophie's bodyguard left. The snick of the lock felt like an extra slap to the face, as if she couldn't be trusted to stay put. After her blowup with Sophie yesterday, she was feeling particularly sore, and itchy to have this scheme over with. If she'd planned better, she could have left the mansion in the night, maybe stolen Midas as a last cut to the debutante, but that wouldn't have earned her any points. The fact was, she was a wanted woman, and the mansion was the safest place she could be.

She couldn't tell if or when the Pinkertons arrived. The interview was being conducted in a parlor on the other side of the house, and she couldn't hear anything through two floors. She looked out the dingy window, but it faced the back of the house and the luscious gardens surrounding the mansion. The Pinkertons would've ridden or driven up the long driveway at the front of the house.

Despite the protections the Favreau household provided, she felt exposed. She'd lost all of Uncle's talismans and anti-Eye charms, and she couldn't be certain the spells he'd woven around her were still in place. She had no gun, mage or otherwise. Just her and the blades she now kept strapped to her body.

She couldn't stay here. Being trapped in a room meant it'd be easier for the Pinks to find her. Always better to be a moving target. Uncle had taught her that much.

Hettie unlatched the window and crawled out onto the ledge. She was three floors above one of Patrice's many rose gardens. She crept along the ledge to the stone downspout, then clambered down, hissing as sharp thorns on the vines crawling up the wall pricked and sliced her hands.

She climbed into the second-floor balcony of the upstairs salon reserved for family use. She peered through the glass before ducking in, then put her ear to the outer door. No sounds echoed through the hall, so she cracked the door open and stuck her head out.

She planted her nose straight into Jemma's navel.

"I *knew* you wouldn't stay put." She pushed Hettie back into the salon and closed the door quietly behind her.

Hettie scowled. "If you knew, why'd you leave me up there?"

"To prove my point." Her nostrils flared as she shook her head. "You don't think things through. You rush into danger half-cocked. Did you even consider what would happen to Miss Sophie if they realized she'd been harboring a wanted criminal? They'd put her in Swedenborg."

Hettie stayed silent. She didn't think any of them would remain in jail for very long. Sophie's father would send an army of lawyers, and when that didn't work he'd wave money and power under the authorities' noses.

"Still," Jemma added gruffly, "you were smart enough to get out. I may need you to be just as smart now." She led her to the corner of the room, moving a table out of the way. "I don't trust these Pinkertons. I need your help to listen and watch Miss Sophie."

"Won't she punish you for disobeying her?"

"Can't say I didn't do my job if I'm right." She drew a curtain back and pushed at the wainscoting. A panel popped inward, swinging open into a narrow crawlspace.

"Of course there are secret passages..." Hettie grumbled to herself, peering into the dusty darkness.

"Follow this route straight, take the stairs down, then make the first two rights. You'll know you're there when you see the red flag. I'll be outside the salon—I can't be in there with them."

"How am I supposed to see?"

"You will. Just stay quiet. The walls are thin."

Hettie sucked in her gut and shimmied through as best she could. The simple servant's dress thankfully did not have voluminous petticoats, so she didn't have too much trouble fitting. Anyone much larger wouldn't make it unscathed—the walls were perforated with rusty nails and bits of wires from which portraits and more hung on the room-side wall.

Jemma closed the secret door behind her, and darkness swallowed her. A dank sweat broke on Hettie's brow. She hated dark, close spaces, and the dust tickled her nose. Slowly her eyes adjusted. The tiniest bit of light seeped through the cracks in the baseboards and through pinholes in the wall, shining like a line of stars in the night. Carefully Hettie followed the route Jemma had outlined, squeezing down a set of steps barely as wide as she was to the ground floor.

Soon she found a red rag tied to a nail just above her head. She put her eye to a bigger pinhole and peeked into the salon. All she could see was a vase of wilting roses. Hettie held her breath as a man's voice came through the wall loud and clear.

"You have to understand, Miss Favreau, that the Pinkerton Agency doesn't act outside of the law, nor can it go against the dictates of the Division of Sorcery." The man's voice was a hair shy of condescending. His words oozed with invitation, though, and Hettie's neck prickled.

"All I'm asking is that my friend be brought home." Sophie's plea hinted at her understanding. "Discreetly, I might add."

"May I ask what the nature of your relationship with this Alastair Fielding is?"

"As I said," Sophie said pertly, "he's a friend."

There was a short pause, and Sophie went on more reluctantly, "You may recognize his name. He's the man who developed the magic transference engine. He's quite clever. I was in correspondence with him before that announcement, you see, and he told me how much pressure he was under. I felt badly for him—he has no family, you know—so I visited him in Chicago and invited him back here to New Orleans to stay with us awhile." She spun the tale expertly, pitching her voice breathily so she sounded appropriately distraught.

"Were you aware he was reported missing while he was in your household?" the man asked blandly.

Sophie gasped. "No! Well...that's not exactly true. He alluded to being under close scrutiny. Said something about sneaking away. I had no idea he meant it literally. I was just...*happy* he was here."

Oh, she was clever, Hettie thought begrudgingly. Sophie was misleading the Pinkerton agent into believing she and Fielding were having some kind of affair. It would make the discretion part understandable.

"Why not bring this to the authorities?" the man asked.

"You read the ransom note. If I get the police involved, they'll kill him."

"And you're certain he's being held in this mountain lair in...Colorado, was it?"

"According to the letter, yes. Why would they lie?"

There came a long pause, and Hettie waited. "I'll have to consult my superior on this matter, Miss Favreau. Be assured we take this kind of threat very seriously."

"Time is of the essence, sir. If the Pinkerton Agency can't help me, I don't know who can."

"Indeed." The man snapped open a pocket watch and glanced at it. "In fact, I think your time may be up."

Suddenly the space between the walls grew cold, and the tip of Hettie's nose went numb. A warning sang through her a second too late.

"Jemma! Marcus!" Sophie cried out.

The unmistakable chill of an opening Zoom tunnel filled the room. How was this possible? Sophie had said the mansion was spelled against remote Zooms—

The doors burst open, and Hettie heard Jemma shout, "Sophie, it's a trap—" but her warning was cut off, and she gave a cry. Something crashed to the ground.

There came a great explosion from outside, like dynamite going off. Footsteps pounded through the house. The resounding boom and arctic whoosh announced the Zoom tunnel's arrival.

She put her eye to the peephole. The flower vase had been knocked over, and now she could see the salon was filled with men in suits and bowler hats facing off against the Favreaus' security team. They shouted at each other, weapons cocked, their bulk framed against the cutout of a familiar street in Chicago hovering in the middle of the parlor.

"Quiet!" A woman's voice cut through the room like a thunderclap, stunning everyone into silence. She stepped into view, an unmistakably feminine figure in a sharply cut dress with a soft chin and narrowed, dagger-sharp eyes.

"Sophie Favreau, in the name of the Pinkerton Detecting Agency, I am placing you and your staff under arrest for the kidnapping of Dr. Alastair Fielding and for harboring and colluding with the outlaw Hettie Alabama."

A buildup of magical power crackled along Hettie's skin—the sorcerers were priming their spells. She suddenly understood the magnitude of their misjudgment. The Pinkertons were not above the law, but they weren't restrained by it either. They'd level the house to acquire their target.

"How dare you invade my home and terrorize my staff like this?" Sophie exclaimed, equal parts outrage and fear quavering through her high-pitched voice. "Who are you? I'll have you sacked for this!"

"My name," the female agent began crisply, "is Jane Pinkerton. My uncle runs the Chicago division, so if you wish to file a complaint, please include a note from me saying hello."

Sophie was stunned into silence for once. Jane Pinkerton went on. "It doesn't take a master truthteller to know you're hiding something, Miss Favreau. I have it on good authority that you and your entourage had an interest in Dr. Fielding's work. I know he didn't leave Chicago willingly—our sorcerers detected traces of influence magic all around the Cumbria Hotel. The question is, where did he go and with whom?"

Hettie cursed. It must have been Uncle's magic leaking everywhere. It wouldn't have taken much to connect the dots between the Mechanik's disappearance and Sophie's involvement with Hettie.

"Our source also mentioned your entourage included a young scarred woman, someone you were apparently passing off as a distant cousin. A Miss Henrietta Wiltshire, I believe was her name." She clucked her tongue. "Not exactly the most obscure moniker for a notorious outlaw."

That source must've been Boss Smythe. He might not have known who Hettie was when they'd first met in Hawksville, but if he'd seen her scar through Sophie's glamor, he would've figured it out eventually. Helping capture a notorious criminal would gain him a lot of support in the polls.

"*Miss* Pinkerton," Sophie said crisply, with all the withering haughtiness money could buy, "everything I've told you is the truth. The Alabama gang took Dr. Fielding to their hideout—"

"I've no doubt that's true," the woman interrupted. "But as my uncle once told me, half truths are as good as lies." She paused, and

Hettie could almost feel her gaze scanning the room. "You and your staff will be detained for questioning. Resist and we will use force."

Magic crackled in the air. "You have no authority here," Marcus growled.

Hettie couldn't help the others. Not without Diablo. She'd be no good to anyone captured or dead—running was her only option.

She hurried along the passageway until it hit a fork and turned right, away from the parlor. Along the way her skirt snagged on several loose nails, and she had to tear it to get free. No more skirts, she vowed angrily.

There came an indistinct shout and then the blast of a gun. Hettie ducked. Suddenly the air was filled with gunfire, and the wall she'd just been pressed against was perforated with bullet holes.

She ran. The boom of a shotgun was followed by blood-curdling screams. The air sizzled as someone threw some kind of paralyzing spell. Some of it must have splashed against the wall, because Hettie's backside went numb. She ran on.

The path dead-ended. Hettie frantically searched the space with her hands, found a latch, and popped open the facing panel. Several crates blocked the door. She put her shoulder into it and wedged herself out past the little doorway, knocking over jars of pickles and preserves as she clambered out. She was in the kitchen pantry.

The house rang with screams and pops that could've been guns or spells. They were under siege. Hettie checked that her bowie knife was secure in her boot sheath and stuck a filet knife from the counter into her apron pocket. As Jemma was fond of saying, you could never have too many knives. She rushed out the back door and into the vegetable garden.

She rounded the house and dove behind the shrubbery as five Pinkerton agents exchanged fire with uniformed Favreau men near one of the sheds. Household staff fled from the building screaming but were stopped and wrestled to the ground by more dark-suited agents with rifles and sidearms. Maids and footmen alike were cuffed, then lined up on their knees among the roses.

The glass windows in the parlor exploded outward, and ripples of blue power threw several Pinks out along with it, bright fireflies chasing them all the way. *Marcus*, she thought grimly. Several more agents ran into the house.

"You there!"

She turned as a Pinkerton agent ran toward her, brandishing his gun. "Don't move!"

She steeled herself and stood up slowly. "Where have you been? I've been waiting out here for reinforcements forever! Didn't Miss Pinkerton tell you to go to the parlor?"

The agent faltered, footsteps slowing, confusion clouding his face.

Hettie didn't hesitate. The filet knife sank into the soft flesh of his neck as easily as butter. The man gave a single surprised gurgle and collapsed to his knees, giving Hettie the opportunity to slide around him. She sawed the shining blade outward in one quick, wet swipe, cutting his vocal cords. He fell down face first into a growing pool of blood.

She wiped her shaking palms on his back. She'd had no choice. He was far bigger and would have shot her dead, or else arrested her. If she was captured, that was it for her and Abby and everyone else.

She checked the man's body. Pinkerton agents kept their talismans on their belts—she'd learned that from Uncle—so she stripped it off his waist. She was no sorcerer, but she might find something useful on it. She left the knife where it was, as well as his gun.

More Pinkerton agents were arriving beyond the estate's main gate. Four automobiles and a number of large metal wagons had pulled up in front of the house. About a dozen men poured from the vehicles, all of them armed. They herded the servants into the wagons like cattle, shoving them and beating them if they didn't move fast enough.

The Favreau security force had pulled back, presumably to protect the comatose mistress of the house and her granddaughter. Considering the number of Pinkerton sorcerers rushing into the mansion, Hettie doubted the Favreaus would be able to hold their ground for much longer.

She wouldn't get far on foot, but it was too risky to try to get to the stables. The Pinks had probably secured the horses by now.

She eyed the abandoned Pinkerton automobiles. If she could get to one—

The snap of a twig behind her had her drawing her bowie knife and spinning around.

"Easy, easy, easy." Horace held out his hands. "I thought that was you, Miss Hettie. Are you all right?"

"For now." She glanced back. "Where'd you come from?"

"The stables. I snuck out the back just as the Pinks came in." He frowned around the besieged grounds. "This is all my fault."

"You can feel guilty later. Right now we need to get out of here." She pointed. "Can you drive one of those things?"

He grimaced. "I've seen it done plenty. Not sure I know how to do it myself."

"We're about to find out." She pointed at the dead agent's gun. "You know how to shoot one of those?"

He wrinkled his nose as he picked it up. "I'd rather not. I don't think blasting our way out is going to work either."

"You got a better idea?"

"Sure." He grabbed her wrist and twisted it around, making her drop the bowie knife, and jammed the gun into her ribs. "Come along quietly."

Hettie's heart shot into her throat. "Horace——"

"You there," he shouted to the man guarding the vehicles. "I've got another one."

"Who're you?"

"Undercover agent. I'm the special liaison to the Division."

Hettie struggled. "You...you lying son of a——"

"Quiet." He slapped her. The openhanded hit was shocking more than painful. And the sound brought two more agents out from around the wagons.

"I've got her. Open the wagon and I'll put her in."

The three men looked at each other, and in that moment of hesitation he let go of Hettie and shot all three of them dead.

Hettie shook. "You...you maniac!" She punched him in the arm. "I thought you were a traitor!"

"Sorry for hitting you," he said. "I had to make it look real. I thought there was more than one guard. Three against two aren't great odds. I needed to draw them out."

She glanced at the smoking barrel. "Thought you said you didn't want to use a gun."

He shrugged. "Doesn't mean I won't."

They opened the wagons and released the captured staff, advising them to run as far as they could to get away from the Pinkertons.

She and Horace climbed into one of the automobiles. "I'm not making you come with me."

"I left you to a mob once." His fingers danced over the dashboard as he took in the controls. "I don't plan on doing it again."

He started the car, pressing down on the pedals. They shuddered forward haltingly at first, but then Horace pulled a lever and the car shot down the long road and out of the estate.

CHAPTER TWENTY-TWO

L ing watched the tong hall's entrance as the last members left for the night. Sometimes a few would stay late to gamble, but he'd been monitoring the comings and goings until he knew the only people inside would be Shang, Ah Chang, and Big Monkey.

Brother Shang sometimes spent late nights drinking or smoking in his office, counting his money or entertaining a girl. He was the most wretched and cowardly of men, and now Ling knew the Division had him on its payroll.

He walked into the tong through the front door, popping the lock off with a simple spell using charcoal and chalk. He'd warned Brother Wu several times to get better protection spells, but he'd never felt the need to: locks only meant secrets, he'd said, and he'd had none to keep. Ironic how that'd turned out for all of them.

The hall was empty. The lingering scent of tobacco and cheap spirits hung in the air. He found Shang exactly where he'd expected, counting bank notes as if they were fish during a famine. Ah Chang sat with his booted feet resting on a low table. He looked up and frowned as Ling pushed the doors open. "I need to speak with Brother Shang."

"Ah, nursemaid." Shang bared his teeth in a humorless smile. "It is very late in the—"

Ling threw a seedling at Ah Chang, whispering the incantation. The hatchet man shouted in alarm as the vines exploded into a burst of green sprouts that wrapped around his legs like hungry tentacles. Another handy gift from Jeremiah Bassett—Ling would thank the old man later.

Shang stood, fumbling with the gun in his desk. Ling vaulted over the desktop and kicked him in the face, dragging him to the ground, but Shang twisted out of his grip and scrambled out the door like a rat with his tail on fire.

"Come back here, you coward!" Ling drew his gun and gave chase. Shang had already made it to the outer door when Ling noticed the movement a moment too late.

His wrist exploded in pain as Big Monkey knocked the gun out of it. He blocked a low kick to his stomach and a knife thrust toward his face. He grabbed the hatchet man's sleeve, wrapped his hand around his wrist, and spun him in a whirlwind movement, dislodging the knife and elbowing his attacker. His nose broke with a sickening crunch.

Big Monkey moaned as he stumbled backward. Ling gave one sharp kick to his shin and snapped it, then punched the man in the chest. He went down hard, gasping.

"I'm not after you," he shouted. But Big Monkey, blind and deaf with rage, swung at him. Ling dodged. He slapped both palms against the man's temples and whispered a sleep spell. His palms flashed with power, and the magic sank into the big man's skull. He went limp.

Shang, foolishly, was trying to flag down a driver on a mostly deserted street. The man never walked more than a block if he didn't have to. Ling whistled, high and sharp, snaring Shang's attention.

"Cymon! Bite!"

From the shadows, the big mutt streaked out. With a vicious snarl, he clamped onto Shang's arm and dragged the man down. Shang screamed, flailing as Cymon's enormous, slobbering jaws worked around his arm, grinding the bones. The tong leader twisted this way and that like a snake trying to escape a hawk's talons.

"Where is she?" Ling shouted.

"Who?"

"Auntie Wu. Brother Wu's sister. You had me followed."

Shang screamed again as Cymon gave his arm a shake. "Call him off! He's breaking my arm!"

"It'll be your neck next if you don't tell me where Ah-Gu is."

"I don't know! I—I don't even know who took her!"

"Liar." Ling grabbed him by the collar and hauled him to his knees. Cymon wagged his tail and started a tug-of-war with Ling, and Shang's arm twisted around in the shoulder socket. He shrieked in agony. "You're working with the Division. You were the one who got Brother Wu and Little Wu arrested."

"All right, yes, that was me. But I had no idea they were going to kill them. They only asked me for the names of the sorcerers in the tong."

"All of them?" Disgust burned through him. "How much were they paying you?"

"Fifty dollars a head. Please, I'll give it to you if you let me go."

A measly fifty dollars to betray his own kind. Disgusted, Ling tightened his hold. "What about Auntie Wu?"

"She...she came to me. She wanted me to step down from leading the tong. I couldn't let the old woman—" He whimpered as Cymon sank his teeth deeper. "I had her followed back to her place and let the Division know where she was."

Ling sorted through this information. "If you knew where she lived, why did you send me to the pier? Why didn't you report *me* to the Division?"

"You?" Shang stared at him. "You're useful. I had no idea you even knew about the old woman."

He wasn't lying. He was too stupid to lie. It sank into Ling's brain like a stone thrown into a pot of boiling mud.

This had never been about him or Abby. This was about Ah-Gu and the other Celestial sorcerers and what the Division was doing with them. Gods, how had he been so stupid? So self-centered?

"Where is she now?" Ling growled.

"Call the dog off," Shang pleaded.

Ling grabbed the man's uninjured hand. He was furious— at Shang, at himself. He'd misjudged yet another situation, and someone else had paid for his mistakes. "I'm a healer." He grabbed Shang's pinkie finger and bent it backward. It gave with a satisfying *snap-pop* like a sugar pea. The tong leader howled. "That means I know exactly what hurts the most, and how to keep you in pain without letting you pass out. So I'm asking you again"—he grabbed the next digit—*"where is Auntie Wu?"*

"They took her to the pier!" Shang shouted.

"Which pier?" He bent the finger back, feeling the tendons stretch.

"Pier 70. I heard them talking about a ship. The *Hardison*. That's all I know, I swear!"

Ling released him. "Cymon, come."

The dog let go of Shang, who collapsed into a sobbing heap on the ground. The big mutt sat at Ling's feet, panting, blood staining his slobbery jowls.

"If you're lying," Ling uttered, staring down into the man's wide eyes, "Cymon will eat well."

Shang didn't respond. He'd pissed himself, the stain spreading down the front of his pants.

Ling started to walk away.

And then Shang called after him, "Wait…does that mean you didn't get my statue?"

When Ling didn't answer, he moaned. "My mother's going to kill me!"

Hettie and Horace drove as far as they could and ditched the automobile by Lake Pontchartrain out of sight of the road, making their way on foot along the swampy edge of the waterfront. It was a while before they came upon a small farm where two slope-backed horses were stabled. When they were certain the household was asleep, Hettie and Horace saddled the old geldings and walked them out of the farm. They rode until the moon was high, heading northwest along the curve of the lake, being mindful of alligators and other nighttime dangers.

It was a long time before they could no longer see the lights of the city, and even longer before they felt safe enough to stop and rest.

"What do we do now?" Horace asked. "They have Sophie and the others."

Hettie had been wondering the same thing the moment that Zoom tunnel had opened. She'd had one goal under Patrice's contract spell: find out what was causing the soothsayers' blackout. Nothing obligated her to look out for Sophie's well-being. Abby was her only real concern, and even though she was far away, she couldn't risk the Pinkertons, the Division, or anyone else tracking her down.

"Sophie's father will do something about this, I'm sure. We can't worry about them right now." Hettie chewed her lip. She did worry, of course, despite her best efforts.

"What about Patrice?"

Hettie frowned. "It's not as if they can arrest her for anything. But maybe they'll find her and wonder what's wrong with her." Or perhaps they'd dissect her, do all manner of horrible tests on her.

Horace made a frustrated sound. "I don't understand. If they suspected Sophie of working with you and kidnapping Fielding, why would they only arrest her now? And why attack the mansion? It's a magical fortress."

"Maybe they needed proof of her involvement before they could do anything," Hettie said, and told him her theory about the Pinkertons' "source" being Boss Smythe. "The moment she asked them to help her find Fielding, they had what they needed."

"As for the protection spells," she went on steadily, "maybe they're not as strong as Sophie thinks they are. Some spells are tied to the sorcerers who cast them. Maybe some of them are tied to Patrice. When Sophie invited the Pinks in, that could've changed the terms of the spell, too."

The night creatures sang their throaty song, whirring and creaking in the muggy dark. Fireflies winked in and out of her peripheral vision like tiny green ghosts. The steady plodding of their tired mounts set an eerie backbeat to the midnight bayou chorus. Insects as big as her hand buzzed around her. Within minutes her legs and neck were covered in swelling bites.

"I'm not convinced," Horace said after a moment, and Hettie glanced at him. Even in the dark she could see his jaw working, the stony cast of his eyes. "I talked to the stable hands every day, and if there was one thing they were all proud of, it was how safe the horses in the stables were. The mansion was spelled so even Mother Nature couldn't get to the house. Gators, rats, mosquitos"—he slapped at one of the offenders with a grunt—"you probably never noticed from the house, but they never got anywhere near the grounds."

"So?"

"So even with Patrice incapacitated, none of those things ever bothered anyone. The protection spells were working. Meaning the Pinkertons had to break through." He met her eye. "We know what Fielding's engine can do. What if people are already using it?"

Hettie shook her head. "We have the only prototype. Apart from the one taken from the university, I mean."

"Fielding had financial backers, which means people knew about this machine for a long time while he built it. He said he had no assistants, but there were notes. And he told me there were failed prototypes. Then there were the people who brought him his meals. People who came to check on his progress. Division agents who reviewed his work, maybe even gave him guidance." Horace's brow was furrowed in thought. "I've been watching this man work, and I can tell you he's not all that together in the head. He thinks way too highly of himself. Overshares to impress people. Thinks no one understands anything he's talking about because he's that much smarter than them." He sighed as if it were a labor to admit it. "Anyone could have stolen his notes and built on his work. So I'm thinking there must be other engines. Other Mechaniks with different engine designs. I've been a horse eight years longer than I've been a Mechanik's assistant and *I* figured out how to work that engine. Someone else could have, too."

"The Division was involved," Hettie added slowly as she started making the connections, "so it makes sense."

Horace nodded. "If I were putting money and resources into it the way the Division was, I wouldn't bet the farm all on one horse. That they didn't immediately come looking for Fielding when he went missing in the first place makes me think maybe they had more success with other Mechaniks. Other engines."

Hettie's skin crawled. It was possible. Still, they could spend days theorizing how or why the Pinkertons came after them. It didn't change their circumstances now.

The rumble of an automobile on the road had them hopping off their horses and dragging them deeper into the muddy woods. They ducked into the underbrush just as the lights of a headlamp slowly panned through the trees. Hettie held her breath as the automobile passed. The horses kept still until the light moved on.

"We need to get out of the woods, find a place to hole up for a while," she said quietly.

Horace thought a moment. "I may know someone who can help us. He's not a...savory sort." Horace cleared his throat. "And it's been years since I've seen him. I don't even know if he's still alive."

"Do you trust him?"

Horace grimaced. "He might not trust me."

Y

They traveled all night till they reached a remote swamp. The property barely had a trail or road to mark its existence, but Horace seemed to know where he was heading, even in the dark.

They tethered the exhausted horses at the edge of the woods. The land around the farm was a bog, pitted with water-filled holes that gradually became a mire deep enough to swallow Hettie. By the time they reached the walkway arching over the worst of the swamp, Hettie's dress was soaked up to her hips and caked with mud. What she wouldn't give for a pair of pants and some sturdy dry boots. She couldn't understand who would ever live out here...unless utter isolation was what they were looking for.

A number of fat pigs dozed in front of the ramshackle structure, their pen fenced off by a high wall of branches planted in the dirt. On the other side of the fence, dozens of alligators lazed in the muck. One of the gators lunged into the air, jaws snapping, as she and Horace navigated across the rickety walkway over the pit of predators. It seemed reckless to have only a few twigs separating the two, but the animals were oblivious to each other.

The house, a worn and faded structure patched and reinforced with branches and whatever wood was at hand, stood on stilts about three feet off the ground. Most of the shutters had fallen off the windows or else had been repurposed to fix the crumbling porch. A well-used rocking chair in one corner had worn a groove in the floorboards. Except for the fresh flowers sitting in a tin can on the railing, Hettie would have thought the place was abandoned.

"You sure it's all right to be knocking in the dead of night?" Hettie whispered. The constant buzz of insects and frog song seemed muted here, as if they dared not disturb the occupants.

Before Horace could answer, a shadow darted out, probing ahead with the muzzle of a very large shotgun.

The woman's wide eyes shone as bright as the full moon. A dark kerchief wrapped her thick hair tight, and her hands remained steady on the rifle.

"What the hell you doin' here?" She kept the muzzle pointed at Horace, but her eyes were on Hettie. "This is private property." Her accent was not like the ones Hettie had heard around New Orleans. It sounded more like what she'd heard in Chicago.

Horace kept his hands raised. "I'm sorry for intruding at this hour. My name's Horace Washington, and this here's my friend, Hettie. We're looking for a friend of mine—Bear Brown."

The woman's eyes narrowed. "What d'you want Bear for?" She shifted her stance, finger over the trigger. "You a spook?"

"Bear's an old friend of mine. We used to work together. I need his help."

The woman held her stance a bit longer. "An' her? What's she got on you?"

"She has nothing on me. We're friends."

Skepticism dulled her gaze, but the muzzle of the shotgun lowered a few inches to Horace's chest. "Bear hasn't had visitors in nearly ten years."

"He was always a private man. Unless you gave him a sip of whiskey." He regarded her with a tilted chin. "You must be his sister, Daisy. He spoke of you often."

She jutted her chin out but didn't respond.

Horace went on. "I thought you were living in Mississippi? He told me you'd found work there."

He must have said the right thing, because she slowly lowered the gun. "I moved back in with Bear years ago. He wasn't doing well." She eyed him suspiciously. "Which you'd know if you were any kind of friend."

"I'm afraid I've been away a long time. Please, we've traveled miles, and while I don't wish to impose, if there's someplace we can safely bed down for some rest, we can talk to Bear in the morning."

"Morning, night, don't matter—Bear doesn't sleep much these days." She jerked her chin toward the house, and they followed her in.

Despite the shabbiness, the inside of the home was tidy, swept and free of cobwebs and mud. Hettie wondered if the exterior of the house had been spelled to deter would-be thieves and mischief makers. The moat full of alligators certainly discouraged visitors.

In the main room, a figure bundled in blankets sat in an armchair. A low fire burned in the potbelly stove. The smell of cooking fat from a leftover meal made Hettie's empty stomach growl. She hadn't eaten since breakfast.

Daisy stooped and spoke to the figure in the chair quietly. Horace waited patiently, looking around the home with interest.

"Horsie?" The creaking voice reminded Hettie of an old millstone grinding wheat. "Horace Washington?"

"It's me, Bear." Horace stepped forward. "How are you?"

The pile of blankets shifted until a gaunt, wizened face peeked out like a half-formed moth from a cocoon. The old man's eyes were milky with cataracts. His dark skin was heavily freckled and lined, the cheeks sunken. He blinked unevenly. "The hell you doin' here, Horsie?"

"I need your help, Bear. My friend and I are in trouble."

"You bring spooks to our doorstep?" Daisy demanded, and paced to the window as if they were already besieged. "What'd you do?"

"It's nothing he did," Hettie interrupted. "It's my fault. Horace hasn't done anything."

"Now that ain't true one bit, is it?" Bear grinned, showing a dark maw with only three teeth in it. "What you do this time, Horsie? Knock up a white girl? Steal some man's wife?"

Horace's countenance became stony. "Those days are long behind me."

"Must be them days that's catchin' up, then. I told you, you can't outrun the devil." Bear's laughter devolved into a fit of coughing. "You bargain wit' Beelzebub, you gotta pay a price."

Horace tensed. "What's he talking about?" Hettie asked.

"Didn't he tell you?" Bear cackled. "Horsie done a deal with the devil hisself."

Hettie stared at Horace. "Is that true?" Her throat was tight. Dealing with the devil was considered the blackest magic. It was risky even for the most skilled sorcerers. She looked the hostler over, trying to puzzle out what he might have given up, what he might have received in return.

Horace grimaced and explained, "It was a small deal only."

"Small!" Bear grinned wide in a silent laugh, his tongue flickering and curling like a curious snake. "Ain't no small deals with Lucifer. Man promised ten years in exchange for... what was it?"

The hostler ground his jaw. "One year of success with my business."

"You can't be much of a businessman to have made that deal," Daisy said with a snort.

"It wasn't just one year. It was one *very* good year that I turned into another twelve."

"And how's it all working for you now?"

"I paid my debt." Horace stood straighter. "A gang of Kukulos turned me into a horse. Eight years I was cursed, until Hettie here helped break the geis."

Daisy muttered an oath and made a sign against evil.

Hettie turned away from Horace. She'd been on the receiving end of not one but *two* devil's bargains, so she couldn't judge. Of course, her situation had been a matter of survival, not profit.

"Don' looked so outraged, dear," Bear chided Hettie. "I'm the one who brokered the deal." He chuckled and sank into his blankets. "Eight years means you still owe two. Devil ain't one to forgive a debt, y'know. So who's chasing you? More Kukulos?"

"No. Pinkertons." He pleaded, "We really need your help, Bear."

Daisy stood behind her brother. "He can't help you. He lent out all his magic."

Horace's face froze in shock. "All? But... you had so much. You could have run your own salon."

"You think that's what I want? To be a dog for the Division?" He struggled to sit upright in his seat. "They been sniffing after me since I was a young 'un, always after what I could do. But I know what they do in their house." He smiled without humor. "Now I got nuttin' they want. It's all out there."

Horace scrubbed his hands over his face. "You didn't have to lend out your powers. If you needed money, I...I would've helped you. You could've written to Jacobi."

"Wasn't 'bout money. The Division chased me from one state to the next. They want what I have, and more. They want to put me in shackles and take my power. Never again." He shook his head violently. "Ain't no one gonna take what's mine. I'd rather give it all away." He half rose from the chair, the blankets slipping to reveal his emaciated frame. His too-big shirt was as thin as his skin, his collarbone and shoulders jutting out like the broken limbs of a felled tree. "I'd rather die than give 'em what's mine!"

"You've gone and upset him." Daisy gently eased her brother back into the chair and wrapped the fallen blankets around him. "You need to leave him alone. Life's hard enough without his power. There's nothin' he can do to help you."

"Nothing *he* can do," Hettie agreed, and took a leap. "But you can."

Horace glanced her way. Hettie pointed. "That table there—someone's used it recently for some spellwork. The runes are still wet. And it doesn't take a sorcerer to know this place has been magicked. Spells like that take a lot of skill and power to maintain."

Daisy straightened. "I don't know what you're talking about."

"No?" Hettie pulled a talisman from the Pinkerton's belt and tossed it at Daisy. The woman reflexively opened a palm and shouted a word, freezing the bit of rock midair, encapsulating it in a sphere of light. Horace startled.

Daisy glowered and peered at the rock. "This is an anti-flea talisman."

Hettie raised her hands. "Sorry. I didn't know what I threw at you. I just wanted to see how you'd react."

Daisy released the charm so it clattered to the floor. "So you know I have magic. Doesn't mean I'm gonna help you." She raised her chin. "I could turn you both into gator food if I wanted."

"If you'd wanted to, you would've already. But I'm guessing you don't want the Division to get a bead on your power." Daisy's lips flattened, and she folded her arms across her chest. "Trust me, the Division are no friends of mine either. They want to take my sister away from me, so I understand what you're going through."

"That's who you're really running from then?"

She didn't want to reveal too much about their circumstances. "Like Horace said, we just need a place to rest and figure out what to do next. A day, two at most."

"That's a lot you're asking." Daisy put her hands on her hips. "I ain't sticking my neck out for some two-bit horse man and a white girl. Not if the Pinks or Division are involved."

"We can pay you," Hettie said. "Not in cash, and not right now. But once we've sorted everything out, we can give you money." Sophie had been generous with her funds, and Hettie imagined she'd reward anyone who'd help them out of their predicament. But there were a lot of ifs in that promise.

"Your word means nothing to me. And money isn't what we need."

"Then what do you need?" Horace asked. "Tell us, and we'll make it happen."

The sorcerer laughed. "What, you gonna snap your fingers and make the Division go away? You gonna keep the Kukulos off our doorstep? You gonna restore Bear's powers and health, make him the man he was before?"

"That's it. The engine!" Hettie grabbed Horace's arm. To Daisy, she said, "We have a machine that can transfer magic in and out of the gifted. If you help us, we'll find a way to give Bear the magic he needs."

Horace eyed her. It was half a bluff; there was no guarantee they could do any of that. The engine had worked, as far as they could tell, but the way it had made Sophie suddenly irrational and wild…Well, that was still a problem. Hettie hated making promises she couldn't keep, but she was desperate enough that she *believed* she could make it happen.

Daisy considered her. "You're not lying." She said it with certainty—truthtelling, most likely.

"I keep my promises," Hettie said, meeting her eye. "We just need to rest and regroup. In return, I'll do whatever I can to help your brother."

Daisy glowered. She glanced at Bear, who'd fallen asleep. She blew out between her lips. "Three nights. No more. Then you leave us alone."

CHAPTER TWENTY-THREE

The following day, Horace went into town with Daisy to find out where the Favreau party had been taken. Because Hettie's face was plastered all over the country, it would be too risky for her to leave the swamp.

She hated waiting, hated even more that Horace would be putting himself at risk for her. She wanted to trust Daisy, but she didn't know the woman. What if she saw one of the wanted posters and figured it out? The bounty on Hettie's head was tempting. The only thing that did reassure her was that Daisy hated and feared the Division more than Hettie did. It was unlikely she'd turn her in.

At some point Bear stirred awake, his glassy eyes blinking open. He moaned and writhed in his blankets for a bit and then subsided. The chair he sat in had a hole cut in the middle, with a chamber pot stowed beneath so he could relieve himself without getting up. When Hettie heard the distinct sounds of it being filled, she waited an appropriate time before emptying it out. She gagged at the blood in the pot.

"You need a doctor," she told him, frowning.

Bear cackled phlegmily. "You think any doc's gonna come out here to see a poor dying negro in a swamp?"

If Ling were there, he would help him. She wondered how he and Abby were doing.

Hettie spoon-fed Bear the thin gruel Daisy had prepared. The soup dribbled from his lips and into the folds of his cocoon, and Hettie did her best to clean him up.

"Not exactly the way you thought this adventure would go, is it?" Bear said as she dabbed at his chin. "I see the fire in your eyes. This ain't what you want."

"I don't mind," she said automatically. She'd said that a lot a long time ago, back when she'd taken on her dead brother's share of the chores as well as her mother's whenever she'd been sickly. When there was work to be done, she didn't shy away from it.

"Maybe so. But you've got a greater destiny, eh?"

"Ain't nothing I need to be doing except making sure you eat your soup," she said with a wry smile. She liked the old man. He reminded her of Uncle, only less crotchety.

In due course he finished his meal. "Tell me, how'd you and Horace become friends?" she asked.

"He was my boss, back when he was just a hostler, before he started selling horseflesh all over the country. I was his go-to sorcerer for the usual protection spells, anti-geis...other tasks."

"Like brokering his bargain with the devil."

"Mm-hmm. He wanted to expand his business, wanted to be a big man. Rich enough that folks didn't see the color of his skin no more. He knew I could do some blood magic, and after he was rejected for a lot of loans, he came to me, asked me to set up the parlay." He laughed. "He's wily, Horace is. Never knew a man could actually *bargain* with the devil, and he drove a hard one."

Hettie bit her lip, trying to figure out how to ask her next question. "You said the devil always comes to collect. Has anyone ever *not* paid their debt?"

He tsked. "You thinkin' you can cheat the devil?" She startled, and he extracted a bony hand and waved. "Bear don' have magic no more, but he can see you *twice* touched." He narrowed his eyes. "What'chu get in return?"

Hettie sighed and pushed up her hair to show him the scar. "I got shot in the head. My uncle made the deal to keep me alive, and the devil took my love for my parents."

Bear clucked his tongue. He regarded Hettie more seriously. "And the second time?"

"It was for my sister's life. She...she didn't come back the same. She drinks blood to sustain her, but she's not a vampire."

"That be her price. What about yours?" At her confusion, he scoffed. "You don' go t'hell an' expect to come back without payin' the toll, do you?"

She hadn't even considered she'd have paid a hell price. In all the trauma of Abby's death and what she'd been through with Diablo and Zavi and the Crowe gang, all she remembered of her time in hell, apart from the soul-shredding agony, was that she'd promised anything the devil wanted to return her sister and her to the realm of the living. Anything...

"Could be the devil hasn't called in his debt yet," Bear said. "Could be he's savin' his favor for a rainy day."

Hettie's skin prickled. She wasn't sure she wanted to know how or when the devil would call in that favor.

Horace and Daisy returned just then. The hostler smiled tiredly. "The engine's safe."

Finally, some good news. "Where is it?"

"It's too suspicious for us to move it all the way back here, and too precarious to take it through the swamp. So I moved it to the Jacksons' stable," he said. At her quizzical look, he explained, "The Favreaus' neighbor. I made friends with their stable master."

Horace's ease with people had always impressed Hettie. Now she wondered whether his ability to make friends with just about anyone had been part of the bargain he'd struck with the devil. "Okay, good. We can go back for it once we figure out what to do next."

He grimaced. "About that. Miss Favreau and Mr. Wellington are being detained in the Swedenborg facility."

The prison for rogue sorcerers. Jemma had warned her this would happen. The most powerful sorcerers went there, and Sophie and Marcus were certainly more than any mundane jail could handle.

Horace continued, "I spoke to one of the footmen who worked in the mansion and managed to escape. He said the Pinkertons Zoomed out and brought them directly to the prison." Horace's jaw firmed. "They arrested the entire household on charges of aiding and abetting a wanted criminal. Servants, maids...even the cook."

Hettie cursed and pushed her fingers through her hair. The Favreau staff was entirely innocent in this matter. "What about Patrice?" They'd left the old soothsayer ensconced in her bedroom.

"Taken, like the others. Transported to Kardec's, maybe, though no one seems to know for sure."

The ball that had formed in her gut tightened, and she reached out to Diablo for comfort. It didn't come. She closed her empty hands into fists and exhaled sharply. Every instinct told her to run away, to leave Sophie and Marcus and the others to their fate. She had no obligation to them—her only duty was to find the cause of the soothsayers' blackout. Patrice's contract spell made that demand clear.

And yet she did not feel its urgent pull now. The fire had been banked, the directive barely an echo in her mind. Was it because Patrice was weakening? If she died, Hettie would be free of the contract.

And would that be such a bad thing? Hettie had a bounty on her head: the best thing for her to do was disappear, find Abby, and run away to Canada. She'd been at the mercy of Sophie's whims for too long. Maybe Mizzay was right. Maybe it was time to break away from all this and settle down.

But Zavi still had Diablo, and he would come after her and Abby again. With Uncle missing and no other powerful sorcerers on her side, she wouldn't last long on her own.

Her hand closed over Walker's talisman. No, she couldn't rely on the bounty hunter, and not because he no longer wielded his father's power. She refused to heap her troubles on him. The comfort of strong arms around her would not save her from Zavi or solve any of her other problems. And she would not put another friend in harm's way.

Daisy, who'd been silent up to that moment, suddenly looked toward the door. "Someone followed us." She pulled the shotgun off the wall.

Hettie's heart sped up, and she went to stand near Bear, drawing her knife. Daisy loaded the shotgun swiftly and aimed it at the door. Horace took up a sturdy-looking walking stick and brandished it like a club. The air went still, and the noises of the swamp faded.

The footsteps were barely audible, soft as the patter of raindrops. The creaking wood veranda gave up the intruder's location, though. Daisy swung the barrel around and blasted straight through the wall, showering wood chips everywhere. In the next instant, the door burst open and a flurry of limbs exploded into action, knocking the shotgun barrel away as Daisy tried to swing it toward the entrance. A long leg whirled and kicked Horace in the stomach like a coiled spring.

Hettie put herself between the attacker and Bear. Daisy started to recite an incantation, but the assailant whipped a chalky bag at her. A cloud of fine, gray-white dust exploded, and the sorcerer gasped and choked, clutching her throat, before she could get three words out. The crouched assailant slammed a fist down, flooring her, then spun toward Horace.

Hettie recognized the fluid motion first. "Jemma!" she cried in relief, the grip on her knife slackening.

But Jemma didn't stop. She lunged at Horace, bowling him onto the ground and sitting on his chest.

"This is your fault!" she shouted, slamming her fist into his jaw. "You were the one who called them! You let them take Miss Sophie away!"

Horace gave an inarticulate cry as Jemma bashed him repeatedly in the face. He managed to buck her off, but not before a cut had opened up above his eye and his lips were bloodied.

"It wasn't me," he said. "The Pinkertons took us all by surprise."

"Jemma!" Hettie shouted. The bodyguard looked up at her, rage unfocusing her eyes. She blinked, and her emotions went from hot to cold in a flash.

"So . . . *you're* safe." Hettie wasn't sure if that was disappointment or relief in Jemma's tone, but the bitterness was unmistakable.

"How'd you find us?"

"Saw *that one* and the witch making off with Fielding's engine, and I followed them back here." She wrinkled her nose as she stared around the room. "Thought you'd been hauled off. Thought that one was trying to sell the engine for money."

"I'd never do such a thing," he growled. "I'm indebted to Miss Favreau and Miss Hettie."

"Debts mean nothing to traitors." Murderous intent glazed Jemma's glare.

Daisy scrambled for her gun. Hettie stopped her and said, "It's all right, Daisy. This is Jemma Baron. She's Sophie Favreau's bodyguard."

"Don' care who she is. Callin' me a witch an' assaultin' me in my own home!" She pointed, hacking dryly as she wiped the last of the chalky dust away. "Oughta turn you into a toad."

"Enough," Bear grumbled. Jemma startled, as if she hadn't noticed the man in the blankets. "Daisy, be civil. Pretty thing like her jus' doin' what she had to, eh?" He chuckled lowly at Jemma, who regarded him as if he were a crusty, wheezing dog.

"How'd you escape?" Hettie asked.

"The Pinkertons had Sophie surrounded. I tried to get her away—Marcus used Luna and Claire to clear a path. But they got her and him both, and I had to fight my way out. Spent the night hiding out in the Jacksons' carriage house. Then I saw this fool dragging the engine in." She cut Horace a look.

He frowned at her, clearly fed up with being polite. "I thought you were supposed to be a bodyguard."

Jemma's eyes narrowed, but there was pain in her face, too. "I wouldn't have been taken to Swedenborg. I don't have the gift. There's nothing I can do to help her from the inside of a jail cell. They would've put me with the other staff, or worse."

Hettie didn't want to linger on the "or worse." "Surely you've contacted Sophie's father to tell him what's happened?"

Jemma straightened. "Mr. Favreau is...indisposed."

"'Indisposed'? His daughter's been arrested and taken to Swedenborg. I'd think he'd want to get her a lawyer or—"

"Mr. Favreau doesn't *care* about Miss Sophie," Jemma said sharply. She sagged. "They had a falling out months ago, just before we met you in Barney's Rock. She's loyal to Miss Patrice, but Mr. Favreau wrote his own mother off years ago. Thinks she's just a crazy old lady, even though her gift made them all rich. He's mundane, you know, through and through. Resents it like the devil. And he's fallen in with some anti-magic types—the worst you can imagine. He's shunned all sorcerers, including his own kin."

"Why didn't you say anything about this before?" Hettie asked, massaging her throbbing temples.

"It isn't any business of *yours*," Jemma told her pointedly. "Sophie's money's her own, and of course Miss Patrice provides for her. Besides," she added quietly, "it hurts Sophie like nothing else to know her father's practically disowned her. You think she wants to share her disgrace?"

Disheartened, a pounding beginning between her eyes, Hettie pressed her palms together and rested her forehead against them.

"You have to help her, Miss Hettie," Jemma said. "You owe her that much."

"Me?" She sat upright. "What do you expect me to do? I don't have Diablo or any of its powers."

"You've got the engine, though," Jemma pointed out. "You could use it to get Diablo back."

"I don't see how."

"She wants you to juice," Horace said, and cut the bodyguard a sour look. "She wants you to take in some magic and try to conjure Diablo."

"You had no problem using that machine on Miss Sophie," Jemma pointed out.

He met her glare. "I didn't have much choice in the matter, did I?"

"You *always* have a choice." She turned back toward Hettie. "I told you once there are times you fight and there are times you run. This is the time to fight. They have Miss Sophie and Miss Patrice and Marcus, and I don't know what they'll do to them in that place."

"Breaking into Swedenborg is suicide," Hettie said. "Without Diablo, I don't see how we could possibly get them out."

"I've seen you do things I never would've believed of a Montana farm girl. Diablo or no, I have faith in you. If anyone can do it—"

"I appreciate the vote of confidence," Hettie interrupted, "but faith won't get us past the front gate of a sorcerers' prison."

"Faith can do a lot," Bear murmured, almost as an afterthought.

Hettie ignored him. "I don't think you understand what's at stake, Jemma."

"I understand more than you know." Jemma sighed. "Before Miss Patrice was stricken with this coma, she told Sophie the last vision she'd scried. She saw you, Miss Hettie, throwing open the doors to freedom. It was why she called us down to see her in the first place. It's all meant to be. You *have* to free Sophie."

"You can't trust soothsaying without context," Daisy countered, her skepticism thick. "What she saw could've been anything." That they were talking about the Soothsayer of the South clearly did not impress her. "And how do we know you're not just lying to get her to help you?"

Hettie remembered the anti-influence spells carved across Jemma's skin, then remembered from her readings that truthtelling spells were a form of influence magic. It meant Jemma couldn't be compelled to tell the truth by spellcraft, and Daisy couldn't read her.

"Sophie told me I'd bring about 'the end,'" Hettie said, emphasizing the last two words. "And I heard you and Sophie arguing that she'd be risking her life. What if what I do kills her?"

Jemma's lips compressed. "If this is the end, then there's no point trying to avoid it. What's meant to happen will happen. But I'll be damned if I don't at least try to save Sophie." Some of her haughty conviction left her, unmasking the naked anguish beneath. "Please, Hettie. I need your help. I can't do this on my own."

Hettie didn't think she should do it at all. For Abby's sake, she should run and hide, leave Sophie and Marcus to their fates. Surely Mr. Favreau wouldn't leave his only child, disowned or not, to languish in the sorcerers' prison? The Pinkertons had no solid proof—probable cause, perhaps, but...if Hettie was caught trying to rescue her, she'd only be substantiating Sophie's crimes.

She caught her distorted reflection on the surface of a metal plate hanging on the wall and, for a moment, thought she was looking at her brother, Paul. Her conversation with Diablo in the in-between rose from her memory.

You have to stop Zavi.

Regardless of what happened to Sophie and the others, the warlock was still a threat to her and Abby. She couldn't fight him without Diablo...or without any of her allies. Sophie had been right about that.

The debutante might be snobbish and demanding, but she had magic, money, power, and connections that could help protect

Hettie and Abby, even from someone like Zavi. Their alliance might be fraught, but Hettie had to admit she was getting the better end of the bargain. For her sister's sake, Hettie *needed* Sophie. They all did.

Besides, even if she wasn't bound by Patrice's contract spell, she was the reason Patrice was in a coma. She was the reason Sophie and Marcus and their staff were in jail, their home in ruins.

She let out a long breath. "I can't abandon my friends," Hettie said quietly. She gazed around the room, grimacing. "Guess we're planning a jailbreak."

CHAPTER TWENTY-FOUR

Of course, committing to a plan of action was a far cry from actually carrying it out. Daisy was reluctant, but she kept glancing at her brother.

"If it's as you say, and this engine can help Bear…" She looked at Jemma and sighed. "I guess we're all in too deep now to back out."

"None of you have any obligation to be involved," Hettie clarified. She turned to Horace. "You included. This is my fight." She didn't want to see him at the end of the hangman's noose because of his association with her.

"I don't abandon my friends or the people who've helped me in times of need."

He was far nobler than Hettie was, certainly. She felt ashamed her motivation was self-interested. "Besides," he added, "Miss Jemma is right. I was the one who suggested bringing the Pinkertons in. I owe Miss Favreau and the others for that, if nothing else."

She nodded, glad for his friendship but worried for his life. "All right. If we're going to get into Swedenborg, we'll need to get Diablo back."

"What's this Diablo you keep talking about?" Daisy asked.

Hettie pursed her lips. She didn't want to lose Daisy's help if she told her about the legendary cursed gun, but she didn't have much of a choice. "I'm blood bonded to a mage gun. Some people call it the Devil's Revolver…"

"Ol' Elias Blackthorn's little devil?" Bear sat up within his blankets. "By the Almighty. Never thought I'd have to contend wit' that again."

Hettie's heart lurched. "You've seen it before?"

"When I was a younger man." He sank back. "I ran with the Blackthorn Rogues for a spell. Helped with a few jobs 'fore I was picked up by the Division. Ol' Elias broke me outta jail, got me south to hide."

Hettie's mind raced. Bear was in his late fifties by her estimation: older than her father, but not so old that they wouldn't have crossed paths. Uncle had told her that the undying outlaw Elias Blackthorn had actually been a series of different men leading the Blackthorn Rogues. If Bear was telling the truth, he was talking about Butch Crowe's father, the man who'd been Elias before he'd passed Diablo on to her pa.

She swallowed past the thickness in her throat. "Did you ever know a man named John—" No. She corrected herself, trying hard to remember her father's name from his criminal past. "Jack Farham?"

Bear's jaw jutted out. "Skinny kid. Soft heart. Was a good shot, though." He peered at her. "You know Jack?"

A tremor began in her gut. Javier Punta had once said divine and infernal forces were at work where Diablo's fate was concerned. If that was true, then it was no coincidence that she'd picked the big black stallion out of the herd of mustangs in Wyoming; no coincidence that he'd been the cursed Horace; no coincidence that the man they'd gone to for help in New Orleans had run with Elias Blackthorn and had known her father.

"Kismet." Horace's eyes gleamed, seeming to read her thoughts.

"Jack Farham was my father," she told Bear. "The mage gun I'm bonded to is Diablo."

Bear went still, and for a moment she thought the old man had gone and died.

Then his eyes rolled back, and he tilted his face up to the ceiling, mouth agape. He inhaled deeply and let out a long, unnerving holler of a laugh.

"God loves a good joke, eh?" He cackled and stomped his feet, making such a ruckus Daisy shushed him. Hettie found herself smiling crookedly despite herself. It was pretty funny if she didn't consider their actual circumstances. "Tell me how you came to have it, girl."

Hettie launched into her story from the beginning. Her father's past and how her parents had been killed, her sister's kidnapping by the Crowe gang, bonding with Diablo, confronting the Kukulos warlock Zavi, then meeting the mage gun's maker in Mexico. The story poured from her, and Bear, a man who'd known her father, came to life like a wilted plant taking in a storm. He nibbled his lower lip, eyes shining, and said, "Your pa was a real cocky one...he had a quick draw and a quick temper. I'm glad he settled down some. Glad the fates sent his daughter my way so I can see there's always hope for us."

She felt her burden lift and at the same time felt reconnected to the man who'd been her father, despite her missing love for him. "Tell me the rest, girl," Bear encouraged.

She described the Alabama gang's hideout in the mountains in Colorado and the null net Zavi had created to ensnare Diablo. Daisy, Bear, and Horace listened intently, and when she finished, her throat was raw. "I can feel Diablo out there. I try to summon it, but I can't get it. It's...stuck."

"It's where it's supposed to be," Bear rumbled meditatively. "Like a peg in a hole. Ain't no reason to unfix it from that seat, not without a lot of force."

"That ain't it," Daisy said. "It's the null net. That spell's got them both tangled up so they can't find each other. You gotta cut it off."

Bear grumped. "That mage gun's drawn to its wielder—"

"*She's* the wielder." Daisy pointed at Hettie. "Weren't you listening? She called it back through the hell gate. It won't leave her side, not even to go home. And this Zavi doesn't have the hold she does, otherwise she'd have felt him calling for it, too." She gave Hettie a once-over. "She's touched, all right. It's the net that's gotta go."

"So...what do I do?"

"You still got that talisman?"

She fished the bit of bone out of her pocket. She didn't know why she'd kept it on her all this time, especially since it was part of the reason she'd lost her connection to Diablo. But she felt... drawn to it somehow. Maybe because the null net was tailored specifically to her and Diablo's power. Maybe because of her blood bond with the mage gun and therefore with Zavi.

Pa had carried a smooth stone in his pocket. It'd come from the bed of the stream that fed the ranch. He'd said it was a talisman of a different kind—his touchstone. His piece of the earth he'd claimed for himself. Maybe Zavi's bone was that for Hettie, gruesome though it was.

Daisy took the talisman from her and squinted. "That's some juju." She turned the yellowish bone over and over and grimaced.

"Anything you can do?"

"Not me. This is some strong blood magic. The bonds that are tying you up can only be severed by like blood—your blood, to be exact. This net's tied to you."

"But... I'm not gifted. I don't know any spells. I couldn't ungeis myself even if I knew how."

"Maybe you can guide her through interpolation," Bear said. Daisy cut her brother a quelling look. "What? You know you can. I'm the one who showed you that trick."

"We've got the engine," Jemma volunteered. "We can juice Hettie, and Daisy can help her sever the net to get Diablo back."

Hettie pursed her lips. Exactly who was Jemma proposing to take magic from? The engine hadn't worked perfectly: Sophie had lost her sanity temporarily when they'd extracted her magic. And without Fielding to tell them what was wrong with the device, the portable prototype could be dangerous.

She couldn't put Daisy, their only sorcerer, at risk that way. "One thing at a time," she said to cut off any further discussion. "We need to get the engine first."

"There's no easy way to move it here," Horace said. "Not through this swamp. I'm afraid we'll drop it and damage it slogging through the muck."

"So we'll go to it," Jemma said. She turned to Bear and Daisy. "I have a safe house closer to the city and funds to keep you in comfort for years. No one will find you there unless you decide to do something foolish. Help us, and you can live out the rest of your lives there in comfort. I can even send doctors who'll be discreet."

Daisy fisted her hands in her skirts. "This has been our home for years. It's kept us safe from the Division all this time."

"If I found it, the Division will, too." Jemma softened her tone. "I'm sorry for getting you involved, truly. But it's not safe for you here anymore."

Daisy's chin sank. Slowly she nodded her acquiescence.

"A roof is a roof, Daisy," Bear soothed. "An' this pretty young thing wants to put us in a fancy house. How 'bout that? I can finally shit in style."

They trekked out of the swamp the following day. Jemma had gone ahead to bring back a cart to transport Bear. Hettie and Horace still had their pilfered horses, which they would turn loose once they were ensconced in the safe house. Their owners would be looking for them.

Horace and Hettie carried Bear in a stretcher made of two long poles with a blanket slung between them. The going was slow through the bog, but the old man hardly weighed a thing. The bundles tied to Daisy's back were probably heavier.

At the edge of the property, Daisy turned back. She picked up a stick floating in the water, held it above her head, and recited an incantation. She broke the stick over her knee. Suddenly, the dilapidated house collapsed into the water with a great splash. In moments the land had reclaimed the wooden boards, as if a large mossy hand were sliding over the structure and pulling it into the swamp. The pigs squealed and scampered when the paltry fence came down, and the alligators stirred as easy prey rushed into their territory. Hettie turned away from the grisly feeding frenzy that ensued.

"That's that." Daisy sighed. "I just got it the way I liked it, too."

"Ain't nothin' 'bout that place you liked," Bear said. He grinned; he seemed to be glad to be out on this adventure.

They walked about an hour to the road where Jemma waited with a cart pulled by a sturdy-looking pony. She'd also picked up

Fielding's engine from the Jacksons'. Hettie didn't know why she was surprised at the bodyguard's resourcefulness. She could have been planning for this her whole life—she was under the employ of the country's most powerful soothsayer, after all. Patrice might've scried this exact scenario and instructed Jemma to be prepared.

They loaded Bear onto the cart and released the stolen horses. Horace drove the conveyance over the pitted, underused road for what felt like hours, and soon every muscle in Hettie's body ached from the hard jostling.

It was midafternoon before Jemma jumped down and walked up to a wall of green. She rooted through the lush vegetation and moss, then pulled aside a curtain concealing a hidden driveway that led up to a brick cottage.

The cart trundled through, and Jemma let the curtain fall back, enveloping them in a bubble of green. An enormous willow tree stood in the center of the garden, its branches spread wide like an umbrella so that the dangling tendrils created a soft canopy of leaves that draped over the place. A tall wrought-iron fence surrounded the property, but dense shrubbery twined around its posts, spilling over the top in an impenetrable cascade. No one looking in this direction would see the house or even the fence for that matter.

"Mercy," Bear whispered as they stared up at the two-story redbrick cottage. "I've never dreamed I'd live in such a fine house."

"It's all yours rent free once my employer is liberated," Jemma reiterated. She pointed toward the fence. "George Favreau himself put up that barrier spell nearly seventy years ago. Patrice said her grandfather kept a mistress or two in this place. It's housed a number of rebels and fugitives over the years as well, from what I hear. Kept out every ne'er-do-well and invader you could imagine. You'll be safe within the walls."

For all that it was hidden, the garden looked like it had been relatively well maintained. Magic, maybe. The house had three bedrooms, a kitchen, and even an indoor bathroom. It was cozy and warm, and though the air was a bit stale, the place was well stocked with worn linens and a good deal of bourbon. There was even a vegetable garden in the back, though it was currently overgrown with aging and dried-up produce.

Daisy settled Bear in a chair by the window. Despite being uprooted from his home, the old man was humming happily. Everyone took turns cleaning up, and then they ate a cold meal of pickles and preserves from the larder, boiled potatoes dug up from the vegetable patch, as well as some bread Daisy had brought along.

Jemma unearthed a trunk of clothes they could change into. Some of them were out of style, but Hettie would take anything over the torn, mud-caked maid's dress. She changed into a pair of work trousers and a finely tailored shirt. She wondered who, exactly, had stayed here in the past—and what they'd gotten up to for the house to have such interesting and varied garments available.

In the main room, Horace reassembled the engine. He talked through it, explaining to Bear and Daisy how the contraption worked. Daisy's frown deepened.

"You're telling me this engine can take magic out of a sorcerer and put it into a mundane?"

"That's exactly it," Horace said.

"And then what?"

Hettie couldn't lie to her. "Honestly…we don't know. The man who invented this machine was kidnapped by the same people who have my gun."

Daisy shook her head. "I don't even know what to think about you people anymore. Warlocks and devil guns and Mechanikal abominations…" She put up her hands in surrender.

"We'll need to test the engine to make sure it works." Horace slid Hettie a loaded look.

Daisy was the only sorcerer with power there. They should warn her of the possible side effects, but if they did, she might not submit to the testing. Jemma gave the slightest shake of her head from across the room.

"Well, I s'pose I'm being volunteered." Daisy nodded at the machine. "Try it on me and Bear first. Take some of what I've got and put it in him."

Horace attached the clamps to Daisy and turned the machine on. The engine whirred to life. "Here we go." Horace turned up the dial. Daisy grunted as the glass canister slowly filled with light. After only a few seconds, Horace turned the machine off, removed the clamps from Daisy, and attached them to Bear's skeletal hands. Hettie was afraid they might crush his delicate bones.

The hostler flipped the switch, and the light in the canister faded. Bear inhaled deeply. His complexion deepened to a rosy glow, and his hollow-seeming face filled like a slowly swelling balloon.

Hettie watched Daisy steadily. She didn't relish the idea of being turned into a frog or something if Daisy became unstable the way Sophie had.

Horace shut the engine off. "Did it work?"

Bear withdrew a hand from the folds of his blanket. He snapped his thumb and forefinger, and a small flame appeared. His eyes danced. "Heh. Lookit that, Daze."

His sister smiled wanly, and Bear frowned. "You're hurting."

"Worth it to see you back to yourself," she croaked.

Bear pushed some of the blankets off. Hettie was shocked by how much healthier he seemed. She realized then that this was the first time they'd completed a magic transfer between two different people. If just a little magic did this much good for Bear, she could only imagine what it could do for Patrice.

If they could find her. Hettie would have to worry about that later.

"How do you feel?" she asked Daisy tentatively.

"Tired...like I've been wrung out." She huffed. "Was that just a *little* magic?"

"We can't be certain," Horace admitted. "The engine might not be calibrated correctly."

"But it does what it should," Jemma declared. "We can juice up Hettie."

"Hold on," Hettie protested. "We can't just use Daisy's magic. I'm sure you're plenty powerful, Daisy, but I don't want to drain you. If something happens, Bear won't have anyone to take care of him."

"Agreed," Horace said. "Seems like whatever might've been wrong with it before's fixed now, so the risk to the donor shouldn't be too great. We need to find other sorcerers who'd be willing to give up some of their magic for you."

"That'd be about as easy as finding a man who'd cut off his own thumb so you could watch it bleed," Daisy said. "This isn't comfortable. I wouldn't do this for fun."

"Would you do it for five dollars?" Horace asked. She frowned. "Ten?" he offered.

Her brow wrinkled, but she looked thoughtful. "Twenty, maybe."

"Then that's our answer," Horace said. "We can loan money for magic."

At Daisy's confused look, Horace explained, "People always want money, especially easy money. People sell their bodies, their hair, their children..." He pursed his lips. "This is no different from regular magic-lending transactions. An opportunity to make money is what drives this country."

"And exactly where are we going to find this vast fortune to hand out?" Daisy asked. "Do you have treasure buried in the swamp?"

"Of course not. It's in a bank." His gaze cut toward Jemma. The bodyguard stiffened.

"You can't be serious," she protested. "That money's mine, you know. It's for emergencies only."

"I'd call this an emergency. If you want us to help, then you'll need to open your purse."

Jemma huffed and crossed her arms. "You better know what you're doing."

"Leave the details to me. Miss Daisy, we'll need your help with this, too." His eyes glinted. "We're gonna make some money."

CHAPTER TWENTY-FIVE

uail's Hollow was not a rich town, but it wasn't the desperate mudhole others pegged it to be. Yes, it was barely on the road to anywhere, the kind of town you found by accident, with its lone saloon and thinly stocked general store. But it was that reputation that made its residents so fiercely defensive of their home and its citizens; such dogged, misplaced loyalty kept them from thinking too hard about leaving for better opportunities. Any outsider could see it was a dying hamlet well on its way to ruination. But the people wanted to preserve what they had, resisting change in any form. As a result they'd become stubbornly insular, meeting all visitors with suspicion.

When word got around that a mundane was handing out cash to sorcerers who would sit for his machine, everyone came out to see. Most snake-oil peddlers were run out of town before they could fleece the hard-bitten townsfolk of their meager earnings; one look at its denizens was enough to make any fraudster spur their horses on. It didn't matter what color their skin was. That was why no one knew what to make of the night-dark barker and his Mechanikal engine, standing in the road in front of the saloon as cool as he pleased, waving around a fat sheaf of bills spread like a lady's fan.

He faced the crowd fearlessly, his bright smile and brighter eyes gleaming. He had the refined accent of a northerner, and his voice rumbled in your chest and made your breath shiver. It was the kind of voice that could convert heathens. If he sang, he would've made the saltiest veteran weep, though there weren't many there who'd admit it.

His companions looked on from the sidelines. There were two women—one tall and lean with the straightest back; the other softer and rounder with quite a few more years and a stoop to her shoulders that matched the ones of the laborers around her. No one could quite figure out what they were there for, except maybe as lookouts.

And then there was the white boy—or was she a girl? Except for him or her, the barker and his troupe might have been chased out of town. People had decided in their hearts, though, that he must be the brains behind the outfit. Maybe it was the way the scarred hermaphrodite kept a dark eye on the crowd, as if challenging them to try anything. Later everyone would talk about that strange fellow. Something about him had unsettled everyone, reminding them of the wild dog that'd hung around the town a few years back. It'd been shot dead after it had attacked a young girl.

"That's right, my good ladies and gentlemen, the divine Fielding engine can now work for *you*," the barker proclaimed. "God has given us this clean, safe device to preserve and share the magic which has enriched the lives of so many."

He showed off the machine's workings, though no one there could've possibly understood what he was talking about. Mechaniks didn't frequent Quail's Hollow, though a handful of low-level sorcerers lived there. Some whispered their doubts, but no one said "abomination," as the townsfolk were too cynical and pragmatic to make superstitious proclamations. Even so, they couldn't shake the strange feeling just looking at the machine gave them.

The barker called the older of his assistants forward for a demonstration. People watched as the glass canister slowly filled with light. When the machine whined down, the sorcerer stood slowly, looking none the worse for wear. "As you can see," the barker said, "my companion is hearty and hale as before, and she still retains a portion of her power." She performed a simple light spell to show her magic was still intact. The audience shifted restlessly, nervously.

The barker beckoned people forward, challenging any mundane to sample the sorcerer's gift—to hold that unearthly power in their own body. When no one stepped up—and who would?—the younger assistant was attached to the machine. She'd been standing so still and quiet, people had nearly forgotten she'd been there at all.

The barker started up the engine. It whirred to life, and the glow within the glass canister faded.

The young woman breathed deep as her body filled with magic. The sorcerers in the audience gasped—they could feel the change, see the gift pouring into her like a pitcher on a windowsill being filled with water, catching the light and throwing it all around. A few crossed themselves.

The woman stood. She didn't seem so invisible anymore. She performed the same light spell the sorcerer had. People clapped, uncertain, their faith shaken.

"It can't be real," people whispered.

"It has to be a trick," others agreed.

"But why give away money? He's not making any profit."

"If it's too good to be true, it probably is," a few said. "What if those bills are geised? What if there's a rogue sorcerer among them, trying to curse folks?" They glanced at the scarred man—he had to be a man with that jutting jaw.

But the sorcerers in the crowd agreed—the only gifted one among them had been the woman who'd attached herself to the machine. And now the other had magic, too.

The whole process was reversed. The younger assistant returned to mundanity, and the sorcerer reclaimed her magic. The barker made his sales pitch then—he would pay a sorcerer a generous ten dollars for the privilege of storing a tiny fraction of their magic, and would lend that magic out to a borrower for fifteen.

At first no one moved, but then the Rickards brothers decided to volunteer for the procedure, if for no other reason than to expose the man's scheme.

Peter, who was gifted, allowed the barker to put his hands in the clamps. Sweat slicked his palms. When the barker threw the switch, he bit his tongue and refused to show his discomfort, even as the magic was drawn off him, skimmed like whey off a pan of curds cooking into cheese. The machine was on only a few seconds, but it felt like forever. Then it was done, and the canister glowed. Peter did his best to smile despite the tremor in his gut. It hadn't been so bad—those two women had endured it fine. So could he.

His brother, Owen, gamely stepped up, wondering now whether there was any fraud to expose. He was more excited about the prospect of trying his brother's magic. Their parents, God rest their souls, had always had great hopes for Peter, but he'd performed so dismally at the Academy, they wouldn't even assign him as an enforcer. Owen had always said if *he'd* been gifted, he would've done great things and moved on from Quail's Hollow.

As the clamps were attached, he wondered whether he could finally make those pie-in-the-sky dreams come true.

The engine whirred to life once more. Owen felt the trickle, warm at first, then icy-cold, but not in a bad way. It was like drinking from the coldest spring on the hottest summer day. His senses opened, and he *felt* the world around him with a sudden clarity he'd never experienced before.

The rush ended unexpectedly. The barker looked him in the eye. "How you feelin', sir?"

He stared at his hands, the aura of his brother's power subsiding. He immediately knew he wanted to perform a spell, but which one? He'd never done any spellcraft. It was like being handed a sack of coins and not having anywhere to spend them.

"How long will this last?" he asked breathlessly. The way power swirled through him, he thought rainbows might shoot from his mouth.

"Long as you want it to," the barker said with a sincere grin. "You can pass it back to him whenever you want to."

"Ain't this just juicing?"

"No, sir," the barker said, offended. "That is a transaction between consenting adults. This is science applied to magic—the great equalizer between gifted and ungifted. Why have only one sorcerer in the family struggling to keep those protection wards up when everyone in the family can step in and share the load?"

Eyes sparkling, Owen rushed off, eager to learn his first spell. His brother trailed after him a touch sluggishly.

Peter and Owen were not ones to lie or collude with charlatans, and their enthusiasm as they ran off to test their split powers excited and surprised everyone. The sorcerers among them liked the idea of earning ten easy dollars, and the mundanes were curious for the opportunity to try on magic.

Soon there was a lineup of sorcerers looking for cash, and another line of people looking to get juiced. There were a few objections from the anti-magic Mundane Movement types, but their criticisms were drowned out by the charge in the air and the exchange of money for magic.

There'd been twelve low-level sorcerers in Quail's Hollow that morning. By midafternoon, there were forty-three.

"Not a bad day's work." Horace counted out the bills that evening after they'd returned to the house. He split the piles of cash, handing Jemma the share she'd invested into the venture with interest and sliding a second pile to Daisy. Her lips pinched, but then she reluctantly took the bills.

He split the remaining pile in two and held out the cash to Hettie. "I didn't do anything to earn that," she said.

"You did more than you think," Horace replied with a knowing look in his eye. More seriously, he said, "Take your share, Hettie. And demand more when you do earn it."

She accepted the money gingerly. She'd been on the verge of admonishing him about lying to the people of Quail's Hollow. His assurances were based on nothing, and they had no way to know if they could restore the sorcerers' powers after they'd been used. But they'd achieved their goal, and that was all Hettie could focus on.

She supposed they were just lucky nothing had gone wrong during any of the transfers, but they weren't going to return to Quail's Hollow, so they'd never know for certain how the engine would affect the residents in the long term. Sophie's turn for the worse had come almost instantly; perhaps it was because she was a high-level sorcerer and felt the loss more keenly, as those with much more to lose often did.

271

Hettie wondered if, hours after they'd left town, the people of Quail's Hollow were feeling any buyer's remorse.

Jemma certainly showed no signs of guilt. She was focused on saving Sophie. Daisy, however, was pale, and remained thin-lipped as she fussed over Bear and tried to feed him some soup.

"Woman, let me be. I can do this." He took the spoon and bowl himself. The initial burst of energy from the transfer seemed to have worn off some, but he was mobile. Apart from that he showed no other side effects. He slurped his soup and nodded toward the engine, which they'd placed in the middle of the living room. "So how many sorcerers' magic is that?"

"Nine," Horace said, "and it's not all their magic. I had this machine turned up to half the dial, then dialed it down to a mere fraction when I did the transfusion."

Bear hummed and nodded. "Good plan. Mundanes don't know the difference between a spark and a bonfire. No sense givin' them a torch when they're dazzled by a cinder."

"It ain't right," Daisy muttered. "What if they want their magic back? They'll tear each other apart."

Horace held up a hand. "They entered into a business deal with their eyes open. *Caveat emptor*, my dear. Let the buyer beware."

"We got what we needed," Jemma said with a definitive nod. "That's all we need to concern ourselves with. We can return their powers when this is all over."

That wasn't likely to happen, but saying it aloud seemed to assuage some of the guilt simmering in the room.

Hettie glanced at the glass canister attached to the engine. Now it was her turn. Dread and something between excitement and fear balled in her chest. She'd never forget how feral, desperate, and craven Walker had become after he'd given up his borrowed magic. Ma had once warned her that people didn't know their true weaknesses until they were tested.

"Ready to do this?" Horace asked.

Hettie blew through her lips. "No. But we've come this far." She held out her hands for the clamps.

"Best to feed it to her as slowly as possible," Daisy said. "It doesn't feel so great coming out, but it's overwhelming coming in."

"Once you have a hold on that power," Bear told her, "you come sit in this protection circle." He'd set up two rings of markings on the ground with numerous talismans placed at various points. He'd been busy while they were away. "Daze'll sit in her own circle. You listen to her, all right? Then you call your little demon, eh?"

She nodded. The teeth of the engine's clamps bit into her hands, the points not quite drawing blood but the grip strong enough to bruise. Horace fiddled with the knobs and dials. He glanced up. "Ready?"

She nodded again, despite the tremors in her muscles. The engine whirred to life. Almost immediately a cold trickle like ice water slid up along her wrist and into her chest.

She exhaled, anticipating seeing her breath. She wasn't cold, but it felt as if the room should be, and that she was the warmest thing in it. She inhaled deeply, thinking of spring days on the farm, the sun shining on her shoulders, a sweet breeze lifting her hair. She felt light, like a kite on the wind, as if she might soar above everyone else if she let go.

"You all right, Miss Hettie?" Horace asked.

The hostler's voice drew her back to reality, and she dipped her head in assent, thinking of the weight of her shoes, of the mage gun she had to reclaim, of the dangers Sophie and Patrice and the others faced; and of Abby, who would always need her.

It seemed to take a long time to feed the contents of the canister into her. At times she wanted to scream at Horace to turn up the pressure on the shivery drip of magic, to get the juice flowing faster. She wanted it over with. But some small part of her told her it was a bad idea, as if her body knew this was not right.

Finally the flow stopped. Hettie stumbled, trembling, as if her body might fly apart if she didn't hold herself together.

"How do you feel?" Jemma asked.

"I'm not sure." Everything glowed strangely. She wanted all at once to expend the energy swirling inside her, but also to hold it in greedily, like a mouthful of good whiskey that tasted like ripe peaches.

Walker had once said juicing was like being able to hear a symphony. Hettie couldn't hear anything, but she could *feel* it, the

273

way the earth might feel tree roots delving deep for life-giving sustenance.

She dropped down into the protection circle, exhausted and exhilarated. Daisy folded herself carefully into the ring while Bear walked around it, adjusting the talismans and redrawing a few of the lines they'd smudged.

"Take my hands."

Hettie had a flash of memory—she'd done something like this with Patrice. What if Zavi reached out and hurt her, too? What if someone else who'd gotten too involved with her suffered?

"It'll be all right," Daisy said. "You've gotta trust me."

She reached out. Daisy's palms were cool and dry. She laced her fingers with Hettie's.

"Focus on the gun. Every little detail of it—its weight, the texture, the little seams and corners and edges."

Hettie closed her eyes. She thought first about the pricking thorn, the razor-sharp spur that took its blood price every time she pulled the trigger. She'd stroked it often, teasingly, the needle-sharp tip dancing in and out of the puncture wounds it had carved into her fingertip.

She pictured the flat trigger, the trigger guard she rested her knuckle against, the butter-smooth grip and the matte black barrel. Her father had held that same gun at one point. Had it thrilled him to know its power? Or had he been disgusted by it?

How many lives had *he* taken with that gun? It'd never occurred to her to ask Uncle.

"Keep your thoughts on the gun." Daisy's voice interrupted her musings. "The physical aspects of it."

Hettie focused on its weight, the warmth of it after it'd been fired, the strange green fire that poured from its barrel, as if it were imitating a fire-breathing dragon from the legends of old. The last time she'd held Diablo was right before she'd dropped it in Chicago, just before she'd been captured by the Alabama gang.

And then they'd brought her to Zavi.

His cold, empty eyes flashed in her mind. Goose bumps prickled all over her skin.

"I'm here, Hettie." Daisy's voice was hard. "Don't think about him. Open your mind. Feel that net around you. It's like spider web."

She felt it then, clinging, sticky. She twisted and turned, but it was everywhere, snagging at her hair, snaring her limbs. It wasn't like any spider's web she'd ever encountered. It was slick and rubbery and reminded her of the sticky goop boiled soup bones made.

"Stop struggling. Take a breath. You're stronger than the web. It's connected to you, which means it can't stick to you if you can control it. Spiders don't get caught in their own webs." Daisy exhaled, and Hettie mirrored her breathing, filling her lungs, letting the woman's voice flow over her.

It suddenly occurred to her how much Daisy reminded her of her mother. Strong. Calm. Fearless. "You're just a little tangled right now. Pull it off you slowly. Concentrate on slipping out of it. It can't hurt you. You have control."

Carefully Hettie drew her arms up and pulled away what felt like a sheet of webbing. She shook off another layer, and it slid from her head. She turned and unwound herself from long ropes tapering into twine, then stepped out of the loosened snares. In her mind's eye, it was complicated, intricate work, as if she were unmaking a tapestry on a loom. It couldn't simply be cut through or unravelled with a pull.

"Good. Good. Now——"

Well, well. What have we here?

Her hair stood on end. Zavi. She opened her eyes, frantic, but could only see the webbing around her, as if she were trapped in a room, surrounded by it.

"Don't panic," Daisy said firmly. "He's trying to scare you into getting stuck again. He can't get to you here, not unless he wants to get tangled in the net himself. Take Diablo back, quick now."

Hettie set her jaw and closed her eyes once more, reaching for Diablo. *Come here*, she told it firmly. *You know you belong with me.*

Flashes of Zavi's face and long-fingered hands crossed her thoughts, as if he were waving her away. She pushed him out. *Come on. You don't want to be there. Come home to me.*

Her hands closed and flexed as the shadow of the revolver formed in them like mist.

How dare you, you impudent little—

Hettie hissed as something stung her cheek. She gritted her teeth, suddenly furious.

Daisy gasped. "How is this possible?"

Zavi's attention swiveled, wry amusement in every line of his face and form. *Didn't she tell you? I'm an angel. One of God's beloved.* He said the word sneeringly. *I have powers to rival any muck-dwelling witch's.*

Hettie's time slowed as Zavi lifted a hand. A flash of power arced toward Daisy.

"No!" Hettie would not let it happen again. She charged in front of the sorcerer.

Zavi's power smashed into her, suffusing her chest. She grunted as it sizzled through her senses. But she wasn't harmed by it.

What—What have you done? Disbelief pitched his voice higher.

Daisy wrapped an arm around Hettie and swung her about. She pointed and shouted an incantation. Streaks of red power ribboned from her hand, slicing through the webbing around them. The ends of her power struck the warlock true as harpoons, one, three, ten of them lancing through his chest. Daisy whipped her hand around in wide arcs, and the ribbons billowed out and wrapped around Zavi tightly.

"Hurry, Hettie!" she shouted.

Diablo's mine, y'hear? You ain't taking what belongs to me. Not now, not ever.

Zavi growled and lashed out with a wave of his hand. Hettie's other cheek stung. Her eyes were shut, but suddenly she could see everything: in the real world, Zavi had Diablo in his grip. His eyes shifted everywhere, searching, while his soul twitched in the bondage of Daisy's ribbons. But the real Zavi couldn't see them.

Hettie had power over him.

She wound up and slammed a fist into his face. The warlock reeled back, dropping the revolver.

Hettie summoned it, and it leaped into her grip. Zavi and the world of webs dissipated like a puff of smoke. When she opened her eyes, she was back in the house.

Diablo rested in her hands once more. She sensed it purring, almost rumbling with pleasure. If Diablo had a tail, it'd be wagging.

I missed you, too, she thought, cradling the revolver against her heart as tears leaked from the corners of her eyes.

"Daze!" Bear ran to his sister's side. She lay sprawled within the protection circle. "You all right?"

The sorcerer slowly sat up with a groan, and Hettie's gut unclenched. "By the gods…that…that warlock…he's more powerful than anything I've ever seen."

"You hurt him," Hettie said, grinning. "You hurt him with your magic."

"Not so sure about that." She flexed her hand. "He was surprised, maybe. Trapped for a bit. Hurt?" She shook her head.

"You look a little peaked. If you'd like a hit of juice…" Jemma gestured at the machine.

"I don't want any of that. I just need to rest." Daisy climbed shakily to her feet and narrowed her gaze on Hettie. "I've seen him now. I don't know what you did to make him hate you, but I don't want anything else to do with you all."

Daisy's sudden, fearful dismissal disappointed Hettie, but she understood. Bear and Daisy had fulfilled their end of the bargain. Powerful though they might be, she couldn't ask any more of them and risk putting them in Zavi's path again. "Thank you."

Daisy grimaced at the gun. "I hope it was worth it."

"It will be." Hettie clutched Diablo. "Now all we have to do is break Sophie out of Swedenborg."

"Piece of cake, right?" Horace grinned lopsidedly.

CHAPTER
TWENTY-SIX

After leaving Shang, Ling found the *Hardison* at Pier 70 easily. The transport vessel had seen better days; rust stains ran from every porthole like brown tear tracks. The ship was not one anyone would likely want to book passage or transport goods on—it barely looked seaworthy. He stared up at the pockmarked metal hull. It was the perfect prison for sorcerers, he thought. It couldn't have been magicked in any way, but Ling felt *something* emanating from it. Not a protection ward or any kind of hide spell. Just...something.

He watched the ship for a whole day. Only a few men came and went, empty-handed each time, as if only to check up on something. If this was a Division ship, they were being extra discreet about it. That wasn't unusual. The best way to protect assets was to keep them hidden from the rest of the world. The Division worked best when no one was looking its way.

He returned to Li Fa's after the night's stakeout. The young woman smacked him in the arm as he ducked into her apartment. "We were worried sick about you! What kind of foolish errand were you on? We thought you'd died, though Abby was convinced you were fine." She grimaced at the little girl, who watched smoke from a stick of incense curl up from the family shrine.

He told her about Shang's betrayals, about the sorcerers he'd given up to the Division, and about the *Hardison*. "I think I can get onto the ship easily enough," he said, "but getting out Ah-Gu, and anyone else who might need help, will be a problem."

"I can put the word out to everyone who might have lost someone," Li Fa said. "We can get help."

Ling shook his head. "I can't ask people to put themselves at risk."

"Ah-Gu is well-respected, as are Brother Wu and Little Wu. If they're in there, people will want to help them. The On Fook tong may be led by Brother Shang, but the members will not hesitate to help if their countrymen are being held unjustly. And they will take care of Shang once they learn what he's done."

"They'll be jailed if they're caught. Or worse."

"Let them decide if it's worth it," Li Fa said. "You cannot do this alone."

He ground his teeth. He couldn't risk it. This was his fault—he should never have trusted Shang in the first place...

"I can help," Abby said, sitting up. "I can go with you."

"It's too dangerous. I can't let you anywhere near the Division."

She looked at him seriously. "You told me that sometimes, when we try to do good things, bad things can happen because we're not careful, or we don't think of consequences."

He swallowed thickly. "I did."

"Well, I don't think you're being careful at all." She crossed her arms. She sounded exactly like Hettie in that moment, the jut of her jaw reminding Ling of Abby's stubborn older sister and the glint in her eyes reminding him of her father. "I think you're trying to sacrifice yourself because you think you're not worth saving."

He opened his mouth to protest, to admonish her impertinence. She was a child. She didn't know him. She didn't know what he'd been through, the mistakes he'd made...

But the tears gathering in Abby's eyes sealed his lips. She scowled at him. "You can't go alone. I *need* you."

A lump formed in his throat. When he knelt to meet her eye, he suddenly felt very small. Abby didn't seem so much a child when he came down to her level. "Abby, it's too dangerous. I promised your sister I'd protect you from these people. You can't go anywhere near them."

"Sacrifice is giving up something important for something else that's important," she parroted. "Ah-Gu is important, but so are you."

"To her...to both of us, *you're* more important. You know that, don't you?"

Abby didn't respond. Her violet eyes shimmered, and she tucked her chin down. "I want to help."

"You can help by staying safe with Li Fa." He turned back to the young woman. "Please. Stay with her. Keep her safe. I won't be long."

"Just wait *one* hour," Li Fa urged. "I can spread the word—"

"I can't afford to waste time. I've no idea what they'll do to her."

"You're a fool, you know," Li Fa said. She shouted after him as he hastened out, "And fools make terrible heroes!"

Y

Hettie, Horace, and Jemma endured another long train ride to New Mexico, this time in the guise of a grieving household. Horace hadn't wanted to disassemble the engine again for fear of breaking something, so the machine was packed into a coffin along with some ham that had started to turn. Hettie's "husband" was loaded into the baggage hold for the duration of the journey, where it would be left alone.

They disembarked one train stop away from Buck's Ridge in the town closest to Swedenborg. There'd be too many Division agents there, and she didn't want to draw any attention. As soon as they'd unloaded their cargo and checked into an inn, Hettie changed into trousers and a shirt.

"No more skirts." She dumped the heavy dress onto a chair in the corner of the room, much to Jemma's dismay. "I'm gonna need to be able to ride fast."

"We're going to need more than that to break into Swedenborg." She nodded toward Hettie's pocket, where she'd stuffed the mage gun. "There's no telling if Diablo will work once we're inside the prison."

"I'm certain it will," Hettie said. "The null spell over Barney's Rock didn't affect it."

"That's a business town," Horace said. "This is a prison for sorcerers. They'll use whatever suppression magics they can. We need a plan not just to get in, but to get out, too."

They were right. They could ride right up to the prison under the time bubble, but adding Sophie and Marcus would tax her.

The problem was they had no idea what they faced within the walls of the sorcerers' prison. If only Uncle were there. She'd thought the old codger would've caught up with her by now, but chances were he was facedown in a saloon. She couldn't rely on him.

This was *her* plan. They'd need horses, maybe even a cart—but how they would manage all that, even with Jemma's funds, was beyond her.

She glanced out the window toward the shed where the engine in the coffin was being kept. More magic might help her extend the bubble...but she was afraid asking might make her sound like she needed it. She didn't want to juice if she didn't have to, of course. But maybe...maybe it would help them.

"We need more information about Swedenborg," Hettie said. "Building plans. Duty rosters. Anything that could give us an idea of what's inside."

"Maybe we could find someone who works at the prison," Horace suggested. "Daisy said it's mostly Division enforcers and low-level gifted that end up working there. I can't imagine anyone being too happy being assigned to watch that place. So we ply them with a few drinks, some friendly talk, a few promises..."

"They'll have silence spells put on them," Jemma interrupted. "We wouldn't get a word out of them before they keeled over dead."

Hettie thought hard. She stared out the window where a group of men were working on erecting a new building—a new shop, perhaps. The men were just framing the walls now. Then it came to her. "Swedenborg was a mundane prison before the Division took it over, right?"

"Yes." Jemma tilted her head. "Why?"

"Well, someone had to have built it. A project that big had to have some approval from the state, wouldn't they? So where would the blueprints be kept?"

Horace nodded. "Town hall is my guess. Buck's Ridge would be where they would've gotten all the supplies shipped and hired all their men from. Rail line was there before most of the town was."

"Those plans would've been for the original prison," Jemma added. "They won't account for any changes the Division's made since."

"We gotta work with something, though." Hettie stood. She didn't relish what she was about to do, but she couldn't see any other way around it. "All right. Wait here. I should be back soon."

"What do you mean? Where are you go—"

Hettie dropped into her time bubble. Jemma and Horace froze in place. They wouldn't approve of this plan, but it'd be faster and easier for her to collect what she needed on her own. Besides, she'd been itching to test Diablo's powers out while she was on the juice. This would be as good a test as any.

She headed out into the silent town, taking her time to find a strong horse. A grey that looked like Jezebel caught her eye. She was young and well-formed, already saddled and loaded with gear as if she were about to embark on a long journey. Carefully, Hettie drew the horse into the time bubble, holding the reins and shushing the mare as the world around it went silent and Hettie suddenly appeared next to her.

"Hey, girl." She spoke as if they were longtime friends. The mare flicked her ears and greeted her warily, breathing in her scent. Hettie's heart ached. She missed Jezebel. Her father's horse was probably cranky as all get-out in the Arizona heat. "You and me are going on a little trip, okay? I promise it'll be safe and you'll be back with your master before he can say carrots."

The mare was not magicked and could not have possibly known what she was saying, but she didn't protest as Hettie climbed into the saddle and set off to find the blueprints to Swedenborg.

It was a few hours' ride to Buck's Ridge. Not that she had any way of measuring time, since the sun barely moved, but the next train stop would've only been another hour or so. As she rode in, she grimaced. Division badges gleamed on the chests or belts of every other man in town. There were Pinkertons here, too. They often collected rogue sorcerers, delinquents, and gifted truants on bounty for the Division.

Wheeled cages filled with shackled men, women, and children were frozen in the roads, displaying their captives like circus animals. A boy of about fifteen clutched the bars with dirty fingers, his face sporting a large bruise. His glare bored through Hettie, as if he blamed her for his predicament. She looked away, perturbed. There was nothing she could do for any of them right now.

She left the horse by a water trough, away from anyone she might accidentally bump into and draw into the bubble. She stretched her sore muscles but felt otherwise all right. Her tiredness was only from riding. Thankfully the supplies in the horse's pack included cheese and fresh bread. She made up a lunch and ate in the town square, sitting among hundreds of government men, surrounded by wanted posters featuring her face. It was the most peace she'd had in a long time.

It would be so easy to set off sticks of dynamite around these men. Or slit their throats where they stood. It would certainly cut down the number of Division and Pinkerton agents standing between her and the prison...

She pushed those morbid thoughts aside.

After her meal she found the town hall. It was a little trickier getting inside with all the doors she had to open, but eventually she found where building plans and permits were housed. Amazingly, they were filed and kept in good order—the benefits of a town high on bureaucracy, she supposed. She took the file on Swedenborg and tracked down the blueprints. She gathered everything she could on the prison, then left the town hall.

"I know you're tired," she said to the horse as she remounted, "but we've got to make it back onto the road home before we can have a good rest."

The mare obeyed. She plodded back the way they'd come, her gait even and steady, while Hettie studied the blueprints. Splitting her attention between the plans and the bubble was easy with the juice. She barely had to think about it. But she was bone-tired. Minutes might have passed in the real world, but in her time bubble, it'd likely been the better part of a day without sleep.

The sun beat down upon them mercilessly. Soon the bubble slipped as her head nodded in the saddle, and the sudden burst of sound and wind startled Hettie and the horse.

They were still on the road, thank goodness, and out of sight of anyone who might have noticed a scarred woman in trousers suddenly popping out of thin air. She gave the horse a break and walked the rest of the way to town. When she had the strength, she raised the time bubble once more and rode back in. Hettie hitched the horse to the post where she'd found her and gave her a good rubdown before resaddling her. It was the least she could do to thank the horse. The scene had changed some, but the horse's owner hadn't noticed she'd been gone. Hettie left a few bills in the saddle bag to make up for the supplies she'd eaten.

Limbs leaden, she trudged up the stairs of the inn and back into the room. Jemma and Horace hadn't even moved from the sitting area, but their expressions said it all—they were arguing over where Hettie had gone.

She closed the door and released the time bubble.

"—she went. She could be halfway across—" Jemma stopped as she noticed Hettie in the doorway. Confusion wrinkled her brow.

"Got the blueprints." She placed them onto the table. "And I might have figured out a plan. But first, I need a nap."

CHAPTER TWENTY-SEVEN

The *Hardison* was not the impenetrable fortress Ling had believed was hiding beneath the rusted-out shell. He walked up the plank unhindered. No barrier spell stopped him. No armed guards rushed him. He couldn't even detect any booby trap spells to ensnare would-be trespassers.

Abby's tearful frown haunted him all the way there. He was taking a huge chance—as well as breaking his promise to Hettie to care for her sister. But he had to save Ah-Gu. Even if she hadn't been Abby's tutor, he owed her that much.

The upper deck was empty, though he spotted signs of life. A cigarette butt. A mop in a bucket of brackish water. Someone had been here at some point. It wasn't just an abandoned ship left open to the elements.

The door to the lower decks was locked, so he applied the small crowbar he'd brought. He grudgingly admitted that, in this, the Division had trained him well: be prepared to lie, steal, cheat, and break his way into and out of any situation he found himself in. He was armed with a small toolkit—rope, knives, and three sticks of dynamite. If anyone caught him, he could claim he was a simple thief looking for valuables.

The latch on the door gave with a spray of rust. This boat really was a junker. Dry-docking the boat made more sense if the Division was only looking for a magic-proof metal prison to hold Auntie Wu and the other sorcerers. If this vessel could move, it wouldn't go far.

He headed quietly down the steps, gun raised. The deeper he descended, the more he felt his gift stifled, like a heavy blanket weighing him down. He let his eyes adjust to the dark. He couldn't perform any spells down here without exerting himself tremendously, so he kept his movements quick and lithe, his weapons ready.

The stairs went down three more levels. He encountered no one on the way, but the ship echoed with metallic groans and tapping sounds. The air here was close, and a strange smell tickled his nose.

He knew what it was instantly. Urine. Decay. Death.

Something else was bothering him. A...drawing sensation, as if someone had caught a thread on his being and was pulling on it, unraveling him slowly. The deeper into the ship's bowels he went, the harder the pull.

Ling braced himself and followed a narrow hall to the end. The smell was strongest here. The door was unlocked, and he opened it easily, soundlessly.

A sick, overwhelming sense of déjà vu hit him. The lowest compartment of the ship was filled with animal pens like those used to keep goats or pigs. Tied and manacled in each was a man, a boy, or in a few instances a woman. They were stuck with hundreds of quivering acupuncture pins. Each had a spider-silk-thin filament attached. The ropes of filaments were bound and braided and strung from the ceiling, rope after rope surging and crackling with power—magic—all of it feeding into...

Ling wanted to vomit just looking at the machine in the center of the room. It resembled a massive cast-iron potbellied pig with hundreds of teats, only this metal sow was taking sustenance from the helpless creatures in the pens.

He bent to check the nearest man to him. He was unresponsive, not even flinching when Ling pinched him. Then he saw why. He was sucking on a pipe attached to a tube. Following the tubing, he discovered a large central lamp on which a lump of opium as big as a loaf of bread cooked. The enclosed glass bowl over top contained the fumes, and the tubes were attached by a metal cap on top. It looked like some kind of hideous tentacle monster.

Ling stayed low, searching the aisles for Ah-Gu and counting the captives. There had to be nearly fifty people in here. He had no idea how he was going to rescue everyone at once. They'd need to be carried up the steps, but he couldn't do it on his own.

He had to find Ah-Gu first. Hopefully she wouldn't be as far gone as these poor souls. Once they got away, she could rally or at least hire others to help rescue everyone else...

Deep, gruff voices echoed through the corridor, and then he heard Auntie Wu's acerbic reply in Cantonese.

"Quit stalling and hurry up," one gruff voice said. "I hate being down here with that thing."

"This procedure is a delicate one," a more cultured voice snapped back. "I can't just jab these needles in willy-nilly. They have to be placed exactly, and I can't do it while she's squirming like this."

"You want me to knock her out?"

"No, I won't be able to tell if I did it right if she isn't conscious."

Ling peeked around the corner. Auntie Wu knelt on the ground, her arms tied to a heavy yoke set over her shoulders. An anti-magic metal collar circled her neck, and her hands were covered by metal mittens. She jerked every time the man went near her. He huffed. "Why didn't you bring the dope like I asked?"

"Lennox had it." He snorted. "I shouldn't have trusted him. I bet he took the dope and sold it off."

"Well I can't do anything with this one if she insists on making things difficult." He gave a put-upon sigh. More loudly and slowly, he said, "Stay still. Smokee drugee."

Ah-Gu met his eye. "When I get out of this, I am going to cut off your balls and feed them to a dog." She uttered the words in perfect, crisp English, then flashed her teeth. The man inched back.

"Don't turn your back on her, doc." The large blond Division man had an enforcer's badge on his belt. "She took out three good men before I clocked her."

"And I'll get the two of you as well," she growled. "Starting with your disrespectful tongues."

The agent chuckled. "Your ether magic won't do you any good here except to feed the hog."

"I wish you'd all stop calling it that. It's not a hog," the other man protested. "It's an osmotic transference engine."

"Whatever you're calling it, it's nowhere near as pretty as Fielding's engine. S'pose that's why you're in here and not touring around with it out there."

"Fielding." The hatred in the scientist's voice sang across the room. "That fop of a tinkerer is more interested in aesthetics than actual Mechaniks. At least my engine has consistent results."

"With Celestials," the Division man corrected. "And only because we brought you Fielding's notes." He paused. "Try not to be so sour, doc. You're getting paid well enough, aren't you?"

The Mechanik said nothing further, focusing on the syringe he was loading. "Here, I think I've found something that will calm her down enough that I can finish the procedure."

Ling had to act. Gun drawn, he aimed for the Mechanik. The shot boomed through the ship, and the bullet found its mark through the man's hand. He screamed. The Division agent dove for cover. Shots rang out, and Ling rolled behind a row of shelves. Glass shattered everywhere as the beakers and bottles on the table exploded.

"Don't hurt the specimen! Don't hurt the specimen!" the Mechanik cried, grabbing Ah-Gu's yoke and hauling her over the broken glass on her knees. She wrenched back and swung around hard, knocking the man in the head with her manacled mitt and sending him sprawling to the ground.

The Division man unleashed another hail of bullets. Ling peeked out in time to see Ah-Gu scramble for shelter. He had to end this before the ricochets killed someone.

He started toward the gunman's hiding place, but his shoulder exploded in pain as a bullet ripped across his flesh. He rolled to the ground, but too late, the Division man was on him, muzzle aimed center mass—

Three bullet holes appeared in the man's chest, sending a spray of blood outward. His body fell heavily to the ground. Ling looked up, heart hammering.

"Little Dragon!" Li Fa ran through the main door, a pistol in one hand. Abby trailed after her, peeking around curiously, followed by Cymon, who stayed glued to her side.

Ling shot to his feet, anger and fear sluicing through his veins. He clutched his bleeding arm. "What are you doing here? I told you to keep her safe!"

"I tried," she said through clenched teeth, gripping her almost comically oversized Colt. "But then the little one told me we had to come after you or you'd die."

Ling scowled. "Abby?"

"I didn't *make* her," she said, toeing the ground. She glanced up. "I...convinced her."

Did she really believe that? Had she used an influence spell unknowingly? Or was she lying about what she'd done to get Li Fa here? He'd have to interrogate and possibly punish her later. "Are you all right?" he asked Li Fa.

"I'd rather not be here, but the others will join us soon."

"Others?"

"I told you I could get help." She frowned at his wound and tore a strip from the hem of her shirt. She yanked him down to her height, and Ling hissed as she efficiently wrapped the makeshift bandage around his arm. She was done before he could protest. "*One hour*, I said. Did you think I was exaggerating?"

Ah-Gu called from her hiding spot, "Li Fa?"

The girl rushed to Auntie Wu's side. Ling found the keys for the manacles and the yoke on the Division man's body and tossed them to her.

"Are you all right?" Li Fa helped Ah-Gu out of the yoke and onto her feet.

"I'll be fine." She eyed Abby critically. "I thought I told you to stay safe."

Abby said simply, "I'm safer here with you and Ling." She looked around with a frown, her gaze clouding briefly. "The people here aren't, though."

"No, they're not." Ling looked for another exit, but there was only the one. The Mechanik could be gathering reinforcements right now. "We need to get them away from here, but how?"

"There will be carts waiting outside," Li Fa said. "I gathered as many of the business owners from On Fook as I could. They'll spread the word and let others know what you've found."

"They came in the dead of night?"

291

"Have you so little faith in your countrymen, Little Dragon?" Ah-Gu asked.

He supposed he did. Few had extended him a helping hand. But this was about helping the people the Division had kidnapped for these horrific experiments.

Ah-Gu studied the acupuncture needles set in one man's back. "This is not going to be pleasant for any of them, but we don't have time to extract these needles carefully. We should destroy that machine." Ah-Gu nodded toward the hog.

"No. That device is taking their magic. We need to give the magic back to these people before we take them out." Ling hurried toward the hog, feeling weaker the closer he got. The thing pulsed sickeningly, drawing power off him like a leech. He focused on finding the controls, figuring out how the machine worked. He should have captured that Mechanik; he could have told them how the hog worked.

"Ah-Fung!" Ah-Gu knelt by one of the figures in the pen— Brother Wu, only he was painfully thin, barely the stalwart titan Ling remembered. Ah-Keung, her nephew, was next to his father, both of them hobbled like goats and sucking on the opium pipes. Despite his warning, she untied the ropes and lay them on the ground, the filaments still wavering against their skin like shining metal porcupine quills. They both gave plaintive moans. "Ling, help them!"

He stared at the instrument panel. If he touched the wrong button, turned the wrong dial, he could kill all these people. He was a healer, not a Mechanik, and he'd be damned if he took another innocent life because of his hubris.

"They're hungry," Abby said. She stood in front of the large latticed canister, staring into the iridescent glow within. She licked her lips. "We should feed them."

"That's exactly what I'm trying to do." His hands trembled. He didn't know what to do. That doctor could come back at any moment with the entire Division to kill them all...

"I'll help." Abby put her palms over the belly of the hog.

"No, wait, Abby, stop!"

The cast-iron hog spiderwebbed at her touch. Light gleamed through the big front grille, focusing on the place where her hands made contact, as if it were drawn to her. Abby inhaled deeply as her skin began to glow. Cymon barked at the hog.

Ling started toward her, but Ah-Gu shouted, "No, Ling! If you touch her, the magic could jump to you and kill you!"

Panicked, he searched for something, anything, to pry her from the power draw. But then the big glass and iron canister shattered. A wave of power battered him back. Then the surge stopped, hovering like a tentative bubble. He looked up in awe as Abby, arms raised, drew the energy into herself.

Shouts echoed down the corridor. Ling hurried to Ah-Gu and Li Fa's side, and they drew their weapons. "Don't let anyone near Abby!" he shouted.

The first Division agents through were caught in the bottleneck of the doorway. Ling shot the first two, Li Fa the third. Ah-Gu placed herself square in front of Abby, staring down the door as if she might stop any bullet with her glare.

One of the agent's bullets ricocheted and struck one of the prone sorcerers. He barely made a sound.

"We can't keep fighting them in here. There has to be another way out," Li Fa said, reloading her gun.

"The Division will have it covered."

"Well, we can't stay here. I'm running out of ammunition."

Ling looked back toward Abby. She'd taken almost all the power from the hog into her. She turned slowly.

"Ling!"

A man had come through the door, and Li Fa's gun had jammed. The Division agent raised his gun, aiming for Abby.

Ah-Gu sailed across the room. At some point she'd armed herself with a crowbar, and she swung it out in a wide arc, batting the man back as if he were a beaded curtain, the crunch of his face almost as loud. She whirled to meet the next assailant, caught his wrist, and snapped it sideways over the crowbar, then hooked him around the neck and slammed him face down on the floor. Cymon met the next man through, lunging for his arm and dragging him to the ground, where he worked his massive jaws around his neck and cut off his screams quickly.

A resounding boom, and Ah-Gu reeled back. Blood poured from a graze on the side of her face. She was too dazed to defend herself from the man with the shotgun who came barreling in. Ling started to shout, but he was too slow—

In a blink Abby was there. The man with the shotgun barely had time to jump back before she placed a hand on his chest. A flash of light burned between her palm and his shirt.

His face froze in terror, mouth agape, eyes huge. His weapon clattered to the ground. His knees went next, and he slumped over as if he'd been nothing more than a marionette whose strings had been cut.

Abby opened her hand, staring at the wisp of bluish energy swirling over her palm like a tiny dust devil. "That's all he had," she said, almost disappointed. She closed her fist over the light, extinguishing—no, *consuming* it.

Ling swallowed back a gasp. Abby had just taken the man's magic. She'd juiced without his consent, ripping out *all* his power in one go as if it were nothing more than a bit of lint she'd picked off his shirt.

Cymon's hackles rose, and he growled at the door. Abby tilted her head. "More are coming," she said, blinking slowly. Then she paused. "No, wait…they're not coming. They're—"

Metal rang loudly above them, booming, echoing. The hull shuddered, and the floor started vibrating. The engine roared to life like an old man's phlegmy cough. The ship juddered and swayed beneath their feet.

"We're moving!" Ah-Gu exclaimed.

Li Fa stared up, as if she could discern what was happening abovedeck. "Where do they think they're going to take us?"

"They're not taking us anywhere." Ling set his jaw. "They're going to float the boat into the bay and sink it with all of us on board." The Division was more invested in its secrecy than its assets. They'd kill anyone who might try to expose what they were doing here. "Disconnect everyone quickly. We need to get to the lifeboats." If there were any left on board.

"There are too many people here. We can't possibly get them all up those stairs."

"I can help." Abby turned and seemed to take in the room in one glance. She raised her hand and said, "Open."

All at once the manacles on every captive unlatched and clattered away. The ropes hobbling them sloughed off like dead snakes. Abby made a sweeping gesture with her arm, and the needles sprang away from their bodies, the fine filaments recoiling like worms into their burrows.

Then Abby looked at the large opium lamp. She made a fist, and the whole contraption collapsed on itself, as if crushed by an invisible giant's hand. Slowly the captives stirred, groaning and wailing as the numbing smoke they'd been steadily inhaling disappeared.

"By the gods..." Ah-Gu covered her mouth with a shaking hand. She bent to check on her brother and nephew. "They're alive, but they need time to recover."

"We don't have time." Ling licked his lips. He knew what he had to ask, but it could still be dangerous. "Abby...?"

"You want me to take you somewhere safe," she said, staring around the metal room as if she were trying to figure out a big puzzle.

"Can you do it?" She was juiced like no one he'd ever seen, but he didn't know her limits...or her control. "We need to move everyone in here safely out."

"To where?"

That was the question. It usually took a group of at least twelve mid-to-high-level sorcerers with very good Vision to open a remote Zoom. "Wherever you think we'd be safest."

She contemplated a moment and nodded.

Her indigo powers had never been tested like this. Remote Zoom tunnels were already unstable enough on their own, but they didn't fare well near metal.

The floor shook again. A loud bang rang through the ship, followed by a rush of heat and acrid black smoke billowing through the hallway. And then another, closer explosion had them stumbling back. Shrapnel and dust showered down on them. The blast hadn't been close enough to be lethal.

"Dynamite!" Ling shouted. "They're blowing up the steps!" The hull would be next—they'd drown them all like rats.

"It's up to Abby now," Ah-Gu said grimly. Blood ran from her temple, but she met Ling's eye with fierce determination. "Trust in her."

They didn't have much choice. Ling watched as Abby swept a rough circle around her with her toe, pivoting on her heel. The path left a circle of faintly glowing power. She sat down and rested her hands on her knees, palms upward, as if to meditate.

The boat shuddered—more blasts. Ling imagined the agents on board sending bundles of dynamite down every shaft, every doorway. They'd burn the lifeboats, too, except for the ones they'd escape in. Instead of dwelling on their demise, though, Ah-Gu and Li Fa were frantically trying to help their people, gathering them together. He was a healer—he should be doing the same. But he couldn't tear his eyes away from Abby.

The girl had begun a chant, something that was old and familiar yet entirely alien in Ling's ear. It sounded like something he'd heard once a long time ago... and then it came to him, clear as a summer's day.

It was the chant of the monks in the monastery on the mountain a day's travel from his village. He'd heard snatches of their prayers on the wind sometimes, or thought he had. It'd been right around when his gift had manifested—but no one else believed he could hear anyone that far away. His father had, though. He was so proud of his second-born son, had insisted it was a sign he was meant to be a great sorcerer... his brother had always been jealous of him...

His skin prickled as the chant grew louder. Had Ah-Gu taught the prayer to Abby? A glance her way told him no—Auntie Wu was just as surprised.

The boat rocked and listed to one side. Bodies no longer tethered to their pens slid and rolled, but the jolt did startle a few of the sorcerers to wakefulness. Confused and disoriented, they slurred, "What's happening? Where am I?" A few simply broke down in sobs of relief, of fear.

Ah-Gu and Li Fa herded everyone together, and Ah-Gu tried her best to assure them they were safe and would be taken away from here soon. They needed to stay close together as Abby did her spell.

The air grew cold. Abby's eyes opened, night-dark and fathomless as the bottom of the ocean they were all headed for if she didn't succeed. The magic she'd absorbed from the hog swirled beneath her skin, lighting her innards as if she were a paper lantern. She said some words—in what language, Ling couldn't tell.

A pinhole of light appeared in front of her, a tear in the fabric of their world. But it wouldn't open further.

She gritted her teeth. "I…need…more…" she said, her voice startlingly hers, the ten-year-old girl he'd known pleading for another bite of pastry or asking her father to fix her doll…

Ling understood. All that power inside her, and it still wasn't enough.

He slid a knife across his wrist and placed the cut over her lips. Her tongue probed the cut, and she latched on.

His breath left him as if someone had kicked him in the stomach. Ling staggered to his knees. His bones sang with her hunger as she gulped away his magical life force—he was certain she'd slurp the flesh off his bones, too. His vision grew hazy, and the ground tilted beneath his feet. Or was that the boat?

She suddenly let go, frowning. "You're hurting."

"Don't worry about me. Open the Zoom. Get everyone to safety, Abby." If she sucked him dry and killed him in the process, so be it. He would fulfill his promise to Hettie and save her sister. He would die with honor.

Abby unlatched, and Ling looked up blearily. "You don't need to die for us," Ah-Gu said, gently taking Ling's arm out of Abby's grasp. Her own finger dripped blood. "Abby…take what you need. No more."

The young girl nodded and licked the older woman's finger.

The violet of her eyes deepened to an intense glow, and she inhaled sharply. She pointed at the pinhole in the air and said a single word: *"Open."*

The remote Zoom tunnel rent open with such force Ling stumbled back. His nose hairs froze instantly. The air filled with a flurry of snowflakes, and mist pooled around his knees. Instead of the usual flat disc of the Zoom aperture, though, it was a bubble— spherical, only it looked flat from every side. The captive sorcerers all stared in horror, shaken from their stupors by the sheer display of power. *Their* power. All in one little girl.

Ling stared through the gateway. He thought he'd see the Alabama ranch in Montana, or even Ah-Gu's shop in Chinatown. All he saw was a dull, flat blackness on the other side. Where was she taking them?

The floor beneath his feet groaned and tilted. Everyone slipped to the ground and tried to brace themselves to keep from sliding into the far wall. Cymon whined as his paws scrabbled to find purchase.

"We have to go!" he shouted.

"Go where?" one of the more lucid sorcerers cried, staring into the darkness. "We have no idea where that Zoom will end up."

"Go or die, it's your choice!" Li Fa shouted.

Ah-Gu pushed Brother Wu and Little Wu ahead of her. "Show some leadership," she urged. "Show them the On Fook tong fears nothing."

Brother Wu, still groggy, decided it was best to listen to his older sister. He took his son's hand and stumbled into the portal. They sank into the darkness. Li Fa and Ah-Gu herded the rest forward, though gravity was doing a lot of that for them as the boat listed. Water rushed in through the stairwells, sloshing and foaming into the lower decks. In seconds it was up to Ling's knees.

"Let's go, Little Dragon," Ah-Gu shouted as Li Fa dove through the portal. She had Cymon by the collar.

He hesitated. "I have to destroy that machine. If we leave it, the Division will try to salvage it."

She sucked in a lip and nodded in understanding as she jumped through, pulling the reluctant dog after her.

He took out the three sticks of dynamite he'd brought. He didn't have nearly enough detonation cord. He'd have only a few seconds to pull Abby into the portal behind him once he lit the fuse. If he pushed her in ahead of him, he risked being caught on the other side.

He glanced back toward the engine. Water sloshed around the hog from vents in the ceiling and poured from the ducts around the machine. Throwing the dynamite might get it wet and render it useless.

He couldn't let this device survive. He sloshed through the water, set the dynamite in the heart of the hog, and lit the fuse. He fled back across the distance.

"Hettie!" Abby's black eyes were suddenly violet once more. She stared around fearfully. "She's in trouble!"

Her concentration broken, the portal wobbled. The boat shuddered. All at once, the floor jacked up vertically. Ling flailed, trying to grab on to something, but there was nothing in his path. Only the portal.

"Abby!" He scrambled uselessly in freefall.

He had to get to her. He had to pull her in after him—

The deafening boom of the dynamite smashed into him, propelling him on a wave of fire. But just as the flames licked his skin, the frigid suck-pull of the Zoom threw him into a spin.

Darkness engulfed him. He screamed.

He'd left Abby behind.

Ling woke up on a soft pallet in a room scented with sandalwood and incense. His head pounded. His muscles ached. His mouth was parchment dry. He felt as though he'd awakened from a long and terrible dream.

He cracked his eyes open, saw the other beds filled with men and women murmuring quietly to each other, to themselves, looking haggard and drained. Some were rocking back and forth in a fetal position. Others were moaning, sweating, crying— withdrawal symptoms, he realized. That was how he knew he was in a hospital... or a healing place, at any rate.

He pushed the blankets off and tried to sit up, but Cymon had laid his paws and massive, drooling head over his chest. The big dog pushed up, snuffling him briefly as if checking him over, then gave him a slobbery lick and retreated, tail wagging.

Ling reached for his gift, seeking out a sense of what condition he was in. He didn't usually self-heal, but in this case...

He felt nothing.

His eyes flew open. His magic was—

Abby.

Ling was swamped by a grief so black it blotted out his vision. The last thing he remembered was that blast. If the fire hadn't gotten her, the water had. He let out a wrenching cry as his failure crashed through him. She'd taken almost all of his gift in her last selfless act. He would have given ten times as much if it had meant she would live. She'd saved him. She'd saved them all...

"Shh, Little Dragon, you'll be all right." Ah-Gu's voice soothed. She wasn't assuring him—she was telling him. "You came through the portal last. You've been asleep for nearly three days."

He stared blearily as she held out a bowl of lukewarm broth. He sipped the brew, found himself ravenous, and gulped it down. The broth gave him strength enough to let out another wordless sob. "I failed her. She's gone."

"We don't know that. She's not a stupid girl, no matter what you think."

"I was supposed to pull her in after me."

"She could have stepped through that portal at any point after you went through. The spell was... imperfect." She hesitated. "Ling, I said you were asleep for three days. But it's been twelve since the night you came to rescue me."

"Twelve days?" How was that possible? Remote Zoom tunnels didn't travel through time... did they? And why wasn't he dead from starvation if that were the case? He rubbed his temples as his head throbbed. He suddenly registered his surroundings. "Wait, where are we? Where did she send us?"

Ah-Gu pinched her lips but didn't answer his question. "Abby missed something in the spell, I think. Or perhaps she didn't. I can't always tell what she's thinking... maybe that's for the best, for my own sanity." She shook her head. "When my brother and nephew landed on the other side, it was nearly a week after we'd found them on the boat. The others came through hourly. The portal was open for two days before you fell through."

"Where are we?" he repeated, cold trickling through his veins.

When she didn't respond, he got to his feet shakily, stumbled toward the entrance, and threw open the doors.

Sunlight flooded in, momentarily blinding him. There was a gold quality about the air. The faintest scent of flowers and someone cooking pork tickled his nose. A chicken clucked loudly in the middle of the street, and a shower of feathers drifted by on the wind.

The unmistakable babble of the marketplace filled his ears, with people bargaining and complaining about the price and quality of produce. The musical, throaty syllables were alien at first, but then he realized he understood everything perfectly. It had just been so long since he'd heard it...

And over top of all that, the distant chanting of the monks on the mountain.

Ling crumpled to his knees. Abby had sent him to the place *he'd* always felt safest: the hospital where he'd trained in his village, thousands of miles across the ocean.

She'd opened a remote Zoom tunnel all the way to China.

"How...?" He stared at Ah-Gu, whose lips were pinched. "There've never been transoceanic Zooms. Never."

"You told me she once opened a coyote portal through the Wall on the Mexican-American border with little effort," she said. "That spell is, strictly speaking, not a Zoom. The sorcerer who created that spell circumvented the barrier spell in the Wall, traversing through physical matter. I wonder if Abby has somehow figured out how to combine that spellcraft with the longer reach of a remote Zoom. With the power she siphoned from that machine, there's no telling what she's capable of."

Ling placed a shaking palm over his brow. Abby's indigo powers were greater than he could possibly have fathomed. He stared up at Ah-Gu. "What will she do with all that power?"

"She sent us where she thought we felt safest—home." The corners of her mouth pulled back. "It's likely she went where *she* felt safest."

No. Gods, no.

Ling put his face in his hands. He'd failed Hettie utterly.

CHAPTER TWENTY-EIGHT

Before it was a prison for rogue sorcerers, the Swedenborg facility had been a prison like most others—thick stone walls cemented between solid oak timbers, with metal bars on the tiny windows, a labyrinthine interior, and yet more bars inside. When it had been repurposed by the Division, sorcerers spelled the wood beams and wall struts with a faint null spell. Sheets of metal were riveted to the existing structure, both inside and outside. The perimeter had been extended and a detection spell put in place within a two-mile radius. No one passed the outer edge without the guards knowing you were coming.

The gleaming structure sat beneath the unforgiving sun in the middle of the New Mexico desert. Because it was covered in metal, the place got hot as an oven quickly. It was a blessing and a curse; everyone hated the heat, but it kept the inmates sluggish and less likely to act up. Bad behavior risked losing the day's water ration. Out here you could survive a beating, you could survive a few days without food. But you couldn't survive without water.

It was one of the many challenges of servicing the prison—the closest aquifer was located near Buck's Ridge, which was what made the town possible. They'd laid down pipes and set up a pump at one point, but the pressure over that distance had never been adequate, and the system failed more often than it worked. As a result, getting water to the facility involved a nonstop convoy of tank carts that ran day in, day out, to and from the prison. Should one of the wagon wheels break, it could mean serious problems for the inmates and the staff of Swedenborg. There'd been water riots before.

Magic, of course, was forbidden in Swedenborg. Remote Zoom tunnels could not materialize anywhere within the facility's two-mile perimeter. Inmates were ostensibly at the facility to be "reformed." In reality they were subjected to various magical tests to help advance the field of sorcery and science as a "service" to magickind. Of course the inmates signed papers to declare they'd "volunteered" for those tests, and their families were compensated if they died in the testing. The Division wasn't barbaric, after all.

Hettie wasn't certain Diablo's time bubble would go undetected if she walked up to the prison, so they needed a way past the outer perimeter. She'd only use the bubble when they got as close as possible to the building itself. By then, it would be too late for anyone to stop them. Assuming the time bubble did work.

There were a lot of ifs in this plan, but they'd argued over the logistics too long, and Jemma was fretful about Sophie's well-being. As it was, it had taken Horace nearly a week to procure what they needed. How he'd managed it she wasn't sure, though she knew Jemma's dwindling funds had helped expedite the business. Hettie had a feeling she didn't want to know how or where the man had gotten his goods, in case she was ever questioned about it on the witness stand.

When the time came to strike, Hettie found herself strangely calm. Breaking into the Division of Sorcery's most secure stronghold to rescue her friends shouldn't have been something she felt confident about. Part of her wondered if the juice mixed with Diablo's triumphant return had given her a false sense of security. The revolver shouldn't have been so arrogant, though it certainly had dared her to test its mettle in the past.

"One more time," Jemma insisted as she strapped the blades to Hettie's back and waist.

Hettie closed her eyes, praying for patience. "Drop into the time bubble while I'm still in the cart. Exit and go to the records office.

Find out where Sophie and Marcus are. Get them and exit through the southern loading bay."

"Tell me how you'll get to the records office."

Hettie recited the path twisting through the prison.

"And what do you do if you accidentally bump into someone?"

"I won't," she said determinedly.

Jemma glowered. "I should go with you." Hettie had no doubt the bodyguard would have no problem slitting the throats of anyone who came between her and Sophie. Hettie herself was still wrestling with her conscience over the Pinkerton she'd killed in the mansion garden.

"We've already tested this. I can't hold the bubble with more than two people for longer than thirty minutes, even on the juice. I can't even be sure there isn't some kind of counterspell that'll mess with Diablo's powers. And we don't know what we're going to come up against in there."

"That's *why* you need me," Jemma said.

"Someone has to stay with the horses at the perimeter for when we get out," Hettie said. "We're going to need a quick getaway, time bubble or no." She gripped Jemma's arm. "If this goes as planned, we'll be with you in a blink and on our way before anyone notices."

Fielding's engine had been put into storage, sent "away," Jemma said, to a place it'd be safe. For all their sakes, the bodyguard was the only one who knew where it was being housed. Hettie regretted that decision now. An extra hit of magic would've gone a long way to bolstering her courage and confidence. But she said nothing.

Once they got Marcus and Sophie out, they'd all be fugitives. They couldn't lug that engine around with them while they were on the run. Sophie might not be pleased, since they needed it to help her grandmother, but they couldn't be certain Patrice was in Kardec Hospital for the Magically Infirm. They couldn't travel all the way to Massachusetts only to find out she was elsewhere.

Night had fallen when Horace pulled up in an ice wagon. He hopped out quickly and threw open the doors. Cold mist poured out of the cabin. "Time's of the essence," he said. "There's a bit of space in the middle there. You can clear some of the hay, and I'll pile it back after you." He gave her a grim look. "I hope you're wearing long underwear, Miss Hettie."

305

"I wouldn't normally talk about my undergarments with a man, Mr. Washington," she said wryly. "But in this case, yes, I am dressed for this."

"Won't be ice for too much longer," he said. The huge blocks were packed tight with straw, but in the New Mexico heat, the outer layer was turning quickly to slush. "I'm sorry to say you're going to get a bit wet. Here." He handed her a small flask. "Whiskey. To stave off the cold."

She took a swig, letting the fire race down her throat, then handed it back and climbed in. There was just enough space between the thick slabs that she could squeeze in sideways, and Horace and Jemma stuffed the straw back in.

She thought that she might enjoy the cold after the New Mexico heat, but five minutes later the chill settled in, and the damp on her skin turned to a wet, freezing burn. The hay tickled her nose and did little to insulate her from the blocks of ice.

Horace urged the horses on at a quick trot. The wagon rocked and jarred as it rumbled down the road. Hettie shut her eyes, trying not to think about how the ice slabs might shift and crush her on the ride to the prison. She wasn't going to ask Horace to slow down, though. Anyone they might encounter would be suspicious if they didn't expedite their precious cargo.

When she could no longer feel the tip of her nose, the wagon slowed, and she heard Horace holler, "Hey there! Ice delivery!"

A pause. "We don't get ice out here," another voice shouted back.

"Well, then, it's your lucky day. I have some premium ice straight from New England to deliver to…" His voice faded as he walked away from the wagon, and Hettie couldn't quite make out what he said.

It'd been a gamble to bring ice to the prison. The problem was, it would have been extremely expensive to get it out to the middle of the New Mexico desert. A facility like Swedenborg would need some way to store food, even for the short term, though it was more likely that the amount of ice they'd get would only be enough for the warden and other administrators. The prisoners were more likely to get rotting, worm-infested meals. Still, it was almost certain the facility could use ice, even if all it did was thaw out for some very expensive water rations.

"I don't think you understand the value of this cargo," she heard Horace say. "Not only is this the purest potable ice you can imagine, but I'm willing to part with it for a song. Imagine, you could be enjoying a frosty, cold beer today."

"If you're not on the delivery roster, I can't let you in," the guard said, regret touching his voice.

"Sir, I beg of you. I'll be totally honest—I spent my last dollar to have this shipment remote Zoomed in, but my business arrangement fell through. If I'm going to get any of it back, I need to sell this ice."

"Not my problem."

"Just let me talk to your cook—he would know the quality of my product, understand the bargain he'd be getting. Why, if the warden knew about the cost savings this shipment was bringing to this facility, you'd be up for a promotion. Sir, I'm a desperate man, and every second I'm delayed is another penny out of my pocket."

The man hesitated. There were more low murmurs as they negotiated. Then Horace said loudly, "Well, of course you may inspect the merchandise! Please, please, come. I can even chisel you a sample. A little whiskey on the side, perhaps? Or rum, if you prefer..."

Hettie held her breath as the wagon doors were unlocked. The straw stirred a bit, but the guard didn't seem to be all that interested in the contents. The wagon was packed tight, after all, except for those few inches Hettie was wedged into. She was glad she hadn't had a big dinner.

"A fine product," Horace declared, and she heard him scraping at the ice blocks. The doors were shut, and there was a little more chatter. The guard must have been convinced, because the wagon jostled and was in motion once more.

They were past the perimeter.

It was a few more minutes before Horace said, "Now, don't you go doing anything rash. Stick with the plan and get what you came for." His words might as well have been to himself, and she realized why: the Division could easily Eye anyone within the perimeter's barrier. They could be watching him right now as he made his way to the prison.

The wagon stopped once more. Horace spoke to some more guards, but they didn't give him as much trouble as the perimeter guard did. He rapped on the side shortly before opening the doors—his signal that they were as deep into the facility as they could go. Now it was all up to her.

Hettie shoveled the straw out of her way and dropped into her time bubble. She shimmied out from between the blocks, sopping wet and chilled through. It was still dark, and the air was cold. Or maybe that was just her—there was no breeze in the time bubble. The day's heat, which should have soaked the ground, was curiously absent. Perhaps that was because the loading bay they were in was shaded from the hot sun.

She skirted around Horace, who stared expectantly into the wagon, his expression conveying it all. *Good luck. Don't get caught or we're all going to prison.*

She'd imagined a dank dungeon of rough stone, crawling with pests. But the corridors she walked were pristinely kept, with polished oak floors and whitewashed walls. Lamps with blue-white magic glow stones hung at intervals from the ceiling, casting their wan light everywhere. She couldn't imagine how they were keeping up that magic, but then, this was a prison for sorcerers. Maybe there were a handful of inmates whose job was to keep the lights on.

She recited the directions to the records office to herself. She needn't have—there were signs pointing toward it at every corner. A few guards patrolled the halls. Their dark uniforms had a small Division badge sewn onto the front pocket in gold thread. As predicted, there weren't as many active guards on the night shift as there might have been during the day. Most of them looked overworked and worn down. She wondered about the spells they were juggling to do their job.

The records office was locked, of course. But either no one inside thought anything was worth taking, or they didn't have the magical resources to seal this one room. Hettie popped the lock open the way Jemma had showed her with a screwdriver and a bit of force.

Within, row upon row of filing cabinets were arranged in an almost mazelike pattern, with aisles snaking up and down. There had to be tens of thousands of files in here, all of prisoners past and present.

The files were arranged in alphabetical order. She quickly found files for Marcus Wellington and Sophie Favreau. They were being kept in separate wings on opposite sides of the prison, in the men's and women's sections respectively.

She began to make her way out of the office when a flash of movement out of the corner of her eye had her spinning around, Diablo raised.

Nothing was there.

The hairs on the back of her neck prickled. Maybe it was the cold in her bones still playing tricks with her.

But then she saw it again, just out of the corner of her eye. A flash of darkness, like a man with a cape, or large black bird...

The place could be haunted. Hundreds of inmates must have died here. There were bound to be restless spirits seeking justice...

She was about to turn away when the shadowy figure swooped directly in front of her, then turned a corner down the aisle. Icy tendrils feathered across her skin. Whatever spirit was stalking her, it was determined to get her attention.

She decided to follow and see what it wanted.

The way the cabinets were arranged, she ended up near the beginning of the alphabet. The shadowy figure had disappeared. Ahead of her, a drawer slid open on its own. The corner of a file slowly edged up, as if being plucked up by a bird. Hettie hesitated. Despite Diablo's bubble, she didn't have time to dally. Plus, every item she took into the time bubble put more pressure on her to maintain it.

She heard something like the flap of wings taking off.

She gritted her teeth and reached for the file. Blinked as the faded name on the thick file came into focus.

Bassett, Jeremiah.

With trembling hands and a foggy head, she opened the file and read the top page twice.

Her stomach bottomed out. Uncle...

He hadn't been out looking for her. He hadn't been getting drunk in some saloon.

He'd been caught by the Division just after she'd been taken by the Alabama gang in Chicago. And he'd been imprisoned here the whole time.

CHAPTER TWENTY-NINE

Hettie's stomach churned as she hurried out of the office. Now was not the time to feel remorse. She'd get the old man and everyone else out somehow. Unfortunately the file didn't say which cell Uncle was being kept in; the space labeled "Confinement" sported only a big zero. She'd have to search the men's wing until she could locate him.

First things first. She went to get Sophie. The locks on the cell doors would not open with a screwdriver, though. She needed keys, which meant taking them off a guard.

Hettie finally found a man with a heavy set of keys attached to his belt. She grimaced at the arsenal of knives strapped to her body, wondering which Jemma might have used for this. As many men as she'd killed, though, she couldn't just slit his throat like a hapless animal at slaughter.

One way or another, she'd be forced to take him into her time bubble.

She positioned herself behind him and tried to lift the ring off without touching him, but it was no good. The guard stumbled as if he'd just tripped on his own feet. Hettie wrapped an arm around his neck, cutting off his air supply, and squeezed hard, pulling him to the ground and cinching her legs around him as he struggled to get a word out, a breath in. She hung on, setting her hooks into the time bubble, locked her ankles together, making sure she did not let go. The man's panicked thrashing and bucking did him no good. Finally he slackened. She squeezed hard once for good measure, then untangled herself, limbs shaking, muscles aching. She could not do that again.

She hurriedly tried every key on the ring until she opened the outer door to the wing. The inmates slept soundly, the barred doors to their cells reminding her of hundreds of dark, empty eyes. It smelled strangely of lilacs here, though it did not completely hide the acrid tang of fear and degradation.

She found Sophie curled up on a cot in her assigned cell. A dirty, poorly sewn sackcloth dress was layered over her petticoats. Dark circles hung heavily beneath her eyes, and her golden curls were limp and dishevelled. A bruise marred the underside of her jaw.

A pair of thick, heavy bracelets painted with blue stars adorned her wrists. At first Hettie thought they were an unnecessary adornment, but then she realized the decoration must have been there to indicate what kind of sorcery Sophie specialized in.

Hettie opened the cell door. All the doors she'd brought into her bubble were weighing on her now. She hadn't thought there'd be so many.

She touched Sophie's shoulder, bringing her into her time bubble, and then gently called to her. "Sophie."

The debutante's eyes snapped open. She sat straight up in bed. "Hettie!" It came out on a sob, and Sophie flung her arms around her and started to cry.

"Shh, shh. It's okay. Jemma and Horace are waiting outside for us."

"Marcus—"

"We're getting him next. C'mon. Stay close to me and don't touch anything." The press of Sophie's presence in the time bubble made it feel like a balloon filling with water, bouncing pendulously with each step she took.

They hurried to the men's wing. Hettie told Sophie in brief about everything that had happened and how they'd arrived in New Mexico. The sorcerer marveled as they passed a few guards frozen in time.

Thankfully the keys Hettie had taken worked on these doors, too. They found Marcus's cell and unlocked the door, the weight of yet another object in Hettie's time bubble making her feel a little light-headed. Sophie touched his shoulder. He woke more slowly than she had, but as he laid eyes on Sophie, he shot to alertness.

"Who are you?" he demanded, backing up against the wall.

"Marcus...it's me. Sophie."

His eyes were huge, but no spark of recognition came.

"Oh, no..." Sophie put her hands to her mouth and looked to Hettie, tears filling her eyes. That was when Hettie realized that in the firefight with the Pinkertons, Marcus had used Luna and Claire, and the mage guns had taken their blood price: his memory of the one person he was sworn to protect.

They couldn't just leave him there, though. "You are Marcus Wellington," she said sternly, and he turned to look at her as if she'd popped out of thin air.

"Miss Alabama..." He glanced between her and Sophie, confused. "I don't understand..."

Well, at least he remembered her. "Do you know how you got here?"

He hesitated. "There are...gaps. But I know the Pinkertons arrested me. I was in a mansion in New Orleans..." He trailed off. If all he'd forgotten was Sophie, then Hettie could only imagine how confused he must be about why he'd been in the Favreau mansion in the first place.

"You used your mage guns and lost some of your memories." They must have confiscated his little book. "This is Sophie. You used to know her. I'm here to get you both out, but first, tell me—have you seen my uncle?"

"Mr. Bassett?" He blinked. "No. Why?"

She told them about the file she'd found. "He hasn't been missing all this time. He's been here. But his file didn't say where he was being kept. There's just a big zero in his cell allotment."

Marcus's jaw firmed. "I've heard rumors of an underground confinement level reserved for the most dangerous sorcerers. They call it Level Zero." He wiped a hand over his mouth. "No one who has been sent down there has ever returned."

313

Hettie set her teeth. Uncle had pulled her from the brink of hell. She supposed it was her turn to save him.

"You can't mean to go looking for him," Sophie said. "Can you even hold this time bubble…" She trailed off as she looked closer. She gasped. "You're juicing."

"It was the only way," Hettie said a touch defensively. "And yes, I am going to go find Uncle. This is the only opportunity we'll have. I'll drop the two of you off past the edge of the perimeter first." She gestured for them to follow.

"The Division might sense you," Sophie warned.

"Nothing has interfered with Diablo yet." They turned the corner and carefully skirted around some guards. "If they even knew how to stop me, it'd take them time to cast a counterspell or put up their wards." She gestured toward the nearly stock-still guards. "They can't catch up."

"What about Luna and Claire?" Marcus asked. "If we have time…"

"I'm sorry, Marcus. I can't go rifling through any more files looking for your mage guns or anything else. Everything I touch comes into my time bubble, and I can't hold it forever. I've still got to get Uncle."

"Can't you just step out of your time bubble and step back in?" he asked.

She understood his anxiety. It was Sophie who explained, "The detection spells have probably already been triggered the first time Hettie used the bubble. The null spells will take effect soon."

"But…Diablo's different, isn't it?"

"We can't take the chance, Marcus. We need to leave now."

He pursed his lips, dejected. She understood his anxiety, his loss. She vowed to make it up to him somehow.

They walked out of the prison unhindered and through the dusty desert toward the perimeter. The whole world seemed to be holding its breath. Every step became more and more difficult, and she reminded them to stay close. Maybe the null spell on Swedenborg was being deployed. Or perhaps her juice was running out.

"There." Hettie pointed toward a gap in the trees. "Jemma's camped about a mile that way. Take the horses and go. Horace will rejoin you at the rendezvous. I'll go back for Uncle."

"I don't like this," Sophie said. "You can't be sure they really have Mr. Bassett. His name is common enough…"

"It's him," she said with surety, remembering the details on the file. "I can't leave him here." Something had made sure she would find him. Ignoring spirits never ended well.

The perimeter of Swedenborg's field of influence was marked by a string hung with talismans. The moment they crossed the line, the bubble burst, and Hettie stumbled to her knees with a gasp.

"Are you all right?" Marcus touched her shoulder, and she flinched. Pins and needles buzzed across her skin.

"I…I don't feel…" *Right* wasn't the word she wanted to use, but it was the only one she could think of. Something was off, as if a piece of her were missing. Had she used up the juice?

"It's the barrier." Sophie studied the talismans with narrowed eyes, the way one might examine an ancient language. "It strips off any magic a person might have taken out of the prison—my guess is in case someone tried to juice off a sorcerer inside." She frowned. "Can you still use Diablo?"

She conjured the revolver easily and exhaled in relief. "I'll be fine. Just get going. Get as far from here as you can. Uncle and I will rejoin you as soon as possible."

Marcus looked skeptically at Sophie. The debutante bit her lip and held out her hand. "Mr. Wellington, please. I can't do this on my own."

"Please, go with her, Marcus," Hettie implored. "I'll explain everything as soon as I can. You can trust Sophie."

"If *you* trust her, Miss Alabama, then I suppose I can, too." He nodded and followed the debutante but kept a little distance between them. Would he remember Jemma? It would be odd if he could remember one but not the other.

Hettie stepped past the perimeter once more and dropped back into the time bubble. From a distance Swedenborg looked like a wedding cake frosted with steel, gleaming beneath the moonlight. It was a sprawling facility, and she didn't relish the thought of searching every broom closet for Uncle in her syrupy time. On the one hand, at least she'd unburdened the bubble of her passengers and everything she'd taken into it. On the other, reestablishing the bubble felt a lot harder. The juice was running out, and the prison's counterspells were probably taking effect. Jumping in and out of time would not help her.

She walked toward the prison. Her body grew heavy. Her bones ached with fatigue. She wanted to lie down to rest…

The time bubble wobbled. Something was wrong. She bit the inside of her cheek to wake herself up and gripped Diablo tightly. *Hang on long enough for me to find Uncle*, she told it firmly. She drove her trigger finger against the thorn, letting the pain feed her need, letting her blood power the mage gun's magic.

The golden syrup of time rippled around her, crystalizing. Sweat broke out all over her body. She could barely take a step without the whole bubble collapsing. She knew then she wouldn't be able to hang on long enough to find Uncle and get them out of Swedenborg.

I can't do this alone, she thought bleakly.

Diablo pulsed in reassurance. Something hissed in her mind. She looked all around her, expecting the bubble to have dropped, but it hadn't. The world remained frozen in time.

The sound came again. It sounded like…sand. Or a snake? No, a bird. The rustle of wings and a dry, rasping caw, as if a crow were rising out of the earth.

And there it was. A shadowy shape on the ground, not quite there, yet its empty eyes were fixed on her. Its black beak snapped and opened, and it made that sound again.

"Are you a ghost?" she asked it plainly. She'd read that ghosts sometimes forgot about their human forms and took on animal ones. She'd heard plenty of stories of animal guides who helped people…and other stories of spirit creatures who were tricksters, leading people to their deaths.

The black bird—she wanted to say it was a raven, but its misty form shifted like smoke—ruffled its feathers, shivering in the wind. She could barely distinguish it against the night sky. She almost wondered if she were seeing things. It took off suddenly, flying in a wide arc around her, its form cutting a circular swath against the star-studded sky, blacking out the pinpoints of light with its diaphanous midnight wings.

With a shudder, she realized she hadn't brought that thing into the time bubble. It had *followed* her there. Perhaps it had some connection to the same magic that Diablo used. Or perhaps...

"Paul?" she asked quietly. But the bird didn't respond. She shook her head, chastising herself for being a fool.

The bird angled down and sailed closer to the ground, around shoulder height. Hettie said, "You were the one who showed me Uncle's file, weren't you?"

The bird didn't reply. It simply flew on, leading Hettie vaguely west until it landed on the ground in the lightest puff of black dust. It tapped the ground with its beak, banging a hard, hollow beat against something that definitely wasn't earth.

Hettie kneeled and swept her palm over the ground. The large metal hatch was barely visible beneath the sand. A big faded zero was painted on top in white. No, not a zero—it was a protection circle, bisected by a line of runes. Her heart thudded hard as she cleared the dirt off. When she looked up to thank the bird spirit, it had vanished.

Was that you? she asked Diablo. The mage gun was silent.

The door was made of heavy iron. A prybar was set into a groove next to the hatch. She used it to pull the plate up, then wedged it beneath the lip and levered the door open. Her muscles strained as she lifted the door and set the bar into the slot to keep it in place. Beneath, a set of narrow metal stairs led down into the darkness.

Diablo at the ready, she descended. Something foul wafted to her nose, and she covered her mouth. A fly buzzed near her ear, then another. The stench got worse the farther in she went, and so did the buzzing. She realized then that she was walking into a thick cloud of flies and bringing them into her time bubble as she touched them. Small as they were, she could feel their weight on the syrup of her suspension. She wouldn't be able to stay in here for long before the bubble gave.

She froze, unsure whether to go on. *Death, death, death,* the feasting flies hummed. *That* was what she was smelling. This place wasn't just a prison—it was a tomb. And Uncle was down here somewhere. How long had he been here? Would he even be alive? Her steps faltered. If he wasn't, did she want her last memories of him to be of some bloated corpse in the dark?

She steeled herself. She had to see. The spirit who'd led her to this place must have wanted something from her.

She kept going, the light from above fading. There were no lamps here. No glow stones or lanterns or anything to give her any sense of how much deeper the stairs went, how large the space was. It was like walking into the belly of a whale.

Slowly her eyesight adjusted. No, wait…it was Diablo, glowing a faint green. It wasn't exactly a comforting light, but it was enough to see by, to see the walls around her, the bottom of the steps and the wet, gritty sand on the floor of the hole.

The space she entered was large enough to swallow what light Diablo did give off, so she couldn't see the ceiling or the walls. The stench of rot was unbearable here, and she pulled the bandana tied around her neck up to cover her nose and mouth. Flies buzzed her ears, flickered against her eyelashes, and she flinched and swatted at the air, inadvertently bringing more of the critters. Her steps crunched over what she soon realized was a carpet of maggots and other bugs. Hundreds of little lives slipping into her bubble only to be crushed underfoot.

The flies didn't know not to leave her space. They stretched the time bubble in all directions, making Hettie grit her teeth. Damn flies. She would have to let go of the bubble, but she feared what she'd encounter the moment she did.

She didn't have a choice. She took a deep breath and released it.

The buzzing became nearly deafening, and the horrid smell wafted upward into her nostrils as the odious fumes rushed to escape up the hatch. She listened for something other than the discordant song of the flies, heard nothing.

"Uncle," she said into the dark.

Nothing.

She summoned her courage. "Jeremiah Bassett," she called more loudly. She tasted the foulness on her tongue and coughed, struggling to contain her gorge.

A shuffle in the dark was followed by a moan. Hettie stood her ground, raising Diablo. "Uncle?"

Something lurched toward her, a stumbling, shambling shadow. She almost screamed as its half-rotted face pressed in close. He'd been a man at some point, but now he was melted flesh crawling with maggots.

Everything inside Hettie clenched and recoiled, and in doing so, she pulled Diablo's trigger.

The muzzle exploded in a flash of green fire, pouring out and illuminating the space. And in that oubliette of death, she saw what she wished she hadn't. Dozens of bodies—alive, half-alive, nearly dead, or otherwise perished—stirred in the dark. Empty, hungry eyes stared her way as Diablo's blinding hell flame blazed.

The man-thing howled and stumbled back, clawing at its tattered clothing and flaming skin and muscle.

Hettie realized what she'd just done, and the moment the man-thing crumpled to the ground, agony tore through her.

She dropped like a stone as her whole body seized, screaming as Diablo sheared a year off her life. It'd been some time since the Devil's Revolver had taken its blood price, and it was *starving*.

It wasn't just the physical pain that made her scream. She could see by the hell-green embers of the now dead man-thing that the other figures were coming toward her, drawn by the fire, drawn by Diablo.

She knew then what she had recognized in the far depths of her mind: that craven look in the man-thing's eyes was *hunger*. More specifically, the hunger of a man desperate for juice. For magic.

And Diablo was that in spades.

The twitch of her muscles finally eased, and she shakily scrambled to her feet as the first of the man-things reached her. He pawed at her, mumbling, grabbing, tugging. Hettie pushed him off, and when he rushed her more angrily, she kicked him in the stomach.

She had to get out of there. She struggled for calm, to pull the bubble around her. It caught—snagged. Why wasn't it working? She fought off another—a woman in a tattered smock whose eyes had been clawed out. Hettie kicked her feet out from under her and fired Diablo at her legs, melting the sand around her and encasing the creature's limbs in molten glass.

Someone grabbed her from behind. Another gripped her wrist. Diablo glowed bright as hands shot out from the dark and pawed at her. One of the creatures grabbed her hand and bit her wrist.

She screamed, twisting in her captor's hold. Her finger spasmed and pulled the trigger several times. Fire blasted up to the ceiling, punching holes all around her. Clods of melted earth dripped down on her assailants, and they cried out as they were buried. Hettie tore herself out of the man-thing's grip and unleashed a spume of flame, drawing it in a wide arc around her. The desperate creatures didn't seem to care—they waded right into the hell fire, got stuck in the melted earth. The whole cavern glowed green-white.

The air was so thick with flies, it was as if she were standing in a hellish blizzard. The man-things surrounded her, blocking the way to the stairs. Frantically she searched for another way out.

She reached for the time bubble again. It wasn't coming!

Think, Hettie, think!

She looked up. She could shoot her way through, but the moment she killed one of these creatures, she'd be a goner. They'd tear her limb from limb.

She holstered the gun and drew one of Jemma's long daggers. The creatures were closing in, climbing over their fallen comrades stuck in place. She slashed at the first one that reached her, slicing a long gash across its face, but the man-thing barely flinched. She stabbed at another stumbling toward her, the blade sinking deep. And still the man-thing scrabbled for her.

She backed away, heart hammering.

They didn't feel pain. They didn't feel fear.

They wanted her magic. They wanted *her*.

Someone grabbed her wrist, and she screamed.

"Damn fool girl!" Uncle's face was sallow and haggard as he tugged her toward him. "C'mon!"

CHAPTER THIRTY

Hettie's heart nearly exploded with relief. His insult was the sweetest thing she'd ever heard. She followed him as he plowed through the moaning horde, slashing and hacking off grasping limbs with a rusty machete as if he were an intrepid explorercutting his way through a jungle.

They reached the stairwell. Uncle toed a semicircular line around the foot of the steps and handed Hettie the machete. "Brace yourself."

He opened his hands and spoke an incantation, then slapped them down on the ground. Power radiated out from the lines, and the oncoming man-things shied away, buffeted back.

Uncle groaned and slumped down. Hettie held the machete at the ready, but their assailants hesitated. "What'd you do?"

"Barrier spell," he gritted. "Hurry. I can't hold it."

She slung an arm beneath him and half carried him up the steps. He reeked of horrors untold.

"How long have you been here?"

"You'd be the better one to answer that," he grumbled as he hobbled up the stairs. "The Division boys caught up with me three days after you disappeared. I found the traces of a remote Zoom but couldn't find you. I tried to track you down. Did one spell too many and ended up flat on my back in a hospital. Division got called in on account of me being a high-level sorcerer. They didn't like my answers and dragged me off. They didn't even check me in at Swedenborg. They just put me here."

"No charges? No trial?"

"They knew who I was." He snorted. "That's all they needed to know."

"What are those…things?" she asked. His weight put a lot of strain on her back, but she kept pulling him up. There seemed to be more steps on the way up than there had been going down.

"Sorcerers. At least they used to be. The Division's used lifetime inmates in all kinds of experiments, mainly ones to do with eternal life. Fountain of youth potions." He nodded. "This batch is different, though. Been drained of their magic—most of it, anyhow."

"Drained? Like they loaned their magic out?" She thought of Bear Brown, but as decrepit as the old man was, he hadn't become one of these mindless creatures.

"This is something else." He gave her a steady look. "Hettie, I don't think Fielding's engine is the only one of its kind. I think whatever this program is, it's been in the works for a long time. These people…they've been here years, wasting away but not quite dying. They were experimented on and thrown down here…maybe because the Division didn't know what else to do with them, but more likely because they wanted to see how they'd do after the experiment was over."

Hettie's head spun. "But…that's horrible. How can they get away with this?"

"They won't."

As soon as they got to the surface, she was going to melt the door shut. She glanced at him. "Why didn't you try to escape before now?"

"You think I haven't? No one can open that door from the inside. Not while those things are clawing at me, and not in my condition."

She couldn't imagine the hell he'd been living these past weeks in the dark, trapped with these creatures. She didn't want to even think about what he'd eaten or drunk to survive.

The hatch loomed just above, the gap showing the clearest and most beautiful slice of open sky she'd ever seen. She boosted Uncle up first, then climbed out herself. As she rolled out onto the dust, she kicked the prybar out so the door slammed shut with a resounding boom. She pulled in a deep, clean breath of cool night air.

"Gods," Uncle breathed, and gave a weak laugh. "I thought I'd never see the stars again."

In the moonlight, which seemed so bright compared to that dungeon, she could see a distant stream of dust making its way toward them from the jail. "We gotta git!" Hettie pulled Uncle to his feet.

They only made it a few steps before Uncle stumbled and fell to his knees, wheezing. Hettie slung his arm around her shoulders. "Don't die on me now, old man. You have a lot to answer for."

"Don't you worry, I'll do that in hell," he griped, moaning.

They hurried toward the edge of the perimeter. If she was lucky, Horace would find them and pick them up. Or perhaps Jemma had left her a horse. The way Uncle was gasping, she didn't think he'd last long on foot.

She reached for the time bubble—and stopped dead in her tracks.

"My time bubble's still not working." She closed her eyes, trying to calm her thundering heart. Every second they wasted, the Division got closer. *What are you doing?* she screamed silently at Diablo. The mage gun didn't respond. It must have been the null spell, or some other magical protection that was stifling Diablo's powers. Unless...

Her steps faltered, and she stared into the night. A cloying sense of déjà vu hit her as shadows flickered through the dark just outside of the perimeter, racing and darting in and out of her vision. The full moon was huge and pale above them, a fear-widened eye staring blindly into the void.

"No..." She sucked in the freezing-cold air. Of course. How had she not noticed it before? The air was unnaturally chilly. The tips of her fingers and nose were numb. This wasn't just regular nighttime damp. They were in the desert. Someone had opened a remote Zoom here recently.

She had a pretty good idea who.

"Hettie..." Uncle felt it, too, a second too late. He stopped and squinted into the night. "What—"

A gunshot blast exploded out of the dark.

Hettie's world slowed down, but not because Diablo's time bubble was working, and not because this was a vision. The light was yellowish, not gold; more the color of pus, putrid and decaying. It sliced through the air sure as an arrow—

Uncle barely flinched. At first she thought it'd missed.

Jeremiah Bassett fell to his knees. He stared, stricken, and then slowly a smile formed on his lips. "Huh."

He went slack and collapsed facedown into the dirt.

Hettie didn't think she screamed, but she couldn't be sure. The blood was pumping so thick through her veins, squeezed by a heart that was about to burst, she couldn't hear anything. Her vision clouded. She thought for a moment that a susurration of starlings had taken off all around her, their cries filling her head, their dark feathers blinding her.

Diablo was in her fist. She clung to it as if she were in a storm. *Uncle. Uncle!* She clawed her way across the dirt—when had she fallen?—and turned him onto his back. Blood welled up from a deep gushing gash in his chest, stretching from hip to shoulder—a cut more perfect than a surgeon could make with a scalpel. The smell of death hit her again—a flash of memory, of Paul with his heavy head in her little lap, telling her it would be okay...

Uncle raised a shaking hand. "H-Hettie..." He pushed a blood-soaked sachet into her palm and murmured something. Her skin broke out in goose pimples as the last of his magic trickled over her like a benediction. She heard the hiss of an animal, the release of breath...

And then his eyes were empty, staring up at the stars, tracing the path before him to a place she could not follow.

Jeremiah Bassett was dead.

The pain came. So quick, so sharp, it was like a nail being driven through her throat, her heart, her stomach. It was worse than the agony of Diablo swallowing a year of her life. A wordless sob rose through her, morphing into a cry of pure rage that vibrated through every fiber of her being. Her ears rang with her scream.

She staggered to her feet and stared all around, seeking her target. She knew the gunshot that had pierced the old man's heart.

She knew that yellowish light, that sure aim. Why hadn't Mizzay aimed for *her* instead?

To cause her pain. To make her lose focus. The woman was insane and bent on becoming Hettie for some convoluted reason.

"Mizzay!" she roared into the darkness. She didn't see red, she saw green—the color of Diablo's power. The color of envy, the color of death and the vengeance she'd wreak.

She would kill Mizzay. She would gladly kill her ten times over and let Diablo gobble up every one of those years. *"Mizzay!"*

Only the sounds of night greeted her…and for some reason they sounded like snickers.

Hettie shouted, "Come out here and face me, you cowardly bitch!"

"She won't come."

She spun and pulled Diablo's trigger, but the mage gun's blast splashed harmlessly at the feet of the warlock Zavi. He stood against the night, pale skin aglow with nearly the same intensity as Diablo. The mage gun quavered. It did not want to go back to him.

Zavi glanced down, smirking. "Mizzay's out there somewhere, hiding in the bushes. She's not like you, you know. She'd never go toe-to-toe with you and Diablo. Not even to prove herself. She just wants your legacy to be hers."

"*You* made her do this. This is *your* fault!"

"I didn't do anything," he said matter-of-factly. "I made her mage gun, but she's the one who pulls the trigger. I didn't tell her to kill the old man." He gestured toward Uncle. "He means nothing to me."

Rage boiled over inside her. "Don't you talk about him like that! Don't you even look at him! He wasn't nothing! He was the greatest sorcerer—" Her words caught in her throat. Uncle was dead. He wasn't blood, but he was family.

Now all she had left was Abby.

Zavi looked genuinely sorry. Sympathetic, even. Hatred scorched through her blood. She raised Diablo, the weight of its intent straining her wrist. She needed to kill someone right now.

"We already know that won't work." Zavi nodded at the Division guards. They were closing in fast. "I'm here to offer you a deal.

Relinquish Diablo to me, and I'll take you out of here and as far as you want to go."

She snorted. "You want me as dead as everyone else."

He lifted his chin. "Perhaps. But can you guarantee those men won't do worse?" His gaze flicked toward the rapidly approaching line of dust. "Don't be foolish. Come with me and I can help you."

Hettie stepped back from the pain and anger swirling inside her, her survival instincts sharpening her intuition. Something had changed. Zavi, with all his power, was trying to coax her to come. And he still wanted Diablo. Why, when he'd always had the upper hand? Why didn't he just kill her now, open the gate to hell?

Because she had something over him. As long as she didn't go along with him, she'd continue to have the advantage.

She waited, her grip tight on Diablo. The time bubble wasn't working, which meant the Alabama gang surrounded her. She'd thought she'd cut the null net, but maybe that was only temporary.

They hadn't presented Jemma, Sophie, or the others as hostages, so they wouldn't have that leverage over her. The Division would be here soon. Would Zavi try to interfere if they arrested her? Would they try to arrest *him*?

He could probably kill them all with a wave of his hand. She didn't feel a single bit of remorse over that. The Division had taken Uncle and made his last days a living hell in that hole. They were experimenting on inmates. They were doing all kinds of atrocious things to people...

They would do the same to Abby if they got their hands on her. And Hettie would rather die here than let any of these people near her sister.

Let them do their worst, she thought with cold conviction. *Let them destroy each other. If I get caught up in this...so be it. Open the gate. I'm ready. And I hope they all rot in hell.*

Diablo smiled in her mind.

CHAPTER THIRTY-ONE

*Z*avi's serene countenance changed to one of mild annoyance as Hettie simply stood there, staring, waiting. The approaching hoofbeats shuddered through the ground, up into her bones through the soles of her feet. She turned to face the Division men who'd come to bring her in.

They launched glow stones into the air to hover above them in a brilliant multicolored arc. Hettie squinted against the sudden glare that flooded the area and cast its awful light over Uncle's body.

"Miss Alabama." She recognized that voice as well as the straw-colored hair and big mustache. Her grip tightened on Diablo as the man tipped his hat.

"Captain Bradley." He'd led the army that'd rousted the Crowes from Sonora station. She lifted her chin, meeting his eye, a kind of flat serenity smothering her emotions. She spoke remotely, unaffected. "I see you've been demoted to guarding a bunch of criminals."

His lips twitched. "I'm only here as a special consultant to Swedenborg on account of my previous dealings with you and Mr. Bassett." His gaze canted toward the body, and his lips pursed. "Damn shame. He was a fine man."

"Fine enough for y'all to throw into that hell hole?" She raised her gun. "Did you know about Level Zero?"

"It was an administrative error I came here to correct," he said mildly. *Lies*, she thought. The coward was staring down Diablo's barrel and would say anything not to have a hole blown through his face. She could see the fine sheen of sweat glimmering on his brow. "How about you come back to my office and we'll sort things out? I can arrange for a proper burial for Mr. Bassett."

She glared, not answering. He knew just as well as she that she could blow them all to hell before they could blink an eye, but they weren't about to shoot. Even shooting her in the leg could be dangerous. If she was killed, the gate to hell would open.

"With all due respect, captain," Zavi said quietly, "Miss Alabama has yet to refuse *my* proposition."

Bradley glanced up as if just noticing Zavi for the first time. The six men with him gripped their sidearms in surprise.

"Who are you?" The captain shook his head. "Never mind that. This is Division property, and you're trespassing. You'll have to come with us."

"Trespassing?" Zavi blinked. "This land doesn't belong to you or anyone else." Zavi tilted his chin. "You're nothing but squatters. Vermin. Parasites."

Hettie tensed along with Bradley's men. Clearly they could sense his power, knew that he was above and beyond their combined skills as sorcerers.

"I've got business with this one, Captain," she said, drawing the men's attention back to her. "You'll have to wait your turn."

"I'm afraid not, Miss Alabama. You're wanted in fifteen different states for crimes including murder, theft—"

"I can clear that up, Captain. That wasn't this Hettie at all, but her doppelgänger."

Bradley shook his head again, as if he couldn't seem to keep Zavi's presence in mind, like a man trying to stay awake. "Dop... doppelgänger?"

"A woman I met in my travels. A gifted actress. I employed her to assist me in my quest to acquire the Devil's Revolver—to find Miss Alabama here. The real Miss Alabama. I'm afraid my version is a pale imitation."

"'Pale imitation'?" Mizzay appeared out of thin air, and the Division men pulled their guns on her, but she didn't flinch. She was in full outlaw regalia, with her black embroidered split skirt, frilled blouse, and leather vest. A bandolier was slung across her chest, although with her mage gun she didn't need it. Her eyes—Hettie's eyes—blazed as she marched up to Zavi. "How dare you! I've been everything you asked of me and more!"

"Sweet holy honeysuckle." Captain Bradley looked between them—nearly identical except for their clothing and posture. He didn't seem to know where to point his weapon.

"I didn't tell you to come out of hiding." Zavi gave a put-upon sigh. They must be using some kind of hide spell—a variation on glamor magic. The rest of the Alabama gang was likely surrounding Hettie in the same fashion. How many of them had guns trained on her right now? Judging by the twitchy horses and fidgeting, the Division agents knew how much danger they were in, too.

"*You* don't order me around," Mizzay said. "This is my gang, you hear? You owe us. You owe *me*. All I wanted—"

"Was what? For me to love you?"

Mizzay's cheeks turned scarlet. Zavi gave her a pitying look. "You poor dear. I tried to discourage you. I'm not even human. Surely you know that."

She gave a manic smile. "I don't care. You *have* to love me. You gave me the General!"

"I don't *have* to do anything. The mage gun was a tool for you to use, nothing more."

Zavi had masterfully manipulated whatever twisted feelings she'd developed for him in order to take over her outfit. He'd offered her the General, and the mage gun had chipped away at her mind—or maybe there was some kind of influence spell on it that made Mizzay fall in love. Those facts didn't soften Hettie's heart.

"It's her, isn't it?" She swung her dagger-gaze to Hettie. "You're obsessed with her. Maybe I should just kill her, and then you'll be mine."

A cold fist seized Hettie's heart. She raised Diablo. "Mizzay."

As her double turned, she pulled the trigger. The outlaw fired at the same moment. The power of the two mage guns splashed against each other, rocking them back.

The Division horses danced away, whinnying.

Mizzay only laughed. "Is that all you've got? You think Zavi would make something inferior to Diablo?" She unleashed a barrage of pus-yellow fire that sliced through the air. Hettie just barely dove out of the path; a beam caught her pant leg, slicing through the fabric like a knife through water.

Hettie sent a jet of green flame out to splash on the ground around Mizzay, penning her within a horseshoe-shaped crescent. "Why'd you do it?" she shouted. "Why'd you kill Uncle? He never did anything to you!"

"Everyone's done something." Mizzay trained her gun on Hettie.

"Enough of this." Captain Bradley rode his horse between them. "Two young ladies shouldn't be using guns, much less—"

A yellowish flash, and the top half of his head toppled off in a spray of blood.

The Division men drew in a panic, shouting, "Put your guns down! In the name of the Division of Sorcery, *put your guns and talismans down!*"

Mizzay only laughed. "Or you'll what? Arrest us?" She gestured, and the hide spell dropped. At least fifty armed men formed a loose crescent around them. The Division men's heads swiveled around and around, eyes wide.

"Your efforts are futile, gentlemen," Zavi said. "Whatever protections you think your null spells and barrier afforded you are pointless. I undid them all minutes ago."

Hettie got a bad feeling. "What are you doing, Zavi?"

His lips lifted in a humorless smile. "Nothing that need concern you, Miss Alabama. That we met here has been entirely coincidence…if you believe in such things." He tilted his chin. "I don't. But maybe for once the fates are smiling upon me. I'm owed that much."

In the distance the Swedenborg facility lit up, and a siren sounded. Glow stones flared to life around the gantries. The land was suddenly flooded with light, revealing the shadows darting toward the building on fast legs.

"You geised my men?" Mizzay cried in outrage. "We had an agreement!"

"We did. But your men can make their own decisions. I simply offered them the chance to *survive* this mission." He said it as if he were reciting alternatives to a recipe.

Distant gunshots echoed from the prison. An explosion rocketed against the walls in a splash of multihued flames—magic cannon fire, like the kind that had been so destructive during the war. Swedenborg was besieged.

The Division men watched helplessly, completely at a loss without their leader. Then it didn't matter, because Zavi said, "Kill them."

Hettie dove to the ground as a hail of bullets perforated the six men and their horses. They landed in a gory heap upon the ground.

"A waste of magic," Zavi said, gazing at the prison in the distance. "But I'm rather eager to get this over with."

Plumes of fire bloomed over the prison, the percussive blasts rippling over them a moment later. Hettie gripped Diablo tightly. "You're freeing the prisoners?"

"Freeing?" Zavi chortled. It sounded like a bandsaw wobbling. "I suppose you could call it that."

"The device is in place, Zavi," a man's voice said near her ear. A strong amplification spell—the gang members must've been juiced. "We're ready."

"Good." He glanced over his shoulder. "Dr. Fielding?"

Alastair Fielding was pushed into the circle of light. He looked thin, haggard, his clothes torn and soiled, his hands shaking. His spine was stooped as if he'd been crushed underfoot like a tin can and couldn't be unbent. His huge eyes lit on Hettie. There was no hope or relief in them. Only fear.

"W-we sh-shouldn't be doing this," he stuttered. "We c-can't be certain the ch-ch-chain reaction won't stop. M-my c-c-calculations..."

"You're doing it to further Mechaniks," Zavi soothed, his voice like treacle. "If this works, imagine the papers you'll publish. The awards you'll win. Your colleagues will look up to you. You'll be a true hero in the fields of both magic and science."

Fielding's shaking head gradually rolled to the side until he was nodding. "Y-yes, yes, I s-suppose that's t-true."

Hettie wanted to believe he was under an influence spell. But she could see from the way the Mechanik was trembling that he was only fighting his own inner self.

"What's going on, Alastair?" She addressed him by his first name to get his attention.

"Miss Wiltshire!" He acted as if he'd just noticed her. "Oh, you should see the strides I've m-made in my work. This Mr. Z-Zavi has given me s-so...so much..." A single tear dripped from his glassy eyes. "So much to work with. The engine...the engine can now work without the leads. It can draw magic wirelessly! Through ether! I'd never thought it p-possible, but..." He giggled. More tears rained down. "This is our f-first test of the Ether engine."

"Fielding's Ether engine," Zavi preened. "It has a nice ring to it. The patents will make you a very rich man."

The Mechanik nodded eagerly.

Horror dawned on Hettie slowly. They were testing that thing in the middle of the greatest central gathering of sorcerers.

She thought of the man-things in Level Zero. "Fielding, no! You can't do that!"

"It's for science," he protested almost petulantly. "This will be the greatest discovery of our time!"

"If you'll do the honors," Zavi said, flashing a red-gummed grin at Hettie.

Someone handed Fielding a box inscribed with runes. The Mechanikal abomination radiated the same feeling the engine did, pulling at Diablo, making the mage gun shrink away.

Fielding slit his hand, waved it over the box while enunciating an incantation. He put his bloodied palm over the box.

Hettie felt something like a kick in the chest. Diablo gave a plaintive moan in her mind. Her vision blurred briefly as a shock wave rolled over her, and she stumbled back.

The Swedenborg prison glowed with sickly bluish light, almost in the same way that the engine's canister did when it was filled with magic. The glow stones had all gone out, but the land was bathed in the ambient glow and the baleful moon.

"Beautiful," Zavi breathed.

And then there came a sucking sensation, not unlike the draw of the Zoom tunnels, tugging at her skin, at her heart and her very being. The glow faded and she felt it being drawn in like a bedsheet being pulled through a barrel's bunghole. Diablo gave a cry in her mind, and Hettie realized that the null net the Alabama gang used was no longer working.

She dropped into her time bubble. The deafening silence gave her a moment to breathe, but then Zavi's head turned her way and he said, "Where do you think you're going?"

She pointed Diablo at him. "Stop this. Whatever it is, you have to stop it."

"*I* didn't do anything. You keep blaming me for these disasters, but I haven't interfered at all in your human affairs. That's not my role here."

"You kidnapped those children. You drank their blood. You handed a woman a weapon that made her lose her mind. You juiced these men and made them do these terrible things."

"No one had to do a thing I said. I was simply taking advantage of their charity."

"You may not pull the trigger, but you sure as hell are holding the gun." She found her voice, her conviction. She lifted her chin. "What possible reason could you have for doing all this?"

Zavi glared. "I was ripped from my home, Hettie Alabama. A land of diamond palaces and cloud floors. A place where the air was always warm and sweet and the wind was always soft. All of that and everything I ever loved was taken from me when I was dragged here by that worm, Javier Punta." Hatred carved deep lines in his face, and for the first time she saw his age, the cynicism of a mortal life without mortality—without an end—to temper it.

"At first I thought I'd do some good here. I thought I had a purpose among you mortals. Instead, I've found nothing but pain and suffering and utter futility." He clenched his hands as if he might strangle humanity.

"All your kind are driven by the same base instincts you crawled out of creation's womb with. Greed. Lust. Hatred. Every single person I've met on this earth has betrayed me, betrayed their fellow man, betrayed themselves and their whole race. The universe gives and gives, and all you do is take, take, take. You consume and destroy everything you touch. Your kind are the most selfish, most self-serving, most wasteful beings in all of creation."

"Guess it's good we excel at something, then."

Zavi snorted. "Where I'm from, we would watch your little existence for amusement. You're like maggots, gorging yourself on a carcass in the pointless pursuit of becoming a worthless insect. Of all the realms, this one is the most base and reckless, the one that threw all its potential away. You've squandered the divine powers gifted to you in this world." He paced in a tight line like a caged cat. "Your kind are worse than locusts, and the moment you find a way to open the doors to the other realms, you'll take what's there, too. The only way to make sure you never do is to take magic out of this world. Take away the keys to the kingdom."

She glanced toward the prison. "You made Fielding's engine into some kind of...bomb to take magic away from the gifted."

"Not just the gifted. Out of everything in its blast radius." He looked toward the fading magic light, a twilight world slowly turning to midnight. "I realized I don't have to end the whole world. Opening the gate to the place you call hell is a messy business, and it would do me no good to end up *there*. No, for the good of all the realms, I'm making sure your kind never breaches the other worlds. Maybe then they'll notice me and take me back. I would be a hero."

So this *was* all about Zavi getting home. Diablo was right—Zavi was trying to get attention, the way a child throwing a tantrum would. Only he wasn't a child; he had a plan. And his delusion of heroism teetered close enough to insanity that she believed him capable of anything.

"This could be the solution to your curse, you know," he went on. "If we take all the magic out of the world, Diablo will no longer have a hold on you, and my tie to it will break."

"And Abby?" She remembered everything Mizzay said, everything Zavi had insinuated. "She could die if magic left the world."

"An unfortunate possibility. But it's not personal. Not anymore. Vengeance is empty, Hettie Alabama. I realize that now. I was being petty. I lost sight of the bigger picture, became selfish and self-centered. Clearly, I've spent too much time among your kind."

She didn't believe him. "Why the change of heart?"

"It was thanks to you, actually. First you had the audacity to nearly die when I set that golem on you. It wasn't supposed to kill you—it couldn't have, the way I designed it—and yet somehow you wriggled your way to the brink of death anyway. You had the ability to go where I couldn't, against all odds.

"And then you wrenched Diablo back from me. That was quite a feat, you know. We're connected, after all, by the same powers that drew us out of our dimensions." He stared into the middle distance, pensive.

"I had an epiphany then. A little thing like a mage gun can be made and unmade like that." He snapped his fingers. "Diablo and I are refugees in this realm. Once magic has been purged from this land, our ties here will be broken, and we can be free to return home."

"If that's true, why do you need it? Why can't you let us be?"

He smiled, almost impressed. "There's no telling where we'll go once magic disappears from this place. The demon inside Diablo is a natural finder—it can navigate through any realm. Javier Punta didn't tell you *that*, did he?" He scoffed. "I don't want to be lost and wandering the realms, searching for home for eternity. Diablo can lead me there, and then it can go back to where it came from. But for all that to work, I need you to relinquish it to me. It's stubbornly loyal to you."

Perhaps parts of that were true, but she couldn't be certain which. Hettie did not trust a word out of his mouth.

"You don't need to do this," Hettie said. "Whatever it is you want—to die, to go home…there must be another way. You can't just take magic from the land."

"If not me, it'll be the Division." He gestured toward the prison. "Mechaniks all over the country have been developing these machines for the Division for decades. Centuries, even. Apart from one small accident in England, Fielding was the first to make a breakthrough." He glanced over his shoulder, but the good doctor had been herded out of sight. "That's why I quietly invested in his work. An anonymous donation to push his research forward. He was the closest to getting it right, after all."

"You don't call *that* interference?"

"What, giving money?" He snickered. "This is why your kind are so amusing. You have such pedestrian obsessions. Do you know why the Division wanted these engines?" He flashed his teeth. "Because they want to concentrate and redistribute magic to the people *they* deem worthy…or at least those who can pay." His lips curled. "Can you imagine that? Stealing divinity from the chosen in exchange for some pieces of paper. They'd kill their own gods if someone gave them a coin to do it." He laughed unpleasantly. "And you think *I'm* the monster."

Everything inside Hettie shrank with fear and loathing. "How do you even know this?"

"I've been on this world for over two hundred years, and observing it for much longer. I've traveled all over the globe, searching for Diablo, for a way home. I've studied your histories, discovered your magic secrets. I even lived as a human for a while in a misguided attempt to understand your kind better. I learned everything I needed to about the Division in that time, and believe me, they are no more noble than a pile of ants scavenging for scraps and defending their hill."

Hettie knew the Division wasn't to be trusted. Even so, a war had started in her about who to trust less. "That's not proof of anything," she said.

"I have no reason to lie. You know deep down your fellow man is as mindlessly selfish as I've described. Even you aren't immune to that thinking—I can smell the borrowed magic on you." He sniffed. "A rather pungent and weak bouquet, no doubt wrung from some damp-sponge sorcerers. Tell me, how is what you've done any different from what I've done?"

Shame welled up inside her at her own hypocrisy. No matter what reasoning or justification she came up with, Zavi was right. She'd bilked the people of Quail's Hollow out of their magic for her own personal gain. She felt ill.

"You can't be faulted. You're acting on animal instincts, after all." His tone wasn't condescending exactly—pitying, perhaps. Maybe even sympathetic. He pressed on. "Give me Diablo, and I will leave you and Abby and that plot of land around your Montana ranch alone. Your own little magical oasis where you can live out the rest of your days. I don't need either of you. Just the mage gun."

The time bubble shimmered around her, and Diablo quivered in her mind's eye. She was so tired of running, of fighting, of looking for ways to resist…it was tempting to just give up.

You can't trust him.

She thought of Abby. Zavi could not promise the bomb wouldn't affect her sister. Selfish or no, she had one job.

You gotta protect Abby now.

She raised Diablo. "I can't let you do this."

Zavi's eyebrow notched up, as if he hadn't expected resistance. "What do you think will happen here? You can't shoot me dead. You could run away, but where to? Even if you tried to hide, I'd find you again. And I wouldn't be kind about taking Diablo from you then. That motley crew of yours would be my first targets. Patrice Favreau, for instance..." He tsked. "Well, she's hanging on to life by the skin of her teeth. I could destroy her soul, you know. For her sake, you should relinquish the gun to me."

The manic gleam that she'd come to know so well had returned to his eyes. He was lying, making things up. If Patrice was any kind of threat to him, and if he had the ability to harm her, he would've done so by now to get leverage over Hettie. He wanted Diablo, and he would say anything to get it from her.

She looked him dead in the eye. "I don't believe you."

Hettie pulled Diablo's trigger, melting the ground at his feet. Zavi shrieked as he sank into the molten earth up to his knees.

It wouldn't buy her much time, but it would have to do. Abby's life was threatened by Zavi's device and the magic drain, and as long as Hettie had Diablo, they were both in danger. She had to run.

As she turned to go, the air turned frosty. Her breath clouded. She spun around. What was Zavi—

He looked stricken. His black eyes blanked, turning to regular human eyes with dark irises and milky whites. His mouth slackened as a pinhole of darkness formed between them.

A remote Zoom tunnel was opening in their bubble of time. How? Hettie backed away, prepared for anything—

The Zoom exploded open, a sphere of light and dark. A surge of water smashed into her, submerging her and Zavi briefly. She flailed, but just as quickly as the wave had hit she landed back in the mud with a splash, grit in her eyes and mouth as she coughed salty water up. The chill of the Zoom froze her skin almost instantly.

She looked up. Her heart expanded and contracted painfully as joy and fear squeezed through her.

"Abby!" she gasped.

CHAPTER THIRTY-TWO

The little girl blinked as she took in her surroundings. All around her the Alabama gang lay splayed out on the ground, some of them drowned, some of them bowled over, many of them groaning and spluttering. The time bubble had burst.

Abby knelt by Uncle's body and touched his forehead. Her lip wobbled, and she hung her head. "He's gone."

"Abby." Hettie rose on shaky limbs. "What are you doing here?" No need to ask how she'd managed the remote Zoom—she'd done it before, and her powers had obviously grown under Ling's care. "Where's Ling? You were supposed to stay with him."

"He's safe. They're all safe." She smiled a little sadly.

Hettie didn't have the heart to admonish her. She'd missed her so much. She hugged her tight. "We have to go, okay? Can you—"

Abby was staring toward the prison. "Hungry."

Unease churned through Hettie. Of course she'd still have blood cravings. After opening that remote Zoom, she must have drained her powers.

"Abigail." Zavi's liquid voice slithered through Hettie, and both she and her sister turned. The warlock smiled. He was soaked head to toe, bedraggled, and still rooted in the ground, legs encased in glass and melted earth. Damp locks hung limply over his face. "I'm glad to see you well, dear."

Abby's face scrunched up as if she'd smelled something off. "You're not my friend anymore," she told him sternly. "You hurt my sister. You hurt me."

For a moment Zavi looked aggrieved. "I made mistakes. But look how much you've grown! And your remote Zoom—"

Abby turned away, ignoring him. "I'm hungry, Hettie."

Hettie almost smiled at the way she'd dismissed their foe. "We'll get you something to eat soon, okay? But we have to leave this place."

Abby looked doubtful, her eyes glazing, and a whimper escaped her.

"You're not going anywhere." Mizzay got to her feet. She drew her weapon and smirked down at Abby. "Well aren't you cute as a button? You must be the little sister I've heard all about."

Abby stared up at her, processing what she was seeing. "You're not Hettie." She lifted her hand as if she were pulling up a skirt to see what was underneath. Mizzay gasped and reeled. When she looked up again, Hettie's face was gone. The woman's face beneath was revealed—beautiful and naked and angry.

"How—how dare you?" She brought up her mage gun.

"Abby!" Hettie dove in front of her sister and fired half a blink faster than Mizzay did. Diablo's green flame exploded outward with a roar like a dragon breathing fire. She sent her heart out with it, her fierce need to protect Abby shielding her sister while her anger and hatred and everything she felt about this woman wearing her face lanced toward her enemy.

The revolver's flame surged, swallowing the General's pus-yellow glare. Mizzay lit up like a match thrown into an inferno, and her shriek curdled Hettie's blood. It was over in a second. The General evaporated with her, and when the flames receded all that was left was a smudge on the ground.

Instantly Hettie's flesh shredded apart as the Devil's Revolver took its blood price. But overtop the agony was…satisfaction. Her scream morphed into an empty laugh as the pain dissipated. *I got her, Uncle. I got her for you.*

Tears leaked from the corners of her eyes. Hettie didn't realize the pain was over until Abby turned her face up. Her sister was cradling her head in her lap. "Shh. It's okay," she whispered. "It'll all be okay."

Hettie smiled up at her sister. "I'm not going anywhere, Abby."

"I know." She looked off to the side, frowning.

Hettie felt the rumbling, sensed the bitter cold a moment later. The wind whipped up, and the sky darkened. The light over the prison had gone completely out, and only the moon lit the desolate landscape.

As if coordinated, the air blossomed with remote Zoom tunnels. Icy crystals filled the air in a blizzard, and Hettie's nostrils burned with cold. The tufty grass around them frosted over, and the wet ground crackled as it crystalized into a carpet of furry ice. The Alabama gang members who hadn't been knocked out by Abby's deluge got to their feet shakily, turning every which way as the Zooms disgorged hundreds of armed men. Division men. Soldiers and sorcerers on horseback, in automobiles. An army that rivalled the one that had taken out the Crowe gang. Some of the Alabama men dropped their weapons and fled. Others opened fire and were cut down immediately. They were corralled and surrounded, suppressed by woven nets weighed down with talismans, with magicked ropes that kept them penned like cattle.

Hettie dragged Abby to her feet and ran for an opening in the crowds. Her sister stumbled behind her. They had to get out of there.

She reached for the time bubble—it didn't come.

She looked frantically around. Why was the net still working? But no, it wasn't Zavi's null net—it was something else suppressing her ability to use Diablo. Or maybe the shock wave from Fielding's bomb had rolled over them.

She had to think. How would they escape? She couldn't afford to kill anyone else right now—she'd drop like a stone.

Escape...freedom...what had Jemma said about throwing open doors? She looked back to where the hatch to Level Zero lay.

She impaled her finger on Diablo's thorn and unleashed a blast of green fire that swallowed the dirt, melting the door like hot water being poured over ice. Horses and men scrambled out of the revolver's path. The gaping slag-crusted hole sat like a festering wound in the earth, glowing faintly green and fading to a slightly more mundane orange.

"Freeze!" a man shouted. She whipped around. The man had his gun aimed at Hettie's head. His horse panted, blowing clouds of steam into the cold air. The mare's eyes were huge, and she lifted her hooves high, sensing the wrongness all around her. Her rider struggled to hold her still while keeping his weapon trained on Hettie.

And then came the moan.

She knew from the shock on the Division agent's face that the first of the man-things had crawled out of the hole. The stairs leading down were intact, she was sure—Diablo's firepower was precise, doing exactly what she'd pictured in her mind.

Throwing open the doors to freedom.

She drew her sister close. The man-thing shambled to its feet, head twitching left and right as if seeking... something.

Its eyes lighted on her, on the mage gun in her hand, and it burst into motion, hurriedly limping across the stretch of scrubby land, slavering as if it were running toward a clear, cold stream after a long walk in the desert.

The Division agent yelled in panic—something between "Stop!" and "Hold it!" so that it came out as a jumble of syllables. The creature didn't stop.

A gunshot split the air, and a hole exploded in the man-thing's shoulder, but it kept coming. Another shot directly to its heart, and still the man-thing came. Only now it was angry. It swerved and went directly for the agent, dragging the rider off the horse despite his furious kicks. He screamed as the man-thing sank its teeth into his wrist, blood squelching between its rotting lips.

The agent scrabbled for his gun and blew a hole through the creature's head. Its body collapsed onto the ground, and he gasped in horror, in pain.

And then there were more moans as three, five, ten, twenty of the man-things piled out of the hole, crawling over each other like ants trying to escape a flooding nest.

The agent met her eyes, condemning her and telling her to run all in one horrified look. He got to his feet and started shouting

342

at the others to rally and refocus. Most of them were too busy struggling with the Alabama gang.

"We gotta go!" she said to Abby, pushing her toward the perimeter. Those creatures were drawn to magic, and she and Abby were the clearest targets standing out in the open.

Abby ran ahead of her, seeming to know her thoughts. She pushed her hands out and clapped them together. Ahead, a knot of men grappling with each other were knocked aside by an unseen force, their bodies flung high and far so that a path was cleared for her and Hettie.

And then Hettie heard something she never thought she'd hear. At first she'd thought it was a horse. But no.

Zavi was screaming.

The man-things had found him, stuck fast to the ground. Hettie was wrong—she and Abby weren't the clearest targets. The warlock was pushing them off with magic, bashing through the horde arrowing toward him, but they overwhelmed him, grabbing his arms, biting, clamping down on his flesh in a futile effort to gorge on his wealth of magic.

He screamed so she felt it in her gut. Screamed so that the world knew what horrors existed. Screamed and screamed.

The other Division agents who'd been too busy rounding up the Alabama gang finally noticed the new threat, and they turned their guns toward the hole where dozens of the man-things clambered out. Fire and light whizzed through the air as the Division tried to beat back the tide of creatures, but where they had numbers, the man-things had monstrous hunger, an inability to feel pain, and nothing to lose.

Well, they were the Division's problem to deal with.

A riderless horse cantered past, and Hettie grabbed the reins. "Abby, let's go!"

Her sister vaulted on without help. Hettie climbed into the saddle and grabbed the reins.

"Giddy—"

Her vision burst in an explosion of stars and grayness, and the ground rushed up at her. The world spun as the horse squealed and bolted. She tried to say something—*run*, maybe—but the words flubbed through her twisted tongue. What'd—

Shot. She'd been shot. In the head. Again.

She caught only flashes through the fronds of grass in front of her eyes. She felt as though she were swimming down, unable to surface, as if in a bad dream. She heard more than she saw, but couldn't make anything out. Not in any way that made sense.

There were shouts. Gunfire. A few bone-chilling screams that reminded Hettie of cattle being branded. Abby was there, standing over her. Abby! Why hadn't she stayed on the horse and run? She reached out toward her sister, but Abby wouldn't budge, glaring around fiercely. Protecting her.

Get away, run! She tried to shout. Her lips wouldn't move.

She wanted to roll over, to wake from this nightmare, but she couldn't. She was having trouble breathing, and she realized it was because her mouth and nose were filling with blood. Maybe she was dying...

Above her, Abby raised her hands. Hettie didn't know how she knew, barely able to see through her swollen eyelids. But she knew it, and she felt her power gathering around her sister, drawn to her like lightning to a rod. The pressure on Hettie's body grew until she felt crushed by its weight.

A pulse juddered through her bones, then another. Hammer blows. Great, sweeping motions that brushed men and man-things away like gnats. Every flick of Abby's hand knocked bodies over like they were toy soldiers. Every swipe drove Hettie's body into the ground like a stake. The pounding intensified. She coughed and groaned as her ribs cracked. The next blow dislocated her shoulder. She whimpered and gritted her teeth. Something popped in her skull.

Abby's magic was going to kill her.

Diablo ticked in her hand. No. No! She wasn't going to shoot her sister, not even to save her own life. *Abby*, she called, but it came out as a gurgle. She tasted blood. It was trickling out of the corner of her flaccid lips, filling her lungs. She'd drown in it if Abby didn't stop.

All around her there came shouts. The next bone-shattering pulse didn't come, though. Abby had stopped—why? Hettie tried to open her eyes, but they were swollen shut. Her face felt puffy, numb. Her whole body sang with pain, beaten to a bloody pulp.

Abby might as well have been raining those blows on her. And she'd only just realized what she'd been doing.

"Oh, no. No!" Abby cried. "I'm sorry, Hettie! I'm sorry!"

Hettie couldn't reply. The grayness was fuzzing over her mind. Was this it? If she died now, the hell gate would open. She couldn't let Abby get caught in its pull.

"Get...away..." If this was it, she had to make her sister go. She'd happily let hell claim these Division agents and the evil she'd unleashed. "Go...Abby..."

More shouts all around her. Magic bristled through the cold air. Abby gasped and was dragged back. Someone had thrown a lasso around her. Another sailed out and cinched her waist. Men were shouting all around her. More lassos, and Abby gave a cry and thrashed.

"Abby!" Hettie summoned the last of her strength and drew. A wave of fire rushed out of the mage gun, its weight unbearable in her broken hands.

Diablo found its mark. Many marks. It always would. Death was its purpose; blood was its price. And Hettie was bleeding out.

The Devil's Revolver gulped her years down. One. Two. Three. Four. Five. Six. Seven. Eight. Nine. Ten. Eleven...

Her bones were already broken, and now they were shards twisting between her joints. Her flesh had to have sheared right off in places. She was bleeding. The wetness was from more than her body emptying itself. The pain didn't stop. The years were peeling off her as if she were being flayed alive.

Please let me die, she finally thought, unable to cry or scream for mercy. All she wanted was for the pain to end.

Something curious happened then. Hettie wasn't sure what she was seeing, but a warmth spread through her chest from the inner pocket of her coat. The little sachet Uncle had given her was...expanding? She could barely tell, though she thought she saw a great black pair of wings rise up and spread protectively over her, blotting out the stars.

The pain suddenly stopped. Diablo was a solid weight in her hand, but the rest of her was a steaming mass of prickly feeling.

And still the men's voices came. The lassos again, and then nets! Abby fell to her knees. Someone threw a blanket over her, and she started screaming as she was tackled and dragged to the ground. No! Whatever they were doing to her—

Hettie wouldn't let them. *Help me*, she begged Diablo, the Devil's Revolver, the devil himself. *Help me save my sister, and I will do whatever you ask.*

The rustle of feathers shushed in her ears, or maybe it was just the rush of blood as she pushed herself up with what she thought was superhuman strength, as if she were in a dream. With broken fingers, she pulled Diablo's trigger again. And again. And again. Every shot found a mark. Every pull ended a life.

Another tidal wave of agony washed over her. But this time she surfaced quickly, buoyed by sheer willpower. She pulled the trigger again, blasting a man holding one end of a lasso into nothingness. The wave smacked her back, but she got up again, pulled the trigger, ended a life. And again. And again...

"Abby!" She unleashed Diablo, slicing through the lassos, burning through the men, cutting down anything and everything that held her sister in thrall. Diablo's thorn had pierced cleanly through her finger—which was when Hettie realized part of it was missing.

The men left holding the ends of the ropes retreated, and the men who'd nearly had Abby tied up vaulted back as Hettie approached. She pulled the blanket off her sister, saw the tears streaming down her red cheeks. A fresh scrape marred her cheek, and her lip was split.

Rage filled Hettie. *They'd hurt Abby.*

She faced the Division army, feeling strong, feeling bold, feeling the knife edge of death and the blackest eternity pressing in on her from all sides. All around her, she heard the rush of wings, as if a flock of birds circled. No, it wasn't wings; it was the sound of guns cocking, of spells nervously whispered, of prayers being said.

She was surrounded. The man-things had been cut down. Those harbingers could not help her now. That they hadn't shot her dead yet meant they knew who she was, what she held, and what fate befell them if they killed her. The question was, how many Division agents could she kill before they decided they couldn't take any more losses?

All she had to do was get Abby away. All she had to do to fulfill her promise to Paul and her ma and pa was die to save her sister.

"Listen up, y'all," she said, trembling under the weight of her broken body. "You know who I am. You've seen what I can do. You wanna take me in, that's fine. But you know I will unleash literal hell on you if you try to touch my sister. So the deal's this: you let her go, and you get me instead."

Silence. Maybe they were trying to figure out who was in charge, if she'd already killed their commander. "Deal," a man finally shouted.

She huffed. They'd capitulated far too quickly. Of course they wouldn't let Abby go—they'd capture her the moment they had Hettie and Diablo in custody. She wouldn't let that happen.

"Abby," she gritted, "you're gonna get on a horse, y'hear?"

"No."

"Abby," she said more sternly, and coughed. She spat a mouthful of blood and teeth. "You're gonna get on a horse, and you're gonna ride it as far and as fast as you can. Get some more blood. Juice up however you need to. Keep the Division and anyone else who tries to hurt or control you away."

"I know what you're gonna do," Abby said back. "You can't, Hettie."

"Don't argue with me. Just do it. Go."

Abby circled around her. Tears flooded her eyes. "No. You can't. You have to be the one to save us." She cupped Hettie's cheeks, and for a bleary moment, Hettie thought she was looking into her mother's brave, smiling face. Blood stained Abby's palms. Seeing all that red was making Hettie queasy. It was all hers.

"I'm doing what I have to," she said.

"I know." Abby sniffed. "And so am I." She licked her palms. Her pupils swallowed her eyes. Her blood-stained hands glowed.

"Good-bye," Abby whispered. She stepped back and slapped her hands down on the dirt.

The ground opened beneath Hettie, and she screamed as she tumbled down, down, down until she didn't know which way was up anymore. The gritty grayness around her was like slurry, cold as the earth. She waved her arms, suddenly afraid the cold intangible grip would claim her completely. And then she knew—her sister had opened a coyote portal to save her life.

"Abby! Abby!" There was no answer.

Hettie howled. Her tears darted out every which way, like startled fish. The fist around her gut clenched and unclenched until she vomited, and that, too, dissipated into the not-quite-solid matter she traversed.

A peculiar emptiness invaded every pore then, as if her soul had left her. The air was thick and cold, suffusing her lungs like a rainstorm in the last days of winter. Her body was nothing here. She might as well let the earth claim her. She didn't care anymore. She'd failed her family utterly. She was alone.

She stopped moving and felt the dank, clinging fingers of the earth probe her, embrace her. This was where she deserved to end up, melded into the dirt and rock with no marker. Buried slowly and agonizingly, screaming in the ground.

She *deserved* hell.

Diablo kicked in her palm, sticking her finger with its thorn. She gripped the gun automatically and fired.

The hell-green blast cleared a path, and she tumbled down it. She gave an angry cry, denied her end.

You! She flung the weapon away. *This is your fault!*

Diablo reformed in her grip instantly. Contemptuously.

She hit the dirt like a cow pie and groaned. Everything hurt. It didn't matter. Her heart was broken. She wanted to cry, but the tears were locked inside the tight bud of pain in the center of her chest, with all its broken ribs. Why had Abby saved her? What point was there? She was going to die out here...among the long, soft grasses...

The sky was just lightening to a damp, gray morning. It'd be the last dawn she'd ever see. She would've preferred to die in the night, unable to see the sky or her injuries. That she could see at all through her puffy eyes—

But they weren't puffy. And her ribs weren't broken. She wasn't dying. She was sore, but...gingerly, she sat up and examined herself. Not a scratch on her. Barely even a bruise.

Abby had healed her. Her sister had done her one more undeserved favor.

The distinct sound of a shotgun being chambered met her ears. "Whoever you are, get up slowly."

Her heart stuttered at that gruff voice. No. No.

Abby, why would you do this for me?

She turned.

His silhouette was broad as ever, his ice-blue eyes narrowed. The wind lifted his black duster briefly, revealing his familiar black attire, boots to hat, carrying the scent of leather and horses to her nose.

Recognition flickered over his face, but he hesitated. Slowly, he lowered the shotgun. "Hettie?"

Hettie's chest caved, and the dam of emotions broke. She crumpled, unable to even say Walker Woodroffe's name in relief, in greeting, in anything but abject misery.

Her sister was gone. The Division had taken her.

To be concluded in the final Chapter of the Devil's Revolver series,

THE LEGEND OF DIABLO

AUTHOR'S ACKNOWLEDGMENTS

My deepest thanks to all the readers and fans who've stuck it out this long with Hettie. If you've gotten to the end of this book screaming (in a good way...?), let me know on Facebook or Twitter that I've done my job. I hope you'll be back for the final installment of the series, *The Legend of Diablo*.

As always, I'd like to thank my editor and publisher, Mary Ann Hudson and Ruthie Knox, and the rest of the team at Brain Mill Press for believing in Hettie and the Devil's Revolver series.

To my agent, Courtney Miller-Callihan of Handspun Literary, for being a rock, finding Hettie a home, and for all her awesomeness.

Thanks to Cassandre Bolan for her fantastic, visionary work on the Devil's Revolver book covers, and to Ann O'Connell for her beautiful interior drawings.

I'd like to acknowledge the funding support from the Ontario Arts Council, an agency of the Government of Ontario, for the grant that helped me continue work on this series, and specifically *The Devil's Pact*. Support for the arts includes genre fiction, and I am honored to have received this grant.

A tip of the hat to Bakka Phoenix Books in Toronto, Canada, for being a terrific host for my book launches through heat waves and ice storms alike.

To my mom and dad, immigrants who came to Canada decades ago for new opportunities and to provide better lives for their children. Thanks for all the years of free room and board, and for teaching me about hard work.

To my sisters, Fiona and Jenny: thanks for your cheerleading, marketing, and sales pitches to friends and colleagues alike, and for everything you do for the family.

To the Irrational Biped who teaches me something every day: you've shown me how much room there is for love and patience in my heart. I hope I can make the world a better place for you.

Finally, to my husband, John: I don't have enough words with which to express the gratitude, appreciation, and love I have for you. I'm afraid any attempt at articulating it would only lead to verbal off-gassing, so instead I will simply say thank you. Or in the Irrational Biped's words: "Poot. Butt."

One more book to go and this cowgirl can ride off into the sunset...for a while, anyway.

ABOUT THE AUTHOR

V. S. McGrath is a published romance author (as Vicki Essex) and has six books with Harlequin Superromance: *Her Son's Hero* (July 2011); *Back to the Good Fortune Diner* (January 2013), which was picked for the Smart Bitches Trashy Books Sizzling Book Club; *In Her Corner* (March 2014); *A Recipe for Reunion* (March 2015); *Red Carpet Arrangement* (January 2016); and *Matinees with Miriam* (November 2016). She has been featured in the *Globe and Mail*, *Metro Toronto*, *Torontoist*, *Inside Toronto*, and Canada.com. *The Devil's Revolver* is her debut young adult fantasy. You can find her on Facebook, Twitter, or her websites: vsmcgrath.com and vickiessex.com. She lives in Toronto, Canada.

Made in the USA
Lexington, KY
24 December 2018